NOWHERE BOYS

MASCOT BOOKS
an imprint of Amplify Publishing Group

www.mascotbooks.com

Nowhere Boys

For more information, please contact:
Mascot Books, an imprint of Amplify Publishing Group
620 Herndon Parkway, Suite 220
Herndon, VA 20170
info@amplifypublishing.com

Library of Congress Control Number: 2023906021
CPSIA Code: PRV0623A
ISBN-13: 978-1-63755-595-8
Printed in the United States

NOWHERE BOYS

A NOVEL

MARK ASAY

CONTENTS

CHAPTER 1

The house had the same pictures as my parents' house; the Mormon temples were respective to their location, mine being Seattle and theirs, Los Angeles. The framed picture of Jesus Christ was there—white robe, long hair, bearded with hands clasped praying, eyes open while looking up to the heavens.

The board games and playing cards were stacked in the corner—no face cards, as even the appearance of the cards was considered too close to gambling. The bookshelves had the typical series—*History of the Church: The Complete 7 Volume Set*, Bible study companions for both Old and New Testaments, and multiple copies of the *Book of Mormon*, bent and frayed—which were recycled each year for early-morning seminary before high school started.

It was all the same but different. This was their home and their family; mine was 1,200 miles away. But this was my new home, and it felt like it, looked like it, and sounded like it. I watched Mike flip through the movie section of the *Los Angeles Times*. "What do you feel like seeing?" Rachel asked her brother as she leaned over to see the paper.

"I'm up for anything," Mike said.

Rachel was nineteen; I was nineteen. The back of my head tickled, "Control your thoughts!" I heard the words from the Mission Training Center (MTC) resonating in my ears: "It's really the devil working on you!" I combatted the words by thinking, "No, it's a pretty girl with an incredible smile, and at the moment it's all I can really enjoy."

"Elder Dorsey, what do you want to see?" Craig asked. I blushed, and I felt my sweaty fingers, leaving wet imprints in my lap.

"Aaahhh, you're kidding, right?" They laughed; they knew missionaries couldn't see movies.

"Hey, you guys! Don't give Elder Dorsey a hard time. He just got here!" Sister Barrett said, coming to my defense. She smiled at me, and the redness in my face ebbed away.

After the introductions, the questions started.

"So, Elder, where are you from?" Brother Barrett asked. Elder: I didn't even get the pleasure of hearing my own last name. It was a non-descript time. I was intimidated by Barrett's six-foot-three frame and full head of hair. He stood at the kitchen counter; he had just gotten home and was working on a ham sandwich.

"Seattle," I said with confidence.

"Are you going to miss the rain?" he asked, looking up from the partially mustarded sandwich.

"Yeah," I said, "but I lived in Texas the last couple months, so it shouldn't be too bad, with the heat and all."

He looked down at the sandwich and finished the elongated **S** of mustard squeezing out the bottom of the bottle, the watery mix spitting and farting its way free. "How do you like California?"

"I like it. I've only been here a day, but so far I like it. It's Hollywood."

Rachel seemed to have it made—her brother's friends, two years older than she, were staying over, and all wanted to go to the movie. That is, if she was going.

Sister Barrett was pretty. She'd bleached her hair to a not-quite-natural-looking blond. It hung down a little past her shoulders, showing off her face. Her smile made the situation better. She understood my situation and tried to make the best of the brief visit. Mike played basketball for the community college. Craig was in tenth grade and played varsity basketball for his school. The little one, Wayne, was eight years old—the baby of the family.

The Barretts were a favorite family of the missionaries. It was the first place I visited after two months at the MTC in Utah. All Mormon missionaries came from there, as it was like boot camp for the army. So I'd gone from the MTC, to the home of President Carlson, then to the Austins (from whom we rented the room), and finally to the Barretts—each one providing as much awe as the last; each one being its own pinnacle.

I knew that I was where I should be.

CHAPTER 2

I was one of the 43,395 missionaries worldwide serving for the Mormon Church in 1990. I had thought many times about how these first few days in the field would be. I'd sung songs with the lyrics:

I hope they call me on a mission, when I have grown a foot or two.
I hope by then I will be ready to teach and preach and work as missionaries do.

The mission was in the thoughts and dealings of my family, extended family, friends, and ex-girlfriends; decisions had been made by me, my parents, and leaders of the Church to get me to the point where I would be ready to go. I'd gone through four different interviews to establish the fact that I was a "“worthy”‘ nineteen-year-old male who would represent the Church in a way consistent with the standards set forth by God himself, passed down through his prophet on earth, Ezra Taft Benson.

Armed with only four things—a copy of the King James Version of the Bible, a black leather-bound *Book of Mormon* (with highlighted passages guiding me through six Discussions we taught to each and every person showing interest in coming unto God's true religion on the earth), a spiral-bound flip chart with pictures of Jesus Christ (describing the Plan of Salvation, including big words instructing his followers not to commit adultery and a picture of coins stacked on one another, illustrating the law of tithing, (full-time Mormons must pay a 10% tithe on their gross net income to stay in full participation in the Mormon Church), and finally my unfaltering testimony of the truth of the message I brought. This is a testimony I had agonized over during years of study and prayer to finally have the affirmation of the Holy Ghost that all these things were true.

And why was I given the task of bringing people salvation? I had the authority from Jesus Christ, the Melchizedek Priesthood—the same priesthood that Jesus gave to John the Baptist before he baptized Jesus. This was what set me apart—the restored priesthood on the earth, the only priesthood on the earth, the power to heal and give the gift of the Holy Ghost; the only true interpreter of Jesus Christ. These few but powerful tools would act as my wielding sword over the next two years as I worked each and every day to rid the world of the gentiles (anyone not Mormon or not baptized into God's Church). Those who would convert would be welcomed into the fold. Those who would not would be thrust down to hell at my very words—as I was taught, so I believed.

CHAPTER 3

It was November, sunny yet cold. The mellow afternoon sun and light breeze had turned into a fierce, penetrating force, making its way through my several layers of clothing. The sudden drop of nearly ten degrees, shortly after the sun hid itself behind the low hills surrounding the San Fernando Valley—the Valley—prompted us to ask Sister Barrett for a ride home.

"It was nice to meet you, Elder Dorsey," Sister Barrett said, turning around from the front seat to make eye contact with me. Elder Fischer grabbed the front door handle and tried to reach it before Sister Barrett. When there were two missionaries and a woman, both missionaries had to sit by each other. With bucket seats, this had left us both in the back.

"It was nice to meet you," I said, crawling out in my stiff suit. I pushed the seat back. "Byes" were said as we shut the door. The little black Chevy two-door pulled out of the driveway, straightened, and sped off in the direction from which we'd just come.

We walked up the brick path to the door of the Austins. There was a wagon wheel upright in the front yard and old driftwood for steps. Elder Fischer got out the key and opened the sticky door.

"It takes a little work to get this open, but it's never been a problem."

"OK," I said.

I walked in, immediately facing an obstacle: the Austins' dog. I was attacked by a German shepherd at age five, leaving me with a scar on an otherwise perfect leg, a remnant of the chunk of flesh tugged off by the dog. I didn't trust dogs, especially ones that growled when they saw a person. His teeth were huge. His *head* was huge. I wanted to hug the wall and say,

"What the heck is that doing here! Put it outside!" I didn't say anything, though. At least nothing I *wanted* to say.

"What a pretty dog! What kind is it?" I asked, showing no signs of my loss of composure within.

"It's an Akita," said Sister Austin, smiling down at the dog as if it were her first born. "Don't mind the growl, she's harmless."

My first city had a huge, growling dog that I lived with—indoors.

"Well, Elder Dorsey. How do you like California so far?" I was quickly getting accustomed to answering the same questions from everyone I met, from both missionaries and members. The trainers in the MTC didn't mention anything about answering the same questions time and again, but maybe this was just the natural way of things, when nothing was known of a person.

"Love it," I said. "I've only been here for a day, but I think I will really enjoy it. I'm sure I will miss the rain and the cloudy days, but I'm looking forward to it." I wasn't sure who or what I sounded like, but it wasn't myself. Then again, *Elder Dorsey* didn't seem to be my name, either. Outwardly, I sounded positively tickled to be on a mission, when in reality I would have rather been home with a girl on the couch, making out and watching a movie. Why didn't someone ask *me* how I liked mission life? Are you going to miss swimming? And going out with your friends? And dating girls? Asking these questions is how they *tried* to get to know me, but this small talk—where I'm from, how I'm liking my new area—these questions meant nothing.

"Miss the rain, huh? You must be from the Northwest?" Brother Austin asked.

"Seattle," I said proudly.

"Seattle?" Brother Austin asked as we finally moved from the entry hall and got a little further away from each other. "Wasn't Elder Westra from Seattle too?" He asked.

"I just learned that. Different city, though. We don't know each other."

"Well, if he is any indication of what elders from Seattle are like, we are looking forward to having you here."

"Actually, I'm from a little town north of Seattle called Ballard," I said.

Sister Austin went into the kitchen while talking over her shoulder at us, "You hungry, Elders?"

"No, we just had ice cream at the Barretts," I said. Then something happened: her walk, her tone, or maybe just the lack of any kind of genuine response told me that something was wrong. It reminded me of when I'd mention my father's name to my mother, even though it had been years since the divorce, or when an ex-girlfriend's name would come up in conversation with another girlfriend.

Elder Fischer looked down at his watch. "Well, we'd better get ready to turn in for the night. I'm sure Elder Dorsey is looking forward to unpacking."

Elder Fischer seemed a lot older than me, maybe because he was six-foot-six.

We said good night and walked towards the bedroom. With the door shut, I finally felt a little relief. I wasn't one to feel as comfortable around other people as I did when I was by myself.

"This is your closet and that's your desk," Elder Fischer instructed as he pushed one of the glass doors open on the double closet, pointing to one side of the desk.

I was the proud owner of a half-closet and a portion of a desk built into the wall in the back of the room. Everything was fashioned in thick, rough, dark wood. It looked like someone had spilled shellac on a piece of wood, ruined it, and tried to hide it in pieces of furniture—the whole house was that way.

The closet had plenty of room and the desk, as thick and dark as it was, made up for in size what it lacked in aesthetics. I enjoyed unpacking all my new things—the first time in a real area versus the MTC. I think Elder Fischer enjoyed it too. He watched me, commenting on each item as I pulled my newly purchased belongings out of my garment bag and suitcase. I thought he might be reflecting on when he had first come out on his mission, when all things were new.

"You'll like those shoes. They're very comfortable," he said, as I pulled out one of two brand-new pairs of Rockport dress shoes, or at least what somewhat resembled dress shoes: they had rubber soles; real dress shoes have wood soles. Rockports were the favorite among missionaries, though, due to their light weight and staying power.

“Pretty comfortable so far,” I said, looking down at black wingtips still on my feet. “They’re so light.”

“Hey, you want to play a quick game of pool?” Elder Fischer said, his voice lacking excitement and complacent in tone.

“Really? There’s a table here?”

“It’s in the back. I can show you the bathroom and you can put your stuff away while we’re back there.”

“OK.” I left the packing. I had already hung up my shirts and suits, but the rest was put off for another time.

I followed Elder Fischer through the sunken living room into the hallway, leading us to the back of the house. We came out from the hallway to a long room with sun rays casting off plaques, framed photos, macramé, and large pinecones hanging on the walls from top to bottom—one of the finest dust collections I’d ever seen. At the back of the room, the pool table stood. Fischer quickly turned to the right and showed me our personal bathroom. If members wanted to have missionaries living in their home, they needed to provide them with their own entrance and bathroom. Technically, the current arrangement passed but was questionable. The bathroom was the size of a closet with a sink, toilet, and shower. Small, but would serve the purpose. I’m not sure what Elder Fischer meant by putting my stuff away in the bathroom. There where no shelves or cupboards, not even a medicine-cabinet mirror. The toothbrush holder was it. So I put my toothbrush away, lost a game of pool, and went back to the bedroom.

“Would you like to say the prayer tonight, or would you like me to?” Elder Fischer asked.

“Oh, feel free,” I said as we knelt down, elbows on his lower bunk.

After the companionship prayer, I got into the top bunk and said my personal prayers while kneeling on my bed. I went to sleep with thoughts of what had happened over the past few hours, wondering how long this mission was going to feel.

Sister Austin drove us to Rusty Bikes the next day. We left at nine thirty.

We couldn't leave any earlier because we had personal study, companionship study, and breakfast. Elder Fischer gave me a bowl of Rice Krispies and a glass of orange juice. He didn't have to do that; it must have been his gesture to make me feel somewhat at home in a strange place.

"So...what kind of bike are you looking for?" asked Russ.

"Well, I want a mountain bike. And I'll be on it every day for the next two years."

"What's your price limit?"

"About two-fifty."

While Russ started looking around for the right bike, I asked him questions about his store and how he got into the bike-selling business. He had a nifty little answer about how much he loved bikes and had always wanted to do something like own a bike shop. He hoped to expand someday, maybe the next year. He was friendly and good with customers. I wondered if he would give me a deal for talking with him. I didn't ask or expect a deal, though.

He had two bikes in my range. I picked out a red one without straight handlebars. I didn't like red, but it was a little stronger than the black one, the only other bike in my range. I didn't need any accessories, except for a lock. I quickly picked out a titanium U-lock that could only be torched apart. I wrote a check and rode out of the store.

Other than occasional borrowing of a bike at the dorms to get to class when I was late, I hadn't been on a bike in years. The majority of my bike riding had been when I was a young kid. I now pulled wheelies next to Elder Fischer, jumping off curbs and bunny-hopping every crack in the road.

"Where are we going?" I asked Elder Fischer, slowing down to talk with him.

"We are going to run by the grocery store so you can get some food to last you until P-Day." P-Day was short for Preparation Day—it was every Monday, the only day during the week that missionaries could go grocery shopping and do laundry. It also turned into a day when missionaries would meet up with each other, play basketball, or just hang out.

I had my backpack with me to carry my copies of the *Book of Mormon* and my scriptures; it probably added an additional 20 pounds to my load. I filled it up further with my frozen meals, climbed back on my bike, and followed Elder Fischer out of the parking lot towards what I hoped would be home. I really didn't want to be carrying frozen food around with me all day.

It wasn't that Elder Fischer kept things from me; it was more that he was quiet. Since I didn't ask a lot of questions, he kept to himself. When we got back to the Austins, I unpacked my food in the mini-fridge set aside for the missionaries.

"We are going to go to the Johnstons for dinner, but before dinner, we are helping Brother Johnston put up Christmas decorations," Elder Fischer said as we walked into the room to change into our P-Day clothes. Unless we were doing a service project, we needed to be in our shirt and tie at all times. Helping put up Christmas decorations would count for service, something we were asked to do each week.

Brother Johnston picked us up about eleven o'clock. I squeezed into the back seat of the little Honda Civic wagon and tried to take in the little car. It was built in the seventies, and the sounds that erupted from it suggested that it had not been tuned up since coming off the assembly line. I kept pushing the headliner up to keep it out of my hair while trying to answer a barrage of questions asked by Brother Johnston.

The seat flaked when I touched it: the imitation leather's shelf life had expired, and the vinyl was decomposing in between my fingers.

The clutch grinding with every shift, we pulled in front of a little one-story house on a busy street. Hopping out, we yelled at each other over the traffic, saying, "Here we are!" "Elder, come on in!" and "Elder, you first." Inside, coats were taken and we were handed Canada Dry seltzers, the flavored kind. I chose black cherry.

Sister Johnston quickly got into an explanation of her family's genealogy. She was on the way to get a printout of the family tree when we headed out the front door to the garage. It was hardly a garage, rather a storage facility for junk. With an assembly line in place, we started pulling down the reindeer from the two-by-four eaves above the mess on the floor. There was a narrow path for us to get in and out. First, of course, there was

Rudolph. "Careful with the nose; it's glass!" Brother Johnston said, carefully handing a life-size plywood reindeer to Elder Fischer. Elder Fischer relayed the message to me by looking into my eyes and letting his eyes speak to me, "Elder Dorsey, you heard what he said…so I won't repeat it each time…look."

I nodded, acknowledging that the eye-contact communication was understood. We eventually had all the reindeer lying on the grass, which was warmed by the sun, next to a busy street.

We watched as a man thought intensely about how reindeer—plywood reindeer—should be displayed. I held back suggesting possible places that I thought would look good, knowing that our suggestions were not what Brother Johnston had in mind when asking for our help.

"How many years have you been decorating like this, Brother Johnston?" I asked.

"This is the twelfth year."

"Whoa, that's a long time!" I said surprised, letting my emotion show.

"We enjoy it," he said.

When the last reindeer was pulled out of the garage, we stepped back to look at the different pieces of the puzzle that we had just laid over the lawn. Brother Johnston took on the role as overseer, as Elder Fischer and I proceeded to put the different parts of the puzzle together. Just about the time the sun started to fall, we stood back and saw the picture we had created.

Santa was getting out of the chimney, with the elves helping him. The North Pole ladder went down to the front flower garden, which acted as the makeshift runway. The reindeer were lined up in a row, waiting for Santa, Rudolph in the lead. We each commented on how nice it looked as we walked inside for dinner.

"Canadian seltzer, Elder?" Brother Johnston asked. "Sure." I said.

I took the blackberry seltzer and put it at my place on the table. Elder Fischer followed suit with his apricot seltzer. We helped carry the rest of the dinner to the table and sat down. Brother Johnston asked me to say the prayer, and I accepted—outwardly gracious, but inwardly regretting my acceptance. It was my first dinner prayer with a family in the mission field. Little went into learning about praying in the MTC. Most missionaries had been brought up in the Church and were accustomed to praying out loud at the dinner table. Automatically, I recited one of the family prayers I'd grown up with.

My dad, of course, had the most elegant prayers. He always sounded so grateful for his family and God. His prayers were reverent and respectful, his deep, strong voice resonating throughout the house. The beginning of each prayer was about the same: "Dear Heavenly Father…" When I was in Seattle before the mission, I had a good friend from school and church. His name was Tony. He ate over at our house all the time. Most the time it was just he and I hanging out while our parents were working. At one of the few dinners when my parents were around, we were sitting at the kitchen counter, getting ready to eat, as my Dad asked me to say the blessing. After the blessing, Dad looked at me, rolled his eyes a little, and asked me to try and put a little more effort into my prayers. Pretty innocent, actually. He never really went off too bad. Tony—understand that Tony was a bit of a smart ass and my parents thought his parents were bums—piped in and said, "A prayer is a prayer and you can't tell him how to pray". My Dad, in shock, replied, "In our house we have certain rules." Tony was dismissed from the table and from the house thereafter.

An important part of prayer was saying the person's name. Even if the message wasn't important, it at least sounded good—I knew this much. I thanked the Johnstons for having us over for dinner and asked God to bless them. Missionary prayers were a big deal to most families. As we were full-time ordained ministers of God, families felt that our prayers were answered when theirs might not be. I believed this, so I asked God to bless them. I didn't know exactly what they needed, so I blessed them with whatever they might need at the time.

The Johnstons' son, Michael, was on a mission in Dallas, Texas. He had about a year left. Sister Johnston passed pictures around the table so we could see him. Michael and his sister Megan (Megan was sitting next to me) were adopted, we learned. Brother and Sister Johnston seemed a little old to have kids their age, so it made sense when they mentioned the adoption. Sister Johnston was so proud of her son. Well, the whole family was. But Sister Johnston's eyes just lit up when she talked about him. It meant everything to parents to have their sons go on a mission. It meant a lot with daughters, but not as much. Generally, the girls who went had no chance of getting married, so they needed a mission on their résumé to improve their odds. They had to serve for only a year and a half versus the two years that men served.

When the different bowls and platters reached their final resting place, we all began to eat. I ended up with a piece of oven-roasted turkey, a little overdone, going through several glasses of water once the seltzers stopped coming. After dinner, once the table was cleared, we moved over to the living room and all had a seat. We licked our teeth and held our stomachs, thinking about naps and sleeping.

"Elder Dorsey and I would like to leave a message with you as thanks for having us over tonight," Elder Fischer explained to the Johnstons.

"As always, we would love it," Brother Johnston said.

Elder Fischer had mentioned this to me as we were heading out the door of the Austins towards Brother Johnston's car.

Apparently missionaries, or at least ones with Elder Fischer, shared a message with the members after dinner. He told me that we would be sharing the First Discussion with them. Even though I'd spent the last two months studying the Discussions and had memorized them straight from the pamphlet, my hands got sweaty. I was not looking forward to it at all. The First Discussion was exactly that: the first discussion we had with gentiles. I didn't tell gentiles what we meant by *gentiles*, though. The term seemed to have a bit of a negative connotation and implied heathenism. I surely would never want to be called a heathen. The Discussion went over the plan that God had for us here on earth, explaining that if we lived according to the plan, we could live with him forever after we died. So we shared this with the Johnstons, even though they knew it. Members liked to hear the missionaries recite the Discussions so they could rate us on our eloquence. I was sure Sister Johnston was thinking about her son Michael out there, doing the same thing we were doing. Although she was looking at me, I knew it was her son she saw.

We recited the First Discussion, Elder Fischer making it sound like a poem he had written, while I read directly from the book. I looked up occasionally to make the important eye contact (explained to us in the MTC) and kept reading away.

We had to be home and studying by nine thirty. It was a quarter after nine when we headed out to the worn Honda.

Once home, it was time to get ready for bed and do our nightly study and prayers.

"Is that what we do with members as a message to leave them? Share the First Discussion?" I asked.

"It's always something you can do. There are missionary videos that most members haven't seen, and any article that you might read in the *Ensign* or *Friend*,"—the monthly Church-published magazines—"but always try to leave something. The Discussions are things we have with us all the time, so they are easy to share. *And* it's good practice for new missionaries."

"So do we go over to the Johnstons a lot?"

"They usually have us over a couple times a month. So yeah, that's more than some families. You will start to get an idea from the dinner calendar of the different families that have us over more than others."

The Church had come out and said that each family should have the missionaries over once a month. There were families we could count on who didn't need to sign the dinner calendar, like the Barretts. We could call them any night that we didn't have a dinner appointment and they'd tell us to come on over. Or most the time, we could just show up and get fed.

Missionaries didn't get any hungrier than other people, but everything seemed to be so centered on food that I wondered if, in the past, a missionary had starved to death. We were nineteen-year-old boys, though—and therefore always hungry. I figured that because the monthly check we got from the Church factored in dinner appointments with members, less money was budgeted for food. The members were inclined to feel obligated to feed us.

After our morning showers and personal study, Elder Fischer and I needed to do our companionship study. Each morning, companionships read out of the Missionary Guide, teaching us about love and empathy, and how to express them to each person we talked with. I thought it was funny that a thing like empathy was taught when God probably intended it to be natural. Some things are not learned, but rather understood. I knew I used empathy *before* my mission. It would be hard to have any friends if empathy wasn't shown in some form. I'd felt sad for people and what they were going through, but now the Missionary Guide put a name to it. So each day we would study a different concept of the Missionary Guide and put it to use with the people we came in contact with that day. We role-played a Discussion we might have with someone we met, trying to show empathy with what they told us. I didn't agree with the whole role-playing act. It's all we had done the last two months in the MTC as missionaries in training, and it had lost its luster.

The Missionary Guide explained empathy as "the ability to put yourself in another's situation and share his thoughts and feelings. Empathy is also looking at things from others' point of view rather than yours." I knew that this was impossible, that all a person could hope for was that in trying to understand another, he would only prolong the time before a final judgment was made as to whether he liked someone or not. But I still continued to study, learn, practice, and act as if it was God himself who wrote the Missionary Guide. I thought of God's finger, with flames burning into a stone wall, like in the movie *The Ten Commandments.*

Elder Fischer didn't act out his characters. I bet after being on the mission for two years, I wouldn't either.

The role-play for the morning involved Karen, an investigator, being taught by sister missionaries. Karen was having a hard time praying. Investigator Karen said, "I'm sorry. I didn't pray. It's hard for me." The Missionary Guide gave us three different scenarios of what the sisters could say in response, and we had to pick the right answer.

"Karen, I want you to know that prayer is very important. It's the only way we have of talking with our Heavenly Father. If you don't pray, then you will..." Generally a missionary would put in something fun and smart like, "then you will go to hell" or "you will be spanked," all with the straightest face possible. It wasn't nearly as fun when it was only one of the missionaries playing with it, though, so the clever insertions were not part of our study.

After doing that for thirty minutes, we headed out. I put my backpack on with my scriptures in it. Elder Fischer then put five copies of the *Book of Mormon* in it and we were off.

I had my pant leg in the leg wrap I bought with my bike, a little black Velcro strap with a strip of reflecting yellow so cars could see me. Elder Fischer's pant legs were stuffed into his socks. They would both be protected from the chain.

We had already gone over the plan for the day when we looked at our blue planners. The blue planner was one sheet of card stock: a glorified spreadsheet; lines and times for everything.

Missionaries were to keep track of their schedule with the blue planners. Even if an elder or a sister had a day-timer, or Franklin Planner, the Church still wanted to see the missionary standard blue planners.

"Where are we going? Tracting?" I asked as we headed down Devonshire Street.

"It's about twenty minutes from here. I haven't tracted there since I've been in the area, so thought you and I would start out in a fresh spot."

"Great!" I said, pedaling to keep up with my long-legged companion, wondering why I was always trying to keep up with him. If it were just his long legs, then that would mean he got through life quicker, too much of an advantage for God to give to only a few.

After about ten minutes of riding along Devonshire Street, with cars passing us at forty miles an hour, we turned off onto a side street where we rode side by side.

"Have you had much luck tracting?"

"I've taught people when tracting, but never baptized anyone. But the Spanish-speaking missionaries rely on tracting to find the majority of people they teach and baptize."

"Do you like tracting?" I asked.

"It's alright. You'll have to tell me what you think of it today when we are done. There is a lot more to tracting than just looking for people to baptize. I think it's also about just getting out and working.

If the Lord sees that you are working hard, then he will send people to you. We could go to a member's home and they may have a neighbor that wants to hear the Discussions. I think that would be a blessing from hard work. If we weren't out tracting, we wouldn't have met that person to teach."

Fischer veered over to the curb and hopped up on the grass, just under a street sign.

"That makes sense. Sort of like anything—if you work hard, eventually something will come of it," I said, as I followed suit and hopped up the curb by the sign.

We locked our bikes together with both the cable lock and the titanium U-lock. I asked Elder Fischer to take a picture of me with the bikes and the sign, as it was my first day of tracting; I thought I should capture the moment. With a backpack full of copies of the *Book of Mormon*, a pen, and a blue planner in my shirt pocket, I walked with Elder Fischer up to the first house on the street.

"What are these? I've seen them all my life and never knew what they were." I said, pointing to a little emblem on the door jam about six feet up.

"It's called a mezuzah. There is a tiny roll of paper with commandments on it inside. It's from a scripture in Deuteronomy that God said to put his commandments on your doorpost. Or at least that's what the Jews took it to mean. I think they touch it with their kissed fingers when they come and go."

"Should I have known that?"

"No. How would you know that if you haven't really been exposed to it? I didn't know it before I started tracting. It's in the glossary of our Bibles, though. You can look it up."

"I will, when we get back."

Nobody was home at the first five doors. At the sixth house, a man opened the door. He was from the Czech Republic. He told us he could not speak English. In the little broken English he could speak, he said that he lived there with his brother, who wasn't home at the time. I pointed to the cover of the *Book of Mormon* and asked him if he could read English. He smiled and said no, but he could read Czech.

I told him we would come back with a Czech *Book of Mormon* that he could read. We set up a time two weeks out to come back and give him the book. I checked with Elder Fischer to make sure that we would be able to get a Czech book by then before telling the man we would come back.

Walking down the gravel walk from the house, I asked Elder Fischer, "Have you ever taught someone in a different language?"

"I don't think we could teach him. It would be tough when we don't speak the language. We can get him a *Book of Mormon*, but that's about all we can do. If he is really interested, then we could try to get some missionaries that speak Czech to come teach him. It was good that you offered him a Czech book, though. At least he will have it in his hands."

"That's true; hadn't thought that it would be tough to teach him not knowing the language," I said, feeling a little embarrassed at my poorly thought-out question. Of *course* someone couldn't be taught when there was no common language.

The next house had a mezuzah on it, and when the young woman opened the door, she simply pointed to the emblem on the door, smiled, and shut the door. It seemed the mezuzah served a second purpose as an antitracting device.

"Maybe we should look for an area that isn't so Jewish?" I asked.

"It isn't for us to choose who or where we teach."

"Elder, my first tracting experience of my lifetime as a full-time missionary, and you pick a ninety-percent Jewish neighborhood. That's not really fair."

"Well, we will be done soon with the area, and then we can move on to a more encouraging neighborhood. One thing to think about, though: at least the majority of people in this neighborhood are familiar with religion and Jesus Christ, so it might make it easier."

"Jewish people seem so serious about it, though. I bet not many Jewish people convert to other religions."

"Probably not, but they are still familiar with Jesus. Why don't we try a different approach? Let's try to talk about modern-day prophets on earth today."

"Why would that make a difference?" I asked with an inquisitive look.

"The Jewish religion believes that Christ was a prophet here on earth, not the savior. By going into modern-day prophets, it builds on common beliefs. Like in the Missionary Guide, building on common ground. Let's try it."

"That makes perfect sense. I think that's a grand idea. You take the first one so I get an idea of how to do it."

Elder Fischer looked over at me with a little smirk, "OK, but you will try it after that."

It took four more attempts at knocking on doors until someone finally opened. I could hear people behind other doors, even saw the light change in the peephole, but they wouldn't answer. I wouldn't have either. I thought our message was important—in fact the most important message a person could hear in his whole life—but I wouldn't open a door to people I didn't know. Also, with our being in white shirts and ties, in our early twenties, most people recognized us and knew what we wanted to say to them. When a young woman answered the door, Elder Fischer went into the new approach.

"Hello Ma'am. We are missionaries for the Church of Jesus Christ and Latter-day Saints, and we would like to spend a few minutes with you and share a message about modern-day prophets."

"No thanks. Not interested."

"Have a nice day," Elder Fischer said as the door was being shut.

"Well, I think our new approach is a hit," I said.

"It's only one door. It takes hundreds of doors to find people."

"I know. I was just giving you a hard time." "I'll take the next one," I said.

Our new approach didn't get any new members. We found only two people home the rest of the morning, before we took a break for lunch.

We walked back to our bikes and headed home. The sun was out in its madness, showing the winter chill who truly was boss. The heat helped work up a sweat. The wind from cruising about fifteen miles an hour on the bike helped keep the sweat from pouring off my body, but I knew as soon as we slowed down, I would be dripping. The seventy-degree weather would take a little getting used to. Living in both Utah and Dallas before the mission helped with tolerating the heat, but I never really got to like the hot weather. Especially while riding a bike in a tie, heavy pants, and a collared dress shirt. Underneath it all were garments—sacred garments, as part of the calling (one's job within the Mormon Church). It felt like wearing long underwear under everything else.

We coasted into the Austins' front yard, locked our bikes to the wagon wheel, and went inside. We had an hour for lunch. I wasn't sure what it entailed, the hour, but figured I'd follow along with Fischer.

"A little macaroni and cheese today, I think," I said, as I pulled one of my bonus-buy, six-for-a-dollar boxes from the cupboard set aside for us. Looking at the directions, I noticed that it asked for milk.

"Elder Fischer, have you ever made this without milk? I asked, holding the box up for him to see.

"Yeah, it works. Not quite as creamy, but it will work. Put a little extra butter in it. That should help."

"Do we ever have this at dinner appointments?"

"Sometimes. But there are big differences in the types of macaroni and cheese that you can eat."

"Oh really? I didn't know that. I look forward to learning about the different kinds." I made my macaroni and cheese and sat at the kitchen table across from Fischer, working on his second bowl of cereal.

"I take it that Sister Austin works during the day?" "Yeah, she is a county auditor for machinery."

"Really?" I said surprised, thinking she wasn't all that sharp.

I recovered, saying, "That sounds like a neat job."

"I haven't asked her much about it, but she seems to like it." "So how do you like it here? I mean the area where we live?"

How many different places have you lived since you've been out?" "Let's see,... I served in Bakersfield for the longest time. One year out of the two that I've been out."

"Is that a popular place to serve?"

"If you are Spanish speaking, then you have quite a bit of success. But for regular missionaries like you and I, it's not as nice. It's really hot there. It's east of here, in the desert. I've also served in Atascadero, up the coast about two hundred miles. It's nice there. You're right on the coast and it's pretty small, so you really get to know the area and the people."

Elder Fischer was running out of milk and cereal in his bowl, so I figured lunch was almost over. As he got up to wash the dish, he said we had about thirty minutes left on our lunch break. He headed into the bedroom as I got up to wash my bowl. If the Austins had been home, then he would have had to wait for me to finish, as missionaries couldn't be alone with anyone other than their companion or another missionary. If Brother Austin had been home, it would have been all right according to the mission rules.

The window over the kitchen sink looked out on a large backyard. In the far corner, there was a garage or shop. A driveway ran to this shop from the front of the house. An old brown Ford F150 truck was parked there. A skinny strip of grass lined the side of the shop, separating it from the concrete slab that took up the remainder of the yard. It looked like a tennis court, but small, so it turned out to be a big pickleball court. Brother Austin had mentioned something about it earlier and said he had originally wanted a tennis court, but once it was built, there just wasn't enough room to really move around. He probably shouldn't have tried to put it in himself. There was a door off the kitchen that let the dogs in and out; dog hair all over the frame of the door and outside on the patio.

The dogs were outside, so I didn't even attempt to go out. I finished putting my things away and headed to the bedroom to see what Elder Fischer was up to.

Beep! "Hi, Elders, this is Sister Williams." Just calling to remind you about dinner tonight. Give me a call if you need a ride, otherwise we will see you around five- thirty." *Beep!*

"Elders, this is Brother Erickson from the Second Ward, reminding you about this Sunday. It's missionary Sunday, and I would like to talk with you as to what your plan is for Sacrament Meeting. Give me a call and we can go over it. I know at least the three of us will be speaking, but anyone else that I haven't thought of? Number is 640-8908. Need to have final names for the program by tomorrow. Talk to you later." Beep-beep!

"Are we talking this Sunday?" I asked.

"Yes. Didn't I tell you? I guess I hadn't really thought about it," Fischer said while flipping through his organizer with the blue planners folded up in the back.

"That's OK. What are the topics, or the theme of the meeting?"

"It's missionary Sunday. It's the time that we make sure the members know who we are, talk about some of the work that we have in the area, and ask them for their support. This ward is pretty good about keeping up on them."

"Do you have any suggestions on what I can talk about?" I asked.

"Well, you need to introduce yourself. That could be the majority of your time. Since you just got here, you really don't know too much about the work going on, but you will by Sunday. So tell about yourself, maybe tell a story of something that has happened since you have been out."

"OK. How much time are we taking?" I asked.

"About fifteen minutes."

"OK," I said.

"Will you call the Williams about dinner tonight and let them know that we will need a ride? Here is the ward directory," Elder Fischer said, handing me his organizer with pages inside that had been retrofitted with the ward directory. "Make sure and tell them that we have appointments afterwards, so we will be picked up from their house around seven."

"Sure," I said as I sat down at my side of the desk and reached for the phone. After talking with the Williamses for a minute and doing a preliminary introduction, a ride was set up with them and we were back on our bikes for the rest of the afternoon.

"Where are we headed, Elder Fischer?" I asked after I'd finally caught up with him.

"We are going to visit Heavenly and George. They are a couple of people that were baptized last month. We are teaching them the New Member Discussions. They live about two miles up, on the left. After that, we will run by the Hickmans; they are members in the Second Ward. You can meet them. They are a neat family."

"No more tracting for today?"

"Probably not today, unless everyone that we have set to visit isn't home."

Overhead I heard the familiar sounds of a jet plane. It was easy to see in the clear sky a big 737 from Boeing.

"Elder Dorsey, how far away is that plane?"

"I have no idea. Thousands of feet."

"About 25 days," Elder Fischer said just before a smile crept across his face.

"Oh, that's right! I forgot that this is your last month out here. That's an interesting way to calculate the distance to the airplane. Very clever, I must say."

"You will hear it all the time. Not from me—I was just kind of getting you ready. You'll get missionaries that use different things like that, though."

"I can't wait. Do you think about it a lot?"

"Well I'm trying not to, but it can definitely distract a person pretty easily."

"What are you going to do when you get home? No, wait! What are you going to do the day you get home to Pocatello?"

"I haven't even talked with my parents as to what they have planned, but I imagine I'll have my grandparents and the whole family at the airport. From there, we will probably go home and have a big dinner with everyone."

"What are you going to have for dinner? One of Mom's favorites?"

"No request has been made, but I'm sure it will be good."

"Fischer! You are going home after two years! You must be craving for something, whether food, or maybe to see some friends?"

"Elder Dorsey, I've really tried not to think about it too much. You can imagine how hard on you and the other missionaries it would be if I talked about home and what I'm going to be doing."

"Yeah, that makes sense. I'm still writing you and finding out what you did those couple days after you got back though."

"OK. You can write and I'll let you know."

Fischer took a sharp left turn into a narrow alley, leaving me going down Cornelius Street. I quickly got turned around and caught him as he was locking his bike to a pole in the back parking lot of an old apartment complex. The titanium U-lock wouldn't fit around the pole that Elder Fischer had picked, so I proceeded to lock my red mountain bike to his borrowed

1960s ten-speed.

"I hope they don't just cut the tubes on my bike to get to yours," Elder Fischer said, concerned.

"If they want it that bad, let them have it," I said, looking back at the bikes. As I turned back, I leaned a little to the left and brushed up against an old, dirty blue truck with a nice clean spot where my white shirt had just swiped it.

"Shoot!" I said, as I pulled my shirt away from me and patted out the dirt.

We went through an outside door into a dark, deep-shag–carpeted hallway with orange lights that looked liked lanterns hanging on the wall. A musty smell permeated my nose. I imagined that the walls and carpet in the place were saturated with the odors, hair, and skin flakes of people and pets that had made their home there over the past forty years. A potent smell of garlic was mixed in with everything else.

"Man, what is that?" I asked, looking up with my nose. "It smells so good."

"Yeah, it does," Elder Fischer said.

After going up a flight of stairs, coming out to another hall with the exact same look and feel, we were standing in front of a door with the number 2-1-3 in gold. A little black button with the word *push* and a peephole lit with light stared back at us. Fischer knocked on the door. I heard a dog bark in response.

"Who is it?" A voice from the other side of the door came back.

"It's the Elders," Elder Fischer replied.

"Oh, hang on a minute."

The deadbolt clicked, the chain lock was undone, left hanging on the frame. The door was opened and we were invited in.

"Hi, Heavenly. How are you?" Elder Fischer asked as we walked into the little apartment.

"Good. How are you?"

"Did you remember we were coming for the Third New Member Discussion?"

"That's right. We talked about it Sunday, didn't we?"

"Yes. Is now still a good time?"

"Sure, this works fine. Are you guys hungry? We just finished having lunch and still have everything out.

"Thanks for the offer, but we have a dinner appointment later, so we will take you up on it another time."

"OK. Whose house you going to eat at tonight?"

"They are members in the Second Ward. Their name is Williams."

"Well that was very nice of them to invite you over for dinner," Heavenly said as she looked over at me and put out her hand. "I'm Heavenly, young Elder Dorsey." She said, looking at the black name tag hooked over my short-sleeve shirt's pocket. "It's nice to meet you."

"Nice to meet you too."

We proceeded into the living room and were pointed to a couch. There was a man who looked like Shaggy from *Scooby-Doo* bouncing a baby on his legs at one end, and a teenage girl at the other. Elder Fischer and I squeezed in next to each other while Heavenly introduced me to the rest of the people in the room. I wondered why no one was at work or school,

The man on the couch next to me was George Thompson. He was either overly friendly, or just liked to smile. He gave me a big "Hello, Elder Dorsey!" The young girl at the other end of the couch was named Star, and on the La-Z-Boy was Jack. Jack had a huge, curly head of hair that *may* have been combed. It was a mop. Jack took an instant liking to me and hopped up to shake my hand. His eyes were innocent, even for a twelve-year-old boy.

"It's nice to meet you, Elder Dorsey. I look forward to seeing you around."

"Nice to meet you too, Jack. I'm sure you will see me around," I said while looking up from the couch.

Over the next hour, we talked about their recent conversion to the Church. Heavenly talked about all the different churches she had been involved with and how she had been on the search for the true gospel and God her whole life. She had even had a stint of devil worshipping. She had her rosary beads around her neck and looked back a little while rubbing them, explaining how nice it felt when she used to sing with the beads in the congregation. She said she still wears them and feels comforted by them. Star changed the baby about halfway through our visit and cleaned up the kitchen from lunch. She did it quietly, trying not to disturb herself or us.

When it was time to go, we left with a prayer and walked out with George.

"Thanks for giving us a ride back to the Austins, George. Otherwise, we wouldn't have been able to make it in time for dinner."

"No problem. I was going to head over to the church tonight anyway and water the vegetables. You don't mind if we stop off there on the way, do you?"

"That's fine," Elder Fischer said, as he loaded his bike into the back of the truck.

After I loaded my bike in the truck, I hopped in the old blue truck with the clean spot on the door.

On the way to the church, George explained how he took care of the vegetable garden in the back of the church in exchange for fresh vegetables for his family. Once there, he showed me the compost bin, carrots, and squash. Watering took about ten minutes. I think George wanted to show off the garden instead of there really being a need to water it.

Back in the truck, George asked me questions about Seattle. He wanted to know all about the rain. I told him that it didn't rain as much as people thought. I said, "It is overcast a lot, but very few years are there consecutive days of rain into the twenties or thirties."

George asked genuine questions that he didn't know the answers to, like he knew he would never visit Seattle, so it was his chance to learn first hand. George seemed from another time, with his long hair and scraggly beard. He looked like he'd had a tough time with life. The deep creases extending from the corners of his eyes made me wonder when he had spent time in the sun or the wind.

Whatever his past was, his mind was clear and he enjoyed the thoughts and words of a young, nineteen-year-old boy.

"How much time until dinner?" I asked Fischer as he pushed open the door to the Austins.

"Ride should be here in about ten minutes."

“I’m going to change shirts. This thing is pretty dirty,” I said as I walked off in the direction of the bedroom, checking my armpits for freshness with Elder Fischer close behind.

I pulled out one of seven clean, white, short-sleeve shirts from my closet, still pressed from the ironing job I did at the MTC before leaving. I bought the neatest garment bag that allowed me to put shirts and pants in it and strapped them in so they didn’t move during travel. It hung from the door, an invention I thought so clever. Once I got the new shirt on and another layer of deodorant, Brother Daniels arrived and we were out the door to dinner.

The Williamses lived about twenty minutes from the Austins. We went through the usual question-and-answer period on the way with Brother Williams. It was cold, so Brother Williams had on a trench coat. It looked like he had just gotten home from work or was picking us up on his way home. Sister Williams called while we were on the road and asked Brother Williams to pick up a loaf of garlic bread from Von’s. We had just passed Von’s about two miles back, so we did a quick U-turn (quick for a minivan), and headed back towards the store. As we pulled into the parking lot, Brother Williams looked down at his watch, almost hitting another car. He had to slam on his brakes to avoid a collision. We didn’t say anything when Brother Williams said, “Oh, fuck!” and neither did he. Once he recovered from the near accident, Brother Williams asked us what time our appointments were that night. Elder Fischer told him that Brother Schultz would be picking us up around seven thirty.

“Well, I think everything else is ready, so it should go pretty quick. I know Sister Williams wanted to have it all ready before we got there, but something came up earlier that put us a little behind.”

“We should be fine,” Elder Fischer said, looking at his watch and shuffling through his daily organizer. Most the missionaries carried organizers. I’d noticed the Franklin Planner as being the most popular and one of the most expensive. Although the company was owned by a Mormon in Utah, missionaries didn’t get discounts when making purchases. I thought that since the organizers were helping in spreading the word of the Lord, the Franklin people should be handing them out. Apparently they didn’t think so, though. Oh, if only I ran the world and each person thought as I did.

"This should take just a minute," Brother Williams said as he was getting out of the car.

"We'll come in with you," Elder Fischer said, opening the passenger door and looking back at me. I pushed open the big sliding door, grabbed my backpack, and followed Brother Williams and Elder Fischer into the store, again following and trying to keep up. Fischer would take about one step to each of my two, and Brother Williams was walking faster than I had ever tried to. Walking too fast turned in to a waddle, and then the craziness started. I had on a backpack and a short-sleeve, white dress shirt and was the shortest of three people, rushing to keep up—it was a confidence builder.

Brother Williams grabbed a loaf of French bread and paid cash for it. I said "Hi" to people in line. Only one person out of three said "Hi" back. I figured it was the badge.

When we finally reached our destination, I noticed a banner on the front of the Williamses' house.

CONGRATULATIONS ON A NEW BABY GIRL!

"Oh, you just had a baby?" I asked.

"Well, my wife did. Yes. Actually the baby is about three weeks old, so the sign's a little old," he said.

"Well, congratulations anyway," I said.

"Thanks Elder," he said as he reached for the front door.

Brother Williams liked to keep things up for a while, I could tell. He still had his Christmas lights up from last year.

"Hello, Elders. We are all ready!" we heard from the kitchen. I guessed it was Sister Williams from the sweet voice.

"Elders, can I take your coats?" Brother Williams asked. "Thank you," Elder Fischer said as we handed our coats over.

A couple kids were poking their heads around the corner from down the hall. Giggling came from the same place. We went into the kitchen and sat down at the table. The food was already on the table. Brother Williams handed over the foil bag of French bread to Sister Williams, and she put it in the oven, bag and all, after opening one end.

"Elder Dorsey, would you offer the prayer tonight?" Brother Williams asked.

After the prayer, I met each of the kids at the table.

I helped myself to one of the hot pieces of bread from the oven and was surprised to learn that it came from the store all buttered with garlic on it. What a concept! It was really good. I filled up on the bread. I liked it more than the dry pot roast that I washed down with water.

After dinner, our split picked us up and we went to visit members' homes. The whole idea of splits was to involve members with the hope of getting twice as many converts. It served as a time for regular companions to split from each other for an evening and take a different member with them to teach and preach to the neighborhood people.

Visiting members' homes was what we planned when we had no teaching appointments for the evening. We set up a couple of appointments with members and shared a message with them on how important it is to share the gospel. Brother Schultz was visibly bugged that we were visiting members and not investigators. I empathized with him. If I had a night planned with the missionaries, I would want to teach Discussions to investigators and explain the gospel. It would have been a chance for him to open his Bible and *Book of Mormon,* putting into practice everything he had forgotten about his mission twenty years prior. Brother Shultz was a trooper, though. Even though he knew everyone we visited, he contributed to the Discussions we shared and even admonished the members to get their friends and neighbors introduced to the Church.

It was only nine o'clock when Brother Schultz dropped us back at the Austins. We thanked him for going out with us, said a prayer in the car, and headed inside.

Since we had to be in by nine thirty each night and in bed by ten thirty, on the nights that we got home early, we had a chance for personal study or for just hanging out. There wasn't much to do just hanging out, so I opted for personal study. Elder Fischer had his head buried in his sketchpad, so hanging out wasn't even an option. As I flipped through the *Book of Mormon*, I asked Elder Fischer what he was drawing.

"I'm into caricatures right now," he said.

"Can I see some?" I asked.

"Sure."

He turned his chair to face me and started flipping through his sketchpad.

"Who is that?" I asked after he just flipped past a man with big dark glasses.

"Elvis Costello," he said.

"Who's that?" I asked, recognizing his name, but having no idea who he was.

"He's a singer and songwriter," he said.

He rattled off a few songs that he thought I should have heard, but nothing came to mind. I watched plenty of MTV in high school but must have missed the afternoons with Elvis Costello.

"When did you start drawing?" I asked.

"I guess I just always have. I want to be a graphic design major, so I've taken several art classes at Iowa State already."

"What do graphic designers do?" I asked.

"Marketing and advertising for companies. Most companies that sell something have graphic designers," he said.

"Did you draw that?" I asked, pointing to a devil-looking, hairy-faced man framed on the wall above the desk.

"Yeah… I did that when I first came out and just hang it up wherever I'm at."

"What is it for?" I asked.

"It's this ancient Indian guy that supposedly scares away the demons. I don't believe in it but thought it was a cool thing to draw."

"It's great. Man, have *you* got a talent! I've always wanted to be able to draw."

"You can. Have you practiced much at it?" He asked.

"Well, no. Whenever I draw, though, it sucks."

"Well, then try drawing something that you might enjoy. And keep drawing it until you get good at it. That's a way to start. Even if you start by tracing things."

"Really? Tracing will help? What should I draw?" I asked.

He picked up a Calvin and Hobbes cartoon book and held it up. "Just getting your fingers and your hands used to doing something different will make a huge difference."

"Do you like Calvin and Hobbes?"

"Oh, yeah. Love 'em," I said, with a deep, grunting Tim Allen voice.

"Work on drawing Calvin for a while. See how good you get." I set a mental goal to become a Calvin artist.

I finally got around to writing my talk on Saturday night after a long day of tracting and visiting members. It didn't take me long. In school, I'd formed a habit of thinking a lot about what I would talk or write about throughout my days and weeks before a talk or paper was due; when I sat down to write it out, it was all there. I made my talk into an outline form; mainly a few key words that I knew would trigger the flow of the talk, allowing me to speak naturally versus just reading in front of the two hundred people in the congregation. I'd planned on starting out by talking about myself—where I was from and what I did before my mission. I wrote a little joke about the rain in Seattle; thought it would be a nice icebreaker. I ran some of it by Elder Fischer, who said it sounded great. I asked him what he was going to talk about. He said he would doctor up the First Discussion to make it sound like natural talk and then, at the end, would bring it around as the First Discussion for investigators. The idea was to show the members how easy and innocent it was to talk about the Church.

Hopefully, this would prompt the members to get out and get everyone they knew interested in the Church.

By ten o'clock, I was done with my talk and began thinking about the next day. I would be meeting the members of the Sixth Ward for the first time. These were people I was to keep in touch with for the rest of my life. Our families would exchange Christmas cards for years to come. I might even meet my wife (of course not knowing it at the time) and tell the story of how we met, how I was stricken with awe and a sense of knowing her in the preexistence. Had I never gone on a mission, I would have been alone with no wife, no family, searching and wandering the world for the lost love that was never to be found.

We had a Ward Mission Meeting before church, so we got there about an hour early. Brother Robson, the ward mission leader, was a few minutes late. I drew a perfect Calvin on the inside cover of my *Book of Mormon* while waiting.

The meeting lasted only about a half hour. After the meeting, we greeted the members and scoped the congregation for anyone who looked new. We weren't expecting any of our investigators to come, yet there was always a chance that one might show.

The brethren were thrilled to meet me. The wives seemed to be disinterested, which I attributed to the kids they were trying to keep at bay. I probably shook over a hundred hands yet didn't remember one name. It was really nice, though, when the Barretts and the Austins came through the door, familiar faces. Sister Barrett gave me a melting smile. Rachel said "Hello" and shook my hand; I wished I could have kissed her. I was meeting hundreds of new people, talking to absolute strangers, yet the only thing that made me sweat and blush was seeing Rachel. The Barrett women's smiles, were intoxicating. The thoughts that went through my head were far from missionary work, yet in my vulnerable state as a greenie, I felt good.

Brother Austin, with whom I was becoming fast friends, shook my hand just like all the other members and invited us to sit with them. I thanked him for the offer and explained that the Barretts were already saving a place for us. I'd never been so polite in my life. "Thank you" and "Nice to meet you too!" were commonplace phrases by the end of the day.

My talk went off without a hitch. I was nervous, but I didn't think anyone could tell. For the rest of the day, everyone who passed me in the hall said, "Enjoyed your talk, Elder," or ""Looking forward to having you guys over for dinner soon."

It seemed like the missionary spirit was in the air. I asked Elder Fischer, "It seems that everyone loves the missionaries here. Why don't we get more referrals?"

"Most people don't feel comfortable talking to their gentile friends and neighbors about the Church. Did you talk with your friends about the Church and try to get them to come out?"

"No, but I'm a kid. I don't have to; the members have to. It's part of being in the Church. It's a commandment."

"I know. It's still hard to do, though."

"I guess, but I'm still hitting everyone up." I said assuredly. We got our dinner calendar back from Sister Jensen, the Relief Society president, and thanked her for handing it around. I saw that the Robertsons had us scheduled for tonight. Sister Robertson walked up as we were looking it over and asked us what time we would like to eat. She looked down at her watch and said, "Elders, It's two o'clock. How does three-thirty sound to you?"

"That would be fine," Elder Fischer said.

"Did you warn Elder Dorsey about us?" She chided.

"Nope, but I plan on it before we get there," he said, not missing a beat, his soft eyes smiling.

"Do you guys need a ride? I can have John run over to get you," she asked.

"That would be great if he could. We have an appointment afterwards, so it would save us a little time," he said.

"OK. He'll be there around three. How'd you make out for dinners this week?" she asked, looking at the dinner calendar in my hand.

I turned it towards her so she could see all the squares marked with *X*'s. "We did great. I think we have dinner for the next three weeks," I said, thinking it may have been due to my exceptional personal skills, my natural ability to talk in front of people, and my overall appearance that filled the calendar.

"Now, you know if there is *ever* a time that you don't have a dinner, call me. You are always welcome at my house. When my boys go on missions, I never want them to go hungry."

"Thank you. That is very nice of you, and we'll be sure to take you up on it," I responded. I wondered if people ever did things simply because they were nice people, or was it because they were looking at the residual blessing for themselves and their family?

We got a ride home with the Austins, then relaxed for a few minutes before Brother Robertson picked us up.

Brother Austin turned on the television. The coverage of the war in Iraq was on every channel. Brother Austin shook his head back and laughed in disbelief, "What does Saddam Hussein think he is doing? We are just going to kill 'em! I can't believe he's going up against the U.S. in this."

"Well I don't think that's what he intended. He just wanted to take over Kuwait, not take on the United States," I said.

Saddam Hussein was a madman who had taken control of Iraq ten years earlier. He was instantly disliked for killing twenty-one of the cabinet members from the existing regime. After he took over Kuwait and was in control of 24% of the world's oil, the United States stepped in. We asked him to get out, with a deadline of January 15th. He wasn't abandoning his regime, so we were going to bomb him with everything we had. Very impressive show by President George Bush, and great timing as Bush had just taken office.

"He had to figure, though, that the U.S. would get involved when oil is in jeopardy," Brother Austin said.

"That's true. I hadn't thought of that," I said, grateful for being the receiver of such insightfulness.

I'd followed the war a little bit before I came out. We couldn't read the paper or magazines while on the mission, so I was just going off what I saw when we came in at night and the news was on and what I had remembered hearing before I went into the MTC. We weren't allowed to watch television either, even the news, but if it was on while we were passing through the room, it was OK to stand a minute and watch it—as long as we didn't sit down and put our feet up. If Brother Austin was in the room and we talked with him, it was really OK.

Brother Robertson was five minutes late. He apologized, said "Hi" to Brother Austin, and then walked out the door with us.

Once in the car, Brother Robertson told me how much he enjoyed the Sacrament Meeting.

"That was one of the best Sacrament Meetings I've been to in a long time! It's always nice when the elders get up and talk about their work. And Elder Fischer, I really enjoyed the First Discussion today. It took me a few minutes to figure out why it sounded so familiar, but even in Spanish, you just can't forget something that you taught every day for two years."

"Where did you serve, Brother Robertson?" I asked from the back seat.

"Spain. Boy, it's been about fifteen years now. Man, that's not fun to think about."

"Your mission isn't?" I asked.

"No, my age. The mission was great. Wouldn't trade it for the world," he said.

"Oh yeah?" I asked.

"Yeah. You know, I still have people that I keep in touch with in Spain."

"Really? Have you gone back to visit yet?" I asked.

"No, not yet. We want to wait until the kids are a little older so they can really enjoy it. It's so expensive to travel there. If I hadn't gone there on my mission, I don't think I would have ever been able to go overseas to travel. Although we hope to in the future."

"It would be expensive, especially with a family," I said.

"You stateside guys have it made. You can keep in contact with all the people and friends you meet forever and not lose touch. I would really like to see the people I baptized, more than anything."

"You still write to them, don't you?" I asked.

"Just one family that I baptized. We exchange Christmas cards. But there were hundreds that I will never now what happened."

"That would be tough," I sympathized.

Dinner was ready when we arrived at the Robertsons. Everyone had a plate set in front of him, except for me. After Fischer said the prayer on the food, Sister Robertson got up to get my plate.

"There you go, Elder Dorsey. Enjoy!" she said as she handed me a plate full of roast beef, mashed potatoes, and cauliflower—all green.

"Whoa, what is this?" I asked in shock.

"Green, because you're a greenie!" three-year-old Jacob blurted out.

I had a big smile and started rolling my eyes back.

"I would never have thought that this would have happened to me. I've never even heard of this," I said, laughing with the kids.

"No, Elder? I thought all greenies got at least *one* green dinner on their mission," Sister Robertson said.

"Nope, this is a first for me and probably the last. It looks very good, though. Really," I said as I scooped up a green spoonful of mashed potatoes. "The first green mashed potatoes that I've ever had in my life. Here they go!" I said as I held the spoon mouth height and put it in. The kids were really getting a kick out of it. I chomped on the potatoes, making grunting sounds of enjoyment. I think the kids would have liked green food.

After dinner we went into the living room. While we were sharing a story out of the *Book of Mormon* about the prophet Alma and his brothers, Sister Robertson breastfed the baby, right there. I'd never been around breastfeeding, and to me, a boob was a boob. Whether a kid is sucking on it or not, a boob was a boob. Why couldn't she go into another room? Why couldn't she at least use a towel and cover up?

No, she just pulled her boob out. She did this without me even knowing that she was going to feed the baby. I thought she was just pulling it out. All I could do was phase out everything. I did it, phased out everything except the sucking sound of the baby on the orange nipple. I refused to look over at Sister Robertson the rest of the evening, quite awkward when we were there another hour. When she finally put her breast away, I was able to at least say goodbye to her.

"What was that all about, Elder?" I asked Fischer once safely back at the Austins.

"What was *what* about?" he said.

"Sister Robertson's bareness?" I said.

"She was just breastfeeding. Get used to it; you will see it all the time," he said.

"I don't want to get used to it."

"Well, a lot of women do it. You'll see it while on your mission. It's mainly the members that do it, so if you spend most your time with investigators you won't have to worry about it," he said, slyly suggesting that I should spend most of my time with investigators.

"Well I don't want them to. Can't we say something while we are in their house?" I asked.

"Key word there, Elder Dorsey: *their* house. We are in their house. If they want to breastfeed, then they should be able to. Some people feel they should be able to do it anywhere they like. Don't worry about it too much. Believe it or not, you will get used to it," he said, as if patting me on the shoulder, telling me everything would be OK.

"I hope so. It's really hard to concentrate on anything when that is going on," I said, concerned with myself only.

P-Day consisted of doing laundry in the morning, with plans to go with Sister Barrett to the mall in the afternoon. I secretly hoped that Rachel would be there.

We were lucky to have a washer and dryer in our house. Most missionaries had to go to the laundromat, where they'd waste their time on a P-Day when they could have been enjoying themselves. We'd already done our laundry and been to the grocery store by the time Sister Barrett picked us up to go to the mall. I learned that we weren't going to the conventional mall, but to a flea-market mall. Rachel didn't go.

A huge tent had been set up in a parking lot four miles outside of our area. The tent was packed full of adults, kids, and tables. It felt like everyone was selling something, whether it be a pair of sunglasses that blocked UV rays like no others, or a spray-on carpet cleaner to clean up after pets messed on the carpet. There was a man selling wigs, a lady selling painted-on fingernails, and couples selling homemade jams and crafts. Christmas was coming—decorations and crafts promising to make the Christmas holiday unforgettable were everywhere. I would have loved to buy a back massager made to fit a chair or shoe inserts that were virtually invisible (to make a person look an inch taller), but I didn't end up buying anything. Sister Barrett let us wander as soon as we hit the front door. After we had looked around a little, we started looking for her.

We found her beside a stand full of professional sports jerseys signed by their very famous wearers. There was one signed by Derrick McKey, a forward for the Seattle SuperSonics, and another by Clyde Drexler of the Portland Trail Blazers. Too expensive for any gift that I might give, but

Sister Barrett had already picked a couple out.

With three boys at home, all playing basketball for their respective schools, I imagined they would make great gifts.

"You guys all finished looking around?" She asked, as we stood outside the shop of jerseys. Looking down at our empty hands she commented, "Hey, you guys didn't even buy anything!"

"I know…" I said with remorse in my voice, "I've already done my shopping for Christmas" (which I hadn't).

"I won't have room to carry it on the plane," Elder Fischer said, with an easy, pleasant tone.

"Oh, that's right, Elder Fischer! You will be home for Christmas this year. Won't that be nice. How exciting!" Sister Barrett said.

"I think so," Elder Fischer said with a soft smile. "So, are you guys ready to go then?"

"Sure."

"You want to stop and get some lunch before we head home?" Sister Barrett asked as we walked back to the car.

"Oh yeah; I'm starving," I blurted out before Elder Fischer had time to answer.

"There's an In-and-Out Burger on the way home. You want to stop there?" She asked.

"That sounds perfect! I've wanted to go there before I go home. And, well, if I don't go today, with it being out of the area and all, I may not get there before I go."

"Oh, no. I'm a terrible member. I took you outside your area," Sister Barrett said, looking over at Elder Fischer with concern in her eyes.

"No, you're not. We go out of our area if we need to, and going out a few miles to spend time with a member on P-Day isn't a big deal," Elder Fischer said. And I wondered where he got his boundaries from.

"You're sure? We can just head home now, and that might make it better," she said, squishing her face up in anticipation. She wanted to take us out. What was it about Moms wanting to see boys eat?

"No, going to In-and-Out will be fine. I promise," Elder Fischer reassured. I was a little surprised with Elder Fischer, as he was a stickler for the rules. I thought how many investigators would be turned away from us for breaking even the least of the rules. This thought confused me and instantly started swimming in my head, around and around, until I had to throw it out completely or be a zombie for the rest of the afternoon.

I hadn't been to In-and-Out Burger and was looking forward to it. I enjoyed eating at new places, even if it was a fast-food restaurant. Nothing could have prepared me for how good the burgers were, though. They were the best burgers I'd had, even better than Dick's Hamburgers back home! I ate three of them with a small milkshake and water. Sister Barrett bought them for us. We offered to pay, but she refused.

Members had this thing about taking care of the missionaries. They thought if they took care of us when we were in their area, then other members would take care of their sons while they were on their missions. I hoped God didn't work that way; it would be more pressure than I could ever handle.

We ate inside the restaurant, in our P-Days.

When we got back to the Austins, we played a couple games of pool and wrote letters.

"Who you writing to?" I asked Elder Fischer after he beat me in both games of pool.

"My Mom."

"Man, what do you say when you will be home in less than three weeks?" I asked, secretly envying his going home.

"Tell her how the work is going…tell her a little about you. And tell her not to worry about me coming home."

"She'll worry no matter *what* you tell her. She hasn't seen you in two years."

"I know she will. But it's still nice to hear."

"Are you writing any girls at home?" I asked.

"No. I had some friends before I left, but no girlfriend."

"You are so mellow about going home, Fischer. It's like you aren't even thinking about it."

"Oh, I'm thinking about it," he said, looking up from his letter, "Aren't you looking forward to just starting your mission, Elder?"

"Well, yeah. But I look forward to when it's over and I'm back having some fun. I mean, this isn't the most fun I've had," I said, surprised at what I'd just shared.

"I know what you mean. Well, it will be here before you know it," he said.

"I know. I know."

I wrote a letter to my mom. I told her all the new things in my life—all about my area, the members, and the Austins. I wrote my little brother David. He was going on a mission in another two years. He would actually leave about a month before I got home, so I wouldn't see him for four years.

We had a dinner appointment at five with the McDonnells. Elder Fischer tried to describe them from our meeting on Sunday, but I couldn't remember. After dinner, the McDonnells invited us to stay for Family Home Evening—an evening once a week, generally on a Monday, set aside by the prophets as family night. Everyone in the family was to stay home together, involving him- or herself in a lesson and activity. The Church had a manual for members to teach from, with the activity mapped out along with a simple, cheap treat to look forward to afterwards, like layered pudding. Most families with little kids adhered to this regimen each week, without fail. Families with grown children in high school or college tended to let Family Home Evening slide

Family Home Evening with the McDonnells was super. Benson, the two-year-old, was on my lap all night long. He was the cutest little kid. He had big brown eyes that looked at you like a cocker spaniel's, sad and tired. He wasn't sad, though; just had those eyes. We had a lesson from six-year-old Braden McDonnell, who taught us about when Jesus was baptized and a dove came down from heaven. The game was orchestrated by Jason (he went by Jay). He had us all on our hands and knees in a circle, telling the person next to us, whose eyes were closed, where to throw a little sponge Nerf ball into a basket. The point was to show how we needed help from our Heavenly Father through life, or we would go through life blind, thus missing the basket and missing the point of life.

The only thing they asked us to contribute to the night was the closing prayer. Benson held my arms folded around him while I said it. I thanked God for the lovely evening that we had with the McDonnells. I named each one of the kids and asked God to bless them. It was only a minute or so long, but by the time I was finished, Benson was asleep on my lap.

We had a busy week planned. District Meeting was scheduled for Tuesday, and Wednesday was Zone Conference.

District Meeting was for the missionaries in our district; it consisted of Elder Ryan and Elder Proude, who covered Woodland Hills. They lived in a gorgeous home of fellow members who were rarely home, as they traveled the world. We had sisters in our district also; they covered all the deaf people in the whole Valley. Just like missionaries who learned a language in the MTC, these sisters learned to sign. The other companionship, Elders Nestler and Booth, covered two of the Spanish-speaking wards.

We met at the ward building of Elders Ryan and Proude. It was closest to being in the middle for everyone. The sisters and the Spanish-speaking missionaries had cars but with limited allowable miles. They had to monitor how far they drove and understood that miles were better spent in search of new members rather than getting together with fellow missionaries.

District Meeting was like any other meeting within the Church. We had a prayer to start it off, a spiritual message shared by one of the companionships, along with some sort of activity or game that was to represent fun. I was introduced to everyone in the meeting. I took about five minutes, answering questions about where I was from, my experience at the MTC, and my time at Brigham Young University (BYU). The Spanish-speaking elders shared a spiritual message, and Elder Fischer gave a lesson out of the Missionary Guide on follow-up with potential new members.

Afterwards, we played a game of bump on the basketball court. The idea of the game was to shoot a foul shot and make it before the next one in line got his ball in. It was called *bump* because you could bump the other person's ball all the way down to the other end of the court if you were able to hit it in the air, not off a bounce. It came down to Elder Proude and me as the last two. I missed, leaving Elder Proude to be crowned as King of Bump, the last thing I thought he needed, as he already thought he was a king.

"Hey, Dorsey! I noticed you didn't have any sunglasses?" Elder Proude said.

"No, I don't," I said matter-of-factly, "I'll need to get some, though."

"I have a pair of Frog Eyes. You know, the Oakley ones. I'll sell 'em to you for fifteen bucks."

"That's not a bad deal. Sure, I'll take 'em."

"I have them in my bag here," he said while reaching into the bag on the back of his bike.

"OK. I think I have fifteen dollars on me too," I pulled my wallet from my back pocket and handed over a ten. "I only have ten. Can I owe you five?" I asked.

"Sure. Just give it to me next time you see me."

We rode back towards our area and I looked through my new glasses over at Elder Fischer. "That wasn't a bad deal, was it?"

"No, I don't think so."

"Enjoyed your lesson on Follow-Up out of the Missionary Guide," I said with a touch of sarcasm.

"Oh, OK. Sure you did. Elder Dorsey, have you been out long enough to tease me?" He asked.

"Probably not. I really did enjoy it, though," I said with a grin, "That part about calling the investigator back later: couldn't you use that when you are home dating?"

"OK, OK. Enough about the Missionary Guide. And yes, most missionaries find the Missionary Guide the *perfect guide* to dating and getting married."

We rode the rest of the way home, enjoying the breeze. After splits that night, we got home around nine o'clock. When I came in the bedroom, Elder Fischer was writing another letter. "Oooh...writing letters on a Tuesday?" I asked, teasing.

"Just catching up on some I didn't have a chance to get to yesterday."

"Fischer, it's OK," I said.

"Elder, you need to get out of the habit of calling me Fischer. You really need to call me Elder Fischer," he said.

"Are you serious?" I asked, a bit taken aback.

"Well, yes. That's what we are out here. We are *Elders*. We need to remember that. And calling each other by our last names, we forget that we are different."

"What do you mean?" I asked.

"Well, it's easy to think that we are the same people we were when we were home, just in a different place."

"Dang, never thought of it like that," I said.

"Something to think about. It doesn't bug *me*, but it's a good habit to call everyone out here *Elder*."

"I'll work on that. I don't see it as such a big deal that I can't work on it," I said, feeling enlightened.

Zone Conference came once a month. Several zones coming together to hear the latest inspired word from God via President Carlson.

The topic of Zone Conference was Helping Others Feel and Recognize the Spirit, a topic right out of the Missionary Guide. I feverishly took notes as President Carlson talked from the pulpit. I noticed most of the missionaries around me weren't taking notes; they must have heard it already. Sister Carlson gave a talk on keeping clean, how a clean home or apartment invited the spirit. I thought it was very interesting and that there must have been a little hubbub somewhere in the mission to warrant such a talk. I didn't take notes on it.

I didn't see Elder Nelson, the only missionary I came out with. I'd heard he had been sent to Bakersfield, which was too many zones over to be invited to the Valley's Zone Conference. There were ten zones in the mission.

Each zone had a zone leader, who passed on any pertinent information from the president, or passed on pertinent information to the president. zone leaders served many facilities: they could interview elders as needed, or they could interview investigators on certain matters concerning drugs and alcohol before a baptism to determine if the investigator was truly worthy to be baptized. This didn't happen often, but often enough that there needed to be someone in place for it. Within each zone might be several districts. Each district had a district leader, like Elder Fischer. If a missionary had any one of these titles, he was thought to be a smarter, and an all-around better, missionary. Any leadership roles would have the accompanying letter sent home to the parents. In the upper echelon of the mission leadership roles there were the Assistants to the President (APs). They wore the crown of God among members and other missionaries, at least the greenies. After the mission, they had their pick of the litter in dating and ward callings. They were the future bishops, stake presidents, and apostles of the church.

The assistants worked daily with the president in keeping the mission running smoothly. They went to the airport, picking up all newly arriving missionaries and dropping off those departing. Any "problem missionaries" needing to be transferred to a different location would be handled by the APs. They worked in the office with the senior missionaries, traveling to all the Zone Conferences and giving workshops on missionary topics. Parents wanted their sons to be an AP on their mission. This hat ensured he would marry into the perfect family, with the most beautiful wife imaginable. Parents received a letter signed by the mission president himself, congratulating the parents on raising such a magnificent young man who could be ready to serve in such a capacity as his assistant. I imagine that some parents would take this letter and frame it, tell the ward, and have it announced in Sacrament Meeting the following Sunday after receiving the letter.

The crowned AP's whom I had met coming off the plane stood before me in a workshop, teaching me how to tract and get better results. It looked like they teamed up; they were both teaching it. They gave me a handout, so I didn't take notes. They called everyone "Elder" because they didn't have every elder's name memorized the way the president did.

After Zone Conference, we went out on our splits. I went out with Brother Edwards, a short, slight, bald man. He was intense and looked directly into my eyes during any trading of words. Elder Fischer and I had set up an appointment with one of the people we had met while tracting. The majority of the time, when people set up an appointment to see us, they forgot or just meant to get us off their doorstep. Candice was there and let us in. She and three-year-old Bobbi were watching reruns of *Bay-*

watch. She turned the television off and told Bobbi to come sit by her. Bobbi's long, curly, blond hair was in front of her face when she turned to look at the television after it had been turned off. She brushed her hair back; there was a look of "Who would dare turn off my television?" She didn't cry; just looked at us in wonderment.

I introduced Brother Edwards to both Bobbi and Candice and thanked them for having us over. We hadn't even had a chance to talk with Candice when we knocked on her door the first time; she was on lunch and just about to walk out. I was shocked she invited us in, surprised she even remembered us from the quick visit on her doorstep.

We asked about her and her family. She moved to Chatsworth about six months earlier from Minnesota after she and her husband had what sounded like a rough breakup. When she was in Minnesota, she occasionally attended mass at a Catholic church on the corner. She hadn't grown up Catholic nor had any feelings towards one particular church or religion, but at the time, she thought it would be nice to go and introduce religious traditions to Bobbi. We explained a little about who we were: that I came to California from Seattle, Washington, to share what I believed to be true God's Church. Brother Edwards explained that he lived in the Valley with his family and attended his local Mormon Church. She seemed to be genuinely interested in what we were saying, asking questions not only about the Church, but also about what it was like leaving our families for two whole years.

We taught her the First Discussion and set up a time the following week to come back and teach the Second. I had taught the First Discussion numerous times since being out, yet Brother Edwards hadn't taught one in twenty-five years, since he had been on his mission in France. It was pretty rough. Luckily, Candice didn't have any questions or show signs of minding that we sucked.

Elder Fischer was excited that Brother Edwards and I were able to teach a First; he was surprised Candice had been home and let us in. "Well, we are now actively teaching an investigator," he said.

"She's our only one, huh?" I asked.

"Yeah, she's it. We have a few that are stuck on the Second. It's hard to go any further in the Discussions if they don't commit to being baptized, so we tend to have a few just sitting out there. I've tried to get in touch with them to introduce you, but if I can't, we may want to move on. We will go by tomorrow and leave notes on their doors."

"You told me about a young guy that was in an accident on his motorcycle. What about him?"

"We'll go see Daniel tomorrow. You never know what kind of mood he will be in, but I do think he enjoys our visits. I know I enjoy them and him."

* * * * *

"Hello, Elders! Oh, we got a new one today," Daniel said as we walked into his room.

"Hello, Daniel. Nice to see you again. This is Elder Dorsey," Elder Fischer said.

"It's nice to meet you," I said.

"What's your name? Elder…?" Daniel asked, looking at me.

"Elder Dorsey," I said.

"No, No. What's your *real* name?" He asked.

"What do you mean?" I asked.

"Daniel thinks it's funny—excuse me, not *right*—that we hide ourselves with our name tags instead of using our real names," Elder Fischer explained gently.

"My name is Ray," I said, not waiting for any hint of how to answer from Elder Fischer.

" Ray Dorsey…now *there's* a name! It's nice to meet you too, Ray."

"Daniel, you know we would prefer it if you called us 'Elder,'" Elder Fischer said with his soft eyes looking into Daniel's.

"I can call you anything I want. Don't forget, you're the ones that came to visit *me*."

We talked with Daniel for about a half hour. He was twenty-one and pissed off. He had been in a motorcycle accident six months earlier that left him paralyzed from his neck down. He was a good-looking kid. On his wall, he had pictures of him with friends and past girlfriends. At least I assumed they were, as he had his arms around them and was in some way embracing them. They were all very pretty.

It appeared he had quite the life before, although any other life would have been quite the life compared with his present state. Elder Fischer told me a little more about him after we left.

"We met him by visiting the home off and on. The house always has people that are bedridden. Since I've been here, three people have moved out of there."

"Man, that's gotta be hard to see. How often do you go visit the house?" I asked.

"I've tried to do it once a week. On busy weeks, though, it slips," he said. I thought that if anything couldn't be missed or slip through the cracks, it would be Daniel and anyone else in that house. I was sad yet thankful for my own health in my thoughts.

"Have we had any success?" I asked.

"Well, that depends on what you mean by *success*."

"You know what I mean. Have we baptized any of them?"

"No, but I think they enjoy the visits. It's hard to tell. They are pretty pissed off, for the most part. Elder Dorsey, we don't really go there to teach them the gospel. Although I enjoy it, it's been counted as service with us."

"Oh. Why don't we try to teach them?"

"I don't think it's the time or place. Plus, when we start pushing Discussions on people like that, we may not get invited back by the people in charge. Just be careful and go there to say "Hi." If they ask to be taught, then teach them."

"Have you taught Daniel any Discussions?"

"We taught him the First about two months ago. He tends to fight or disagree with the things taught. I just don't think this is his time."

"Why don't we try and teach him the Second next week? It will be like a going-away present for you," I said.

"We can try. Go ahead and schedule it for next week, sometime during the day."

When we went back the next week, Daniel was in high spirits. He was thrilled to see us. He was listening to the rock band Boston on the radio.

"Hello, Elders. Two visits in two weeks; what's up? You running out of people to teach?" He asked, the lyrics of Boston's "Oh What a Feeling" blaring in the background.

"Hi, Daniel. How are you today?" I asked.

"I'm not bad. I took a shit this morning. Stunk up the *whole* god*damn* house! It was pretty funny. Last week, after you left, my girlfriend called and broke up with me," he said, almost laughing. I thought I had misjudged his high spirits. I thought *any* emotion in *his* state should be considered good, though. Had I been in his position, I'd insist on a constant heroin drip into my IV. I wanted to ask him what he would do with legs for just one more day. Would he run and run until he collapsed and then crawl? I wished I could have given him *my* legs for a day.

"Sorry to hear about that. Had you two been dating for a while?" I asked.

"Three years. Thought we might get married. Can't really blame her, though. Look at me."

I didn't know what to say.

"What else is going on in your life? Tell me what you do to keep busy," I didn't know what to say and was stumbling over the words that were coming out.

"Keep busy? How busy can I get? I watch television," he said, his tone changing dramatically from the minute before.

"What do you like to watch?" I asked.

"Elder Dorsey, do you not see it? All I can do is watch television. After the first month, I'd already seen everything twice. It's not a matter of what I like to watch, it's what I haven't seen for the longest time."

"Good point. I imagine you do watch a lot of television. I thought maybe the nurses or maybe your family came to visit. Maybe they read to you?"

"No. Why would I want someone sitting here reading to me? Hell, I didn't even like reading when I had legs. Why would I want to read now?" He said with disgust.

"Hey, Daniel, it was only a suggestion. No reason to get mad about it," Elder Fischer said.

"Fuck you guys! You ask me if I *read*? Hell, I can't even hold a book. Get the hell out of here!"

"OK, OK. I'll give you a call next week, Daniel. Maybe we can come visit you then," Elder Fischer said.

Daniel didn't say "Bye" as we walked back to the front door, where the nurse let us out.

"What was up with that, Elder?" I asked.

"That's happened a couple times. I think it might be his medication. Sometimes we sit and talk for an hour and Daniel is quite pleasant, and sometimes," shrugging his shoulders, "he's really tough to talk with."

"Well, hopefully next week will be better." I said.

A week later, we got onto our bikes and headed over to Candice's. She wasn't home when we had tried the previous week to give her the next Discussion. We didn't have her phone number—she hadn't wanted to give it to us—so we stopped by every other day, hoping to catch her home.

"We should leave her a note today. Just to let her know that we are still here and want to see her again," I said.

"Good idea," Elder Fischer said.

When we got to Candice's, she wasn't there. Elder Fischer kept one of those miniature spiral notebooks in the pocket of his white shirt. It only had three pages left, enough to get him through the rest of his mission.

The note read:

Candice,

Looking forward to seeing you again. Give us a call when you have a chance. Our number is 425-9870.

Elder Dorsey & Elder Fischer

We tracted for the next few days and visited members in nearby neighborhoods. Elder Fischer had a few members he wanted to say "Bye" to, but not many. There were, of course, the Barretts, whom we were accustomed to seeing anyway, along with Heavenly and George. We gave Heavenly and George the last of the New Member Discussions. His final Discussion was for members vulnerable to leaving the Church within the year in further search of God's true religion on earth. Once involved in the Church, the feelings of the spirit risked being abandoned, causing new members to continue their search. I thought it similar to first love, a feeling so intense in the beginning, then gone with the passage of time.

We played pool every night after splits. Elder Fischer was quiet, probably engrossed in thoughts of a new life. He let me use his scriptures one day, when teaching a new-found investigator. The scriptures were well worn, easily flipping open to the designated verses that we shared with each investigator. He had marked his scriptures with the same precision and natural ability that his drawing took on. Some elders crinkled the pages of their Bibles and *Book of Mormon*s, page by page, then straightened them again, making the pages easier to flip when Bible bashing. Their scriptures took on the appearance of untamed curly hair. Elder Fischer didn't ever do this, though. His scriptures were worn from hard work—morning and nightly reading—for the past two years.

Elder Fischer wore his green suit to church. All the kids called him the Jolly Green Giant; even I did. He had bought the polyester suit from another missionary going home. The suit's bright color forced Fischer to wear sunglasses with it. Even I, standing next to him, had to shield my eyes, the shine was that intense. The Bishop asked him to bear his testimony in Sacrament Meeting. He thanked everyone for the time he had spent with them, telling everyone how much he believed in what he had done over the past two years. I felt he was talking to me, letting me know his feeling of importance for the job he had done, a job I was just beginning.

Elder Fischer never talked about members. He never talked about other missionaries. His profound statement was, "While you're out here, you might as well work hard."

We hugged goodbye. He was wearing his green suit for the last time.

CHAPTER 4

The first thing Elder Elliot gave me was a Czech *Book of Mormon*.

"Here you go. I take it we are teaching a Czech?" he asked.

"Oh, hey, thanks," I said as I took it with one hand and stuck out my other hand to shake his. He had already gone to the back of the car and was pulling his bike out. I quickly put my hand down so I wouldn't look dumb.

"Can I help you unload?" I asked.

"Sure, grab my suitcase," he said, looking up from putting the front wheel on his bike. He had one of those quick releases. My bike didn't have that.

"This is Jim," he said, pointing his head towards the tall man who was driving.

"Nice to meet you, Jim," I said.

"Nice to meet you."

"You can put your bike on the side of the house," I said, pointing to the gate in the back of the driveway. "That's where we put them at night. It's always locked."

"Hey, this looks like a pretty cool place to live!" he said.

"I think so," I said. I grabbed the suitcase, and Jim followed me inside. He put the suitcase down in front of the closet.

"So, how is Bakersfield?" I asked Jim as we went back outside.

"A lot hotter than here. Man, this is nice."

"How hot is it there?" I asked.

"About eighty degrees."

"That is hot. Isn't it real dry heat too? Or is it humid?"

"Pretty humid. You get used to it. But this is nice."

"I bet."

Elder Elliot put his bike at the side of the house and stood in front of the car. The trunk and passenger doors were shut. There was a duffle bag on the ground at the side of the car. He brushed his hair back with his free hand, the other out in front of him.

"Well, Jim. I guess this is it," he said while Jim reached for his outstretched hand.

"Call me when you get home," Jim said while they shook hands.

"Oh, I will. Don't worry. You're going to set me up, remember?"

"I will! You better call. We are only a couple hours away," Jim said.

They hugged and said "Love you" as Elder Elliot looked at me while Jim pulled out of the driveway.

"Elder Dorsey, good to meet you," he said, sticking out his hand.

"Nice to meet you. Let me show you around a little," I said. The dogs scared me, so I showed Elder Elliot the outside from inside.

"That's a shop," I said, pointing from the kitchen window. "Believe or not, that's a tennis court."

"That's a pretty small tennis court," Elder Elliot said.

"That might be why they don't play on it."

"We are welcome to play pool whenever we want. Elder Fischer and I played pretty often. It's a nice way to relax at night."

"Sounds nice," Elder Elliot said.

The bathroom and laundry room also extracted a "nice" from Elder Elliot.

"So, do you see Elder Proude very often?" He asked.

"At District Meetings and Zone Conferences," I said.

"Well, let's see what they're doing."

"OK. Here's a number. You want to call them?" I asked.

"Sure. Thanks."

While Elder Elliot and Elder Proude talked about other missionaries and members, I went over the night's appointments.

Elder Fischer and I discussed everything I would do for the next two weeks with Elder Elliot—tracting, visiting members, dinner appointments, even agendas for our weekly Ward Mission Meeting; I knew exactly what we were doing.

Elder Elliot pulled the phone away and asked me what we had planned for this evening. Dinner and splits was my answer. Elder Elliot told Elder Proude that they'd have to do it some other night and said "Bye."

Our dinner appointment was scheduled for five o'clock. Elder Elliot spent the time unpacking and getting organized. He didn't have much. The suitcases had his shirts and suits in them, but other than that, it was all basketball shoes and T-shirts. I thought how cool it would be to have an athlete as a companion, although Elliot didn't look like one.

The first Sunday he seemed comfortable with everyone he met. He greeted all the members, even those on the other side of the chapel. Looking over occasionally, I noticed he always had two or three members just waiting to meet him and shake his hand as he held back in the crowd with a constant smile on his face. I thought it was a smart-alec smile, but it worked. Within a week the Barretts loved him. On our first P-Day together, we met the rest of the zone at the Hillsboro Building and played ball. Elder Elliot was harsh with ballplayers; he felt he was as good as the next.

Elder Elliot was six-three though he didn't look it. He wasn't fat; just carried a lot of weight. He wasn't even out of shape; just didn't have the body of an athlete. I wondered how I would look after a year and a half on a mission. On the court, Elliot was best inside, inside the key. Like all big men, he wanted to shoot threes, but he was best inside.

P-Days changed: we played ball. It seemed that the majority of the elders enjoyed playing ball. With Elder Proude, who claimed to be a walk-on at Rick's College in Idaho, and Elder Jenkins, who was a walk-on with Indiana, there were battles. Elder Proude had the sweetest stroke from three-point range. It made me sick with envy.

We'd split up into two teams. Sometimes we picked them, but after all the missionaries had played with each other, we divided up based on what we knew would be the most competitive. Also, I think everyone felt bad for missionaries who wouldn't get picked until last, or not picked at all.

After playing ball for about three or four hours, we would all go out to lunch at In-and-Out Burger. I was making a few friends. It was nice talking with missionaries about the work going on in their area and with the cool members. Most missionaries were nice, yet surprisingly some were a little snobby, like Elder Proude. A mission just didn't seem the place to be a snob. We were all there doing the same job, all struggling with the same things. Maybe some elders felt the need to be snobby so that other missionaries would think that they gave up more to go on their mission than another missionary might have.

After eating, we would either go home or go shopping at the mall. It was a real treat to wear shorts and sandals. People didn't stare when we dressed like them, as they did when we were in our mission attire.

Elder Elliot told me that if we didn't schedule any appointments on Monday nights, we could relax and stretch P-Day a little longer. I agreed; it seemed like an innocent thing. So we played pool or chess. Mostly chess.

Elder Elliot brought a full-size chessboard with him to the Austins. He said he got it off another elder going home. I'd played as a kid, one of those all-in-one checker/chessboards. Elliot picked up the game on his mission; he really liked it. Our longest game lasted three hours. The games didn't start out that long. At first, they were maybe thirty minutes. We were well matched, neither of us winning more than the other. There was always a game waiting for us when we got home. Sometimes the games would stay half played for three or four days until we had time to finish them.

It was comforting to see the elders and sisters each week, verifying we weren't the only freaks in the world. I looked forward to when I'd be out past my first area and had other missionaries that I would see at Zone Conferences. Maybe I'd even have missionaries from past areas get transferred into my area. All the old-timers would joke around and even hug when they saw each other. Elder Elliot and Elder Proude seemed to be friends. They always wanted to go on splits together, which was fine with me. Elliot didn't really like tracting and going all day anyway. He would always tell me in a matter-of-fact way, which at first bothered me, but I was forced to be OK with it eventually.

On one of the P-Days that ran into Monday night, Elder Elliot told me he would be heading back with Elder Proud that night, and for the next two days we would be on a split. Generally, splits were done with a senior companion and either a zone leader or a district leader. However, if the two seniors wanted to go on splits alone, then it happened. Elder Ryan had brought his clothes for the next day in his backpack, so he had obviously known about the two-day split and just figured I had too. The funny thing about it was that before Elder Ryan and Elder Proude got to our place, I was asking Elder Elliot about the plans the next day, and he was going right along with what I had planned. I was a little surprised that he would go through a whole day's plan with me, knowing we would be on a split. He acted as if nothing would change; I guess it really wouldn't. Elder Ryan and I would end up doing exactly what Elder Elliot and I would have done.

Later, I asked Elder Ryan, "Did you and Elder Proude have a big day planned tomorrow?" Elder Ryan just smiled a little and told me that their day would have consisted of getting out of the apartment by eleven or twelve, then heading off to either a member's home or to Vine Street to grab a bite to eat.

"Vine Street isn't that full of restaurants. I mean, nice sit-down restaurants," I said, a little confused. We all had money, but only a hundred and thirty a month. I'm sure some of the parents liked to add a little extra for their sons, but not too many could afford to go out and eat like that.

"Yeah. Good food there. We just get appetizers and sit and munch on those. We will hang out there for a couple hours, out on the patio in the sun. I think Elder Proude really likes the sun, because whenever he can, he sits back and looks into it," Elder Ryan explained, respecting Elder Proude by not coming out and saying that he was just lazy, not a true sun god.

Elder Ryan continued to tell me about the days that he and Elder Proude had. He told me how Proude didn't like to go to members' homes to eat, so they didn't pass around a dinner calendar on Sundays. They would sometimes go to dinner at the Moores, but only if they had been hanging out there all afternoon and the Moores happened to invite them to stay for dinner. And the singles ward they covered had about three or four guys who liked to hang out with Elder Proude, so they would go out to eat with them sometimes. As for Discussions, tracting, and splits with members at night, they tried to avoid it. Elder Ryan said it was pretty easy with a singles ward since you got hooked up with guys the same age, guys who understood the confining conditions of a missionary and were eager to let missionaries break out when they were around.

"Do you like this area and Proude?" I asked Ryan, not showing the alarm that I felt inside as to the description of the companionship.

"It's not bad. It's not the *worst* I've had. Proude isn't that bad, he's just a little trunky. He looks forward to going home."

It was my first real insight into another companionship since I'd been out, and I was a little surprised. I might have felt different had I been placed with a different training companion. I imagined what it would have been like having Elder Proude as a training companion. I don't know if it was his face and his pinched lips that made him look like Tom in the movie *The Great Gatsby*, or if it was how he treated anyone who couldn't dunk a basketball or drain a three-pointer like they were less than him. Don't know exactly, but he just bothered me. There was a kid I went to high school with who always wanted to be my friend; his name was Aaron Stoddard. I really didn't want to hang out with him. He was nice and all, but I just didn't hit it off with him. So it was like that: I wouldn't have hung out with Elder Proude if we weren't out on a mission, forced together. Elder Ryan seemed to tolerate him, and that was what really mattered. I thought I had been lucky with companions. Elder Fischer, from what I could tell in my limited exposure to other companions, was not only a great trainer but also a real pleasant guy to be around. Elder Elliot was a guy I liked to pass the hours with playing chess.

Elder Elliot and I weren't friends, but we'd both stop and say "Hi" on the street if we were to meet each other after the mission. I couldn't say that for *all* the missionaries I'd met.

CHAPTER 5

Elder Ryan and I finished our morning Missionary Guide role-play. It was "Resolving Concerns." Elder Ryan played Mr. Hansen, a forty-two-year-old construction worker who wanted to come to church but couldn't because he would miss his cigarettes too much. It was my job as the missionary to find out why Mr. Hansen didn't want to come to church. After I asked several questions using the words *preventing*, *feel*, *commitment*, and *respect*, Mr. Hansen finally told me his reason for not wanting to go to church and the concern was resolved.

As we ate breakfast, Elder Ryan asked about the plans for the day. I pulled my single blue planner out of my shirt pocket and took a look at it while trying to finish the milk in my bowl of cereal.

"Well, this morning we have tracting. We get the beautiful area of Brier Terrace, a community of split-level homes filled with occupants anxiously waiting to convert to the Church," I said, trying to hold back the smile. "And after that, we can grab some lunch back here, then head out and visit members and two inactive families." I folded my planner up with my free hand, the other holding the last of the Honey Nut Cheerios that I poured into my mouth. I was excited to go tracting. Elder Elliot and I didn't talk much when we tracted, but then again we didn't tract much. I think we'd gone twice in the past three weeks. When we did go, it was just the two of us walking up a street, knocking on doors.

After breakfast, we headed back to the room and ran head on into Maverick, the Akita. He was sitting in his usual spot, right off the kitchen. I thought about putting him outside, but I didn't think quickly enough. He saw me hesitate and flinch a little when I realized that he was in my way.

I'd heard that animals can smell when a person is nervous or scared, so no matter what you did, you were screwed. Once they know you are scared, they will attack, no matter what. It's just instinctual for them.

"Shoot! It's Maverick! Let's go this way," I said, and turned to avoid the direct route to the bedroom, opting instead for the long way around the living room, through the front entry.

"Elder, you are funny!" Elder Ryan said while we walked into the bedroom. "Walking all the way around Maverick; I've been here so many times and he's never even *growled* at me."

"That's because he knows you're not scared of him. You see, ever since I was attacked by a dog as a kid, I've been scared of them. And once you are scared, the dogs can sense it and will prey on you."

"Are you sure about that?"

"Positive."

"I'm gonna have to check on that. I've never heard it before."

"Well the reason for that is the only people with the fear or the experience are the ones that can tell about it, so there aren't tons of people around."

"I'm still checking on it."

"Go for it," I said as I sat down in my chair. "Well, let's see…," I said, changing the subject. "We have about an hour left for getting ready and personal study. I don't really care who takes the first shower, so make the call."

"I'll go, that's fine," he said.

When Elder Ryan got back from taking his shower, I shut my *Book of Mormon* and grabbed my towel and shave kit.

Maverick? "Shoot—every morning!" No, the problem this morning was Shanine, Maverick's companion. Shanine had come in and planted herself in the other doorway heading into the kitchen. I insisted that Elder Ryan come out with me and walk past the dogs. Not arm in arm or anything, but just close. I remember when I used to walk home from school. If I heard a dog bark, I'd grab the arm of whoever was closest and hold on.

The bathroom was steamy, so I wiped down the mirror and opened the window as far as it would go. There wasn't a fan in the bathroom. I took a quick shower.

When we were both done with studying and doing our companionship prayers, we loaded up the *Book of Mormon*s for the day and went up to Brier Terrace.

We started tracting on the main street going into Brier Terrace. The area was sitting on the low hills, overlooking the rest of the city. Nice place for a decent view, but hard on the legs for a morning of tracting. Tracting went by quickly—that was one reason I liked it. You could kill a good three hours without even realizing it. The sun on my face, nothing to really worry about, just hoping for the next person to say, "Sure, come on in! I'd love to hear your message," even though it didn't happen often, We were walking up a hill, knocking on each house's door when we came to this nice split-level home. It looked just like all the other homes on the street.

Elder Ryan knocked on the door and we waited patiently. It was my turn for the introduction if the door opened. We tried to go every other one, but sometimes we just decided right when the door was opening.

The door opened and one of the most beautiful women I could have imagined said, "Hello!" She was truly stunning.

"Hi, how are you today?" I asked.

"I'm fine. What can I do for you?" She asked.

"We're missionaries for the Mormon Church," I said while waving my hand in front of Elder Ryan and myself. "We are here to take a few minutes of your time and share with you God's plan." The whole time I was talking, I tried looking directly into her eyes. I had to try because below her neck she had on a small white teddy that she tried to hide under a small white robe. The robe was unbuttoned and went down to her waist, then stopped....

"I have a few minutes. Sure, come on in," she said as she moved aside a little and let us in.

"Great!" I said, wondering if it could have been one of the first answers to my prayers.

The three of us congregated on the little entry landing that all split-level homes have. It was cozy until the door shut and she went up the stairs. We followed.

“Can I get you anything to drink? A beer?” she asked us as we stood at the top of the stairs waiting until she invited us to sit. “Sit down, guys; make yourselves at home.” She walked over to the couch and pushed the cushions up so there was room to sit. “OK, what can I can get you to drink?” she asked as she walked into the kitchen.

“Water is fine,” I said.

“And what about you?” She asked, looking back at Elder Ryan from the kitchen doorway.

“Oh, water is fine for me too. Thanks,” Elder Ryan said.

“No beer? Man, on a hot day like today, couple of guys like you—I was sure you'd want a beer,” she said.

“Well, we don't drink,” I said, loud enough for her to hear in the kitchen.

“You don't drink? Why?” she asked while coming back in the room with two tall glasses of ice water. As she handed the glasses to us, I told her that part of the plan we wanted to share with her that day would go into why we didn't drink. She sat down in a chair across from us and curled up her legs, her robe still untied but hiding what it needed to.

“Let me introduce ourselves. I'm Elder Dorsey and this is Elder Ryan,” I said. “And what is your name?” I was taking control as I had been the first one to talk and it was my area.

“I'm Natalie,” she said as she stood up from her chair and reached her hand out. We did a little half-stand to meet her halfway across the coffee table and shook her hand. As she sat down, her robe brushed against the side of the chair and we had a full view of her leg. I quickly looked down, acting like I was trying to get something out my bag while talking to her; doing anything not to make it obvious that I wasn't trying to look at her.

I asked Natalie what her experience in the past was with religion. She told us that she was baptized Catholic and that she was now a holiday Catholic.

“I like to go when I can, but it seems I only go on the holidays, Christmas and Easter—or when the family is visiting or I'm visiting them,” she said. She looked a little like she was being scolded from us for not going to church. “I really should go more, but it seems that there is always something that comes up.”

"I understand," I said. " It's not like when you wake up on a Sunday morning, especially a sunny Sunday morning, the first thing you want to do is go to church. I can't say that *I* always want to."

"Yeah, so you know what I mean. It's not just that either. After working all week and then running errands, sometimes Sundays are the only day to relax," Natalie said as she lit up a little, knowing that I felt like she might. I was simply using my empathy training from the Missionary Guide.

We talked about Natalie's job as a dancer. She said that she had always wanted to be a dancer and had come to LA to give it a shot. She danced for a club downtown. She didn't go into details as far as what *kind* of dancing or *where* she worked, but I thought it was the neatest thing that she had a dream like that and was working to make it come true. I loved it when people really went after what they dreamed, at any cost. It gave me hope. They were the people who seemed the most successful; the ones who never let anything get in the way of their dreams. After we talked about her work and where Elder Ryan and I were from, we asked if we could teach her the Discussions.

We explained the Discussions consisted of seven lessons explaining the beliefs of our Church. Throughout the Discussions were commitments that would need to be kept in order to continue on to the next Discussion. I didn't tell her that I had just learned the Discussions myself in the MTC a few months earlier. I gave her an overview of the Discussions, explaining that they started with the plan that God had for each person on the earth, and through the Restored Gospel that we were bringing to her that day, we were able to do *exactly* what was needed to be with God and our families for eternity. As for the time factor, I explained that Discussions could be taught in a matter of minutes. But with questions to be answered and stories told, the Discussions had no real time limit. She wanted to move ahead with the First Discussion right then and invited us back for the Second the next week. As Natalie went to grab her Bible, I looked over at Elder Ryan with a huge grin on my face and asked, "How often does *this* happen?"

"This doesn't happen very often," Elder Ryan said, knowing I knew the answer when I asked it.

Natalie came back into the room with her Bible. I could tell that she was very proud of her Bible by the way she was holding it as she walked into the room, with both hands holding it in front of her. It had an embroidered cover on it, tied with a little bow, the kind of ribbon bought at craft stores.

"Hey, that's a neat cover, Natalie. Where did you get it?" I asked.

As she looked down at it, she fingered the small bow and said softly, "This was given to me by my grandma when I was tiny. I don't remember her giving it to me, but I know she is the one that made the cover and wrote on the inside." She opened the front cover of the Bible and handed it to me. I read the inscription out loud:

Dear Natty,

Always remember that God loves you and will always be there when you need him. Keep his words close to you and your heart will always feel safe. Read it daily and rely on it for answers when it seems there are none. You are very special...

Love, Grandma

"That is nice, Natalie. Your grandma sounds like she is very close to the Heavenly Father," I said.

"Well she died a few years ago, but I know she is sitting up there with God right now."

I handed the Bible back to Natalie and asked her if she was ready to start the Discussion. My question seemed out of place, but I didn't know what else to say.

"Sure, I'm ready," she said.

Elder Ryan and I pulled out our Discussions. All seven of mine were bound together in a spiral binder with laminated covers. Elder Ryan's were singled out, strewn about his scripture case. He fished the First Discussion out of what seemed a myriad of notes, Sacrament Meeting programs, and teaching paraphernalia within his scripture case. I looked over at Elder Ryan and asked him if I could go ahead and start. He gave the nod.

"Natalie, God has a plan for us on while on this earth so that we can live with him and our families for eternity after this life. Does that sound like something that you would like to strive for?" I asked.

"Yes. I mean, I want to see my family after I die, of course," she said, and I thought how wonderfully it was going.

"Of course you want to see your family," I said, noticing my perfect restate. "I too want to be with my family after this life."

We continued on with the Discussions, outlining the plan God had laid out for us, touching on some of the different steps that needed to be taken in order to get there. I used everything that I could remember from the Missionary Guide: empathy, resolving concerns, finding the real problem, building relationships of trust, helping others recognize and feel the spirit—I used it all. Natalie would nod her head after each concept we talked about, so we just kept going. After we were finished, I asked Natalie if she had any questions.

"No, it's not that much different from what I've grown up with," she said.

"No, it isn't that different. There *are* some things in the next few Discussions that you may not have heard, but not really all that different from what you've been taught in the past."

We set up a time to see her Tuesday of next week. We gave her a reading assignment in the *Book of Mormon* for the next Discussion. I explained a little about the reading, 3rd Nephi, the part about when Jesus Christ comes down from heaven to visit the people in the Americas, the ancestors to the American Indians. I put a bookmark in the spot to read and handed Natalie her own copy of the *Book of Mormon*, covered in blue synthetic-looking leather. Natalie showed us to the door, where we told her we were anxious to see her next week and that we'd be calling her in a few days to see if she had any questions on what she was reading. She kept her robe together with her free hand, the other shaking ours. She was still holding her robe together as the door shut and the bright sun greeted us. We tracted for another two hours with no success, but that didn't matter. With the find of a lifetime in Natalie, we didn't allow ourselves to get discouraged. The rest of the day, we talked about how the Discussion went and how excited Natalie was about hearing the Gospel. We made a few comments on how pretty she was, but that really wasn't what we were excited about. A companionship could track all day—all week—and not find anyone to teach. Natalie was the first person I had found solely on my own. Well, Elder Ryan was there, but I picked the area and led the way. I couldn't *wait* to tell Elder Elliot about Natalie.

We met Elder Elliot and Proude that night. I could tell that Elder Proude and Elder Elliot had a good time together and would have liked to just stay together.

While Elder Elliot and I headed down the road on our bikes back to the Austins, I asked him about what he had done during splits.

"We relaxed," he said.

"Sounds nice," I said, not looking over at him, just riding next to him.

"We work so hard, Dorsey," he said.

"What do you mean? I mean I know we stay busy, but really what else is there to do other than tract, visit members, and just try to get out?" I asked, looking over at him, gladly keeping my thoughts in my head instead of sharing them with an ill-tempered Elder Elliot.

Really, what was there to do? It wasn't like missionaries could go to the movies or out to a club. That was the stuff that was *really* bad. We had to be in our white shirts all the time, with our name tags on.

Whatever we did, people saw us. More importantly, God saw us. I really didn't know what missionaries did when relaxing during work hours. I wanted to sit down and read a book. For days I would have liked to, but we were allowed to read only church books. And even then, the list included only the Bible, *Book of Mormon,* and *The Doctrine and Covenants*. Even on P-Day, all we could do was play basketball and do laundry.

"Dorsey, we just relaxed a little. It's no big deal."

Elder Elliot was so excited about Natalie that he invited Elder Proude and Elder Ryan to accompany us when we taught her the Second and Third Discussions. The Second Discussion could be a little nerve racking as it was the Discussion where we committed the investigator to "Follow the footsteps of Jesus Christ, and enter the waters of baptism." It seemed so early in a person's learning of the Gospel, which in some cases the person had been introduced to just a few weeks prior. Yet here we were offering them the key to eternal salvation. Could anyone really comprehend the decision they were making and the consequences of not following through with the commitments that were made when entering the waters of baptism? I didn't think so. I thought back to my own baptism and how little I knew, understood, or even cared. It was like another birthday: special treatment for a day. It was fun; I remembered that. But why *wouldn't* it be fun swimming in an indoor pool that had been looked on since birth as the untouchable waters? Of course, a young boy would find this intriguing and covet the day when he, too, could join the elite group of people. Even as a young boy, I could understand the significance of being baptized into the One and Only True Church of God. I'd laugh to myself when my friends who weren't Mormon would say things like "Oh Yeah, I was baptized too," or "I was baptized when I was a baby." My friends—these kids, my contemporaries—didn't know they *weren't* saved, and here I was saved. There was no way Natalie or another investigator could understand this. They would come away with the same thoughts and impressions that I had come away with. But that's what we were out there to do: teach the Discussions—the inspired Discussions—and follow them in exactness, not making statements on a whim when the feeling within prompted one to do so. No, that's not what we were to do.

After all, we were only young men in our twenties—or some, like me, still teenagers. We knew only how to follow and teach as we had followed and been taught. I talked with Elder Elliot about my concerns. He said that usually the investigator would commit to hearing the remainder of the Discussions but would hold off on getting baptized right away. We talked a little about what to do with Natalie, and he responded by advising us to play it by ear and see how it felt at the time. I thought how nice it would be to have a personal prophet advising you on the investigators, as it was clear Elder Elliot had.

Elder Proude and Ryan met us at the Austins around two o'clock, and we headed over to Natalie's for the infamous Second Discussion.

Natalie was thrilled to see us. I'd called her that weekend to ask how her reading was coming along. She said that she hadn't read it yet but would have it completed before we came on Tuesday.

"Hey, guys! Come on in," Natalie said as she opened the door. This time she had on jeans and a T-shirt. Not surprisingly, she looked great in them. I felt bad for even *noticing* her body. I wondered why I couldn't look at women's bodies without thinking about whether they had a nice body or a bad body. If there was ever a place in my life when I should be able to look beyond physical attributes and not base my opinion on them, it should be in the mission field. Natalie showed us in.

"I know that none of you drink beer, so how about some ice water?" she said, going to the kitchen.

I looked over at Elder Proude and got a big grin on my face. He returned the grin. It wasn't that any of us had never seen a pretty girl before, but missionaries didn't usually find pretty girls wanting to hear the Discussions.

"Oh, I need to go grab my Bible and the Bible you gave me. I'll be right back," Natalie said as she put the glasses of ice water on the table for us.

"Did you enjoy the reading, Natalie?" I asked as she walked back into the room with both books clutched to her chest.

"Well, I don't think I understood all of it—any of it," she said, looking sheepishly up from her bowed head. "It sounded just like *my* Bible. I did read my bible each night, though. Talking with you guys last week got me excited about it. I can see why my grandma enjoyed it so much. It's kind of relaxing. I don't understand much of what I read in my bible either but still enjoyed it and felt good after reading it."

"Do you have any questions we can answer for you?" Elder Elliot asked.

"No. I enjoyed it, but I can't think of any real questions."

"What about the First Discussion that we had last week? We went over God's plan that he has for us on this earth," I asked.

"No. Like I said, I think that was the same as I've learned and grown up with."

"OK. Well, throughout these Discussions, just write down any questions you have, and when we see you next, we will answer them for you," I said. She nodded like she understood. I thought, "What if I didn't have the answers?" and then I realized I had *all* the answers.

"Well, why don't we start with the Second Discussion?" I asked.

"Elder Dorsey, we should probably introduce ourselves since Elder Elliot and I weren't here last week," Elder Proude said as he reached over to shake Natalie's hand.

Shoot! I forgot to introduce everyone. I didn't even tell Natalie that other missionaries would be coming. I was nervous. This was my first investigator, after all. Elder Elliot and Elder Proude should have been running the Discussion anyway. They were veterans, and in such a crucial spot as the Second Discussion, with such a crucial investigator, the beautiful Natalie, it would have been appropriate for them to take over.

"My name is Elder Proude."

"And I'm Elder Elliot," he said, reaching over for Natalie's hand.

Elder Elliot explained that he and I were companions who were on splits from each other last week. Natalie had lots of questions for Elder Elliot and Elder Proude. We talked all about Elder Elliot being from Orange County, just a few miles south. Natalie couldn't believe we all came from so far away, yet Elder Elliot got sent to the next county over. Elder Elliot was pretty good when investigators asked him about it; very pleasant and would even laugh. When missionaries or members asked him about it, though, he was straightforward He would say, "Well, this is where the Lord needed me" or "There are people that need to be taught in the Ventura mission also, aren't there?"

Elder Elliot and Elder Proude moved right into the Second Discussion. It was such a smooth transition that it took Elder Ryan and me a minute to realize that we were already teaching. We recapped a little about what we had talked about last week while previewing the Second Discussion. I had to get my Discussions out of my backpack, flipping around until I found them. Within an hour, we came to the part of committing Natalie to "enter the waters of baptism." It was my turn to teach.

I paused before speaking. A missionary learned in the MTC that pausing, looking down and then up again, was very effective. I then explained the importance of baptism and how God wanted all his children to be baptized. I paused again, then looked up from my Discussion right into Natalie's eyes. "Natalie, will you follow the example that Jesus set and be baptized by someone with the authority in God's eyes?"

"I was baptized. Remember, I told you that last week?" Natalie said, awakened finally from her confusion of the priesthood concept (and possibly thinking she had just saved us considerable time and effort and now we all could get on with our lives). She could go back to enjoying her Sundays and we could all go home to our families.

"Natalie, when God came down to visit Joseph Smith, he bestowed the priesthood on him. It was the same priesthood John the Baptist held when he baptized Jesus Christ. That is what we mean when we ask you to be baptized. To be baptized by someone who has the authority from God. Understanding that, Natalie, will you be baptized into God's one true Church on earth today: the Church of Jesus Christ and Latter-day Saints?"

There was a pause as Natalie looked down. "Well I don't want to commit to that right now. It seems a little early, and I don't know if I really understand what you are saying. I think I need to hear more and maybe talk with some friends and my family."

Elder Elliot took over finally, seeing me struggling with the commitment.

"Natalie, if you don't feel comfortable with making a decision today about baptism, we will go over it again later this week or next week when we see you again. Will that work? Will you give it some thought this week while you are going over what we talked about?"

"I would be more comfortable with it if we could wait. But I can still get the rest of the Discussions, right?"

"Sure, that's not a problem. That's what we are here for: to share God's plan with you," Elder Elliot said. "Why don't we go ahead and teach you the Third Discussion today if you have time. Do you?"

"How long will it take?" Natalie asked.

"Maybe thirty minutes," Elder Elliot said.

"Sure. I don't have anything going on until work tonight. You guys are fun to talk with. How many women get four young men in their house anyway?" Natalie flashed a smile at each one of us. It lit up the room and lifted my spirits after her recent nonconversion to the Mormon Church. I knew we had lost her. It seemed the baptism commitment was almost placed in the Second Discussion as a surprise tactic. It caught them off guard. Hell, it caught me off guard when I asked it.

Elder Proude suggested that we move on to the Third Discussion. Instantly, I thought about what it would be like to sleep with Natalie or talk with her about her sleeping with other men. This thought quickly passed, though, and I thought about the commitment to not drinking and whether she would be able to do it. The Third Discussion had commitments to abstain from premarital sex and from drinking. It was easier to get the commitments when there was already the underlying commitment of baptism hanging out there. I wasn't sure why we were moving forward when we really had nothing, but luckily my lack of experience was overshadowed by both Elder Elliot's and Elder Proude's desire to teach.

"Natalie, we are going to talk with you about the Word of Wisdom and the Law of Chastity. First, the Word of Wisdom is the guideline that God has given us on what to take into our body and what to keep out. In *The Doctrine and Covenants*, Joseph Smith received translation from God as to what these things are that we are to keep out." Elder Proude was moving along with the Third Discussion like he might have with any other investigator. I wondered if he had even taken notice of the glass ashtray sitting on the coffee table in front of us. I wasn't sure how it would affect his presentation, but I thought it should. "We believe that tobacco, alcohol, and hot drinks were not meant for the body. These include coffee, tea, cigarettes, chewing tobacco, and alcohol—any alcohol."

It was a strange feeling to reprimand a beautiful woman I had just met a week earlier—telling her that pretty much everything she did was shit; that she lived a shitty life and needed to change it or we wouldn't welcome her into God's Church.

"You mean no coffee? I couldn't do that. I like my morning coffee. You guys don't drink coffee?" she said, truly surprised when she realized these commitments that Elder Proude was asking of her were the same guidelines that we lived by each day. "Do you mean wine also? Doesn't God drink wine in the Bible?"

"Nope. No coffee for us. Or tea or alcohol," Elder Elliot said. "And as for wine, the wine talked about in the Bible is different than the wine we drink today. In the Bible, it wasn't fermented."

"It wasn't? I didn't know that. I'll ask my Mom about that. We even drink wine in church when we are taking Communion. I can't imagine it being that bad when it's passed out at church."

I saw that Natalie was struggling with the concept of not drinking. It wasn't just that she wouldn't be able to go out with friends on a Friday night and enjoy some beers or a Long Island ice tea, but also the foreign concept that drinking itself was bad. I noticed that people who didn't abuse alcohol truly didn't see anything wrong with drinking, almost to the point that it was absurd to think about going without. I could imagine people growing up with parents having wine on the dinner table and having a glass with their meal. I often thought how nice it would be to have a glass of Merlot with a heavy meal of steak and potatoes. And here we were, telling her that it was the devil's drink.

"Wow! You guys are kinda missing out, don't you think?

Coffee doesn't seem *that* bad," she said confused. "But I could give it up to get baptized. I'll give it some thought."

"Great, Natalie," Elder Proude said, "Also, would you give up cigarettes? You would need to do that before getting baptized."

"Oh, I don't really smoke anyway."

Moving only my eyes, I looked down at the cigarette butts in the ashtray. There was lipstick on some of them, "My roommate smokes. These are her cigarettes. I occasionally have one if we go out and are having some beers, but not enough to worry about stopping. I could give the few I have up."

"Good, Natalie. You really seem to understand the importance of the Word of Wisdom. There are also some guidelines as to things that are good for the body. Things such as meat and dairy, all in moderation, of course," Elder Proude continued. "We will go over in more detail as to what can go into the body and what needs to be kept out. Remember, we feel the body is a gift from God, and we are simply trying to keep it clean for when we see him again."

"I understand," Natalie said, seeming to take in the Word of Wisdom Discussion. Elder Proude was skating around the question; he was going to get a weak commitment from her. "I take *good* care of my body. I eat healthy and work out every day. I don't think God would turn me out of heaven for my body." Smiling, I thought no one would kick this woman out of *anywhere* because of her body. It was incredible—God at his best work.

"Elder Elliot, you want to take the next commitment?" Elder Proude asked.

"Sure," Elder Elliot said, looking down at his Discussion pamphlet. I wanted to say something, to interject and get a commitment of "yes" or "no" from Natalie as to whether she was going to keep drinking. I kept silent, hoping that both Elder Elliot and Elder Proude were using wisdom that I didn't have in not getting the commitment.

"Natalie, we are going to talk about the Law of Chastity. We believe that the act of procreation is sacred and is something that should only be done between husband and wife. We believe it's one of the greatest gifts that God has given us and that we need to treat it accordingly and only have those relations with the one we love."

"Oh, I agree with you. I believe it's special. Only shared with those you love," Natalie said, looking at Elder Elliot.

"Good, good. Well that's it, then. You have a real grasp of the principles we have shared with you today."

"Again, it isn't all that different from what I've learned in the past."

I wasn't going to let Elder Elliot wimp out on a commitment—not one as important as the sex one. I finally interjected and said, "Natalie, I just want to make sure you understand the commitment that we are asking from you." Everyone was silent and only Natalie was looking at me. The other elders were too damn scared. I was bothered that *I* had to get the commitment when I wasn't even the one teaching the principle. It was in the Missionary Guide. We read about it every day: how to get a commitment, how to phrase the question. Elder Proude and Elder Elliot were so far off, I was going to have to ask them what Missionary Guide they were reading each morning.

"OK, Elder Dorsey. I think I understand," Natalie said at my statement.

"Natalie, in order to get baptized, will you commit to not having premarital sex? Will you commit to not having sex until you are married?"

"What?!" Natalie said, surprised. She hadn't gotten what Elder Elliot was saying. "Ohhh no, I can't commit to that. No sex? I like it too much," she said. We all smiled and turned red with the impressions we got in our minds and between our legs. Of course, she liked sex. She was perfect, and liking sex fit in perfectly with perfect women. Talking about sex with Natalie was awkward. She was hot, and we all wanted to have sex with her or with a girl who looked like her.

"It will be hard." I instantly wanted to retract my statement. "I mean… it might be difficult." It was too late, I turned red at ""will be hard" and quickly tried to keep the Discussion on a serious note. As I was sputtering my words out, Natalie's face lit up and she pointed at us. "You guys, you mean that none of you…? Oh my God! You guys are all *virgins*!" We all smiled and laughed quietly. "Oh my God, you guys are all little virgins!" she said with concern, sadness, and shock. I wished she was willing to take us back to her room and resolve her concern, but I kept the thought to myself. "So you guys have never had sex?" she asked, expecting an answer. I didn't know what to say. The question was put to all of us. Elder Elliot finally spoke with wisdom that I didn't have.

"Through repentance, we are all virgins," he said.

"What does that mean?" Natalie asked.

"Meaning that in God's eyes, we are virgins," Elder Elliot said.

"I want to know, though. Elder Ryan, are you a virgin?" she asked, looking directly at Elder Ryan sitting next to me.

"I am."

"Elder Dorsey?"

"Through repentance, I am."

"Elder Proude?"

"Through repentance, I am."

We had all just admitted to a stranger, a woman we were trying to share the Gospel with, whether we had slept with women before our mission. It felt strange, but good to be honest. It instantly bonded us with her and with each other as missionaries. I was proud of Elder Elliot for using the repentance principle in his explanation. If we had to lie to her, I don't think I would have felt as good as I did.

"Wow, so you guys aren't going to have sex until you get married? That might be a *long* time."

"You get used to it after a while," Elder Elliot said.

"I don't think it's something *I'd* want to get used to. You know, guys, to be honest with you, I could give up drinking and cigarettes and coffee, but I don't want to give up sex. I don't even think it's bad. I do it with boyfriends, people I love. I don't think that's bad."

We had nothing to move forward with. The idea was to have an investigator read the *Book of Mormon*, feel the spirit, and get a testimony. A testimony that they couldn't deny because the promptings of the spirit were so great after reading the *Book of Mormon,* they *had* to commit. With Natalie, she never understood what she read. We had nothing; she had nothing. We lost her, if we ever had her.

We had nowhere to go but home. We asked Natalie to consider what we had talked about, to consider the commitments that we asked her to keep. We asked her to pray about what we presented. We marked another passage in the *Book of Mormon* on prayer in hopes that the spirit would leap out and grab her. Although I had doubt before we even knocked on her door to give her the Discussions that first day. People didn't get the gospel; they didn't feel the spirit. I was a terrible portal for God to be moving through, and I wondered why. *I* didn't even feel the spirit. How could I expect others to feel the spirit? These thoughts consumed my mind as we said goodbye to Natalie. I knew we would never see her again, even though we set up a time the next week. She was now a number on a whiteboard on the wall of the room of two young men who couldn't understand why she didn't want to be Mormon. Or did we?

It was a relief to report to Brother Jenkins we had found a new investigator and were working on two investigators that we had tracted out. He knew we were working hard. Brother Jenkins was interested in the investigators. He was a podiatrist; I thought this could have something to do with it. He was used to working for what he had. He saw the fruits of labor in tracting and saw that within the past four weeks, we had added two people to our previous investigator pool of zero. Elder Fischer had just come off baptizing Heavenly and George and their family, so that was still fresh in the minds of the ward members. But anything new to report was good.

We explained that Natalie worked at night, so we wouldn't be able to use a split for teaching.

"Elders, there are some members that are available during the day. In fact, maybe we could get Sister Luke over there for one of the Discussions?

"I'm not sure if we are ready for that," Elder Elliot said.

"You know that the sooner we can involve the members, the success rate of conversion skyrockets."

"I know, I know. But I just don't think she is ready for the Relief Society President yet. Give us a couple more weeks until we consider involving the members," Elder Elliot said. I was glad he was showing some backbone, something habitually missing in his teaching and committing.

"Oh, of course. Just let me know and I'll make the call." We informed Brother Jenkins that the New Member Discussions were finished with George and Heavenly. What we didn't inform him of, or ask him about, was why they were able to get baptized while living together. I'd learned the baby wasn't George's but that they shared a room in the small apartment. They had to: it was only a two-bedroom apartment and there were four people living in it. Elder Fischer didn't share any facts on this, even after I had prompted him for them. I was sure they had had an interview before the baptism and this would have come up. I hoped, at least. But then I started wondering why I even cared.

We went to the McCulloughs for dinner that night. They picked us up about five thirty. We had taken a few hours to relax after church. We were right in the middle of a game of chess that had lasted three days. Elder Elliot had my queen, but I had just about everything else of his.

Brother McCullough had his fourteen-year-old daughter Lisa in the car. She was really pretty, with long blond hair. I think he knew his daughter was so pretty. She sat in the front seat of the Nissan Pathfinder but didn't say anything to us. Brother McCullough talked the whole time, asking us how the work was going. He liked the fact that we had two investigators we were teaching the Discussions to, and both of them were found from tracting, something we shared with as many members as we could.

The McCulloughs lived on the outskirts of Chatsworth, a new housing development on a hill. No streetlights, so I couldn't look at the other houses around us. Their house was new, with high ceilings and small rooms. I didn't see any of the bedrooms, but the family room and living room were small. They had six kids. I didn't think they were old enough to have that many kids. At dinner I asked how they ended up living where they did.

"We liked the house and the area," he said with a little derision. "How else do you decide to buy a house?"

"Those are the best reasons," I said.

I don't know how Elder Elliot picked up on it so soon from serving in the area, but he let me have it when we got home.

"Dang, Dorsey. Why did you ask him that?"

"Ask him what?"

"Why he moved there!"

"Because I wanted to know."

"Don't you *know* that it is a predominantly black neighborhood?"

"No. How would I know that?"

"Haven't you been up there before?"

"I don't think so. Even if I had, how would I know that just by tracting?"

"Is that all you think about? Tracting? Man, you need to think a little before you ask something like that."

"I don't see anything wrong with asking someone how they came to live where they live."

"Well you should."

"I wouldn't care if someone asked me that."

"Not everyone is like you."

"There is nothing wrong with it."

"Obviously there is."

"That's dumb if he gets hurt or sarcastic because someone asks him why he moved somewhere."

"Dorsey, think a little before you say things. You will meet all kinds of people out here. They are different than you, members or nonmembers. Just think about it."

I was so mad. I couldn't believe a comment like that would have offended anyone. I thought, if I had to be careful about something like that, then I didn't want to be on this fucking mission.

Elder Ingstrom and Elder Johansson picked us up for basketball the next day. Elder Elliot and I didn't talk much that morning. We never talked much. Elders Proude and Ryan were already in the car as we tried squeezing in the little Ford Escort wagon.

"Dorsey, get in the back hatch," Elder Elliot said when it was obvious that we weren't all going to fit in the back seat.

I rode in the back of the wagon without a seatbelt to the Chatsworth ward building. Elder Proude turned around from the front passenger seat and looked at Elliot. "Elder Jensen's going to be there. This is going to be fun."

"This *will* be fun." Elder Elliot said. "What should we do for teams?"

"We'll just split up. Let's just pick them; it takes too long to try and shoot for teams," Elder Elliot said.

"I agree," said Elder Proude

Elder Proude and Jenkins split up the teams between the fifteen elders there. I ended up on Elder Jenkins' team with Elder Elliot.

I was never an all-star with the basketball team or anything, but I could shoot threes if I was open, and inside I thought I was pretty deadly. I played high school ball but was primarily a bench warmer. It was a triple-A school, and a person had to be *quite* the player to start for it. I was small and never had the weight to be a huge force inside.

The ball started on the side of Proude's, and right from the start it looked like they had the advantage.

Missionaries were serious about ball. We had only one day out of the week to do anything but be a missionary, and all we wanted was to make the best of it. Elder Proude stroked a couple of threes the first two times down the court.

Elder Jenkins stayed inside for us, but he wanted to get outside from the start by the weak side he was playing on offense. They took a quick 10–0 lead over us.

Elder Elliot then took a time-out and looked over at Elder Jenkins in the huddle.

"What should we do?"

"Let's go, man. Let's just start shooting and shutting down Proude."

"Yeah, we need to shut Proude down. He's hanging outside, but he will get inside if we let him. And if he does, we will be better off."

"I agree," Elder Elliot said.

The huddle broke, and we sauntered back onto the court. Elder Jenkins finally got the ball inside and put in three lay-ups. We were able to shut Proude down for a while, it seemed. Because Proude was playing off-guard and Jenkins was playing center, they didn't have to guard each other. Elder Elliot also played off-guard and was guarding Elder Proude unsuccessfully, as his teammates saw it, but possibly he was just being lazy.

We exchanged baskets the next few times down the court. By the time we took a half-time break, the score was tied and tension had arisen.

Elder Elliot, Jenkins, and Proude hung out at one end of the court talking, while I shot free throws with Elder Ryan. The rest of the missionaries talked at the stage until halftime was over.

As I shot there by myself at one end of the court and ran after any missed shots, I thought about Daniel. Thought how he wasn't able to shoot a basketball. I imagined he would be thrilled, even without playing, if he could just shoot the ball. I thought if I didn't have legs, I wouldn't want to live; not even for a short time to say goodbye. I would just want to be taken back to heaven, never having to go through the trial of living without legs. I wondered if I thought that way because I was young or because I was wise. I wanted to ask Daniel about it, ask him if he would have rather died. I knew we would need more time together before I could ask him something like that, but I hoped we would grow close. I knew he was probably the only paraplegic I would ever know, or ever take the time to know.

Elder Elliot and I hadn't been over there in a few weeks, and I felt we needed to soon.

Elder Jenkins put in the call to arms, and we huddled together as a team on our end of the court.

"OK, let's beat these guys. Try to get me the ball down low. No one can guard me down there with Elder Proude hanging out in three-point land. He doesn't like defense anyway. They won't be able to stop Elder Elliot and me down low," Elder Jenkins said. I knew they couldn't beat us if we stuck to his plan. "Elder Dorsey, you bring the ball down and we will get set up around the key."

"OK," I said, feeling important that I was entrusted with the ball anywhere on the court. There were some big bodies in the game, and I felt small. I wasn't a guard. I couldn't handle the ball well enough, but people always assumed from my size that I was just naturally a guard. I probably would have been and would have had more success in the game had I learned to handle the ball like a guard. Yet, with a younger brother who could handle the ball like an NBA guard, I never had to develop my talent. I could fake out most players as long as I wasn't pressured, and I just got rid of the ball soon after passing half-court.

Elder Jenkins's game plan was working flawlessly. We were able to score the first four times down the court, taking a slight lead over Elder Proude's team. The frustration showed in the passes and shots of his team. It seemed inevitable that the only way they would be able to stop us was to foul. Elder Proude caught on quick and started fouling Elder Jenkins on every possession. Luckily, Elder Jenkins played hard but kept his smart *and* his cool. He realized it wasn't an NBA game. No bonuses depended on who won. It was, after all, just for fun. Unfortunately, Elder Elliot didn't react in the same way. Elder Elliot was fouled twice by Elder Proude in the paint, his hair flopping over his eyes and the sweat rolling off his arms. After a missed three-point attempt by Elder Proude, I corralled the rebound and saw Elder Elliot at the half-court line. Elder Proude was there with him, his long legs making his backpedaling effective in positioning himself on the court for cherry pickers. I flicked a double-handed pass to Elder Elliot at half-court, and he was dribbling in for an easy lay-up when Elder Proude hard-fouled him. It was a cheap shot and wasn't necessary. He stopped the ball from going in the hoop but pissed an irritable Elder Elliot off even more.

"Foul!" Elder Elliot yelled and threw the ball to me at the top of the key to check it in for another possession. I checked the ball and quickly found Elder Elliot under the hoop.

"Foul!" Elder Elliot said.

"Come on, Elliot. I hardly touched you," Elder Proude said.

"But you still *touched* me!"

"Well, it's basketball. It's a *contact* sport," Elder Proude said.

"And I called a foul."

"Fine."

Elder Elliot wanted the ball with each possession and made it clear. I accommodated and passed it to him. I thought he was being a pain. The atmosphere in the gym and on the court had changed and wasn't fun, the way it should have been. Elder Elliot started hanging behind the three-point line and launching them. With every possession, Elder Elliot either went straight at Elder Proude or stood two or three feet behind the three-point line, then tossed the ball up. Elder Proude counteracted by launching his own three-point balls. Neither of them even looked for any open teammates. Elder Elliot's frustration was further heightened by the fact that he couldn't compete with Elder Proude's three-point prowess. He hit one in five three-pointers, and Elder Proude hit as many as Elder Elliot missed. Elder Elliot called another foul with no one around.

"Stop being a baby, Elliot," Elder Proude said.

"Fuck you," Elder Elliot said. The two of them—the two friends, the two elders in collusion with each other to avoid missionary work, split with their companions, and sleep the days away—couldn't even get along on the hardwood. Consequently, they ruined an afternoon of basketball for an entire zone.

Elder Elliot walked off the court, done for the day. The game ended, and he didn't say a word until we got out of the car after being dropped off by Elder Ingstrom. There were six of us in the car, and we had all agreed to go to In-and-Out Burger after the game. Elder Elliot hadn't said a word, and it was assumed he just wanted to be dropped off. I wanted In-and-Out Burger but got out of the car as well. I was mad, and it showed on my face. Ever so slightly, but it showed.

"Good luck today, Dorsey," Elder Proude said, rolling his eyes as Elder Elliot's big backside was getting out of the back seat.

"Thanks," I said, with resolution in my voice. I wish I could have gone with the rest of the elders in the car, but when I proposed this to Elder Elliot, he said, "No."

"Come on, Dorsey. We're not going. Get out of the car."

I didn't say anything except "Thanks" to Elder Proude, after his rare moment of being empathetic. Elder Elliot and I played chess in silence for the rest of the afternoon. I looked forward to a quiet night of reading the scriptures and writing some letters.

We got the call in the afternoon. The assistants were lucky to catch us in between basketball and laundry. I answered the phone to an excited "Hello, Elder Dorsey. How are you? This is Elder Biggs."

"I'm fine. Thanks for asking."

"Hey, is Elder Elliot handy?"

"Sure, I'll get him. Hang on one minute."

Elder Elliot and Elder Biggs talked for about ten minutes. Elder Elliot took notes with addresses and names on it. I thought this might have to do with transfers, but I'd been in the area only two months and Elder Elliot had only about two months left, so I couldn't see either one of us getting transferred.

After Elliot finished, he looked over at me with a grin. Not a grin of happiness, but rather a grin of "I've got some news for you that will surprise you, and I can't wait to see the look on your face."

"Elder Dorsey, you are getting transferred," he said.

"Me?"

"Yep. You are going to Van Nuys, in the Valley. Your new comp is Elder Bell."

"When do I go?" I asked.

"Wednesday. Elder Ryan is being transferred too. So Elder Proude and I will just plan on hanging out while you guys get transferred." I wondered how he was able to say "Fuck you" to an Elder and then look forward to hanging out during transfers. Strong words to make up from.

"How will I get to my new area?"

"Eric could probably take you, or Sister Barrett."

"What about our investigators?" I asked.

"They'll be fine. I'm still here. I kinda know what I'm doing, you know."

"I know. I didn't mean it like that. I've only been here two months. I was hoping to spend a little time and get to know everyone."

"Hey, this is part of being on a mission: transfers. It was nice knowing you, Elder Dorsey."

CHAPTER 6

We loaded up the 1970 F150 on Wednesday morning. It was a regular workday so I had on my short-sleeve white shirt.

Packing was easy. I still had some shirts and socks in the packages from Mr. Macs, the missionary supply store in Utah.

Van Nuys was a slum of a city in the middle of the San Fernando Valley. The San Fernando Valley was famous for a few rock songs that streets were mentioned in, and also for the cult movie *Valley Girl*. The lingo of Valley Girl talk came from the Valley. When we drove over the hill into the Valley, the smog hung like a dirty pillowcase with snot and drool stained from years of use and inconsistent washing. The I-5 was refreshing. I reminisced of home for a minute until we hit the bumper-to-bumper traffic I would later learn was a prerequisite for travel preparation anywhere in the Valley. Eric pointed out the Santa Anas to the East, and I thought about the chilling winds that came off them in the late afternoons: cooling after long bike rides, pleasant when one was hot and sweaty, and torture when riding into them after a long day of work.

The Hollywood Hills, off to the south, were full of big mansions and wildfires. Driving through the Valley to the apartment complex that I would call my home for the next few months reminded me of South Rainer Avenue in Seattle—also a slum of an area. I saw more blacks and homeless on the drive than I had seen in my whole life. We pulled in front of the España Apartments and parked in a loading zone. "Why don't you run up and find your place? I'll wait here," Eric said.

I buzzed the "Missionaries" button on the intercom. "Hello?" A scratchy voice said.

"Hello, this is Elder Dorsey. Is this Elder Bell?"

"Yeah, I'll buzz you up."

The buzz opened the iron gate, and I walked into the courtyard. A big square in the middle of the towering four-story apartment complex was my welcome. I thought it was a little like Central Park with the New York skyline looming over it. It was run down. It needed to be weeded and raked, and it smelled rotten.

I saw a short, stocky, and bushy-haired young man in a white shirt up on the 3rd-floor landing. He had just come out of an apartment. "Elder Dorsey, up here! I'll come down and help with your stuff."

"OK!" I yelled back.

Elder Bell met Eric and me out by the truck and told Eric to move around to the side alley. As he moved the truck, Elder Bell and I introduced ourselves and shook hands.

"You're right on time. Brother Jacobson just left. He was hanging out with me until you got here. I told him that you should be here any time and thought it would be OK if he left. It was his day off," he said it as if making sure with me that it was OK that he was alone for a few minutes.

"That was nice of him to wait with you. How is it here, the work? The members?" I asked.

"Well, members are the same in all the areas. You have your nice ones and your not so nice ones. You'll actually meet a really nice one tonight, our Ward Mission Leader, Stephen Day—or Brother Day—but we just call him Stephen. He's coming over for dinner tonight. I thought it would be good if you met him and we went over the area and what's been going on."

"What do you mean? What's going on in the area?" I asked.

"Well, this area just got missionaries after not having them for a year. They had a companionship that was covering new contacts and current investigators, but the ward hasn't had its own. I've been here about two weeks. But I was in a threesome with the elders in the Third Ward, next area over."

"Did you get a chance to do much work here, then?"

"No. We pretty much worked their area, knowing that I would be here full-time in a couple weeks. I did meet Stephen, though. And he is really excited about having his own missionaries for the ward. He said the whole ward is really excited."

"So how long have you been out?" I asked.

"About a year and a half. How about you?"

"I've been out a whopping two months."

"Hey, you've gotta start somewhere," Elder Bell said, easily reassuring me.

We unloaded the truck, each of us taking an item up. I traveled with a bike and two bags. With one trip up to the third floor, the truck was empty. Eric wished me the best of luck and was out the door, back to Chatsworth.

The little apartment was a two-bedroom, one-bath setup. Elder Bell and I shared the smaller of the two bedrooms. There was a single bed on one side and a set of bunk beds on the other. I had the luxury of living on the lower bunk. The living room had a television in it that belonged to our unseen roommate, Bill. He was unseen except for about once a month when was traveling through town. He lived in Nevada, a traveling salesman who made frequent stops in L.A. The Church subsidized his rent for letting the missionaries live there. It was a good setup for all involved. All the pots and pans were his, along with the furniture, a big burgundy L-shaped couch that reminded me of one my Dad tried to get at the dump in Seattle before someone threw it into the dump truck. Bill had just been here the weekend before, so he wouldn't be around for another month. Elder Bell said he had complained the place was a mess and that we needed to keep it clean. The three missionaries had been living in the apartment until the other companionship got an apartment with two other missionaries.

Stephen Day showed up around six o'clock with three tubs of food: lemon chicken, creamed green beans, and corn. Sister Donaldson, a member in the ward, owned Spatulas, a restaurant in Hollywood Hills. On the way home from work, Stephen grabbed the food. Stephen said we could stop by there anytime and get food, or call him up when we didn't have dinner and he would stop by and grab some for us on his way home. We dished out the food and sat around the dining room table for our first Ward Mission Meeting. Stephen explained there were currently no investigators and that the missionaries in the past had been lazy. We went over a map of the area, marking where some of the key members lived. Key members were Church members who provided missionaries with an open invite for lunch or dinner, or referrals for potential new members. Stephen told us how excited the ward was to have us.

"Last Sunday Bishop Hatch got up and gave a talk about missionary work. He told all the members what a blessing it was to have missionaries in the ward again and that they all needed to go home and consider people in their area, whether it be friends, neighbors, or family, and invite the missionaries over to their homes and have their contacts there. So you guys should get lots of dinner appointments and hopefully lots of referrals," Stephen said.

"What about inactives?" I asked.

"We have some inactives, of course. There are always those that feel their Sundays are more precious than doing the work of God. There is a fine line between giving a member a calling to keep them coming to church each Sunday and giving them a calling and they avoid it and don't come. What I'll do is get a list from the Bishop before Sunday, and we'll meet and go over that list. Maybe the Bishop has some insight into different members that we can take to visit them that might be more welcoming than others," Stephen said, his mouth full of juicy lemon chicken. He was a messy eater and didn't notice he was missing a napkin.

I had my planner opened, trying to retrofit the new ward directory into it. I flipped over to Sunday so I could schedule a time.

"What time are we meeting on Sunday? Before or after church?"

"Why don't we meet after? I have meetings before and that would make for way too early of a morning to have the Ward Mission Meeting also."

After we officially ended the Ward Mission Meeting, we cleaned up after dinner then relaxed on the sofa as Stephen explained doctrinal secrets we were cautioned never to bring up or talk about with members or investigators.

He told us about *The Salamander Letters*. He told us of the theory going around Salt Lake regarding these letters. Supposedly, Joseph Smith didn't see God in the woods that day he went out to pray and ask, "Out of all the churches in the world, which was the right one?" God didn't come down and see him; a salamander did. The letters that were going around Salt Lake were supposedly written by Joseph Smith to a friend, describing what had actually taken place in the sacred grove. That he had seen and talked with a salamander, not Jesus Christ and God the Father. I asked Stephen if he believed this.

"Well, it doesn't really matter what Joseph Smith saw that day. He had a spiritual experience that ended up bringing God's Gospel once again back to the earth," he said while stuffing a piece of chocolate cake into his mouth.

"Good point," I said.

"There is no way to really prove whether these letters are real or not, but it sure is causing some concern in Utah right now. I heard the Church is trying to buy these letters. They've had the letters examined by specialists to determine whether the paper quality dates back to the late 1800s, and it does."

Stephen talked for another hour or so about the news out of Salt Lake and different rumors of what it all meant.

"Now, Elders, you shouldn't even worry about any of this. This won't change your work at all. If you run into someone that has questions or wants some answers to all these things, set up a meeting and I'll talk with them. Oh, almost forgot: the Bishop has set apart about twenty minutes for you to introduce yourselves in the new ward. Plan on taking it at the beginning of Sacrament Meeting." Stephen left with those parting words as Elder Bell and I turned out the lights and went to the bedroom.

As we were getting ready for bed, I asked Elder Bell about the next day's plans.

"We don't have anything planned yet, but we can work out the details tomorrow morning before we leave," he said.

"Do you like to tract?" I asked him.

"I don't mind tracting, but we have a bonus here." He went over to the closet and pulled out a stack of paper a foot high. "These are all requests for the *Book of Mormon*," he said while flipping through them. "Bounce-back tapes, and missionary visits. Some of these are two years old, but hey! They are somewhat warm referrals."

The referrals had come from the "Brought to you by the Church of Jesus Christ and Latter-day Saints" commercials on television.

"No way! What did the missionaries do here before? Stephen wasn't kidding when he said they were lazy. This is a gold mine!" I said.

Elder Bell got a big smile on his face from my greenie excitement. "Well, remember, some of these are old, and most of the time these don't pan out."

"Yeah, but still. With that stack, just from sheer numbers, there has got to be a few of them."

"Let's hope so," Elder Bell said.

While we were lying in bed, I asked Elder Bell all about his last area, Bakersfield, two hundred miles east of the Valley. He told me how much he liked it and how the members there were really nice. He told me about several of the investigators that he was teaching. One in particular, named Darla. She was a single mom. She had a two-year-old kid named Stanton. "Man, the ward just *loved* these guys. We had all the member support, just like it says in the Missionary Guide. Members sat in on the last three lessons. I didn't feel bad about leaving them in the other members' hands, but I'll miss seeing them. We probably went over there two or three times a week."

"Well, hopefully we can find some investigators like that here. You know they're out there, we just gotta find them," I said.

I silently prayed to God, telling him how thankful I was to be in the area and how much I wanted his help in finding the people who were ready to hear the gospel. After the prayer, I thought about my new area and my new companion. I never asked Elder Bell why he was transferred two weeks before the rest of the missionaries.

Elder Bell liked to sleep. At least on the first day of a new companionship, he liked to sleep. We should have been up by six thirty doing companionship study and getting ready to leave by nine thirty. We did companionship study around eight and didn't get out the door until ten thirty. We didn't have a well-stocked kitchen due to the transfers, so we opted to go to the grocery store before doing anything else. Elder Bell led the way to a Von's supermarket about three miles away. He rode fast. He had a monster mountain bike called a Giant. It was made for someone about six-five, and with his five-five frame, his butt would rotate about six inches each time he pedaled. It was funny to ride behind him and watch. Most of the time he just stood up, which seemed to suit him better. While stopped at a red light, I asked him why he had such a big bike. He said he'd borrowed it from a member in his last area. He was in such a hurry when he got transferred that he didn't have time to call the member and let him know, so he just took it with him. He said he would call him and return it eventually, though.

Once at the store, I loaded up on Top Ramen noodles and lunch meat. The store was a little less expensive than the Von's in Chatsworth. In Chatsworth, Top Ramen were six for a dollar only when the store ran a special. Elder Bell told me they always had the special going on here. Elder Bell went for a bag of chips and Quaker instant oatmeal packets. I tried to get into a conversation in line while checking out, but the lady in front of me told me that she wasn't interested. All I said was "How are you today?" She must have taken that to mean "Would you like to be baptized into the Mormon Church?"

As we headed out of the store, Elder Bell suggested that we run by home and drop off our groceries. I said that would be fine, and I followed profound Butt-Waddle-Bell back to the apartment.

"Well it's already 12:00," Elder Bell said while looking at his watch. He'd looked at it about five times on the way home but figured doing it now would make it look like it hadn't even occurred to him what time it was and how little we had accomplished by noon. "We might as well have lunch and take a break."

"OK," I said.

I made a couple of bologna sandwiches and sat down on the couch. I'd bought a map of the city and surrounding communities at the store and started going over it with the stack of referrals. We would be riding all day if we didn't get some kind of route to the referrals. I sorted by zip code, then street, then house number. Once I had six stacks, I took the east side of Van Nuys and started locating the different streets from the referrals. Within two hours, I had about twenty referrals located within seven miles of each other. Knowing the streets by then, I went into the ward directory and picked out five members who lived within those seven miles, ready to meet some people. I woke up Elder Bell to explain what I had done.

"Elder Dorsey, this is great! Let's go!"

All the referrals were requests for the *Book of Mormon*, so I loaded ten into my backpack and looked around trying to figure out what to do with the other ten.

"Elder Dorsey, we probably won't get to all twenty today, so the ones in your bag should be sufficient."

"Yeah, you're probably right."

The first five referrals greeted us with solid doors that never opened. We didn't hear anyone behind the door, so we concluded that no one was home and we set up a follow-up visit. These people had no idea they were now being scheduled for visits each morning in two missionary's morning-planning meetings. We would talk about them each morning and get to know each one by name and description of house, without their ever realizing it. They would become a vital part of our day and our mission as they went right on doing exactly what they did everyday.

A woman opened the sixth door we knocked on. She looked like she had just woken up. A television was on in the background with a commercial about debt consolidation—it was loud.

"Hi! We are missionaries from the Mormon Church and would like to talk with an Amanda Halquist about a *Book of Mormon* that she ordered," I said.

"Well, I'm Amanda but I didn't order no *Book of Mormon*," she said.

"It was some time ago; it looks like you ordered it about a year and a half ago. Do you remember? You may have seen it on a commercial or possibly visited one of our temples?"

"No, I think I would remember visiting a temple or a commercial that I ordered something off of. I'll take it, though."

"Great. Do you have a few minutes now? We could sit down and explain a little about the *Book* to you?" I asked.

"Now is not a good time, but I'll take it anyways."

"OK, no problem. Is there a time when we could come back during the day later this week, or would night work better?" I asked, using the commitment process I'd learned in the MTC and studied in the Missionary Guide. I didn't ask her whether she *wanted* us to come back. Rather, I asked what times would work so it took a possible "no" out of the conversation.

"Oh, definitely during the day. My kids are home after school and I wouldn't want them around," she said.

"Well, we do feel that our message is for the family, so it might be a good idea to have the kids here when we come back," I said.

"I'd rather it was just us," she said.

I opened my planner and flipped through the pages to later in the week. If anyone looked closely, it had no appointments scheduled at any time. I had a few notes from Chatsworth, but that's it. I flipped to the following week and scheduled her in for next Tuesday.

I asked if she would like me to point out some particularly interesting chapters in the book, and she said no. As we walked down the steps after her door shut, I looked over at Elder Bell and said, "Well, at least we have an appointment for next week. That's a start."

Elder Bell agreed that it was a start and continued his positive attitude, the only attitude I had seen as of yet. Bell was a pretty laid-back guy; so far, we were having a good time. Throughout the days of following up on the referrals, I would ask him questions about his home in Ogden, Utah, and what it was like to grow up in Mormon country.

"Dorsey, it's not any different than any other place. You have people there that do everything you could imagine. The only difference is that most of these people have Mormons in their family or were born into it and just fell away. You don't meet too many people that have never heard of Mormons, though."

I was fascinated with living in Utah. I went to a semester of college at Brigham Young University before the mission, the biggest college in the state, and also the main Mormon college in the world. If a person was any kind of Mormon, they went to BYU before and after their mission. It ensured getting the prettiest wife and a prosperous life in the Church. I equated it with going to Yale or Harvard, as the gentiles were so fond of.

We went by a couple of the members' homes that I had listed. Neither family was home, so I scheduled a follow-up visit for the next day. It did occur to me that if someone wasn't home at a certain time one day, to try another time another day, but we had the time and anything to fill it up with was nice.

It was six o'clock; we were leaning up against a streetlight pole, wondering what we wanted to do.

"I'm hungry," I said as I flipped through my planner, making mental notes of the doings of the day. "I don't show that we have a dinner appointment tonight, so looks like we are on our own."

"We'll have to make sure and pass around a calendar on Sunday to get some appointments," Elder Bell said.

"Good idea. Do you know any women in the ward that can take it into the Relief Society with them to pass around?" I asked.

"We'll just give it to the Relief Society president. In fact, will you make a note to visit her before Sunday? You can write it in your planner," he said.

Elder Bell's hair was very fuzzy. He didn't use any gel and didn't comb it. His hair made him look like Fozzie Bear from *The Muppet Show*. I couldn't help but laugh a little when I looked at him. I'd already started calling him Fozzie. He didn't mind; he seemed to enjoy it and I liked calling him it.

"We have a choice. We can either go home and eat some lemon chicken or stop by one of the members on your list," Elder Bell said.

"Either is fine with me. I think it might be a little late to drop by for dinner, though."

"OK, it's lemon chicken," Elder Bell said as he pushed himself off the pole and started across the street.

It was dark on the ride home, but Elder Bell knew the streets well. He flew down them like he had ridden them hundreds of times. I kept up with him as best I could. It was hard to see him, and my eyes were watering profusely from the wind. We finally pulled into an alley that took us behind our apartment building. I didn't even realize we were there until

Elder Bell hopped off his bike, threw it over his shoulder, and started for the stairs.

"Elder Bell, you ride fast. Is that how you've stayed in such good shape on your mission?" He wasn't in the greatest shape, but on a curve scale for missionaries, he wasn't doing too badly.

"I've been on a bike most of my mission; maybe that's it."

We lugged our bikes up the stairs and took them inside the apartment. We checked the answering machine; no one had called. It was nice having a night off from splits with members and from dinner appointments. I looked forward to curling up with the *Book of Mormon* or studying one of the books written by one of the twelve apostles who accompanied the *Book of Mormon*. All the twelve apostles wrote books about the Church. They weren't paid for being a full-time apostle, but they made bank off the books they wrote with all the die-hard Mormons eating them up. Mormons seemed to engross themselves so much in the religion that they had to have every book from anyone writing on the Church. It was a treat to go to the Mormon bookstore and look at all the companions to the bible, the *Book of Mormon*, church history, countless titles by countless authors. These bookstores were usually owned by one of the pillars of the community of Mormons. My Mom had a library full of all the latest books and study guides that went along with all the standard works, but I never read any.

We met the Morels for the first time when they invited us over for dinner on Sunday afternoon. They had three kids: four-year-old Jacob, two-year-old Joan, and two-year-old Erika. Erika was the daughter of Sister Morel's sister, but she was in rehab in Los Angeles and couldn't take care of her. I never asked what she was in rehab for. Sister Morel never talked about her. It was probably crack since Sister Morel had mentioned Erika was born addicted to crack and that was why she cried all the time. Erika cried no matter who held her, so I held her the whole time we were there that night. After dinner, Brother Morel took us for a walk around his yard. I was instantly impressed with the size of the lot, but the state of it kept me from commenting too highly.

There was a '75 Jeep CJ7 buried under years' worth of sprawling blackberry brambles.

"Brother Morel, that's a nice Jeep. What's the story with it?" I asked, walking over to it, carefully picking my way to the driver's-side window and peering in.

"Oh, that's one of my many projects," he said. "With the addition going on the house this year, it will have to be put off for another year again."

"How long have you had it?" Elder Bell asked.

"I bought that my freshman year at BYU. I took Myrna on dates in it when we first met."

"This has the V8, right?" I asked.

"You bet it does. It's a monster on the road; it really moves."

"Does it run?" I asked.

"Well, it did when I parked it there."

"You should get it running again. Even if it's just a second vehicle," I suggested. Being a fan of Jeeps since I was a kid, I hated seeing something that was meant to do so much sit tangled in the very brambles that it was made to tromp over in the mountains.

"Then I'd have to license it and try to keep it running. I don't want to have it to worry about when I'm getting ready to pour the foundation for the addition later this week." Brother Morel turned and looked to the clearing in front of his house with forms waiting for the concrete, "This," he said walking over to the edge of the closest form, "will be taking all my time for the next year."

Elder Bell stepped inside the forms and started pointing out the different rooms of the addition just from what he saw from the rough-in of two-by-fours. "Couple bedrooms and a bath, Brother Morel?" Elder Bell asked.

"Yep. The house is just too small now with the five of us living here. It was fine with just three of us, but it would be so nice for the kids to have their own rooms and Myrna and I to have a big master bedroom with our own bath, finally."

"Man, this is going to be nice," I said.

"We are really looking forward to it. I got a raise about six months ago, and we had been waiting for that to start. The weather has gotten warm enough that I'll be able to come home after work and put in a few hours each night to get this done."

"Are you going to be building it yourself?" Elder Bell asked.

"Yep, all me."

"Would you like some help?" Elder Bell asked, not looking over at Brother Morel but walking around the forms.

"Well, sure. Any help you guys can give would be great.

Maybe you could count it as a service project to help the needy in the ward?" he said, cracking himself up.

"We'd love to, Brother Morel. We have P-Days also that we could come over."

"Elder Bell, have you done this kind of work in the past?" Brother Morel asked.

"Before my mission, this is what I did. I worked for a local contractor, and we did some remodels but mostly new homes. I imagine with the two of us framing, we could have this done in no time."

"Hey, don't count me out!" I blurted in. "I can wield a hammer as well as the next man."

"And Elder Dorsey, you will learn how to frame," Elder Bell said, smiling at me.

We agreed to come over the following Thursday and help with the pouring of the slab. Elder Bell was really excited about the chance to do a little work, different work from missionary work. I looked forward to wearing a tool belt. I'd always wanted to be a cowboy, and wearing a tool belt was the closest thing to having two six-shooters slung low on my hips.

It was eight miles from the Morels house to our apartment.

The night was warm, warm enough to enjoy the breeze from the cruising speed of our bikes. The Morels lived on Dexter Avenue, about four blocks off of Sepulveda Boulevard, one of the main streets going through the Valley. We were able to stay on Dexter for about five miles before crossing over to Sepulveda, taking us the rest of the way home. Dexter was lined with 1950s-style homes. I thought when I finally bought a house, I would like one similar to the humble homes we rode by. Some of the homes even had white picket fences against the sidewalk. Surprisingly, for a pleasant night there were no people out, the sidewalks were clear, and the lack of streetlights made it easy to see the glow from the few lights coming from the houses. I was sure a newly married couple in their early twenties was sitting in one of these homes reading their favorite books to each other in between jaunts of making love in their living room. I couldn't wait until I was there. The mission would make me a prime candidate for all God had to offer in marriage and families, and I looked forward to it. The thoughts of young married couples vanished, though, as we made the turn up to Sepulveda. The lights from the passing cars lit our way on the sidewalk as we covered ground. The Sunday night macaroni and cheese wasn't the best food to peddle eight miles on. I felt the ache inside my stomach. Of course, we didn't slow down as the light turned yellow.

Elder Bell put his bike in low and cruised through the light. I barely made it before a dusty sedan moved into the intersection on its green light.

That night Elder Bell taught me about engines. It had come up when I started asking him about Brother Morel's Jeep. He told me what happens to cars when they sit for years outside without even a tarp on them. He said that most likely the carburetor would need to be rebuilt because it had old gas in it and that the linkage was probably all corroded together. He said it would be more work than it was worth. I didn't like hearing that it wasn't worth it, so I didn't believe it. I could see myself in that Jeep when I got home, a returned missionary cruising around BYU in a Jeep. Elder Bell explained the differences between the small-block V-eight and the big-block V-eight. He told me about the rings and how the fire from the spark plugs pushed the piston heads down, turning the cam rod, giving the engine its power to turn the drivetrain and move the wheels.

As I fell asleep, I thought about Myrna and Brother Morel. I enjoyed meeting them and looked forward to spending time with their family. They were different from hanging out with the Barretts or the Austins or any of the families from Chatsworth. Because Elder Bell and I met them together, they seemed like my mission family. I would be the one introducing missionaries to them, not the other way around. I also thought about the next day and how nice it was going to be to have P-Day. We didn't have any plans. Laundry was always fun. I loved laundromats: what other people talked about, the different laundering techniques, the different clothes, the hum of the washers, the smell of fabric softener, and the talks with others while sitting on top of washers.

It was nice to sleep in on P-Day. When we got to the laundromat, I took my bike inside; Elder Bell didn't care about his bike, so he left it outside. It was a little awkward with each of us taking a big bag of clothes on a bike to a laundromat, but we managed with me dropping mine only once. The laundromat wasn't far from our apartment. We would be able to drop our clothes off and cruise home if we wanted to—but we didn't. There was an automotive supply store across the street. Elder Bell suggested we go in and look at the motor they had on display. They had a small block on display, pulled apart. The manifold was off of it, allowing a person to look right down into the cylinders.

Elder Bell pointed out all the parts from the discussion we had the night before. Once again, I stood amazed at not only what I was learning, but also that this young man, only a few years older than me, knew so much about everything. We walked up and down every aisle in the store, finally purchasing a small brush to clean my sprocket. We then left to put our clothes in the dryer. With the dryer being the longer of the two cycles, we had time to run to the mall down the block. Going to the mall on P-Day was a treat. People didn't stare at us since we looked like them, in street clothes without name tags on.

We got back from the mall in time to pull our clothes out of the dryer before anyone else got to them. I had learned from experience that if clothes were folded when warm, they wouldn't need to be pressed later. With seven white shirts, this was an invaluable trick to know. Even rolled up in my backpack on the bike ride back to the apartment, they would still come out mostly wrinkle free.

After we got back to the apartment and hung up our clothes, Elder Bell decided on a nap before our shopping expedition. He went into the room and shut the door, per my prior request, as he was a snorer. Through the closed door, expecting to hear his snores, instead I instead heard him talking on the phone. I assumed he was talking to people from his previous areas. I didn't think I would do that, even when I had more than one previous area.

I went to the couch and started drawing the engine parts in my journal. The journal had a black leather binder with my name embossed in silver on the cover. I thought it would be heartening if years later my kids could read my journal and look at the drawings I had of engine parts. I had a drawing section filled with pictures of Calvin and Hobbes. The engine parts seemed a nice addition. I wasn't a very good artist, so I took my time to avoid mistakes. I didn't want my journal messy for the many admirers I was sure would be reading it someday—after I was made prophet.

The phone woke me up. It kept ringing. I thought it was a phone from my dream.

"Elder Bell, answer the phone!" I yelled, when I realized it wasn't in my dream but in the apartment.

He finally sauntered out of the room, a smile on his face, and answered the phone after it stopped ringing.

"Elder, why didn't you answer the phone?" he asked.

"I was sleeping. And you are senior companion, so who ever it was would have needed to talk with you anyway. And you've been here longer."

"OK, Dorsey," he said walking over to me. "Get up; it's time to go grocery shopping." He was making his way over to the couch to sit on me and give me a jostle.

"I'm sleeping. Let's go in a little bit."

"No way; you woke me up. Now I'm ready to go," he said as he sat on me and waited for me to push him off.

"Fine!" I said, pushing him off in fun.

After shopping, our outwardly uneventful P-Day was winding down and we were getting ready to go to the Morgans for a dinner appointment. They offered to pick us up when we called to remind them of dinner, but we opted for the bike ride. Elder Bell liked to ride to our appointments, even when members offered. I was looking forward to the ride myself as I had cleaned my sprockets that afternoon and expected my bike to be fast enough to pass Elder Bell.

Riding to the Morgans was pleasant, coming off of a relaxing day looking forward to a nice meal. I hadn't met the Morgans. Or if I had, I didn't remember. The usual questions from members didn't seem to bother me anymore. Maybe it was because I had some of my own to counteract with.

CHAPTER 7

I met Tara riding home one night after an appointment canceled, or rather, wouldn't open their door. She was walking down Londelius Street by herself, with several books under her arm. There was still enough light for our faces to shine, so I felt that stopping wouldn't be a problem. I made sure to make a little noise as we came up behind her on our bikes by talking loudly to Elder Bell.

"Hello, how are you tonight?" I asked as I rode up next to her, being careful to stay several feet away, though. People already thought we were creepy and weird just being Mormon, but add two guys riding next to a girl at night, we had to watch it.

"I'm fine. Is there something I can help you with?" She asked, her long dark hair shining from the slanting light on the street.

"My name is Elder Dorsey, and this is my companion, Elder Bell."

"*Oh*, you're Mormon missionaries. I've heard of you, just never actually met one," she said with a little smirk.

"Well, here we are. Now you can say that you've met some," I said.

"Yes, I can."

"So you have heard of us, then?" I asked.

"That's what I said, isn't it?"

"Yes, it is. Do you have friends that are Mormon?"

"No," she said, still walking and making it hard for me to flirt with this cute girl. I always thought that after the mission, asking a girl out would be so easy compared with going through the hell of knocking on doors, cold calling, and talking to people on the street.

"Then how have you heard of us?"

"Well, I think most people have heard of the Mormon Church. Just like you've heard of the Catholic Church."

"Well, we do meet people who haven't heard of us, so I had to ask."

"It's a hobby of mine to study other religions at times." "Have you studied our religion?"

"Oh, is it *your* religion now? I thought it was God's. In fact, I though it was God's *only* religion."

"OK, I mean have you studied the Mormon religion or the Church of Jesus Christ and Latter-day Saints?"

"A little. I read your Bible."

"Oh, the *Book of Mormon*."

"That's it."

"Did you have any questions that we could answer for you?"

"Sure. Lots."

"Would you like to set up a time for us to come over and answer them for you?" She stopped walking and looked directly at me. I stopped and cradled my bike between my legs.

"Are you serious?" she asked.

"Sure, why not? That's what we do."

"What do you mean that's what you do?"

"We talk with people about our beliefs and how they can make a change in a person's life."

"I'm not sure I'm looking for a change. I just had some questions."

"We can answer them for you. You don't have to change. I was just explaining what we do."

"But you do hope to change the way people think, right?"

"I don't know about the way people think. We explain God's religion. We do ask if they would like to join, if so prompted by the spirit."

"'If so prompted by the spirit'? Is that what you call it?"

"Hey, I just wanted to know if you wanted some of your questions answered. That's it. I'm not asking you to become a Mormon."

"OK. Sure, I'll meet with you," she said pausing longer than necessary between words. "My friends live right down this street, last house on the left. Why don't you call me and we will set something up."

"Great. Looking forward to it." I pulled out my planner and turned to the day's date with a flip of my easy page finder. "OK, what's your number?"

"I think I'll just get your number instead. Is that alright?"

"Sure," I said, handing one of my Mormon Missionary business cards to her, "The number is crossed out and written underneath. We move around a lot."

"So where are you guys from?"

"I'm from Seattle, Washington, and Elder Bell is from Utah."

"Of course, Utah."

"You know, I never got your name."

"My name is Tara."

"Tara, it's been nice meeting you and talking with you. I look forward to getting your call so we can sit down with you."

"Nice meeting you too, Elder Dorsey. I'll give you a call." And she walked down the street towards her friend's house.

Elder Bell and I stayed in the apartment only a few months until we were moved to one in our area. The new apartment was in a small complex of only six other units. The complex reminded me of Vegas, something built to look like another place but looking out of place because of its location. It was a miniature little German town. The building itself had little turrets on top of the ridges. The mailboxes were modeled after what looked like the front of a café with an awning hanging over it. It was a fun place to look at and listen to members' comments. When I finally met the owner months later, I realized from his strong accent why it was modeled after a Bavarian village.

Another set of elders, Elders Christopher and Duncan, moved into the two-bedroom apartment we moved out of. They were both from Utah, but they didn't know each other from before the mission. With both naïveté and sarcasm in my voice, I would asked this of all missionaries from Utah. Elder Christopher had been out about a year. He was older than the rest of us by several years, evident in both his speech and the way he carried himself. Elder Duncan was a greenie. It felt good not to be the newest elder in every situation, something I thought would never change but through time, had. I was called as the district leader, the leader over the six of us. The other set of elders, Elders Deeds and Berry, served on the far side of the Valley, bordering Hollywood Hills. When we visited them, my eyes would wander to the hills, dreaming of someday living in them as a famous actor or writer. I had become fast friends with Elder Deeds and Elder Berry due to our mutual liking for P-Day tennis. We had talked about playing the next P-Day.

Brother Morel had built the forms for his foundation on Saturdays for a month. Prior to building the foundation, he had a backhoe come in and clear the section of yard and dig out the foundation. He'd been working steadily on it throughout the spring and planned on getting it framed and enclosed by fall or winter, but he wouldn't make it without help. We planned on going over there to start framing the following Saturday, after the foundation had cured to the walk.

Missionary work was progressing slowly. Meeting Tara was really all we could write about to President Carlson, and I did so in my weekly letter:

Dear President,

Work is going great. Met an investigator while riding home after a dinner appointment.

Elder Bell and I introduced us and almost gave her a First Discussion right there on the street. We set an appointment up for next week and anxiously await her call. We have faith she will. Elder Bell and I are getting along great. Teaching me tons and very easy to work with. Thanks for all you do.

Elder Dorsey

There was a half-page at the end of the weekly stats form that was provided for our letters to the President. We were required to write a weekly letter, and I wrote every week.

Elder Bell sometimes added to what I wrote, but only a few lines saying how much he appreciated the president. He never read my letters and always let me fill in the stats. Stats were hardly impressive for two full-time, very able bodied men who actually worked. We had no commitments for baptism. We counted Tara as our lead investigator and hadn't even given her a First Discussion. And there were two women who lived in a halfway house for retarded people who wanted to hear the Discussions They had ordered a *Book of Mormon* a year earlier, and we delivered it.

We'd only made the one visit to them the previous week and planned on going back in a couple days. Elder Bell thought they might need a little more time to read the suggested readings in the *Book of Mormon*.

Living with other missionaries didn't seem to lessen Elder Bell's sleeping. He rolled out somewhere between seven and eight o'clock. I might have slept a little longer myself if Elder McDonnell didn't come in each morning and jump on me.

"Why do you have to wake me up, McDonnell?"

"You would feel so bad later today if you didn't get up on time, Elder. I'm doing you a favor."

He had since jumped on the end of my bed, reading me a woeful tale of Jarom from his Spanish *Book of Mormon*.

"Why don't you go sit on Bell's bed," I said, bothered because he was just trying to trick me into getting up. I went along because it was easier than not.

"Because you have the biggest bed in the mission and Elder Bell doesn't wash his sheets."

"I have before," a sleepy Elder Bell said, his mattress shaking from his laughter.

"Bell, time to get up," I said, pushing McDonnell once again off my bed.

"Oh, you go ahead, Dorsey. I'm going over the Discussions in my head. I'm very visual like that."

"OK. You will go to hell for this, you know that."

"Will you come visit me?"

"No. You will just be sleeping down there too."

"Sounds like heaven to me," he said pulling his blanket and sheet closer to his chin and smiling, eyes shut.

"Morning, Elder Loughton. How are you this morning?" I said as I crossed the hall and jumped on McDonnell's made bed.

"Dorsey, get off my bed."

"This thing is hardly a bed. This kind of sucks, actually.

How goes the study of Spanish this morning, Loughton?"

Elder Loughton struggled with the language. It wasn't hard to tell how bad he was, because his companion was said to be the best Spanish speaker in the mission.

Elder McDonnell had notes all over the apartment. In the bathroom, eye level while taking care of business, one could read conjugations of the verb *estar*. I'd taken Spanish in high school and college and probably spoke it better than Elder Loughton. I threw out what I knew each day, and Elder McDonnell played along and taught me new words. He kept a small notepad in the pocket of his shirt to write down words he heard throughout the day and then would study them the next morning. I'd gone on splits with him, amazed at his ability to converse with the Spanish-speaking people. He was as fluid as if it were his first language. I modeled my morning study after his example, and it was paying off. My knowledge of Spanish and the studying I did with Elder McDonnell probably further irritated the struggling Elder Loughton, but he didn't let it show. And I wasn't about to compromise one of the few things from this mission that was going to go home with me—what I learned—just to make him feel better about his inabilities.

"My Spanish is going fine, Elder. And how is yours?" he asked with a smile on his face, enjoying the morning and the small break from studying a language he would never truly grasp and never speak again after the day he got home.

"You know, Loughton, I'm comfortable with where I'm at in my studies. You should look to me as an example and not stress so much about the language."

"Yeah, whatever, Dorsey. Easy for you to say when you learn a verb and use it all week in the same sentence."

"Hey, careful, Loughton. I'm giving you a hard time."

"I know, I know."

McDonnell had moved to the couch, getting serious about his morning study. Spanish missionaries had an extra thirty minutes each day to study the language. McDonnell saved this for last and enjoyed it the most. I was jealous of the missionaries who learned a language.

We were all out here concentrating on God's work and trying to spread the Gospel, yet it seemed these missionaries had an outlet the rest of us didn't have. I'd be done with my mission knowing a whole bunch about the *Book of Mormon* and the Bible. They would come out knowing a language they had had two years to perfect.

Watching McDonnell study Spanish was fun. He didn't like to be interrupted at all. While he was reading the *Book of Mormon*, it was fine to interrupt him, but when the flash cards were in hand with his spiral notebook open to all the words he had written down from the day before, it was known one had to keep quiet. Because of this, I'd made the habit of studying at the kitchen table. This also got me away from both McDonnell and Bell, who had no problem letting out huge bubbles of gas, which in a small apartment was shared with all.

It was during this time that I immersed myself in reading the Old Testament. I was over halfway through, working on the book of Isaiah, which at the rate I was going, could take me the rest of the mission. It was like studying a foreign language at times. With no movies, dating, or even looking at women on the street or in church, the only racy thing I could read or look at was the Old Testament. I read it with a study guide, which helped. I'd read and put colorful notes in all my margins, pointing out what verses meant, according to the Church's approved companion to study.

The shower came on; I could hear Elder Loughton's Mormon Tabernacle Choir and his karaoke attempt.

"Elder Bell, you want some breakfast?" I yelled from the kitchen.

"Dorsey, maybe you could walk in and ask Bell instead of yelling across the apartment," Elder McDonnell said from the other room.

"Bell, instant oatmeal mixed special for you?" I said even louder this time. Elder McDonnell shook his head in regret.

"I'm going to get you, Dorsey. You know the move."

"No, not the move!" I rushed over to McDonnell and begged him not to put down his notebook. "You just keep on studying there, McDonnell. See how nice and quiet it is?"

"Told you not to yell, Dorsey!" he said throwing his notebook aside and grabbing my arm.

"No, No! Don't do it. Bell! Help!"

McDonnell proceeded to throw me around the room like a sack of potatoes. He weighed only ten pounds more than me but was All-State in wrestling. The move he eventually got me in was with my nose in his butt—right in his butthole. It was humiliating and, once there, I couldn't move—could hardly breathe.

Once I stopped struggling and assured McDonnell I would never yell across the room, he let me go. This move took the fun out of the morning. I walked back into my room and dove into my bed.

"Wrestling's for fags!" I yelled from my room.

"You want more, Dorsey?"

I kept my mouth shut the rest of the morning and listened to Elder Bell laugh beside me. I made him breakfast in bed. He didn't even sleep all morning. He just liked lying there in bed with his sheets right up to his chin, wallowing in his stench.

When we finally saddled up with our five *Book of Mormon*s in my backpack, I realized we had no plans.

"Let's go tracting," I said. "It's not too hot yet, and we can get it over with."

"OK, lead the way," Elder Bell said.

We had reverted to tracting after all the warm leads from commercials had been gone through. My efficiency and organization of the leads led to getting through them in only a few days. No success from them—too old, too cold.

"We have to stop off and get a Dirt Moto magazine. I'm kinda getting into these dirt bikes, talking with McDonnell all the time."

"Sure."

We stopped off at the little grocery store next to the laundromat. They didn't have the latest issue, but I hadn't bought one yet, so being a month behind was fine for me. Bell waited outside on the steps.

"Let's head over by Morels; that way we can stop in for lunch."

"I want to go home for lunch, though. I want to read my magazine."

"OK. So where should we go?"

"Let's go over by the park. There are houses behind it in that neighborhood."

"OK. Follow me now."

I was always following Elder Bell. He rode fast for a little guy who slept a lot.

We tracted for about two hours and headed home for lunch. We handed out one *Book of Mormon* to a young Spanish woman and wrote Elder McDonnell's and Loughton's number on the inside cover.

I used my broken Spanish to explain that they were Spanish-speaking missionaries.

"Elders, nice to see that you are always on time for lunch," Elder McDonnell said, looking at his watch.

"Wouldn't miss it, and wouldn't miss the chance to read my *Dirt Moto*," I said, pulling my new magazine from my backpack and flashing the cover at McDonnell.

"Whoa, you got one? Let me see it," Elder McDonnell said. "The cover's comparing the 250 class. Isn't that what you have?"

"Let's see it." I tossed the magazine to Elder McDonnell on the couch.

He looked at the cover and that was it. "I can't read this, Elder. And you shouldn't be either."

"Come on, it's a skinny little magazine that I'm reading on my lunch break. I don't think it's that big a deal."

"Oh, are you the one making the mission rules now?"

"It's only the one. Not like I have a shop guide here and I'm studying it each morning."

"OK, OK. You can rationalize it all you want. Looks like you have."

I read it and didn't feel bad. I even told McDonnell about it and asked him questions about the different classes of motorcycles.

"Dorsey, I don't want to talk about bikes either," he said annoyed, turning his attention to his Spanish words that had failed to register their definitions from the morning's conversations.

After lunch (and after McDonnell and Loughton had left), Elder Bell took a quick nap. I tried reading on the couch but fell asleep myself. I finally woke up and told Elder Bell that we needed to go visit some of our investigators.

Elder Bell didn't mind me telling him to get up. He knew he should anyway.

While Elder Bell was getting ready, I checked the messages on our machine. Tara had called. She left her number and told us to call her. She used my name.

"Hi. Is Tara there?" I asked the woman who answered the phone.

"This is. Who's this?"

"This is Elder Dorsey, returning your call. Remember, we met the other night by your friend's house?"

"I remember. So, yeah. I wanted to see when you could come over and we could talk about your church."

"What's better for you? Nights or days?" I asked.

"Nights. How is Thursday night this week?"

I flipped to the empty page of Thursday in my planner and saw only the scheduled splits with the stake missionaries. "Thursday's good. Where do you live? And we can come over around seven o'clock."

"I'll give you my friend's address. Not the one I was at the other night—a different one."

"OK. Shoot."

"One-four-three-nine Roy Street, number seven."

"Alright. We will plan on Thursday around seven, then?"

"I'll have a couple friends over, too. OK?"

"Of course. No problem."

"OK, then. See you Thursday."

"OK, see you then. Bye."

"Bye-bye." And she was gone.

I didn't know if it was the thrill of the chase with possible investigators or the asking-a-girl-out type of jitters, but I was excited about the appointment. And that she was having friends there with her excited me even more. My mind instantly went to a picture of myself baptizing four investigators from a cold-call conversation on a dark street, after hours, riding home. I would be famous in the mission and all would bow to me. It was the stuff mission legends were made of, and those praised were welcomed home as war heroes.

I told Elder Bell all about the phone call and he got excited too. We added Tara to our whiteboard in our room and stood back to admire. It looked full. We had Tara as an investigator waiting on a First Discussion. The other investigators were all hit or miss. If we caught them home, they might let us teach them. And we had Mary and Stephanie from the group home.

"Let's go visit Mary. She is always there and we could teach her a Discussion," I said.

"She doesn't really understand what we are talking about. Let's go read with her for a while and teach her another time. We will count this as review of the First."

"This will be like the third time we've reviewed the First with her."

"I know. But hey, it's better than tracting."

We went over to Mary's and Stephanie's; they had just gotten home from shopping. They didn't invite us in, so we waited in the carport with our bikes leaning up against the four-by-four supports.

The area had no members that I could recall from dinner appointments or splits. It wasn't a nice neighborhood either. The homes visible from where I leaned all needed paint and I'm sure had for years. The blue paint from the neighbor's house curled and cracked, trying to break free from the glue that held it down, showing large sections of inexpensive plywood that made the outside walls of the houses. Most of the homes were built on cinder-block foundations barely visible through the weeds growing up to the level of the windows. Cars that didn't run sat in the streets, and the ones that did run were in the driveways. Music blared from a nearby home, though I couldn't tell which one. It was rap music.

My gaze took me back to the carport with the washer and dryer beside me. They weren't running. Mary's clothes must have all been cleaned recently.

The screen door opened up to let Mary through. Mary didn't come out of a doorway; it was more liked she emerged from it. She was large, possibly four hundred pounds, and eye level with me. She held on to the two-by-four handrail as she made her way down the three wooden steps, the steps and railing bending and creaking from her weight.

"Hi, Mary. Did you get all your groceries put away?" Elder Bell asked.

"I did. Yes." She sat down in a rusty metal folding chair in front of the washer and dryer.

"Is Stephanie going to join us?" I asked.

"Oh, I don't know. Stephanie, are you coming out?" Mary yelled through the screen door.

"No. Not this time," I heard the small voice answer back. "Well you should. These boys came all the way over to talk with us."

"I don't want to," the small voice answered back and was silent.

"Ooooh well, I guess it's just me today," Mary sighed, looking at the ground.

Elder Bell and I had pulled a couple of rusty metal chairs for ourselves in front of Mary.

"How have you been, Mary?" I asked.

"Fine, I guess. I'm waiting to get my medicine."

"What medicine is that?" I asked, immediately knowing I shouldn't have.

"Oh, just medicine."

"Are you going to be OK without it for a few days?" I asked.

"Oh, I should have it later today or tomorrow. The nurse is bringing it over."

"Well that's good. Is there anything we can do for you today?"

"No, No. Nothing. Everything is fine."

"Well, we wanted to see how your reading was coming in the *Book of Mormon*."

"Well, I haven't read it. It's hard to understand."

"Can we read some with you now?" I asked.

"OK, I have it here," she said, holding it up from her lap. "Great. Why don't we go to the spot that we marked for you?" I reached out for her book and opened it to the part in Third Nephi where Christ came down. First, I showed her the picture and explained what we would be reading.

"We will let Elder Bell start out reading and then I'll take over. Do you feel like reading today? Or would you rather just have us read for you?"

"You go ahead. I'm really slow at reading."

Elder Bell went ahead and read for about ten minutes. I helped Mary follow along in her *Book of Mormon*.

We were introduced to Mary through Dianna Clark. Dianna had just been baptized into the Second Ward the month before I transferred in. She was the perfect new member—introduced all her friends to us, had us over for dinner, opened her apartment up if we needed a place to teach new investigators, gave rides to us on Sundays, and picked up any investigators who needed rides. She was just great.

Elder Bell and I had taught Dianna three of the New Member Discussions since I'd been there. Seeing Mary reminded me that we needed to call her to set up the remaining Discussions. She was always at church, though, so I didn't worry about it too much. Most of the philosophy behind the New Member Discussions was to integrate the new members with current members in the ward to provide them with the strong support needed when what they had learned had sunk in and some realized they wanted out. The growth of the Mormon Church was phenomenal, but retaining its new members was notoriously challenging.

We finished with Mary and set up a time for next week to come back and teach the Second Discussion. We asked her several questions about how she was feeling and about what we were teaching her. We felt she was not only grasping enough of it, but more importantly, feeling the spirit. That alone would let her know that the things we were teaching her were true.

On the ride home, we stopped by the Morels to see how the forms were coming. Everything was done and ready for the concrete to be poured the following day. Once poured and cured, we could then frame (and I could wear a tool belt).

We didn't have any splits planned that night, so we stayed in the apartment and ate Top Ramen noodles. After dinner, I read my motorcycle magazine while Elder Bell slept. When McDonnell and Loughton got home, they came in and hung out for about an hour while we talked about Utah. Both of them were from Utah and had stories about living there. McDonnell was a bit pretentious around Loughton, which I didn't understand. Loughton was a totally different type of person and McDonnell should never have felt threatened by him. Maybe he wasn't threatened, though. Maybe he was just a jerk. We got to know each other well living together, tracting and playing on P-Days. We were all from different parts of the country, yet it was enough for us that we happened to share the same religion along with the belief that we would all be saved. We treated each other like brothers; after all, the Church told us we were.

The next morning we got up early and set out to help pour concrete. When we arrived, the other members were already close to being finished. There were Brother Edwards, Brother Nelson, and Brother Ryan helping push the wet cement around. They had all done that type of work before and were pushing the "mud" around, telling the truck driver when to turn on the mixer, when to add water, and where to point the long chute through which the mud came down to the ground.

"Elders!" Brother Morel said excitedly when seeing us coast into his lot. "Well, is it what you thought, Elder Dorsey?"

"Whoa, this is cool. Do you have any boots that I can wear to get in there and move that stuff around?"

"Sure. Over on the porch. I grabbed a few from work."

I went over to the porch and grabbed an old pair of boots. They were gray with red toes and fit tight, curling my feet from the inside. I saw the kids in the window and waved. I stepped into the cement soup and instantly fell in, up to my waist. My boots filled up, I needed the help of two of the brethren to pull me to safety. Apparently I had stepped on the sides of the foundation that went deeper into the ground. After seeing all the rebar in the holes and forms, I was glad I didn't get a surprise visitor up the backside to make it a truly memorable experience.

With my boots off, in a pair of Brother Morels jeans and a T-shirt that read "Proud to be LDS," I sat on the porch and watched the rest of the afternoon while my clothes washed inside. The forms were filled up and then smoothed out by Brother Morel and Elder Bell.

The smoothing-out process was long, slow, and monotonous. Watching wasn't something I enjoyed so much, so I broke up the time by sitting in my future CJ and walking through the Morels' yard. There was a glass greenhouse behind the house that let in as much sun as the sprawling blackberry bushes allowed. Potting tables stood next to the greenhouse. It was a yard that, cleaned up, would have been pristine. But with the cars and bushes, it was just a big lot occupied by a house, not a yard.

After the smoothing was done, the Morels fed us dinner. I held Jacob on my lap until he just got to be *too* much. I had as much food on me as he had on his plate. Luckily, I was still wearing my "Proud to be LDS" shirt.

After putting on clean sets of clothes, Elder Bell and I started for home. He rode slowly with me alongside him.

"Tomorrow we should hook up with Elder Deeds and Berry for lunch. Like a mini–District Meeting. Sound good?" I asked Elder Bell.

"Sure. There is a bike shop in their area down off of Encino Boulevard that a member owns, and I wanted to get my bike tuned up."

"He just does it for free?"

"Well, he has to. We're missionaries."

"Oh, I guess you're right. You think he will tune my bike?"

"Sure. All you need to do is ask once we get in."

We met Deeds and Berry at the members' home where they lived, a one-story rambler: very open with lots of windows. Deeds and Berry had a room in the back, with a separate entrance accessed through the garage. It was a private little apartment with its own kitchen. I left my overnight bag there, as Deeds and I were going to do splits the next day. We then rode to In-and-Out Burger for lunch.

"Four specials, please." I said, handing over a five-dollar bill.

"Anything else with that, sir?" asked the counter person. "Large water, please."

I ate three of my burgers and gave one to Elder Bell. He never had any money but was always up for going out.

We all sat at the table and talked about the different missionaries we knew and who was in the zone now. Elder Berry came out with Elder Bell, so they knew each other pretty well, along with other missionaries in the field. Elder Deeds and I listened as they talked about the different missionaries going home that month, and who the next AP would be.

After lunch, we rode to the bike shop that Brother Donaldson owned.

There were only four new bikes on the showroom floor, none of which were in the class of any of ours, even the freebie that Bell rode. Brother Donaldson, who was in the back room, barely looked up at us from the bike he was working on.

"Hi, Elders. Come on back; I'm just finishing a tune-up here."

The little repair shop in the back was no bigger than the bed of a pick-up. It was stacked from floor to ceiling with bikes of all makes and sizes. There were ten-year-old ten-speeds, and twelve-speeds about the same age. A few mountain bike parts were scattered on the floor: straight handle bars, big knobbed tires. Brother Donaldson's glasses kept falling way down on his nose, pinching his nostrils and making him breathe hard. Sweat poured off his brow onto his greasy hands, making a black paste other hands would have shied away from. His hair fell down over his glasses, while the fan above made more noise than air movement.

"Hi, Brother Donaldson! This is Elder Dorsey and Elder Bell from the Van Nuys Ward.

"Nice to meet you, Elders. I'd shake your hand, but mine are a little greasy now."

"Oh, that's fine. Nice to meet you too," I said. "This is a nice shop you have here. Have you owned it long?"

"Going on three years now. It started out a lot better—meaning I sold more bikes than I did repairs."

"Would you rather sell bikes than work on them?" I asked.

"Yep. But when sales are slow, you have to do something to make money. I pick up these old ten-speeds for nothing and repair them. I make a little off of them. They go pretty quick once they're on the floor. I guess everyone doesn't need those fancy mountain bikes like the *elders* have," he said with a friendly smile, his eyes looking up at me.

"How much do the ten-speeds go for once they are ready to put on the floor?" Elder Berry asked.

"Under a hundred bucks, unless they're just in great condition."

"That's a *great* deal. I think if I'd had that as an option when I came out, I would have gone that route," I said, thoroughly engrossed in this concept of fixing up old bikes and selling them. "Is it just you here?"

"Oh yeah. When it gets slow, like it's been for the last six months, having someone working beside you is a luxury quickly forgotten."

Elder Deeds walked around the front room, looking at the locks hanging on the wall. "Well, we'll start sending the new missionaries down here," he said.

"Thanks, Elder." Brother Donaldson said. "So what are guys up to today?"

"We all went to lunch over at In-and-Out Burger and then thought we would run by here and say "Hi," Elder Berry said.

"So how are your bikes running? You need anything fixed on them?"

"No. They are running good. Thanks though for the offer, though." Elder Berry said.

"You know…if you ever needed anything for them, come see me. Not sure when I could get around to fixing any of it, but I would always get it done."

"Thanks again, but we are fine for now," Elder Berry said with sincerity.

We'd talked about the different repairs that we each had to do to our bikes on the way down. Elder Bell's chain kept falling off and needed to be tightened, Elder Deeds's gooseneck kept getting loose and he was constantly reaching down and tightening it with his hands as he rode, Elder Berry's back tire kept going flat, and my brakes were soft.

"OK. Let me know, though."

"How is your family doing?" asked Elder Deeds.

"Oh, fine. Kerri is getting ready to go off to school after summer, so she is working and saving her money."

"Where is she going to school?" Elder Deeds asked.

"She's going to Harvard."

"Whoa, Harvard! That's cool. I'm sure she could have gone anywhere then."

"She was looking at Harvard or Princeton. She wants to go to law school, so either one would have been fine. But she had her heart set on Harvard."

"I heard that BYU has a pretty good law school. Is that right?" I asked.

"I don't know. I'm not sure she applied there."

"Oh," I said.

"Let's see…Danny, my eleven-year-old, is playing summer league baseball and seems to keep pretty busy doing that."

"Oh yeah? What position does he play?" I asked enthusiastically, as this was something I felt more comfortable talking about than law school.

Parents of smart kids were smart too. As smart as the kid—if not smarter, I thought. They learn everything the kid learns, if not more, as they see through both a parent's eyes and the eyes of their own failed youth. They were smart enough to realize that even though their lives were crap because they chose not to compete with the rest of the world, their kid still had a better chance at life. So they made sacrifices, which made their lives even crappier, to get their kids smarter, when in the end the kids would have been happier having happy parents versus living with the knowledge that their parents gave up so much for their happiness.

"Third base."

"Oh yeah? I played third base as a kid," I said. "Yeah? You play in school?" He asked.

"Yep. Well, high school. That's it. But I played a lot as a kid."

"Hey, why don't you come by and throw the ball sometime?"

"OK. That would be fun for Danny."

"Well, guys, I need to get back to work," he said.

"We need to get going too," Elder Berry said.

I was glad Elder Berry didn't offer to leave Brother Donaldson with a prayer. It didn't seem necessary to get in a huddle in the back of the bike shop, giving Brother Donaldson a blessing that things would start getting better for him.

We said our goodbyes, stating how nice it was to meet each other, as he walked us out. We went out the back door and felt the sudden sting of sun in our eyes.

"Man, what a nice guy," we all remarked, walking to the front of the building to get our bikes.

"So where is that tennis store you were telling me about, Deeds?" I asked.

"This way," Elder Deeds said. I followed him, riding on the sidewalk, going in and out of curb cuts, thinking about where the tennis shop was and why I, as a young man, considered giving a blessing to a hard-working man with kids who were doing wonderfully.

I was riding behind Elder Bell, who was following the leader of our convoy, Elder Deeds. I had my tennis racquet tied to my rack. Two weeks earlier, I had bought a new oversized Head racquet. The factory strings had already broken, so it had to be restrung. I was looking forward to getting it restrung anyway, since I hated the nylon crap those sporting-goods stores put in just to sell the racquet.

Occasionally on P-Days, if I could convince Elder Bell, we would play tennis for a few hours. Elder Bell didn't play tennis, but he would take my old, crappy racquet and stand on the other side of the net, letting me try to hit to him. He would get into it for a few minutes and score some points on me until he lost a few too many. Then he would go back to just hitting the ball back to me.

We pulled around to the back of the tennis shop, a little concrete building with street-facing windows cut into red brick walls. There was a bike rack, which we locked our bikes to. I grabbed my racquet and walked into the store.

The minute we walked in, we were greeted by a :Hi guys!" from a young man behind the counter. I wondered if that was his bike locked up or if he owned the little convertible Fiat. We all said "Hi" and he went into the back room behind a curtain.

"Can I help you with anything today, guys?" He asked, coming back through the curtain.

No one said anything, so I chimed in, "Yeah, I have some broken strings here." I laid my racquet on the counter.

"Oooh, nice! The Head Venison! I like this racquet. How do you like it?" he asked.

"I like it. I've only had it a few weeks, though. I'm not a big fan of the wide bodies, but I'll play with it for a while."

"What don't you like about the wide bodies?" he asked.

"Well, it just seems that I don't have the control like I did with my old Prince Classic."

"Well, what kind of strings have you been using?" he asked.

"I've just had the factory nylon strings."

"Well, try some different strings. Have you ever tried a gut string?"

"No. I've read about it, or seen ads about it." I looked over at Elder Berry, who had made his way to the counter and was listening. "What about you, Elder Berry?"

"I used it a few times in college. It's expensive, isn't it?" he asked, looking up at the man behind the counter. Elder Berry had an honest, inquisitive look on his face.

"It's a little more than you would spend for the nylon, but they make a synthetic that is about eight dollars more that what you would pay for Prince Topspin. You were probably going to go with something like that anyway."

"Yeah, that's true. That's usually what I get. I play with a lot of spin, both on my serve and my forehand. So I need something to grip the ball pretty good," I said.

"Well, I'll tell you what—I'll give you a discount on the stringing, and you can try the gut out to see if you like it."

"Hey, thanks! That would be great."

"No problem. I'm anxious to see if you like it."

"Me, too! So when can I pick it up?" I asked.

"Oh, I should have it done by Saturday. You can come by then, or anytime after."

"OK. I'll plan on it. Do I need to call first to see if it's done?"

"No," he said looking at me. "Just come by."

"OK. Thanks again," I said, realizing I didn't even ask about the price. It was too late.

"My name is Darrell," he said, wrapping a piece of paper around the neck of my racquet and securing it with a rubber band.

"Elder Dorsey. Nice to meet you," I said, throwing out my hand.

"Elder Berry."

"Elder Deeds."

"Elder Bell." Elder Bell walked towards the counter to join the rest of us.

"Nice to meet all of you."

"You too," Elder Berry said.

After leaving the tennis shop, we went back to Elders Deeds's and Berry's place. Elder Bell was taking care of business in the bathroom while the three of us hung out in the living room. I was looking at Elder Berry's racquet while we talked about what time we were getting back together the next day and what everyone planned to do.

"Shoot. We have a teaching appointment tomorrow night that I can't miss," I said, remembering that we had a First scheduled with Tara.

"What do you mean you can't miss it? Elder Bell will be there," Elder Deeds said.

"I know, but I'm the one that introduced myself when we met her, so I've got to be there," I said and then yelled to Elder Bell in the bathroom to see if he would stay over at Berry's place so Elder Deeds and I could go teach Tara tomorrow night.

"Sure!" he answered over the humming fan in the bathroom. "What about my clothes, though?"

"You can wash them and wear them tomorrow," Elder Deeds said.

Not one of us asked what he would wear while his underwear was washing. We went into the garage where Elder Deeds got his little bike-repair kit he let us all use. We all worked on our bikes for the next hour. We already had the short-sleeve shirts on, so we just tucked our ties into our shirts. I tightened up my brakes and oiled my chain and sprockets. I kept my bike pretty clean. It was easy to clean the sprockets and chain while sitting in the front room, talking with McDonnell about Bell.

That night, Elder Deeds was the "new guy" in the house, telling us stories about his mission and life prior. He worked at a camera store in a mall for three years in high school and even worked through community college. He saved up enough to buy a new Toyota Corolla. We all teased him about driving a missionary car.

"Shut up, you punks!" He said. "Hey, you guys hear about Bell?"

"About what?" I asked.

"About why he got transferred," Elder Deeds said. "No. I hadn't even thought about it," I said.

Elder Deeds got a smile across his face and leaned back into the couch. "Well, he got into a little trouble in his last area."

"Like what?" I asked.

"He got caught watching pay-per-view Playboy."

"What!" I almost jumped up from the floor. "You're kidding, right?"

"No," Elder Deeds said, laughing slightly and shaking his head.

"What do you mean, he got caught?" Elder McDonnell asked.

"Well, I guess he was going down late at night, calling up cable and getting pay-per-view. The members they were living with started seeing it on their bill."

"You mean he did it a couple times?" I asked.

"Yeah! He got caught and they told President Carlson about it."

"What happened then?" I asked.

"He told President Carlson and the members that he wouldn't do it again, but he *did*!"

"What a dummy," Elder McDonnell said.

"Man, that would be embarrassing," I said. "It's weird. I thought Elder Bell was a pretty normal guy."

"Well, he is. He just likes beating off to porno in members' homes," Elder Deeds said, smiling.

"Ah, no visuals, please," I said, rolling my hands over my eyes.

"So that's why he was transferred in the middle of the month to Van Nuys, huh?" I asked.

"Yep, that's it!" Elder Deeds said.

"How did you hear about this?" Elder McDonnell asked. "Elder Berry was in Elder Johnson's district back in Canoga Park. Elder Johnson is friends with Elder Ashley, who was in Elder Bell's district at the time."

"I bet Bell wished no one knew," I said.

"So what? He shouldn't have done it," Elder McDonnell said.

"That's funny!" Elder Loughton said while getting up and going back to his room, shaking his head.

Thoughts of Elder Bell kept my mind busy that night as I was falling asleep. I worried about letting him alone with Darla in the old apartment.

I figured he wasn't *praying* in the extra bedroom, like he told me he was. I thought he was having *sex* with her. He told me that Darla was going to come down to the Valley to do some shopping, so she was going to stop by and visit. I didn't think anything of it at the time, but looking back I knew it was out of line for what a missionary should do. She was a single mom, so I knew she wanted to have sex. *And* I'm sure they had talked about it. I was sitting in one room while he was doing a girl in the next. I was even watching her kid! I thought how many times the kid went to the bedroom door and tried to open it. I thought his little hand kept slipping off the knob when he tried to open it. I would get up and grab him, so as not to disturb the spirit from the prayer the missionary was giving the new member he had baptized in his last area. The kid's hand wasn't slipping off the knob: *the door was locked.* I would be sent home if the President knew; I was sure of it. I told myself no one would ever know about it. I quickly turned my attention to tennis, looking forward to getting my racquet Saturday. And that was a nice thought.

The only thing Elder Bell was bummed about by having to stay with Elder Berry the next night was that he would miss the dinner with Sister Shannon. I told him I would bring back leftovers for him, but he knew I wouldn't. Sister Shannon was a single woman in the ward, who didn't have the missionaries over to her house when meeting us for a dinner appointment. This was possibly due to the fact that she was a single woman, or maybe it was just because she liked taking the missionaries out to dinner. Either way, it was a treat for us. It was always our choice too. She would give us two options for dinner, advising us of our choices the Sunday before our appointment. When she picked us up, after we had all week to think about it, she would take us to our choice. That night we went to Red Lobster.

Sister Shannon picked us up about five thirty. We had to get an early start since we had the appointment with Tara after. Sister Shannon was big—short too. While we sat eating, I wondered if this was a big night for her—if on first dates, when asked how her week went, she would talk about taking the missionaries out for dinner, hoping that the guy with her might overlook some of her faults because she was so spiritual and giving by taking an interest in the missionaries.

We prayed in her car when she dropped us off and blessed her that she might have whatever was lacking in her life. I could still taste the lobster in my mouth as I walked up to the apartment to grab our books.

Tara's wasn't far. We were only five minutes late when we knocked on the door and were let in by an unfamiliar woman. Once my eyes adjusted from the bright, late afternoon sunlight, I saw Tara on the couch across the room. They invited us to take a seat on the other couch in the room. We were introduced to Kristen, Tara's friend. They went to church together.

We had to get to know these two before we jumped into Discussions, I felt. As much small talk as I knew, it was greatly limited to my daily activities as a missionary. Rarely anything else was shared. After we explained that Elder Deeds was from Indiana and I was from Washington, they seemed to have had enough of small talk and wanted to talk religion. There was intensity in their movements and words, as if something else was on their minds.

"So, what are we discussing tonight, Elder Dorsey?" asked Tara.

"Well, we have six Discussions that we give investigators. These go through our beliefs and the commitments we make, to help investigators understand the different concepts we present. What we would like to do is share the First Discussion tonight and then set up a time to come back and share the remainder with you. Does that sound alright?" I asked, leaning forward on the couch in an attempt to look more serious.

"Sure. Go ahead and start. We have our Bibles, as you can see."

"Great, because we will be reading from the Bible a little later."

"I would imagine," Tara said.

Elder Deeds started with the First Discussion. I was proud how he had his pamphlet out and was ready to teach as soon as he heard we were going to teach. He wasn't nervous at all, though I couldn't imagine he'd ever be nervous about anything, really. Tara kept interrupting him, making sure she understood some of the words he was using—*Repentance*, *Atonement*, and *Grace*. I felt she knew what he was saying but just wanted to see if *he* did—if he understood the beliefs he was presenting to others.

"The Plan of Salvation is God's plan. The plan he has for us here on earth," I said, helping out Elder Deeds, who seemed to be struggling a bit with the questions asked of him.

"I understand what you are saying, Elder Dorsey. I'm just making sure that you guys understand. I'm comparing it to what I read in the Bible, and it doesn't sound that different yet. It sounds like just what *I* believe."

"Well, there are going to be some similarities between your religion and ours, the Church Jesus Christ and Latter-day Saints," I said.

"What *are* some differences? So far I don't see any," Tara said.

"Well, one may be that you believe that God and Jesus are one person. We believe they are two individual beings."

"Really?" she said, grabbing her bible in front of her. Before I had time to react, she was quoting the Prophet Isaiah "I, the Lord. The first, and with the last; I am he, before me was there no God formed, neither shall there be after me, I am the first I am the last; and beside me there is no God."

"It is a little difficult to understand exactly what was meant when that was written. That's why we also believe in a prophet on earth today that interprets the Bible for us."

"You let someone else interpret the Bible for you? Don't you think it might have been written for *you* to interpret and live by?"

"I didn't mean that I don't read and interpret the bible myself. I meant that when questions such as that come up, we are able to look to our prophets for an explanation as to whether God and Jesus are two beings or not."

"So, when anything in the bible contradicts what you believe, it's because your prophet has said otherwise?" Kristen said.

"No. First, there are not a lot of contradictions in the Bible. We believe the Bible to be the word of God, just as our prophets are," I replied.

"Let's discuss those differences. And you can explain what the prophets in the Bible meant versus what they wrote and what your prophet tells you today," Tara said.

"Those are the things we discuss throughout the Discussions." I said.

"OK, OK. Go ahead with your Discussions, then." Tara said, poised forward on the couch.

"We believe that when Joseph Smith received the priesthood—"

"When Joseph Smith received the Priesthood?" Tara said questioningly, "In Hebrews 5:9, 2nd Timothy 2:2, and John 1:12, it states that Christ brought an end to the Aaronic Priesthood and is the only High Priest after the manner of Melchizedek."

"Well, we believe that the priesthood was taken from the earth and given to Joseph Smith—"

"How can you believe that? The Bible clearly states that's not the case. Don't you think God would let us know about that?"

"He did. Through Joseph Smith."

"If you don't question what you've learned against the Bible, what do you question it against?" Tara asked.

"The Holy Ghost tells us."

"The Holy Ghost that you can only receive by someone with the priesthood? How is the Holy Ghost going to tell me that you are telling me the truth? I supposedly don't have the Holy Ghost."

"He can be a witness to you that what we are saying—" I said, being cut short again.

"So a person can have the Holy Ghost without being Mormon? I'm confused," Tara said. And so was I. I was lost. She knew the Bible better than I did, and I had no recourse to her attacks.

"All I can say is that I know what I am teaching you is true," I said.

"Elder Dorsey, it doesn't make sense. It goes against the Bible, and you even contradict your own self," Tara continued. I knew she was right. I didn't even have the confirmation and testimony that I kept trying to bear. I was taught in the Missionary Guide that in cases such as this, simply to bear your testimony of the truthfulness of what you were saying and the spirit would bear witness to it to the investigator. It wasn't happening. She continued to counteract everything I said: baptism—Mark 16:15-16, the emphasis is on the believer not the priesthood; eternal life—1 John 5:12-13, no mention of parenthood or temple marriage but is given to all Christians; Atonement—Romans….

I was no match for her quickness and knowledge. I said I could get the answers for her, but it would take some time. She said that I was teaching this to people every day and should know what I believed and taught. I felt small—smaller than I had ever felt—and questioned my own testimony and beliefs and mission life and President Carlson and the Prophet.

We'd been there about an hour and covered everything the Discussions could have presented. I looked at my watch and set up a time to come back the following week. We invited them to church, and they said they would go if we went to theirs. It started after our service was already over, so we said sure. They even agreed to pick us up. I thought that was nice of them but knew in their hearts they wanted to lead us away.

On the way home, Elder Deeds laughed and said "dude" a lot, talking about how we just got killed in there. Elder Deeds told me I handled it perfectly, though, by not getting into a bash with them, it being our first confrontational encounter. I didn't tell Deeds that I didn't bash because I *couldn't* bash. I couldn't flip pages like Tara did, knowing where I wanted to go.

When I went to sleep that night, I thought about how pretty Tara was when we first met her and how she wasn't so much anymore. I also thought, in retrospect, how I could have handled the night's teaching. I saw how she pulled me into her plan to bring out the differences in the beliefs. She was so keen; she even had me bring them up. She did bring up lots of valid questions, though. Even questions concerning the *way* I believe, not just *what* I believed.

Elder Berry and Bell met us back at our place the next day. Elder Bell was on his third day of wearing the same clothes, so first thing he did was change when he got back. No one said anything to him about what Elder Deeds told us.

For the next couple weeks, we spent a lot of time with the Morels. Tara had canceled a couple times, and Mary and Stephanie seemed to have disappeared. Candice had yet to be home when we stopped by. Maybe everyone was busy with summer. It still felt like *we* were.

We had been working with Brother Morel on his framing every day. It felt like we weren't working only when reporting our pitiful numbers of investigators in the weekly District Meeting. No other companionship had any baptism planned, so we didn't feel as bad as we might have.

Spending each day there (and sometimes dinnertime too) we got to know the Morels well. I wondered if there was anything we didn't know about them. We played with their kids and held them so Brother Morel and Myrna could eat more easily. I wondered if they had any secrets that missionaries wouldn't know. I knew Brother Morel prayed in Spanish and taught his kids to do the same. That might have been something that no one else knew, but what else? Did they possibly have an interesting theory about the Prophet's admonishment that every member does missionary work? Myrna didn't like to do missionary work, so they had an agreement. Brother Morel would take care of the missionary work, and Myrna would take care of the genealogy. They thought that by sharing the duties of the Church, they would still get into heaven.

We would normally head over to the Morels around eleven in the morning, when Brother Morel would just be getting up. If he wasn't up and around yet, we would just watch cartoons with the kids while Myrna made breakfast. It made sense that they got such a late start because they watched late-night television. Myrna was always cooking like she was trying to catch the sunrise.

Brother Morel had taken two weeks off after the foundation had cured so he could get a head start on the framing. He wanted the addition framed in by winter. I thought we were making pretty good progress. Once the base plates had been bolted to the foundation, it was just a matter of nailing in the walls after they had been chalked out on the pavement. I was amazed that Brother Morel had the insight to sink the bolts into the partially dried cement. With the bolts, it was simply drilling holes and screwing the nuts on tight, and the base for the outside walls was in place. The outside walls were the first to be framed. I learned to double up on two-by-fours around all the doors and window casings for added strength. I learned the term *king stud* to describe them. By pounding what seemed hundreds of nails into two two-by-fours together, a king stud was made. On Saturdays, a couple of the members would come out to help. Regardless who was there, it was always Elder Bell who read the blueprints and showed us where and when to put in a certain wall or doorway. Once the inside walls were completed, Brother Morel moved to the far side of his woodpile and showed us the beam that would run the length of the addition. A four-by-twelve, forty feet long, would support the roof.

The beam took the entire crew three hours to get into place. Not only were we all standing on ladders once we had it in place, but Elder Bell had also designed a pulley system to help guide and alleviate some of the weight when lifting it up. Once the beam was in place, I finally saw how a building was put together. I knew they didn't all go together like this, but the concept of supporting walls to support the beam to support the roof was clear. I was enjoying wearing the tool belt and working on the house. I even entertained the idea of being a builder when I got home.

We had Zone Conference, where I got a change to see Elder Elliot. I asked him about George and Heavenly and the Barretts and Austins. He said they were all the same except Daniel had died. He said he went by one day and he wasn't there anymore. It had been several months since he had been visited. He shook my hand and moved on to conversations with the other elders he knew.

There was a big distinction between the missionaries who had been out for some time and the ones out less than a year. A distinction only in their minds, though. We were really all the same. Could there be a group more alike than us? Or maybe they just knew more of the other missionaries since they had been out longer.

We heard from Elder Sherman, advising us how to drive our cars without wearing out the brakes. He told us about his drive to the building that day. He counted the number of times another car's brake lights came on over a stretch he had driven. He figured that, after about four blocks, the other car touched his brakes thirty more times than he had. He went on to explain how much money we would save the Lord if we drove more responsibly. The mission also had a 120-day run of no accidents. This was a big deal to him. I had a hard time associating money-saving techniques of driving with saving the Lord money. I just didn't see God budgeting the mission expenses, looking for the savings in brake pads. What was he hoping? That it would spare some change to buy some food for the hungry?

Brother Carlson told us about the scripture in Alma 36:3 in the *Book of*

Mormon. "Whosoever shall put their trust in God shall be supported in their trial, and their troubles and their afflictions shall be lifted up at the last day." I didn't have any real problems or tribulations at the time but knew that later in the mission I might. I'd probably need to depend on that scripture if I were placed with a bad companion or if I were a zone leader with a problem missionary. I thought then that most scriptures were about putting your trust in God (and he will help) or you will go to hell—not because of disobedience, but rather because the trials were too hard and they'd turn you into a sinner. So really our only choice was to trust in God because he had given us insurmountable feats to conquer while on earth.

After the motivational talks and additional instruction from the mission office., the 50 or so missionaries all got our bi-monthly one-on-one interview with President Carlson. They were all about the same, I would suspect. At least *mine* were all about the same. Some of the elders really looked forward to talking with him.

"Dorsey," I heard from behind me. We had all moved outside to wait in the sun as the president went down his list. "You're on with the president," it was Elder McDonnell. The list was in alphabetical order, but the president would start from a different place within the alphabet to mix it up each time. I would have gone by height or made it a game that, by the end, the elder who guessed what order the President had gone in got a prize.

"Thanks. Right inside by the clerk's office?" I asked, walking in that direction.

"Yep."

I walked in to the little classroom. The president had two chairs and a desk beside him.

"Elder Dorsey, shall we pray?" he said, kneeling down with his arms on the chair.

"Sure."

"I'll go ahead and offer that, Elder." And he went into a prayer that sounded like it was asking for blessings directly for me. It was amazing that he could do that after saying so many. After the prayer, we sat on our chairs.

"So what can I do for you today, Elder?"

"Nothing, really. Everything is going really good. You get my letters, don't you? Then everything is fine, right?"

"Yes, I do. Thanks for writing each week."

"No problem," I said.

"Well, are you having any problems with Elder Bell?"

"No. We get along really good."

"And the work seems to be going fine?"

"Well, yeah. We've been helping a member work on an addition because he really wants to get it done before winter, but other than that, we have four investigators and keep looking for more."

"Good, good. Any close to baptism?"

"I think so. We are having a hard time getting appointments with them. I think it's just a matter of getting with them to get to the Second Discussion."

"Good. That's great. You like the ward you are serving? The Van Nuys Second Ward, isn't it?"

"Yeah, I like a lot. I love the members here," I said.

"Well good, Elder. OK, I need to ask you a few questions on how you are personally."

I nodded my head in agreement.

"Are you having problems with any impure thoughts?" He asked.

"Nope."

"Have you masturbated since I last saw you?"

"Nope."

"OK, Elder. Anything else you would like to bring up?"

"No, can't thing of anything."

"All right, then. Why don't we finish up with a prayer? Would you offer that, please?"

"Sure," I said as I got down on my knees, resting my elbows on the seat of my warmed chair.

It always felt a little strange going back out to the rest of the elders right after you'd just been asked if you've masturbated.

After Zone Conference we went to Taco Bell. Not all of us, just the "bikies" in our district. So Elder Deeds, Berry, McDonnell, and Loughton went too.

"So, how'd you like the president's talk on Alma? Putting your trust in the Lord in all things?" Elder McDonnell asked, throwing it out for anyone to nibble on.

"Easier said than done," Elder Deeds said.

"Well, of course it is. Otherwise, everyone would do it," Elder McDonnell said. "Put us out of a job."

"I know. Still, I'm not sure how I'm going to use it or how it will affect anything day to day," he said, wadding up his burger wrapper. "And that is really what I hope for with the president's talks: something that I can take back with me and use that day." He pushed his chair back and wiped his hands "Like last month."

"What was it last month?" I asked, wishing I hadn't.

"Relying on the spirit while teaching. I was able to use that, that night. Not that it's made a huge difference, but I got more out of it than I did today," Elder Deeds said.

"I think that's fair," I said.

"They go hand in hand. President Carlson knows what he talked on, and I think this was a follow-up to what he talked about last month," Elder McDonnell said.

"I think President Carlson gives great talks," I said.

"Me too," Elder Deeds said, getting up, "Let's go. We have an appointment later today."

When we got back to the apartment, we changed into P-Days and went over to the Morels. We were almost finished with the framing. I put fire blocks in between each of the studs on the wall. It was a no-brainer task, and I enjoyed the chance to entertain some ideas while I worked, wearing my much-loved tool belt.

We watched *Star Trek: The Next Generation* until late and went home.

Sundays had turned into a day when we looked our best in suits, with a dark scripture bag clutched in our hands. We tried to look and sound like we were working hard. All the work at the Morels, as hard as it might have been, wasn't what we were out here for, and that was starting to sink in. Elder Bell didn't seem to mind, but he was skating on six months left and was starting to show it. The big news of the day was that a new ward mission leader was called. After church, we sat down with Brother Day and Brother Morel. Brother Day formally handed over the calling of ward mission leader to Brother Morel, telling us that he had been set apart, had hands laid on him, earlier.

Brother Morel had a permanent grin on his face. We were pretty happy also. Not only did we know the Morels already, but we also liked hanging out with them. We would have our weekly meeting at his house, and the kids would be there. It would mean we could spend even more time over there. We had already depended on Brother Morel for splits every week. He was called whenever anyone canceled or whenever we needed another male body. Not all elders kept with the mission ratio rule of women to men; sometimes it was impossible. We decided to go over to the Morels that night and map out a new aggressive workflow for the next month. What this really meant was that we would talk about missionary work, hand over a list of investigators, go over what we needed help with from the ward, and then watch *Star Trek*, which I'd gotten hooked on.

Life was lazy. I was rarely exhausted and forgotten what it felt like. That was the only thing I was ever tired of. Days consisted of tennis in the mornings a couple times a week, enjoyable except for the constant razzing from McDonnell on rules. He meant it in fun. He also understood the situation with Bell, and I think he cut me some slack. I was over the greenie stage, but my role as junior companion had plenty of room for play still. I'd gone down to the tennis store and gotten my racquet from Darrell. The gut strings he suggested stringing it with were playing exactly as I'd hoped, the strings grabbing the ball out of the air and holding it on the strings until—*Smash*!—it finally caught its acceleration and got turned back onto the opponent who had sent it over originally. I called him up after the first game and told him what a great job he did. He knew me by name.

Transfers came. Elder Bell was transferred to Bakersfield, the armpit of the mission. He'd been with me such a short time that it must have been a resting place for him until he went on to serve out his mission. I equated it to "spirit prison." He was in between both heaven and hell in Van Nuys, and the decision was made that he didn't make it, so off to Bakersfield he went. Before he left, I took a picture of him with something that would immortalize him in my thoughts. You could see the outline of his small body, the oil, his hair, fart juice, and wear on his mattress sheet as he held it up next to himself, smiling.

CHAPTER 8

Elder Jameson sold his bike in the last area. We had three days on foot before our car was delivered. As a result, we tracted to just about every house within a four-mile radius of our apartment, adding four potentials to our teaching pool and three First Discussions to our weekly stats.

Elder Jameson's doctor was in the Valley, and he needed to be somewhere close—Van Nuys was it. Jameson first realized that there was a problem with his knee after it swelled to the size of a grapefruit after a P-Day basketball game. Four visits to three different doctors later, it was determined that he needed arthroscopic surgery to remove torn cartilage. He wouldn't ride a bike for months and would be on crutches for weeks afterwards. We were assigned a car, a Ford Escort wagon. The Mormon Church had the largest privately owned fleet of vehicles in the country. Within the Ventura Mission alone, there were over fifty cars—forty-five of which were Toyota Corollas, with the remaining being the Escort wagons.

The morning of the operation, while Elder Jameson was packing his bag, I talked with him.

"So, are you nervous?"

"No. I mean, just normal nervous."

"You know, it's OK if you want to cry," I said, while McDonnell came to into the room and jumped on the bed.

"You dork," he said, throwing his shirt at me.

"We want you to know that we are just here to help where we can. And if that means letting you cry on our shoulders, then you go ahead," McDonnell said.

"Would you guys shut up?" he said while we both cracked up on my bed. "Hey, I'm ready. You ready?"

"Let me get that bag for you, Elder. Wouldn't want you to stress that knee," I said, jumping up.

"That's more like it. You should be serving me today," he said.

"Let's not go overboard now, Elder. It's just a little knee surgery," Elder McDonnell said.

"A little knee surgery? They are going into my knee and cutting part of it out," Elder Jameson said.

"That's OK; God put extra cartilage in there on purpose," Elder McDonnell said.

"Whatever, McDonnell," I said,

"OK, Elder. Let's go."

"Dorsey, you bringing your *Book of Mormon* to read while you wait?" Elder Loughton asked, coming to the door of the room.

"Of course. And I'm tracting to all the rooms in the hospital too. Maybe hand out a few blessings while I'm at it. Let's go."

The waiting room was a chance to read all the latest smut magazines. I read *People* and *Us*. I read about Robert Downey Jr. abusing drugs and Bobby Brown going into rehab for alcohol. They seemed like fiction stories, not real, and the partying they did with the women sounded surreal. After I'd read all that I could handle, as my conscience was getting to me, I pulled out my Bible and read part of Ezekiel in the Old Testament. This wasn't nearly as fun as reading the magazines, so I rationalized reading a home-decorating magazine with thoughts of how I could use it on my mission. I thought that someday a member or investigator might need help pulling wallpaper off. I read how if you soaked it with a soapy sponge and let it sit for several minutes, it would come off in large strips with very little work required. Useful knowledge, though I hoped to never have to use it myself. Three hours later, Jameson was rolled out in a wheelchair.

"Elder Jameson, how are you doing?" I asked when the sliding doors opened.

"It hurts. But not too bad," he said, looking down at his knee. "But look at my cool crutches!"

"Those are nice. I like the blue grip. Very 'You.'"

The nurse went over the painkillers with him and told him how many to take for the different levels of pain. She also gave him some Tylenol and said he should stop by on the way home and grab some more for when they ran out.

Jameson was a pro at the crutches. He made it up the stairs to the apartment with little effort. Once inside, he took some of his painkillers and went to sleep. I read my motorcycle magazine on the couch until I heard McDonnell and Loughton coming up the stairs. I then grabbed the phone and started going through my planner for investigators to call. Our schedule was empty. We'd planned it that way so Jameson would have time to recover.

The time Jameson and I spent tracting and visiting investigators had paid off. We were booked up for almost the entire month. Both Mary and Stephanie had been given the Second Discussion, accepting the commitment to be baptized. We did run into a problem with setting a date for the baptism, though. They had both told us of their sexual relations outside of marriage. While that wasn't grounds to dismiss a baptism, their past sexual relations with women were. They started to go into detail about how it happened in one of the homes. It was the same woman for both of them. Then, right in the middle of the explanation, Stephanie blurted out that they had done something together.

"Well, do you still *do* them?" I asked.

"No. No more. It was just a couple times," Mary said, looking into her lap ashamedly.

We set up a time to have President Carlson interview both of them. It also came out that Mary had had an abortion, which always required an interview with the president.

Another appointment was set up with Tara and Kristen. We were meeting them at the church the following week along with Brother Day—bringing in the big guns. In addition, we had almost finished up with the New Member Discussions with Dianna and had talked with her about sitting in on the rest of the Discussions with Mary and Stephanie. She agreed wholeheartedly.

We'd met two other people to teach who actually gave us their numbers to call them to set up a time for the First, José and Maria. They were married and spoke English. I asked McDonnell who should teach them, and he said the Spanish elders. Yet they spoke English well, so I didn't hand them over. I wanted to give the First Discussion, at least.

We'd spent the majority of Elder Jameson's recovery at the Morels. If I thought I was hooked on *Star Trek* before, I sure was now. I'd been gradually brought into *Star Trek: The Next Generation* through years of watching Captain Kirk and Spock battling Klingons, but my interest had been casual. It came after *Kung Fu* and *M*A*S*H* on Jameson's sick days; it was on, so it was watched. Sunday nights at the Morels meant our Ward Mission Meeting. Afterwards, Brother Morel would shed his white church shirt and put on his authentic *Star Trek* shirt with Myrna wearing hers. These shirts were the same ones worn by Captain Picard and Admiral Troy. Myrna didn't look quite as good as Admiral Troy, but the shirt did justice for her ample bosom. I tried not looking over too often during the night.

Once Jameson was healed to the point where he was able to walk with a slight limp, we started visiting investigators again and were able to meet the demands of a stacked-up schedule. President Carlson met us at the church to interview Mary and Stephanie. We had been able to get hold of Dianna, finally. She had gone out of town for several weeks as her sister was dying of cancer. I didn't know anything about cancer, other than a friend's father had died from it, so I didn't ask any questions. But it did make me think how easy it was for a person in Dianna's position to disappear, and I envied her freedom, despite the conditions that allowed it.

"Mary, nice to meet you," President Carlson said, walking up to us and putting his hand out for Mary to shake. He turned to Stephanie and did the same. "Elder Dorsey, nice to see you. Elder Jameson, good to see you. How is your knee doing? Getting ready to get back out there and get some work done?"

"Yep, I think so. Getting around on it pretty good now."

"Good. Good. Well, shall we start?"

"I've got a room set up for you inside. I'll take you to it," I said.

"Thanks, Elder. Mary, why don't you come along with us?" I led President Carlson into a room with two chairs. "Thanks, Elder. I'll come and get Stephanie when we are finished," President Carlson said.

"OK," I said.

After about thirty minutes, President Carlson came in and asked for Stephanie. We sat there and talked with Mary while Stephanie was being interviewed. Not a lot was said. After President Carlson walked out with Stephanie, he asked me to walk with him to the car.

"Elder Jameson, we will see you at Zone Conference," the President said as he shook Jameson's hand.

"Looking forward to it," he said.

The President and I walked out to the parking lot. "Elder, everything is fine for going ahead with the baptism. Good job," he said as he shook my hand, looking into my eyes. "See you later this month for Zone Conference!" He then got into the mission minivan and drove off. I watched him drive away until I could no longer see the car.

Back at the apartment, there were three messages waiting for us. One from Tara, confirming that we were still on for Thursday night; one from Stephen Day, making sure we were still on with Tara for Thursday; and one from Rachel Barrett in Chatsworth. After Jameson got done "oohing" and "ahhing" over the fact that a girl had called me, I called Rachel back.

Rachel wanted to know where we were playing basketball the following P-Day. I told her we'd be playing at the Van Nuys Stake Center. She said her little brother, Craig, wanted to play basketball I hoped she would find me the best ballplayer in the mission, though I had to admit that her brothers were better than me.

"Great. It will be nice to see you," I said.

"Oh, thanks. That's nice. It will be nice to see you too."

"OK. Talk to you later, then."

"OK. Bye." And she hung up. I stood there for a moment, thinking about what she meant by thanking me for saying it would be nice to see her. She took it farther than I had meant it, making it a valued statement rather than the informal gesture it was. I put the phone down and didn't worry about it. Instead, I was going to worry about the fact that I was looking forward to seeing her.

Work slowed down on the framing of the Morels' home.

Brother Morel had planned to have the walls and roof on before winter, and it looked like he was on course to make it, but then his work stopped. He told us he ran out of money and would have to wait until the next year to finish it. While the work stopped on the framing, the mission work was still moving along.

A date was set for Mary's and Stephanie's baptism. The final Four Discussions had been done within two weeks of the go-ahead from President Carlson. The commitments to abstain from alcohol and drugs were made—neither Elder Jameson nor I was surprised. Brother Morel had scheduled the building for the use of the baptismal font and had made up programs at work. Having a double baptism in a ward within the first four months that missionaries had been there was getting us plenty of recognition. When in the halls during church or at the building for meetings, we were constantly being congratulated on our success. The dinner calendar was full. We were getting support for splits every night we requested them. With six people in our teaching pool, two committed for baptism, two preparing to hear the Second, and trying to get appointments with the others, we stayed on the move. Elder Jameson was moving around with ease and even thought he might soon be transferred.

We both had that in mind when we progressed and set the baptism date. Mary and Stephanie had been continually sidetracked with the required readings, interviews and going to church on Sundays, a prerequisite to baptism. With these things resolved, we moved ahead with the baptism.

Jameson had been my favorite companion to date. He was fun and relaxed, and enjoyed just about anything as long as it was done in fun. Although he didn't want to work, he always did. I was sad to see Elder Jameson go. On his final day, we laughed about the things that had happened during our tenure; we mostly laughed about the baptism of Mary and Stephanie.

Mary requested that I baptize her. She was one of the biggest women I had ever seen. Elder Jameson was going to baptize Stephanie. We were each able to put another notch in our belt. After Stephanie was baptized, Elder Jameson did a perfect job on both the closed-eye prayer (half submerged in water) and the dunking of Stephanie, making sure no part of her clothing was exposed above the water. Complete submersion was vital in making the baptism real. I wished I had asked at some point in my life what happened if the witnesses missed a corner of robe that floated to the top of the water and exposed itself? Would the baptism still count? Would the person go to hell for not being properly baptized? Would the person go through their whole life without the gift of the Holy Ghost because a piece of their robe was exposed out of water? I knew these questions couldn't be answered, though. After witnessing Elder Jameson's wonderful job, I wished that I was he. I envied his completion of the baptism; I dreaded going in front of all the people sitting in pews who didn't know me, watching me baptize a woman I didn't know or really care about, doing something to her I wasn't even sure I should be doing. Even if God gives a person the authority, it might also help to give him the balls to use it.

My portion of the baptism was going perfectly until the submergence began. Mary slipped, getting into the baptismal font, stepping down from the top step. She was moving forward and she came down from heaven, landing on top of the small font and on me. Later, after the tables had been filled with food of all sorts for the members and the new members to interact while doing something as intimate as eating together, the brethren compared water spots on the suit coats. When Mary came down on the water, she parted it with more force than Moses could have. Water went up over the small half-window, onto everyone sitting within five feet. It was a wall of water that went up and out, wetting people, the carpet, and microphones. The shock of the water displacement may have prevented one of the witnesses from seeing my squirming arms and legs coming up from under Mary. With most of the water out of the font, any buoyancy that the water could have provided Mary and her weight with was dissipated. I squirmed there, on my back for what felt like minutes, until a witness came down and rolled her off of me. I wasn't injured, and Mary seemed to recover both mentally and physically.

The font took another thirty minutes to refill. I then baptized Mary, after saying the baptismal prayer three times before getting it right. When I did get it right, there was very little water to cover a woman the size of

Mary, so while holding her under water, I kept tucking in her robe and finally, thinking she might not be able to hold her breath any longer, the witnesses said "OK," signaling the end of the baptism (even though I knew there was robe above water). Since the witnesses accepted the baptism as complete, even without a full submergence in the water, my question on the robe-and-hell thing were answered. Yet that just brought up more questions in my head. I tossed my inner thoughts aside as we laid our hands on the wet heads of Mary and Stephanie, bestowing upon them the gift of the Holy Ghost. I didn't feel the Holy Ghost go through me, even though I was taught that I would.

Elder Jameson and I laughed about the baptism afterwards. We laughed every time we told the story. Other missionaries laughed; even Elder McDonnell and members laughed. Although we didn't tell any members, they heard about it and razzed me a bit. I hugged Elder Jameson and thought I was lucky for knowing him. I knew I probably wouldn't see him again, even though we talked about going to BYU together after the mission.

CHAPTER 9

With the stir-up created from the missionary transfers, I was appointed district leader. The "Your son was called as a district leader" letter went out to the parents and it was official—no mistake made by a sleepy God. This meant that I was inspired to assist the other missionaries in my district. Elder Deeds was still around, but Elder Berry was gone. He was a great guy, Elder Berry. None came more polite or life loving. I got a greenie to train, exuberant from clearly seeing the picture of a missionary's power painted in his head from the teachers at the MTC. Another set of elders was brought in to cover one of my wards. They moved into the apartment that Elder Bell and I had lived in. Greenie Elder Hatfield was paired with a veteran Senior Companion, Elder Christopher, who had postponed his mission. He had stories the rest of us didn't have. Elder Hatfield was blond, with high cheekbones that stuck out when we smiled. He was from Utah. I stopped asking what town each of the elders was from as soon as I learned they were from Utah. The towns didn't make a difference to me. I was just being polite and *maybe* a bit dishonest. Asking something like that would allude to knowledge of the surrounding communities, when in actuality I had none. And if I was questioned about specific Utah communities, I would look stupid. So I didn't ask Elder Hatfield where he was from.

After a District Meeting with me in my new role, Elder Christopher came up to me as I was packing my bike bag with scriptures. He asked if we could talk in private for a minute. "Sure, Elder Christopher. Let's go into one of the classrooms right here," I motioned towards the hall, knowing there would be large unlocked classrooms providing privacy.

It was a children's classroom. Elder Christopher and I sat down on miniature chairs. "So, what's up?" I asked.

"I was hoping we could just solve this between us, not go to the president."

"OK, possibly. What is it?"

"Well, Elder Hatfield is taking extremely long showers. I wouldn't have thought too much about the length of his showers until the other night when I caught him masturbating while we were in the room, falling asleep."

"OK. So have you talked to him about it?" I asked.

"I told him he couldn't do it and I wouldn't say anything to anyone if he stopped doing it. I don't think he's stopped, though. I don't think he does it while lying in bed anymore; he just does it in the shower."

"Would you rather President Carlson handled this?" I suggested, realizing that it should probably be handled by the president.

Elder Christopher was a little older than the other missionaries and spoke eloquently to make him sound wiser than he was. I was sucked into his image.

"I think if you say something about it, that would be enough.

I'm sure it would be."

"OK. If you want me to talk to him, then I will. It will probably be enough."

"Thanks, Elder Dorsey. I appreciate this and hope you respect the privacy of this matter."

"Of course. Wouldn't even think of telling anyone about this. I may tell the President, though, if I feel it would help."

"I understand."

"I'll talk to Elder Hatfield today. This is probably something that could build up and really blow up if we aren't careful."

"Thanks," Elder Christopher said and stood up from the small chair, reaching out for my hand.

I walked back to the gym and saw the other missionaries playing a game of bump. When I was close enough that only Elder Hatfield could hear, I said, "Hey, let's talk for a few minutes." After thinking that he was taller and possibly better looking than me, I secretly felt better about myself that he had this problem and I didn't.

"OK, you want to talk now?" He asked casually.

"Sure. There are some classrooms over on the other side. Let's go." I wanted to get the conversation over as soon as possible for both of our sakes. I couldn't imagine a more embarrassing conversation for two men to have.

We sat down in the little chairs. I told him what Elder Christopher had advised me about his masturbating, "So...what will you do, Elder Hatfield? Can you stop now?"

"Yeah, yeah. I can stop. It's been a while now anyway."

"OK. As far as I'm concerned, this is over, and I'll tell Elder Christopher the same. I won't tell the President unless it continues to be a problem."

"Thanks."

"Anything else?" I asked standing, hoping there wasn't.

"I just hope that Elder Christopher will stop bugging me about the amount of time I'm in the shower."

"He will. I'll talk to him. He has done what he needed to do, and he shouldn't worry about it going forward."

"'Kay. Thanks again," Elder Hatfield said, emphasizing the last words. He then said, "I won't let you down on this."

"Well, it's not really me you'd be letting down. You and the Lord, Elder: that's what it all comes down to."

"That's true. Well, that's what I meant."

"I know. Let's go; we can still get the last game of bump, I said, putting my hand on his shoulder as we walked out, something I'd seen the president and other bishops do after someone came out of their office.

Later that night, I replayed in my mind everything that had happened and been said. I thought I'd handled it fairly.

My own greenie, Elder Barney, was happy not to have any of the problems that were evident in other companionships. "Elder Barney, I agree with you. We get along good, but when two elders are obeying the rules—all the rules—there isn't ever a problem. And that happens most of the time." We lay there for a few minutes and I said, "Elder Barney?"

"Yeah?"

"I gotta run over to Encino to get my racquet tomorrow. I know it's not a P-Day, but I'm really excited to get it."

"That's OK. I don't mind."

"Tomorrow's not too busy; we have time. Good night, Elder."

"Good night, Elder."

* * * * *

"Elder Dorsey! Why, that looks like a freshly strung racquet. On a Thursday! Now, how would you have managed that?"

"Oh, come on, McDonnell. You have to draw the line somewhere: picking up a racquet, just driving by, that can't be against the rules."

"I just hope God sees it that way. Elder, I just want to hang out with you in Heaven. And, well, getting racquets on Thursdays isn't going to get you there."

"OK, OK, I get it. I'll tell you what, though. How about I don't hold it until Monday? That will kinda make up for it."

"Well, it seems to be something that you should have thought of before. You are on your own now. Can't help you. Can't look to me for redemption on this one."

"Come on, McDonnell. You *are* my savior."

"Talk like that will get you a whoop'n."

"OK, well you're not really. I'm gonna put my racquet in the closet. I'm repenting. Just to let you know, I was a proselytizer while in the store. Darrell was there—you've met him. Well, we pretty much gave him the First Discussion, and he gave me a three-racquet Nike tennis bag. I think we are getting somewhere."

"He gave you a bag? Let's see it."

I went into my room and brought out the brand-new bag. Darrell had offered it to me after I admired the bags hanging on the wall. He went over to the wall and pulled off the bag I was looking at. "Elder Dorsey, you need a good tennis bag. By the way your strings are looking and breaking, you can really hit that ball," he said, handing me the bag. I wasn't sure initially if he was giving it to me or making a flattering gesture.

"Darrell, I can't afford this."

"Oh no, it's a gift from me to you. I want you to have it."

"Thank you, Darrell," I said, looking into his eyes. I felt wonderful inside; I thought about how perfect life was at the time.

"He gave that to you?" Elder McDonnell asked when he saw me come into the room with a big, bright, shiny red bag shaped like a tennis racquet.

"He did," I said proudly, "And did I mention we taught a First too?"

"Yeah, you mentioned that, Dorsey," Elder Loughton chimed in from the side.

"I have a friend on my mission. Any of you guys have friends? People who you see that you don't want to introduce the Gospel to because you like them the way they are."

"What? Elder Dorsey, are you saying you don't want Darrell to be baptized?" Elder McDonnell asked, surprised, with the *you are stupid* look on his face that he had mastered long before me, although it felt like he had discovered it because of me.

"Well, no. I mean, I don't think the Church would make a difference in some people's lives like it would in others," I said, in no mood for debate on my feelings about baptizing people.

"The difference it would make is that they have the keys to go to the Celestial Kingdom and sit next to God. That's the only difference it might make," Elder McDonnell said.

"He's a good guy, though. He'll figure it out," I said, feeling extremely inadequate in defense of my expressed thoughts. I suddenly remembered why I held my tongue so often.

"It doesn't matter if he's a good guy. First, you should want him to be baptized so you can enjoy an eternity with him. And second, it's your job. While you are out here, it's your job."

"I just want to enjoy the few days a month that I see him. I haven't thought about enjoying an eternity with him. And as for my job—well, that's relative," I said. Elder McDonnell surprisingly let it go. He had never let anything go unless he was really sure everyone else in the room felt stupid or believed as he did.

We didn't have a dinner appointment, nor did Elder McDonnell or Loughton, so we all went out to In-and-Out Burger. We were in our whites and had appointments later, so going out together was nice. It generally happened only on P-Days. When we returned home, we sat on the floor, couch, and chair, eating our burgers and laughing about everything we could.

"What is that?!" Elder Loughton asked, hearing the pounding of steps on our landing—heavy, sudden, and quick.

BANG, BANG, BANG, "Help!" we heard. Elder Loughton was the first to get up off the couch and open the door. A woman fell into his arms; he kept her from hitting the floor. She had blood in—between her legs, on her hands. Her hair was going in all different directions. She was crying and her eyes couldn't focus. Elder McDonnell jumped up instantly and started speaking Spanish with her. We understood "Help," but after that she went into Spanish entirely.

"Elder Dorsey, grab a blanket," Elder McDonnell told me. I grabbed the comforter off my bed and wrapped it around her shoulders; she was sitting on the couch with Elder Loughton next to her and Elder McDonnell kneeling in front of her, speaking Spanish softly. "Elder Dorsey, call 911. Tell them a woman has been attacked and the man was in her apartment when she ran out. Give them our address and tell them she is here."

I quickly ran to the phone and called 911, explaining everything exactly as Elder McDonnell had instructed. Within five minutes, there were bright helicopter lights searching the vacant lot behind our building, shining into our windows, further lighting the already-lit rooms. The police came within minutes, talked with the woman, and then asked us if she could stay in our place a few minutes while they went down and checked her apartment. We said sure. I thought we were pretty good guys to leave a rape victim with: safe and kind.

The searchlights were still shining when the police officers took the woman away to the station, where she would meet friends to get her into bed. She started to take off the comforter, but I put it back on her shoulders and, in broken Spanish said, "No, tú." She barely smiled, turned, and walked down the steps.

It was quiet after the police and the woman left. We only had a few minutes before our appointments started, and we were going to drop off Elder McDonnell and Loughton in one of their Spanish communities and then pick them up later. No one felt like talking in the car. We hadn't talked about what happened before we left; I didn't think we would ever talk about it. Elder Barney asked if something like that had ever happened before on the mission. I simply said that it must not ever happen again in life and that should be our hope and prayer.

With Elder Barney being new and unfamiliar with my habits or habitually lazy missionaries, I decided to get back to my old self and work hard. I counted the hours, watched the clock, and got double-digit stats. We worked hard at missionary work. We tracted, found, taught and then tracted again. When I saw the Morels at church, they asked me where we had been. I said we were busy but that we would stop by soon. I was taking splits with Elders Hatfield and Christopher. They didn't get along. Elder Hatfield and Barney had served together in the MTC. I thought having a friend at a lonely time in the mission would help them. It helped me too. The less the two of them were together, the better. Elder Christopher hadn't let the masturbating issue go and was still counting Elder Hatfield's minutes in the shower. Elder Hatfield assured me there was no problem and that Elder Christopher was too hard to get along with and he wanted a change. I though it ironic that it was what he did that had created the minute-counting monster Elder Christopher. I told President Carlson that Elder Christopher needed to be transferred after I learned from Elder Barney some of the horror stories of their companionship. I didn't tell him that missions were easier the less an elder talked about them. Friendships were made and dissolved within months. The ire that built up between persons lingered, but the friendships didn't. And it wore on you.

Elder Barney's enthusiasm came partly from his greenness, but mostly from his convertness. He was a recent convert, of just a year, the amount of time new members had to wait before going on a mission. He was excited to share the message that had changed his life. And it had changed his life. People might choose a different college or different major at this time in a life, but not many decide to go on a Mormon mission. With the enthusiasm of a convert, we wielded our swords and seemingly conquered the Valley in less than a month.

Elder Barney was having a wonderful time and believed I was sent from God to be his trainer. I too thought maybe I was.

I didn't want to see Tara again, but after numerous calls from her, I felt obligated. It was I who introduced myself and wanted to talk religion with her. Was I so inept that I searched only for people who didn't know anything about other religions? Or had different beliefs? She had given me a nice blow to the testimony, and I didn't want to see young Elder Barney get the same. I was sure that I was the only one on the planet to wonder whether the Mormon Church was *the* Church and that I had gotten lucky enough to be born into it, learn it, live it, and preach it. If there were others, though, they weren't letting people know. I kept my doubts quiet, simply because most of the questions I had couldn't be answered by anyone but God himself. I'd asked him, and he didn't answer, and the people in the Church couldn't. So the Church's beliefs came down to a matter of the heart rather than the mind, because the mind dismissed it long ago and the heart said no, most of the time. It was a sense of obligation, to both their parents and the Church, that I was sure kept most of the young men out on the mission. And yet it was a different obligation that prompted a missionary in the zone to give a homeless man eighty dollars after he asked for change. And the reason for giving eighty dollars versus a buck? The missionary had just cashed his monthly check and had it in his pocket. But knowing him, it was the moral obligation to himself that he felt for the man. So this obligation prompted me to call Tara back and set up a time when we would meet her, her friends, and probably the devil in the big Mormon church on the corner. There we would debate what God meant when speaking through his prophets in the Bible. It would get everyone frustrated since there was no way to prove any of it. They would think that we missionaries didn't know what we believed, because of the overwhelmingly convincing evidence that they would present. It would come down to simple faith and a testimony, where it started for everyone in the room in the beginning. But Elder Barney had to see what it was like, and I had an obligation, so I called Tara back and set up a time later in the week to meet with her and her friends. I told her I wanted to meet at our church. She said she though it was a weird place to meet, but I said it would just easier. I also said we would have one of the members from the Ward there.

"Oh...why not just the two of you?"

"We don't have all the answers to the questions I think you might ask, so I invited someone else in our ward," I said, knowing I was digging myself into an ugly hole.

"Well, OK. We don't have anything that you probably haven't heard before, but if you want to invite more people, that's fine," she said. I could hear the confusion in her words, yet she sounded honest. I thought, what if she felt *she* was a missionary of sorts? What if was presenting to me what she felt would get *me* to heaven, that she was concerned with what *I* was preaching, teaching, and baptizing people into? Maybe she felt as sorry for me as I felt for her. Or she saw something in my eyes that told her I was a Chosen One and she needed to put her efforts towards me. She was very beautiful; maybe it was truly God who put her in my path that night riding home in the dark.

Probably not, but it could be believed as easily as what I preached each day.

The Morels' addition was taking on the look of a bad remodel. Without a roof, through the winter, the cement and the exposed ends of the studs got a worn look that lived under all the remodels, which were started, stopped, and then started again. Elder Barney loved the Morels' kids instantly. With the kids trusting me already, they simply transferred that trust to my new companion. The transference of trust from family, friends, and lovers is a great thing but can end up hurting people in the end due to the complexities of the relationships garnered. It was that simple. The kids were on Elder Barney's lap and in his arms the whole night. I tried to introduce him to the *Star Trek* night—it didn't take off. He was antsy and fidgety the whole night. He was surprised that we were staying at all after the Ward Mission Meeting was finished, but we hadn't been spending time after hours anywhere other than the apartment; it was his first time at the Morels'. I thought about how much he would change before leaving the mission. So when the television came on and I saw Elder Barney look at me, I had to make a decision quickly—respect Elder Barney or respect the Morels. I respected both and chose to go. At the last minute, I realized that watching television was against the rules—I'd forgotten that. I thought how easy making decisions was when rules were in question.

"Elder Dorsey?" Elder Barney questioned in the apartment. "Yeah?"

"So what happens when a member turns on the television? Should we always just get up and go?"

"Oh, I don't know. Don't think you could ever be faulted for getting up and leaving. Members understand and so does the companion, so it's an easy route to go."

"Did you and Elder Jameson watch *Star Trek* with them?" he asked. I thought he sounded a lot like a girlfriend; all of a sudden I was tired of the conversation.

"Elder Jameson couldn't walk for a month, so we probably watched *Star Trek* in that time."

"Oh." Elder Barney rolled over in his bed, thinking about what book he should pick up to read. It shouldn't have been *too* hard; there were only so many options. He rolled back over into my line of sight; he had his Missionary Guide in his fingers.

"Ya know, Elder Barney, you only have to read that in the mornings," I said.

"I know. It's fun to read, though."

"You have *got* to be kidding." I rolled my eyes back, rolled over onto my back, rubbed my eyes, and ran my hands through my hair.

"Hey, how else am I going to become like you? You don't tell me much, so I have to read it."

"What do you mean I don't tell you much? I drop nuggets of gold at your feet. Hell, I probably put them on your tongue."

"Not that much. You give me some rule stuff—'Obey the rules and you won't have any problems'—but you don't tell me about your past comps and investigators."

"I would, but it isn't all that great. I'd have to curtail what I say so much that it wouldn't make sense in the end. Won't do you any good to tell you how tough some comps are," I said, knowing I hadn't had any bad companions. If I had, I didn't know it.

"Can't be that bad. You've done pretty well while you've been out. That's what I want to know: how do you stay so well liked?"

"Well liked? By whom? Members? Other missionaries?"

"Both. Members *and* other missionaries love you. I just want to make sure that I gain some of that from you. Anyone can go out, meet people, and teach them, but it's the missionaries that get through a mission with a positive outlook. And in you, well, other missionaries and members see it in you. You already have the outlook on life—that it's there for the taking. Maybe that's why people are the way they are towards you. Whatever it is, I wish you would share it with me."

"Can't do that. Don't know what it is. If I figure it out, I'll tell you. Good night, Elder Barney."

"Good night, Elder Dorsey."

Elder Christopher was transferred to Bakersfield—further evidence to strengthen my theory that bad missionaries went to Bakersfield, where hell was. President Carlson wasn't happy when I told him that originally the masturbation discussion came up with just the three of us, and I had made the call not to go to him.

"Elder, those are serious matters. Those are some of the most serious matters that go on during a mission."

"President, I understand now. In the future, I'll come to you."

"Good. It worked out for the best, though. Elder Hatfield, for having a bit of a bumpy ride of his mission so far, he sure is strong in desire and ambition."

"Yeah, he seems to be handling it OK. I make sure and go on lots of splits. Sometimes just having a break helps." I wished I hadn't said that "a break helps." This man knew all about whether or not breaks help. He was married. He went on a mission too. And I was telling him how I came to a decision that was probably wrong. God made it clear in the Bible that in regard to sin and redemption, he was the only one whose judgment mattered. For us Mormons, it was the law of *forgive and forget*, except no one ever forgot. That was the problem with God's law: no one forgets, and all hold grudges.

Elder Hatfield got another seasoned veteran I knew nothing about, who came with no instructions. I liked it that way—it was the prejudgments people had that sucked the life out of them. But with his accent and cowboy hat, I thought there might be a little more info than I was given on this Elder Duncan. He had on missionary clothes, but they were so altered to look like a cowboy in a rodeo that I had to look longer to make sure.

"Well hi-ya, Elder Dorsey. Nice to meet you." He had an accent but was from Utah. He had on a hat, boots, and even flowers on his lapel, but he was from Utah.

"Elder Duncan, how are ya? Good to see you. Any problems getting here?" I thought if I put all my questions out, he might forget most of them and I wouldn't have to keep asking him. He would have thought I asked a lot of great questions of him, when I hadn't.

"No problems getting here, nope. Pretty nice place," he said, looking around on the veranda of the apartment I lived in first coming to the Valley. It seemed so long ago that I had transferred to my second area and had experience under my belt with my sword and *Book of Mormon*. I wished people could see experience like tired eyes. If experience was the criteria people were judged on, the world would be gentler.

I hoped that Elder Duncan was going to work hard with Elder Hatfield. Elder Hatfield wasn't going to make it unless he got some breaks soon.

We were sitting, musing over the day's events. It was my favorite pastime of any day, sitting around with a good group of missionaries. Then Elder McDonnell asked me if I had met Elder Dunkin yet.

"Why do you laugh when you ask me that? Something I should know?" I said with a mini-laugh.

"So you met him? Was he wearing his haaaat?" Elder McDonnell asked, his smile growing with as he drew out the word.

"He was. I was going to ask where yours is. I understand that the people in Utah really dress like him. All of them."

"You know that's not true. You were at BYU. What did you see?"

"That's doesn't count. Most of the students were from out of state and

I'm sure the locals went incognito to school."

"Whatever. Duncan is a goof. He is why Utah gets a bad rap. People like him."

"McDonnell, you take off his hat and he's from Utah just like you. You are who you live by."

"You want me to beat you, Dorsey?" Elder McDonnell said, getting irritated at the slamming of his home state and its inhabitants.

"I love Utah and the people," I said, pulling myself out of death's grip.

"Sure, Dorsey. You *love* Utah. You love to do nothing but make fun of people and the dirt in Utah," Elder Loughton said.

"I don't. I *do* love Utah. Think I'll move there someday. Think I'll move next door to McDonnell, and my kids can influence his kids."

"Dorsey, you are getting close to a whoop'n," Elder McDonnell said, looking up from his notebook.

"'Kay, I'm done. Hey, did anyone hear what happened with the lady downstairs? Is she OK?"

"Her Mom came by this morning; you guys were out—that was a surprise. She said that her daughter was able to get out before anything happened. When the police called later, I gave them a statement over the phone on behalf of all of us."

"What about all the blood?" I asked confused.

"I didn't ask, but I figure she was on her period."

"Oh. I think I would have liked to be consulted before a statement was given on my behalf."

"I *don't* care! They didn't catch the guy, and she said to be on the lookout for a black man."

"I'll be on the lookout for a black man. And what should I do if I see a *black* man?"

"I'm just telling you what she told me. I probably wouldn't do anything."

"Then I won't do anything either," I said and dropped it.

Elder Barney and I were going through the motions of a Sunday—going to church, visiting members, and hoping our investigators were picked up by the members we had scheduled—that is, if the investigators even planned on going. I was surprised when more than once I had an investigator tell me that they heard someone knocking on the door but didn't know who it was, so they didn't answer. I didn't want to explain the concept of doors or knocking, so I let them feel that it was a legitimate excuse. I thought a person should be tough, tough enough to answer the damn door and say, "I don't want to be a Mormon." I invited at least five people each week to church. I liked throwing an invite and address into the end of a conversation on a doorstep or street corner. It was presumptuous to think someone would feel comfortable letting a couple of strange guys into their house and have them sit on the couch where you lay your head. But if you could just take an hour out of a relaxing Sunday and visit a church that you would like to see inside of anyway, then there existed a small chance each Sunday, a "Sunday Lottery" of investigators. I thought it a much better approach than the forward, space-invading, obnoxious "boys in short-sleeve button-down shirts" approach that the Missionary Guide taught. When we got home from church, there was a message on the answering machine to call Elder Hatfield. Generally, Elder Hatfield didn't call unless there was a problem. The usual chain of command went through the senior companion, myself, who would pass on pertinent information. I thought there might be something wrong the minute I heard his voice, along with the reluctance to give any details on the machine.

"Elder Dorsey, you aren't going to believe this, but Elder Duncan got a job."

"Like, a job for money?" I asked.

"Yeah, a job for money. He works on P-days here at the apartment complex."

"What's he do?" I asked.

"He cleans up the flower beds and rakes the leaves."

"How much does he get paid?"

"Like, forty bucks."

"Wow. Well, Elder Hatfield. You know that as missionaries, we can't have jobs."

"I know. I think you should tell Elder Duncan that."

"OK. We're coming over to do laundry tomorrow with you guys. I'll talk to him then. Can you wait till then?"

"Sure. You might catch him in the middle of a shift, though."

"Well, I can probably get him to take his fifteen-minute break," I said, perplexed and pleased at the situation. It was very funny to think about. I told Elder McDonnell, with Elder Barney there in the room, and they both laughed. I didn't like to talk about the other companionships around Elder Barney. It would naturally influence his feelings towards others, and he didn't need that. Elder McDonnell, being a Spanish-speaking missionary, was removed from the English elders and companionships. The language barrier carried over to the mission too. Unless an elder had the rare opportunity to live in an apartment with a set of Spanish elders, he might as well have been on a separate mission. My secrets were safe with McDonnell. He was fun to talk with and would never say anything, because he didn't gossip. He didn't talk about people to other people; he had other things to talk about if he talked at all.

I called the president that night and talked with him concerning Elder Duncan's job. He assured me that having a job was against the rules. He asked me what I had done when they told me, and I said I told them I would be over the next day. We were doing our laundry together, anyway, so I would tell him to quit his job, or the president would make his commute to work unbearable. The President laughed. It was the first time I had heard him laugh, and it felt good. For a brief moment, I felt we were on the same level in some way.

"Elder Dorsey, I think you will do the right thing tomorrow. You take care of it. And if he won't quit, call me. Anything else tonight, Elder?" he asked.

"No, that's it. I'll let you know what happens in the weekly letter."

"Great! Thanks, Elder. You guys get to bed; it's late."

"Will do. Good night."

Elder McDonnell looked over at the clock in the kitchen. "Oh Elder, you called him after ten. We should be in bed studying, not on the phone."

"He doesn't care. This is serious mission business. He was glad I called. He probably thinks I'm suffering, having to use my own personal study time to handle district business. Why, I'm a saint actually."

"Get'n' pretty deep in here, Dorsey. Sure your boots are high enough?"

Elder McDonnell said.

"What do you mean, boots? I don't have boots on."

"You are so dumb sometimes, Dorsey. The boots are for keeping the load of shit you've been feeding us off your feet!"

"Ohhhh, I see. No, there's nothing on the floor. I'm not feeding you anything. It's all real."

"I'm going to bed. Ya'll should do the same," Elder McDonnell said.

P-Days were the best day of the week, offering time to oneself, even if it was walking down the aisle of a grocery store. It was still in mission dress, but feeling alone was somewhat possible with unknowns next to you. The laundromat allotted for forty-five minutes of writing and reading, still reading "approved" material, but not reading aloud to someone else, then having to explain what was meant by what you had just read. It was a time of unadulterated space in the head for thoughts to stretch and ideas to connect. Post–mission-life thoughts were clearer on P-Days. Images of me as a student, studying while doing my laundry under a low-wattage bulb in the basement of an old brick building, thick law books opened but thoughts of calling my beautiful girlfriend on my mind. There were times the ideas came to life so clearly that it comforted me and muted the questions in my mind. My disposition changed, and I looked forward to every minute of every day, knowing I could do anything in the world.

Those same thoughts and feelings somehow inspired me in the day-to-day deed of being a full-time missionary. I had no patience when I saw Elder Duncan raking leaves below in the courtyard.

I leaned over the railing and yelled down, with my hand funneling my voice. "Elder Duncan, what *are* you doing?"

He looked up and smiled wide. "I'm working," and he went back to raking in his cowboy hat, with the greasy sides turned up, keeping the sun off his face. I walked down the stairs and stood by him.

"Elder Duncan, having a job is against the rules."

"*It is*? I didn't know that. It doesn't say anything about it in the White Bible."

"It's one of the rules that they don't feel the need to write down. You have to quit now."

"But I need the money. I have big phone bills."

"Work that out with President Carlson, but you can't have a job. Let's go, we'll tell the manager together." I'd worn my white shirt and tie for the purpose of impressing the landlord, although he didn't need to be impressed to let Elder Duncan go. The whole incident lasted only a few minutes. Elder Duncan hardly questioned my authority, and the Church came away looking controlled. I left the landlord with a gift from the Church: "Consider the few hours' pay a gift from the Church of Jesus Christ and Latter-day Saints."

Later that day, Elders Barney and Hatfield talked while sitting on dryers; Elder Duncan and I talked by the washers. Elder Duncan was telling me all about Utah women. He was having a great time talking with his hat on. He wasn't sore at all that I made him quit his job. I thought he was going to have one hell of a story to tell.

Elder Deeds and his junior companion were coming over for splits. I had charmed a car out of the zone leader for Elder Deeds in payment for introducing me to Darrell. The night before, Elder Barney and I went over exactly what he would do with Elder Mackey, and I felt confident in him. We had spent more time on splits than we had together. He was hard working, forever trying to be perfect in all ways. Even when he screwed up, he was confident it wouldn't happen again. He took the jostling and all the fun we could give him, never complaining, only honestly questioning us. He was everything an elder could ask for in a companion.

"Deeds," I said. "Yeah, Dorsey?"

"I gotta run by the tennis shop and pick up my racquet. We can say "Hi" to Darrell too."

"Sure, no problem. You're always breaking those strings."

"I know. It gets a little spendy. I might have to stop hitting so hard, because I can't afford the stringing," I said, hoping to get a thought from Elder Deeds.

"You can't do that. You just wouldn't play. A true athlete can't come down a notch and play."

"Probably right. I'd just stop playing," I said, sadness coming over me surprisingly. "I'll ask Darrell what I can do about my strings or my stroke so I won't be spending my paltry allowance on strings."

"Yeah, he'll know."

"If I was practical like you, Deeds, such as buying the Corolla instead of the muscle car, then I might find myself in a different position with not such a big question looming overhead: To play or to pay?"

"This isn't quite like driving a Corolla. It's different when it comes to sports and gear. A person can spend money on sports gear and drive a Corolla and still be cool. But if you spent on your money on a car and had no sports, then you wouldn't be cool."

"That is some theory, Deeds."

"It'll click with you. Just wrap yourself up in it for a while, and then it will make sense."

"You're a cool guy, Deeds."

"Well thanks, Dorsey. So are you."

As we neared the tennis shop, I thought how perfect the day was. The sun was still drying the roofs of parked cars and crystalizing dewdrops on blades of grass. I took some time to think of what was around me, where I was, who the people in my life were, and how I got to this spot. I followed the decisions that got me to the point I was at physically. I flipped through them quickly, like flipping to a good spot in a well-worn book.

There was an unfamiliar man behind the counter—as good looking and striking as Darrell, but not Darrell.

"Hi, guys. Can I help you with something?" he asked, seeing a purpose in our steps.

"Yeah. I had a racquet strung by Darrell. He said it would be done today."

"Let's see," he said, looking behind the counter at several white slips rubber-banded to tennis racquet necks. "What kind of racquet is it?"

"Head Venison."

"Here it is," he said, placing it on the counter and taking the white slip, punching buttons into the register from what he read on the slip.

"Is Darrell around today? I thought he usually worked on Thursdays."

"Did you know him?" the man behind the counter asked. "Well, yeah. We were kinda friends. We met here at the shop."

"I have some bad news for you," the man said, looking into my eyes for the first time. "Darrell died last night. He was hit while riding his scooter in the hills."

I was stunned. I couldn't speak. I looked over at Elder Deeds, hoping that he could offer me some words of hope to believe in life again. "Oh. Wow…I just can't believe it."

"I'm sorry you had to find out this way. I think I remember Darrell talking about a missionary that came in and got his racquet strung. He liked you."

"Thanks.…Thanks," I said, in shock, and looking down, I saw my vision was blurred. I paid the fifteen bucks for the strings and looked around the store quickly before Elder Deeds and I walked out the back. It would be the last time I ever went to the store.

"Dorsey. Sorry, man."

"Thanks, Deeds. Let's just forget about stuff today and hang out. I don't want to do anything."

"No problem."

I didn't tell Elder McDonnell about Darrell. He wouldn't have known how to react and would probably ruin my own mourning period. So I didn't tell anyone. I didn't tell Elder Deeds *not* to tell people, though. And I didn't know if he would or not. I didn't care either.

I talked with Elder Barney that night. He told me everything was going great, that there were no problems. All the appointments were there today, and Rachel Barrett called about basketball on P-Day. I told him I'd take care of calling Rachel and thanked him for the message. After I hung up, I wondered how I was going to confirm basketball with Rachel. I wanted to, but calling a girl was serious, especially when her Dad was a bigwig in the stake. So I opted not to call her, hoping she would call back when I was there and I could talk with her. I wished I could have called her, gone over to pick her up for a Friday night movie, and then make out a little with her. The thoughts quickly made me feel like shit, so I stopped thinking about how miserable the mission was and how I should at least be able to kiss beautiful girls while participating in this crappy thing God called life.

We were moving so fast, I didn't even see transfers coming. When they told me I was going to be transferred, I was glad. Sad too, but mostly glad. I was going to miss Elder Barney and Elder McDonnell, but I had served a long time in the Valley and was ready to see something different.

What I wasn't going to miss were Tara, her questions, and her perception of my life and me. The meeting we set up with her and Stephen Day was not pretty. Stephen was in a strange mood and insisted on speaking from the pulpit while the rest of us sat down in the pews. With each question that Tara and her friend asked, Stephen would assume a "nose high, hands gripping the podium" stance, laying into them with scriptures and rough tones. Tara started to fight back in the beginning, but by the end, Stephen had worn her down to a nub, making her feel that she had been set up. She *had* been set up, and I felt bad. But I was being transferred and told Elder Barney to do with her what he wanted. I packed up and went away from everything that bothered me and everything that pleased me.

CHAPTER 10

The Santa Clarita Valley had the city of Santa Clarita, which was formed when the communities of Saugus, Canyon Country, Valencia, and Newhall merged. I was called to be district leader over another set of elders. The Valley had one zone, consisting of one set of sisters and six sets of elders, including a set of Spanish-speaking elders, the only set of Spanish-speaking elders for the whole Valley.

My new companion was Elder Basset. He was from England. He ate Marmite on his toast every morning. I tried it the first day and it just felt wrong.

"I don't see how you can eat that, Elder Basset," I said, watching him from my bed.

"Yum, yum. It's good," he said as he took a bite, looked over, and smiled at me.

"It's gross."

"Hey, that's a little harsh. If you had grown up on it, you would like it."

"Does it remind you of home?"

"Well, yeah. But that's not why I eat it. This is like having coffee in the morning for me."

"Hey, we don't drink coffee."

Shaking his head, he said, "I know we don't drink coffee. I mean, it's like waking up and going through the morning ritual of drinking coffee. This is what the English do."

"Does everyone eat it?" I asked, turning up my nose at him.

"Yes. It's like putting butter on your toast."

Elder Basset and I always talked while we did our personal study. We did our reading to ourselves, but neither of us minded the interruption of a question or casual talk. I'd been out a little over eight months. I'd gone through the Missionary Guide twice already and read the *Book of Mormon* straight through, memorizing all the scriptures that went with the Discussions; a little talk in the morning was a relief from the monotony of reading the same material over and over.

"You done reading?" I asked him.

"I think so. I'm going to take a shower now."

"What are we doing today?" I asked him. I was senior companion, but titles rarely meant anything to the missionaries in the daily routine of things. Of course, when the title of trainer was on your head, a little more planning had to be made. Yet, with two seasoned missionaries, they figured out what to do day to day each morning.

"No appointments that I see." Elder Basset had grabbed his planner from the side of his bed and was flipping through the pages for the week. "Why don't we go meet some members? You've met most of them at church Sunday, but we should go visit them at their homes."

"Sounds good. Any in particular?" I asked.

"Well, let's see. I haven't met many myself, other than at church. So we can start with the ones I know and then ask each one we visit who lives around them."

"OK. Good idea. Kinda early, though, to start visiting them at ten o'clock. Let's tract for a few hours first and then start visiting around lunchtime. I bet we'll get a lunch out of it."

"I'm sure we will."

"Dorsey! Coming at you!" I heard Elder Lampson scream from the living room.

"Wait, I'm not ready!" I yelled back as I leaned forward and saw Elder Lampson with the Nerf football cocked and ready to throw. He threw it high and I tried to jump, slipping on my sheet at the last second. The ball went through my hands and right through the window.

The CRASH! was all we heard as the ball shattered a two-by—two-foot jagged hole in the window.

"Oh!" Elder Lampson sighed as he put his hands up to his mouth, in shock and surprise.

"Man, I wasn't ready. What were you thinking?!" I said, looking down the hall, holding back laughter.

"You never miss, even when you aren't ready. Dorsey, you missed a perfect throw."

"*Perfect* throw?! It was high; I was lying down reading!"

"You were talking, and it wasn't that high."

I slowly got out of bed as the others gathered around my window.

"Boy, that's a big hole," Elder Basset said.

"Thanks, Elder. I kinda see that," I said.

"You guys are going to have to pay for that," Elder Keene said.

"Dorsey's paying for it. He's the one that missed it," Elder Lampson said in between laughs.

"I'm not paying for it. You threw it."

"But it was a great throw. Spiral and everything."

"We're splitting it. How much can it be? Hundred bucks, maybe? It's just a single pane window." I said.

"It's an old window. They might have to replace the whole thing," Elder Keen said.

"No way, they will just replace the glass," I said.

"You better call around and find out," Elder Keene said.

"We will. We will. Man, Keene. It's not that big of deal; it's funny."

"Damaging the apartment is not funny. The landlord will see it and call the mission. And then President Carlson will call us and wonder what's going on."

"He won't call the mission. Even if he did, it was an accident and we will just get it fixed."

I looked over to Elder Basset. "Any glass guys in the ward?"

"I can't think of any glass guys, but Brother Larsen is an electrician. He probably knows some."

"Do you know him pretty well?"

"Oh, yeah. We go over there couple times a week and say hi."

"We will stop by there today and see if he knows any, then.

There, Keene. See? We almost have it fixed already."

"It's going to get cold tonight. Better put something over the hole."

"It's like eighty degrees out! We're not going to get cold."

"OK, fine. You just better get it fixed soon."

I grabbed the vacuum and started cleaning up the glass on my bed and on the carpet, while Elder Basset jumped in the shower. "Elder, it's not P-Day. Looks like you are doing laundry," Elder Keene said as I walked by with an armload of clothes.

"I have glass on my sheets. Ox in the Mire, Elder."

Elder Keene had been out longer than anyone in the apartment. I wasn't sure if he was a jerk because he wasn't the district leader, or if that was just his nature. He had straight hair that hung down past his nose, longer than was allowed on a mission, but he slicked it back over his head so no one could tell. He weighed in at around a buck thirty, and already I wanted to put him through the wall. He didn't ever play with us, in the apartment or on P-Days. He was somewhat of a trooper on P-days in that he would go to the gym or the tennis court and hang out so that the rest of us could play. He was the senior companion to Elder Lampson and seemed to enjoy the title and the power he felt it brought.

Elder Lampson was about six-foot-three and reminded me of Lennie in the Steinbeck novel *Of Mice and Men*. He talked slow and moved about the same.

Another thing that set our two companionships apart was that they had a car. In all companionships with a car, one of the two was designated as the driver. Generally, it was the senior companion, as was in this case. Although Elder Keene was a little hard to take at times, having the car meant that he was safe from us getting too mad at him, knowing it would mean having our permanent ride taken from us.

The work had been slow in Saugus for some time. I looked at the whiteboard, noticing that we had two lingering investigators stuck on the Second Discussion. Although it wasn't crammed with names like the whiteboard in the Valley, it was new, and I looked forward to filling it. Before we left that day, I asked Elder Basset about the names.

"Who is Andy Turner?"

"He's one of our investigators," Elder Basset said, smiling.

"Well, I figured that. The heading Investigators above his name gave that away. What's his story? Why are we still on the Second with him?"

"He is a member referral that we started teaching when I came into the area. He's a friend of a young lady in the ward, named Monica. I think you met Monica last Sunday. Do you remember her?"

"No. Describe her."

"Well, she's very pretty."

"Elder, there are lots of pretty girls in the ward."

"Oh, are there? You shouldn't be looking at them."

"It's natural. Now give me more than that."

"She was sitting on the back pew when we walked in. I introduced you to her after you met Sister Woodside."

"OK. Now I remember. She is pretty. So are they dating?"

"No. They are just friends. She sits in on the Discussions, though. Or, *the* Discussion. We've had a hard time getting together so that we can have them both there."

"It's been months, though. Is it that tough?"

"Well, Andy works nights and Monica works weekends. So yeah, it's tough."

"Why don't we go see Andy today?"

"He sleeps during the day, so it's hard to catch him. I'll give him a call and leave a message for him on his recorder. If he calls us back, we can at least set up a time to meet him and introduce you to him."

"OK. What about Clarissa here?"

"We tracted into her one day and set up a time to visit her to teach her a First, and she wasn't there when we went back."

"So we haven't taught her anything?"

"Not yet. We should stop by there today and set up another time."

"It's a plan, then. Did she seem interested?"

"I think so. She didn't say no."

"That's enough for us." I said.

"What about New Member Discussions? Any recent baptisms?"

"No, we took care of all those. There weren't many."

"Who's the dinner appointment with tonight?" I asked.

"Woodside. Do you remember him? Brother Woodside was that really tall guy with a beard."

"Oh yeah. They have the twin boys, right?"

"Yeah, That's them. They are a fun family. Really relaxed when we go over there."

"Cool," I said and turned to talk with Elder Lampson into the other room.

"Hey, Lampson, you guys have a D.A. dinner appointment tonight?"

"No. Not tonight."

"You want to go to ours?"

"Sure. What time?"

"Six thirty."

"OK. Meet you here. Keene? That sound good to you?"

"Well, who is it?" Elder Basset spoke up, "It's the Woodsides. I know you've met them."

"Are they fun?"

"Well, it's dinner. That's what we are going for," I said. "Do you want to go or not?"

"Sure. We don't have anything else planned."

After showers, we got our bags packed with copies of the *Book of Mormon*, a map, and ward directory, and headed to the front door. "So, we will see you guys around six back here?"

"OK. We'll be here," Elder Lampson said.

Part of being transferred and moving in was meeting the other missionaries for lunch, going shopping to restock the kitchen, and visiting members. Sometimes it felt like missionaries were in the field so the members could feel better about not talking to their friends and neighbors. If all the members talked, there would be no need for missionaries. But we were called for it—at least called to go on a mission for two years—and nothing was judged against us in case of lack of success. The success and praise came just by finishing it. We did everything backwards, with no thought to efficiency, such as visiting members—why would we ride around all day, visiting members, introducing ourselves, just so they knew us? We could have taken twenty minutes, called ten members, and asked them if we could stop by that day. But we opted to ride around all day, stopping in. Most of the time they didn't want to see us, anyway. Either they were busy or we reminded them of how little they were doing to share the Gospel and how little interest they showed in their eternal salvation on days other than Sunday. Sometimes members met a missionary they really liked or thought was really sharp, and they would share the names of the neighbors and friends and get involved in splits each week. Most members were just too damn busy to live their religion other than one day a week. We would remind them of the truth and the lifestyle they vowed, to live. Because that's what it really came down to in the eyes of the Church.

Saugus was a two-stoplight town. And one of those was the freeway off-ramp. It consisted of a small downtown strip mall with older neighborhoods butting up to the new neighborhood in the canyon. The canyon was built up with tract homes and views of the nearby neighbors. The distinction in the membership among the neighborhoods was as quirky as the idea of sending nineteen-year-old boys out to teach the Restored Gospel of Jesus Christ.

We could ride across the ward boundaries in thirty minutes. That would put us at the edge of the tract homes in the canyon.

"Hey, Elder!" I yelled from behind Basset as we rode by the strip mall, "Let's check out the bike shop."

"OK." Elder Basset made a hard right into the next driveway. "It's a spendy one."

"Is it?" I asked as we locked our bikes to the chain on the garbage can out front. Inside was full of Cannondales. I fell in love instantly with the large-tube bikes. "Man, these are nice," I said.

"Yeah, but look at the price. Like twelve hundred dollars for these things."

"But they are so cool looking. They're worth it. I wouldn't buy one out here, but when I get home I will. Can you imagine cruising around BYU on one of these?"

"That would be neat."

"Are we going tracting close to here?" I asked.

"Yep."

“Can I help you?” a man asked, walking up to me with his hands folded behind his back.

“Oh, no. Just looking. These are really nice bikes,” I said.

“They are. Have you ridden a Cannondale before?” he asked.

“No. I didn’t even know about them.”

“Would you like to take one for a ride? We have some used ones in the back.”

“I’d love to,” I said.

“Here, let me grab you a helmet and you can take one for a spin.” He disappeared behind the counter for a few minutes and came back with a blue bike and a yellow helmet.

“Here you go. This is the B2000ML3.”

“So what’s this run used?” I asked.

“About six hundred. I could make a deal for you, though.”

“Whoa! Six hundred bucks for a bike? It would have to be some deal. I mean, I’m sure it’s worth it, but I could never spend that kind of money on a bike, at least not now.”

“Well, give it a spin and see what you think.”

It road like butter. It was the smoothest bike I had ever ridden. It had rock shocks on the front, allowing me to ride right over curbs without pulling the front wheel off the ground.

“Hey, thanks for letting me take it for a ride. My name is Elder Dorsey, by the way. And this is Elder Basset.”

“Elder Basset and I introduced ourselves while you were on the ride. Nice meeting both of you. Come back when I can sell you one of these.”

“Nice meeting you too. We will be back. Our bikes are always needing parts, and now we know where to come.”

“Great! You guys have a great day,” and he rolled the bike and the yellow helmet away.

We locked our bikes to a small tree in one of the older neighborhoods in Saugus. It was about ten thirty, and we figured we could tract for about an hour and a half, then start hitting members up for lunch.

“At least we are catching people home,” I said, after knocking on about ten doors. “They aren’t interested in what we have to say, but they are answering their doors and are polite to us."

"Yeah. They are nice, aren't they?"

"Nicer than people in the Valley. They are just rude down there. I had people open the door, look at our name tags, and just shut the door. Worse was when they would just smile and slam it in our faces."

"I've had my share of those too. Hey, this one's yours!" Elder Basset said as we started walking up a driveway to a one-story rambler. We went to the front door and rang the doorbell. No one answered. As we were standing there, a small Mazda truck drove into the driveway with a girl and a man I guessed to be her father. It was always awkward standing at someone's door when they were just pulling in. We then had to try to talk to them while they were in the middle of their getting-out-of-the-car practices. Some had kids they needed to get out of the back seat, and some had grocery bags.

Whatever they had going on, even if it was just locking the doors, it was enough for them to be bothered. Here we were in their front yard, and they didn't want to talk to us in the first place.

"I *hate* it when they drive up like this," I said to Elder Basset as we walked towards the driveway, towards the man getting out his car.

"Hi, my name is Elder Dor—" Before I could finish, the man was out of his truck and pulling up his shirt, showing me his underwear.

"Hello, Elder. Don't worry about me. I'm already one of the Chosen Ones, see?" And he pointed to his underwear that only temple-going Mormons wore. "Hah, got ya! You must be new to the area. Brother Hobson," he said, dropping his shirt back down and sticking his hand out to shake mine.

"Dad, why do you have to do that?" the girl said, standing on the other side of the truck.

"This is my daughter Trina, Elders. I don't think she finds her old man that funny."

Elder Basset and I both shook Trina's hand, and Brother Hobson invited us in for a glass of water.

"So, are there any other members around here that we could visit?"

"There's quite a few of us here. At least four that I can think of. There are the Roberts, Sister Welch, Shane Thomas…." He sat and thought. Then looking up, "That's about it. Just keep tracting; you will run into them.

The only name I recognized was the Roberts. I remembered it because they had four teenage daughters—all pretty. I thought that was a bad reason for remembering them. A guilty feeling washed over me.

"How is the tracting going? Neighbors being nice?" He asked.

"Yeah. We haven't baptized any yet, but they are nice," Elder Basset said.

"Well, I know most of them, and they are pretty set in their ways. You are welcome to point me out when you talk to them, if you want. I know sometimes if they can put a face with someone in the Church, it might open the door a little."

"Thank you. We will throw your name around. It always helps when we can."

"No problem."

He proceeded to tell about the neighbors. Some single, some retired, some Baptist, some wild.

"Well, I need to get back to work. Thanks for stopping by, Elders. Elder Dorsey, nice to meet you."

"Nice to meet you too, Brother Hobson. We will see you at church Sunday."

"Always," Brother Hobson said, showing us to the door. We were refreshed from seeing fellow members as we got back onto the pavement and walked to a neighboring house.

"Man, now *that* was a shock," I said.

"That was funny. I forgot that they lived here. I wasn't trying to trick you or anything."

"I know. It was funny."

"We've killed about an hour already. It's almost time for lunch. Where should we head to?" I asked.

"Let's go up to the canyon. We will go see the Davidsons.

Sister Davidson should be home; they have a newborn."

"OK. Couple more doors, then? You want to visit any of the members around here before we head up there?"

"I don't think we'd catch too many of them home."

"OK. Couple more doors and we will call it good. Don't you just feel good when we start our day out with a couple hours of tracting?"

"Yeah. It's nice. Makes the whole day go better."

"It makes me feel like we are doing something. Even if we don't catch anyone home or teach any Discussions. It's also nice being able to tell the members that we were tracting before we stopped by their house."

The Davidsons lived in a house that looked like their neighbors'. Their yard looked like their neighbors', also. All the yards and houses looked like the neighbors'. Brother Davidson was on lunch break and invited us in.

"So, what have the Elders been up to today?" he asked.

"We've been tracting all morning," Elder Basset said.

"Any success?" Sister Davidson asked.

"No. But we met some nice people."

"Well, that's better than nothing," Brother Davidson said.

"Hey, you guys want some lunch? I'm making Brother Davidson a sandwich."

"Sure," we both said in unison.

As she made sandwiches in the kitchen, Brother Davidson asked about where I was from, how long I'd been out, were I had served before. I learned that he was an architect and was in the middle of designing the new mall in Valencia, a neighboring city about twenty-five miles from their home. He was strikingly good looking. About six-foot-three, with long hair down to his chin. Little round glasses put the final touch on him as an architect. If I were an architect, I would want to look like him. Sister Davidson was petite, with long black hair. They made kind of an odd couple, due to the size difference, but still a very attractive couple. I guessed they were in their midthirties and had it confirmed by Elder Basset on the way home that night.

After the Davidsons, we went eight houses down to the Thomases. Sister Thomas was a beautiful woman. She, too, was in her midthirties. She had a baby in her arms, yet her figure would never have suggested it. She was skinny, with long legs. Her blond hair fell down to her chest on a pair of breasts that I tried to keep my eyes off of. Her tight-fitting cotton shirt didn't help. I'd started noticing in the Valley that new moms always wore tight shirts. When I brought it up to Elder Bell, he told me it was because they were nursing, causing their breasts to become a lot bigger. It made sense to me. It was great when they were pretty to look at, but for the most part, they weren't, so it wasn't really a problem trying to keep from admiring them. But so far, out of the women I had seen in the Saugus Ward, it was going to be hard to keep my eyes off them. I would, though. It wasn't the time or place for that kind of thing, and I knew the more I dwelled on it, the harder it would get.

"Hi, Elders. How are you today? Out visiting some of the members?" She asked.

"Yeah. We were just down at the Davidsons and thought we would stop by and introduce Elder Dorsey," Elder Basset said.

"Elder Dorsey, it's nice to meet you. I'd shake your hand, but they are a little full right now. Aren't they, honey?" she said as she looked down to the little baby in her arms. "This is Jessica. Can you say 'Hi,' Jessica?"

"Hi, Jessica. You are a cutie," I said, grabbing for her finger. She quickly pulled her hand away and buried her head in her mom's shoulder.

"She gets a little shy around people she doesn't know. Well, I'd invite you in, but Brother Thomas is at work. I think we are on the calendar this week."

"Oh you are?" Elder Basset said. "Well, we will come back then."

"I think it's Thursday night. Any special requests?" She asked.

"Oh, no. Anything is great. We just love getting a home-cooked meal," Elder Basset said.

"Well, I can't promise that. We might just get pizza or something."

"We love those dinners too. Anything is better than Top Ramen noodles," I said.

"It will be something good. Elder Dorsey, nice to meet you. Look forward to having you both over Thursday. Thanks for stopping by."

"It was nice meeting you. See you Thursday," I said.

We had killed another few hours by then and thought we should head home and check messages. We were expecting one from Andy about a Second Discussion.

Elder Basset and I rode side by side on the way out of the canyon.

"Are there a lot of young couples in the ward?" I asked.

"Lots of young couples. Most of the women are pregnant with their second or third child."

"Really? That many are pregnant?" I asked.

"Yeah. I was shocked when I first started meeting members here; I thought they were all pregnant."

Their husbands were probably going at it with them all the time. If I had a wife that looked like the ones I saw, I would be.

Sometimes I thought men got a sense of exhilaration knowing that they got a pretty woman pregnant and wanted to show it off to the other men in the ward. Like saying "Look at my gorgeous wife. And you know we are having awesome sex, because she is pregnant."

"So the young couples live in the canyon, and the older couples and families live in the older homes closer to town?"

"From what I see, the houses in the canyon are even more expensive. Everyone wants to live up there. I think another reason it's so popular is that there are so many members there. All the kids can play together during the day, and the wives can hang out while the husbands are working. It's not uncommon to see two or three of the families playing outside on nice days. Follow me. We are going to take the back way home. We will go up this huge hill, but after the hill, it's all downhill to home."

We turned off of the main road and meandered through a neighborhood of older homes.

"That's where the Woodsides live," Elder Basset said, pointing the house out as we passed by. "You're going to like them. Fun kids, fun family."

"Is Sister Woodside a babe too?" I asked sarcastically.

"I don't know, Elder. I don't look at other men's wives like that," Elder Basset said with a straight face—at least a face that was *trying* to be straight.

"Sure, you don't. It's natural, Elder. It's OK to think another woman is pretty. You think when you are married you will never look at another woman? Or another man's wife? It's OK to look; it's *coveting* that we are not to do."

"I know, I know. I will too. Just giving you a hard time. And yes, she is a babe."

Elder Basset started gaining speed on a little downhill jaunt.

"Get some speed, Dorsey. The hill starts right around this corner. The farther we get up, the less we have to push."

We made it maybe thirty feet up before we got off our bikes and pushed for the next thirty minutes.

"You sure this is worth it?" I asked about twenty minutes into it, with burning legs.

"Oh yeah. Just wait. On the way down, you will be using your brakes most of the time. We can coast all the way home from the top."

Once on the top, I was greeted with a view of open fields and grated lots for new cul-de-sacs. We were sitting above the city and had a great view. Below I could see the Saugus High School and the small Ralph's across the street. The homes on the hill were overlooking this also. They were all new developments. I could tell since the houses themselves looked brand new and there were not many finished yards. It appeared that most of the buyers opted to save money on the purchase by putting the yards in themselves.

For almost twenty minutes, we coasted downhill through streets, turns, new construction, and vacant lots. It was a nice change from pedaling all the way home like the way we had come that morning. It was late afternoon when we got to the apartment. Elder Lampson and Keene were there also. They were both sleeping—Elder Lampson on the couch and Elder Keene in his room.

"Hey, guys. Not too busy today, huh?" I asked as we walked in.

"Keene is not feeling well—upset stomach—so we took a break."

"Are you going to be able to make it tonight for dinner?" I asked.

"Oh yeah. You know, he seems to get over it pretty fast."

"Yeah. That's true."

"Hey, Dorsey!" Elder Basset yelled from the bedroom "Andy called. He wants to meet us tomorrow. It's his day off."

"Great. Alright. We are teaching. Boy, Lampson. We tracted this morning, visited members this afternoon, and then got a teaching appointment for tomorrow. And how are you guys doing?" I asked smiling. Elder Lampson knew it was all in fun.

"We went over to the Gardners. Elder Keene wanted to practice work on the program he's putting on next month for the stake."

"Oh yeah! I forgot about that. How is it coming along?"

"I don't know. I'm not really involved, you know. I just kinda sit there and listen."

"Is Keene calling all the shots?"

"Yeah, *I* have no say in it."

"So why do you have to plan it at the Gardners?"

"He's singing a song. Oh, what is it? I forgot. It's in the hymnals, though. You've heard it."

"So he's singing a song? I'm still missing what there is to plan."

"It's not so much planning. He is singing and being recorded. So we go over there, and he plays the piano and sings and then records it on the Gardners' DAT recorder."

"Why doesn't he just sing into a tape recorder?"

"Because a DAT recorder is the best recording device there is. Brother Gardner does this for a living. He has a studio downtown. It's pretty cool. He has, like, gold records and pictures on the wall from the different artists he has worked with."

"Any famous ones?"

"I didn't recognize any. It's mostly rap music, so I wouldn't know."

"Oh. Well that's cool. How does Keene sound?"

"He sounds just like you or I would sound."

"Oh, you think so?" Elder Keene said, coming into the room. "Well, I mean it sounds good. I don't know if *I* could sing that well. I've never really tried being all that serious, singing into a recorder and all."

"This is what I am going to do for a profession. Write music and lyrics. I doubt that you, with no formal training, could do it. I'm not just singing a song from the hymnal. I'm rewriting some of the music to go with my program and the slides that I have planned."

"Keene, I didn't mean anything by it. Elder Dorsey just asked what we were doing at the Gardners."

"Well, maybe if you gave me a little support with this program, you would understand what we are doing and how important it is for the missionary work here."

"I'm sure it's going to be great."

"You know, just because you guys don't have the interest that I do in music, you put me down for being involved in it."

"No one's putting anyone down, Elder," I said.

"I get absolutely no support from any of you guys."

"What do you want us to do?" I asked. "You don't ask us for help."

"I don't want you to do anything other than think that this is going to be a great program. And you are going to bring out your investigators and make sure you tell the members in your ward."

"We will. I just don't know much about it. I was just asking, Lampson," I said. I was at the point of wanting to throw Keene through the wall again. So I went back to the bedroom to talk with Elder Basset. "So what did Andy say?"

"He sounded excited. He said to come by tomorrow around three."

"We don't have anything planned, do we?"

"Just *that*."

"Any other messages?"

"No."

"Shall we take it easy till dinner?" I said, looking down at my watch.

"Sounds good to me." Elder Basset lay back on his bed and folded his arms behind his head. "What was that all about out there?"

"Oh, nothing. We were talking about Keene's program next month. I'll tell you later."

"I'm taking a nap. Wake me when we are going."

"I will." I said. "Brother Larsen didn't call back about the window?"

"No. I'll give him a call tonight."

"Think we need to call and get it fixed? Find someone out of the phone book?"

"No. Let's wait and talk with Brother Larsen."

"I'm not too worried. I just don't want Keene to be a pain about it."

"Oh, he's fine. He hasn't even mentioned it, has he?"

* * * * *

Sister Woodside came to the door, wiping her hands with a flowered dish towel.

"Elders, come in!"

"Sister Woodside, nice to see you," Elder Basset said. "Did you get my message that there would be four of us?"

"I sure did. Come on in, guys. Don't just stand there."

We all stepped into the house, and Sister Woodside turned back and walked to the kitchen.

"You can put your coats on the couch. Hope you like chicken fajitas."

"Who doesn't?" I said. "Sister Woodside, I'm Elder Dorsey. I'm Elder Basset's companion."

"Oh, yes. Brother Woodside told me we got a new elder in the Ward. Where did Elder Clark get transferred to?"

"He went to Lompoc. Do you know where that is?"

"Yep. It's by Vandenberg Air Force Base," she said.

"I don't know that area. I'm not that familiar with California yet," Elder Basset said.

"Elders, you want to introduce yourselves?" She asked while cutting up two tomatoes.

"I'm Elder Keene and this is Elder Lampson. We serve in Valencia."

"Oh, do you know the Browns? Roger and Lisa?

"Yes, they're a nice family. We were just over there about two weeks ago for dinner."

"Oh, what did you have to eat?"

"Uh, I think it was a rice dish with chicken."

"Was it good?"

"Of course it was. Any dinner appointment is good," Elder Sliders said.

"You kind of have to say it was good, huh?" she said.

"Well, yeah," Elder Lampson said.

Their little twins were in the living room, watching Garfield on television. Chrissie, their thirteen-year-old daughter, was sitting at the kitchen table, cutting out big yellow pencils from a pad of colored paper.

"This is Chrissie, guys. Jared and Josh are in the other room, I think."

"Where is Brother Woodside?" Elder Basset asked.

"He's out back fixing something on the porch. Go on out there, if you like. Will you tell him we will be eating in about ten minutes?"

"Sure," Elder Basset said.

The four of us walked through the kitchen to the porch off the back of the house. We couldn't see Brother Woodside, so Elder Basset called for him.

"Down here!" we heard a voice say from underneath us.

"Hey, Brother Woodside. It's the Elders. What are you doing under the porch?" Elder Basset asked.

"The damn dogs keep getting under here and hiding bones and shit. I'm getting all of it out of here and then replacing the slats they keep breaking."

Two big dogs ran around the fenced back yard. One was a light-brown golden retriever, and the other a scruffy black one with a white stripe on its neck. They were chasing each other on the worn dirt paths in the grass.

"Sister Woodside wanted me to tell you that we would be eating in about ten minutes."

"OK. I'm done down here, anyway."

I saw a basketball court and breakaway hoop on the side of the yard and walked down from the porch and started shooting. Brother Woodside crawled out from under the porch and saw me. "Elder Dorsey, right?"

"Yeah. We met at church," I said as I cradled the ball in my arms and walked over to Brother Woodside with an outstretched hand.

"I remember. How do you like Saugus so far?" he asked as he put his hand out to shake mine.

"I like it. Met some more members today."

"Oh yeah? Who did you meet?"

"We visited the Davidsons and the Thomases."

"Oh! The canyon members! I see how you guys are. We aren't good enough for you down here, is that it?"

"No, no. Not at all. We were just up there, and Elder Basset knew where they lived. We actually rode by your house, but knew we would be seeing you later, so that's why we didn't stop by."

"Well, feel free to anytime. I'm usually working, but Sister Woodside and the kids are here. And I know they would *love* to see you. I want you guys around. You are good for the kids and the family."

"No problem, stop by and grab a little b-ball."

"You like to play basketball?"

"Sure do. I can warm up here during the week for the games on P-Day."

"It's adjustable too. Go ahead and dunk on it if you want."

"Aren't you worried that I'll bend it?"

"I said you could dunk on it, not hang on it. I mean, if that's the only way you can dunk, then don't do it."

"Oh, no. I can do it. Don't worry."

"I'm not."

During dinner, Brother Woodside talked about how hard his mission was. He had served it sixteen years earlier in Michigan.

"Not the work, necessarily, but what might have been going on at home. Just all of it, I guess. It was hard to be somewhere doing something that you really didn't want to be doing. I think it would have been cool to hang out with my friends and go to school, but the mission is what guys do."

Brother Woodside had a valid point. I wondered how many of the missionaries were out because they believed in what they were doing, or were doing it because they had to for their family, or just thought it the right thing to do and did it knowing what they were missing out on. And in the last case, was their sacrifice more because they did it longing for a different time? Or was it because they believed what he was doing was his calling and only *he* could do it, believing he would go on to great things because of it, never wavering.

"So do you guys play basketball on P-Day?"

"Sometimes. Let's see, Elder Dorsey plays and I play."

He looked over at Elder Lampson. "Lampson, you play sometimes with us, don't you?"

"Sometimes. Yeah."

"Elder Keene?" he asked, looking over at Keene.

Elder Keene took his hand and made a swinging motion. "Tennis is my game."

After dinner, Elder Keene and I played Star Wars with Josh and Trent. I was a sky trooper with an antispaceship gun with backpack. Elder Keene was an Ewok warrior, and Josh and Trent were changing characters every five seconds. Elder Basset and Elder Lampson sat on the family-size couch and watched the news.

"I killed you, Keene!" I said as I finished making the sound of an anti-spaceship gun.

"You killed me? What does that mean?"

"I just shot you," I said.

"Well, what happens now? In Star Wars?"

"Josh, what happens when we die?" I asked.

"You go with Grandma and Grandpa," he said, pointing up.

Confused, I looked over at Sister Woodside. She wasn't listening, so I turned back to Josh and said quietly, "No, I mean when you play Star Wars."

"You get a new man," he said, handing me another sky trooper. "Here, you can play with this."

"Well, thank you, Josh. You are very fun to play with," I said and handed the sky trooper to Keene.

Keene put his sky trooper on the carpet and started playing with Josh.

"Keene?" I said. "You're dead."

"When did you kill me?"

"You didn't hear the gun?" I said, looking down at my guy. I picked him up and said, "Oh, I had the silencer. That's why you didn't hear it."

"Hand me another guy," he said, throwing the sky trooper over with the Ewok warrior.

"Here you go," I said, handing him a flight-jacketed Luke Skywalker.

As he put Luke on the floor, he said, "Bang. Dorsey, I've just shot you."

"With what?" I said.

"With my guy here."

"Look at your guy," I said, motioning with my head.

"What?! He shot you."

"He doesn't have a gun. He's getting ready for a flight," I said.

"What? How did you know he didn't have a gun?" Elder Keene asked.

"Well, look. He isn't carrying anything. See my guy? He has a big gun."

"Fine," he said and threw him down with the others. He then turned and watched the news while I played with Josh and Trent.

CHAPTER 11

Andy was a handsome guy. His hair was short, above his ears. It was slightly wavy; he wore it pushed back over the top. He smiled a lot. And he was short, about five-five.

Elder Basset had taught Andy the First and the Second Discussions. Both Discussions had gone according to the guidelines except when Andy was asked to be baptized. He didn't accept. He said it was too soon. Monica had sat in on both Discussions and was very supportive in getting Andy to hear them. And that's where he had been left for about a month. He hadn't seen Monica since the last Discussion. He said they had both been really busy over the last month, which was why he hadn't accepted.

Andy worked for a local contractor, painting new houses in the canyon.

"Are you serious?" I asked when I heard about the painting.

"Well, it's me and a crew of guys. But I've been working on most of the homes up there."

"How are they? The homes. Are they nice?" I asked.

"They aren't bad. I wouldn't mind one. They're expensive"

"Really? About how much?" I asked.

"Some go for as much as three hundred thousand."

"Wow, *that* much? I wouldn't have thought. But it *is* California. That's what's expensive."

"Well yeah, but those houses are under a hundred thousand to build."

"Man, that guy's making some money," I said.

"Yep. His name is Larry Night; company is Night Homes. You will see signs all over the place."

"I've seen those already."

"Did you know he is a member of the Church?" Elder Basset said.

"Really? I didn't know that. Is he in our ward?" I asked, looking over at Elder Basset with my eyebrows raised.

"No. He's over in Canyon country."

"Andy, did you know that?" I asked.

"I think I've heard it before. I don't see him very often. Just occasionally at a site. We aren't, like, friends or anything. He probably doesn't even know who I am."

"Do you like painting houses?" I asked.

"It's not bad. I'm finishing school, so it lets me get off early and then get a class in at night."

"What are you planning on majoring in?"

"Communications."

"I have friends majoring in that. What do you do with a communications major?" I asked.

"I'm not sure myself, Elder Dorsey. I'll let you know when I'm done."

"How much longer do you have?"

"About a year. I've been working on it for about two now. I did my first two years originally at Santa Clarita Valley Community after high school but just never went on."

"I know that feeling," I said, and then thought about it a little.

"Well, I *kind of* know the feeling. I went before my mission and plan to go back. So it's like taking time off also."

"A little bit," Andy said.

"Elder Basset, did you go to college before your mission?" I asked. "Where did you go? Oxford?"

"No, not Oxford. Not everyone from England goes to Oxford."

"It's probably like going to Harvard or Yale here, right?" Andy said.

"Yes. It's like that. It's hard to get into and *very* expensive."

Andy must have made decent money painting. He rented a two-bedroom house with a small yard. I got up and looked around the front room, where we were sitting. I looked at some pictures of him with a man who could have been his dad. There were pictures of him skiing. Jumping, really. And higher and bigger than I could dream of. He said he went to Vail every year for about two weeks. I asked him if he ever skied around Seattle, and he hadn't. I told him he hadn't missed out on much, as the snow was either slushy or icy.

"The nicest place I've skied is Utah. Well, I went to Whistler once, but on a regular basis, it's Utah," I said.

"I bet Whistler was nice," Andy said.

"Really nice. Except lift tickets are, like, sixty dollars. I think that's a bit much."

"That's about what it is here. I know what you mean, though. If I went any more than a couple times a year, I wouldn't be able to afford it. So, you skied while you were at school in Utah, I take it?"

"My friends and I would generally go up on the weekends. It's so close, and Sundance is only about twenty minutes from BYU, so it was really easy to get to. We would just be sitting around and say, 'Let's go skiing,' and were on the slopes twenty minutes later."

"That would be nice. I have to plan a whole week's vacation to go."

We talked about skiing, about painting, just about everything but the Discussions and where Andy wanted to go with them. When I finally asked him about it, he said that we could just take over where he had left off. He wanted to have Monica at the next Discussion. I said we would call her. We left with a prayer that Elder Basset offered. We planned to meet the following week, after I'd called Monica and set up a time.

Elder Basset was riding alongside of me when I asked him why he hadn't progressed with Andy further than the Second Discussion. I thought he was a prime candidate for being a devout Mormon. He didn't smoke and drank little. Those were the two biggest obstacles to overcome for most investigators—other than the sex, of course. That seemed the hardest concept to accept and commit to living without, outside of marriage.

Again, Elder Basset explained that the First and Second had gone very smoothly, but Andy just didn't feel the time was right to get baptized. I suggested that we ask him up front about it next time we saw him.

Elder Basset called Monica after we got back from splits. "I set it up for next Wednesday." Elder Basset told me.

"Great. Did she say anything?" I asked.

"No. She was glad that he was still looking at taking the Discussions, but that's about it."

"Man, I wonder what it is. There's *got* to be a reason he fell off like he did." I thought about Andy that night while I tried to sleep. Young, single, good-looking investigators maybe come along once on a mission, and Andy was my chance to get one. I thought that of all people who would *not* want to be members of the Church, it was the young and single. They had so much to look forward to every day. They could date pretty girls and actually go out and have a beer with them. I thought how easy and fun it would be to be able to call a girl and say "Would you like to go grab a beer or something?"—a chance I would never have. Then, if things worked out, a young guy could have sex with the woman. Why would anyone want to give that up? Eternal life? Was that it? I could understand with a family and all, kind of like an extended insurance plan, but for singles? I didn't understand. Of course, these questions would never come up with someone like Andy. I certainly wasn't going to bring them up.

That night we had dinner with the Thomases. Sister Thomas let us in the door this time. Brother Thomas invited us to sit down in the living room, while Sister Thomas busily gathered the kids and put the plates on the kitchen table. There we sat in front of a large-screen television with the Dodgers playing. "These guys are having a heck of a year," Brother Thomas said as he clicked the controller and the ominous buzzing of the television stopped. "But, we will save that for another time. Hate to have you guys break the rules at my house."

"Oh honey, don't give them a hard time. Elders, what would you like to drink? Water or milk?" Sister Thomas asked from the kitchen.

"Water is fine."

"For me too," I said.

"So, you Elders have a busy day today?" Brother Thomas asked.

"We met with an investigator. Maybe you remember him, Andy? He's a friend of Monica Lee's. He's been to church several times with her.

"I don't remember, no. How is he coming along?"

"Well, we are a little stuck. We've taught him up to the Second Discussion, and we can't get a commitment out of him," I said.

"OK, everyone to the table. It's time to eat," I heard from behind me.

Elder Basset and I made our way to the table, with Brother Thomas following. I tried to bring up Andy in discussion several times during dinner, but Brother Thomas kept talking about the mission he served in São Paolo, Brazil. It had been about eight years since he served, yet he talked like it was the day before. Brother Thomas was a big man. Standing nearly six-three, he was built like a boxer: nimble and slender. I'd watched him hit a softball out of the park in the prior week's ward softball game. One of the members told me that he could have been a professional baseball player, which would explain why he could hit and play so well, but it didn't explain why he hadn't become one. Did he opt for going to work eight hours a day and taking a trip once a year with his family instead? The truth, I was sure, was that he wanted to be a baseball player. And in dreaming, practicing, and playing more than most, he got pretty good. But not good enough. It seemed so many of the men in the Church got a majority of their skills at sports right on the wood floor behind them, where they sat in Sacrament Meeting each Sunday. Anytime a member moved into the ward with any sense of athletic ability, they "could have been pro," it seemed.

On our way home, we took the direct route over the mountain—the hard climb uphill, with the long, easy coast home. It was dark and Elder Bassett didn't see the construction sign in the middle of the road. The battery had failed on the sign's flasher, leaving a dark sawhorse. The reflecting tape had nothing to reflect off of since we rode with no lights. We were cruising about thirty miles and hour. I was fifteen feet behind him and skidded to a halt when I heard the sound of scraping metal and fabric against the hard pavement. He tumbled with his bike fifty feet down the hill, taking a load of loose rocks and dirt with him. I laughed. Even when I saw the blood seeping through his white shirt, I laughed. I was in shock. It was the scariest bike wreck I'd seen or heard. Every knuckle was showing raw skin—red. His knees were bloodied, his pants were ripped, his face was scratched. We had to carry his bike home. He leaned against me the whole way. When we arrived, we put Neosporin on every inch of his body. He stayed in bed for several days. I read aloud to him and made him breakfast, lunch, and dinner as he slowly mended. He was tough—toughest I'd seen out of a young man. He was even tough when I scrubbed the raw flesh, extracting small pebbles from the wounds.

Elder Basset was transferred after he mended. We had served together only a month. He had done a great job introducing me to the area, so I wasn't nervous or anxious about his leaving. There was no distinction of power as far as a senior companion or junior went. If I were a mission president, I would want companionships to work and interact as Elder Basset and I had. We worked every day. We understood each other. If one of us didn't want to tract for the last hour of the day, we wouldn't. We were both always ready to go out with members, out to lunch with them, or just about anything it took to stay in the mission field. I don't think he ever questioned whether he would finish serving his mission, nor did I.

CHAPTER 12

Elder Hampton sauntered into the apartment with a duffle bag over his shoulder and a beat-up, blue vinyl suitcase. He was about my size, but not as thick. He had a cocky air about him. I wondered how it would fit in with the pretty, thirty-something couples in the ward. He had on faded blue cotton pants, technically against the mission rules. I don't think he would have worn them in front of the president.

The rules for dress had gone from wearing a suit full-time, to wearing a short-sleeve white shirt with only the suit pants, now classified as appropriate—along with, of course, the mandatory undergarments. Missionaries stretched the clothing rules, as I did, but not on transfer days, when members drove a missionary to his newly assigned area. It was one of the times I was sure President Carlson wouldn't want the rules to be stretched. Stretching the rules was typically reserved for days when the weather reached ninety degrees, when members and possible investigators would understand the lack of thick suit pants. But today was a transfer day, and Elder Hampton still didn't seem to mind what he was wearing. He threw his bags on the bed and asked me to show him around.

He was from Helper, Utah, population two thousand. Ten of whom were Hamptons. I asked him how the town got the name *Helper*, and he explained the town kept the helper locomotives that would attach to the coal trains, pulling them up the mountains to the Wasatch Front. This was all he knew about the history behind the name, and it sounded rehearsed.

If I came from a town called Helper, my history would probably be rehearsed and brief as well, due to the number of times I would be asked about the name. Elder Hampton was going home in five months, when his mission was over, to work for his uncle on his farm in a nearby city. He didn't know if he was going to school or not. If so, he said he'd go to a junior college.

Later, after we each went through our list of the names of companions we'd served with, we concluded that we didn't know any of the same ones. Elder Hampton was "old school" in the mission; he had served with the previous president. I was always a little envious of the missionaries who had the chance to serve under two presidents. With all the guidelines, mission presidents still had their own way of running a mission.

After nineteen months on his mission, Elder Hampton didn't tract anymore. The few times I tried, he refused to talk. I had no problem with this at first, taking every door myself. But after three or four times, I decided to fight with him on a better playing field—the basketball court.

Elder Basset and I had turned into regulars at the Woodsides. I didn't see any need for this to change, especially with such a willing companion. Elder Hampton wanted to fill his days in bed listening to Journey on his Walkman. I liked Journey but had no desire to listen to them under the current situation, that of being a full-time missionary, although I *did* let Hampton play all of their greatest hits for me—all of which I recognized. I explained I liked them but told him to keep the headphones on because I didn't want to listen.

"Well, what do you listen to? he asked.

"Approved music only, of course," I said with fun, so he didn't know whether or not I was kidding.

"OK, Dorsey. You never listen to anything else?"

"No. I wasn't a big music guy before the mission, so this one really isn't a hard rule for me to keep. And you have to go out of your way to hear music out here on the mission."

"Maybe I have something you would like."

"Well, as long as it's approved, I'm up for it." And that's when I was introduced to Amy Grant. We wore out her tape. 'Baby, Baby, I'm taken with the notion….' I was in heaven. She was a gospel singer, and the only one who was approved by President Carlson, along with the Tabernacle Choir. Classical music was also approved, but. I'd never listened to it and didn't see myself picking it up, so I was limited.

He showed no guilt. On the contrary, he personified a man who was forced to go on a mission because his family expected him to, as he was following generations of examples. With the Church being established in 1889, there were quite a few families with pedigrees going directly back to the trek across the Rocky Mountains during the early days of the Church. With so much sacrificed by the generations before, it was not looked upon lightly when younger generations didn't do their part. The part of nineteen-year-old boys in the Mormon Church was to go on a full-time mission, separated from their family and friends for two straight years. For Hampton, I thought his need to fulfill his obligations to the Church was even more prevalent due to his lack of desire in any other direction for the post-mission years. If Hampton completed his mission, he would be hailed a hero at his homecoming and would be ensured the rights to a beautiful, Mormon, virgin bride. No one would ever know that he was a complete jerk on his mission, with so little respect for others that fellow companions would forget to mention him. But none of this mattered in the post-mission years. All appeared in order if a young man was able to go on a mission and then come home after the two years were up. Hampton was putting in his time. Maybe his plan wasn't that off base, other than how hard he made it for companions to live with him.

Hampton was the king of "give an inch and take a mile." When I let him take his time in the morning, even thirty minutes or so, the next day he took an hour. Soon it got to be that we got out of the house when we got out of it, generally around eleven o'clock. When we woke up was, of course, not tracked other than the interviews we had once a month with the President, when he asked if there was anything we needed to talk about. Following in Hampton's footsteps, I quickly started saying there was nothing to talk about and switched the conversation to questions regarding our investigators—the seemingly fictitious characters we visited and who had a place on the whiteboard in our room but were far from investigators.

After a morning of playing basketball at the Woodsides and grabbing lunch with the kids, we visited members other than the Woodsides. Sister Weidermeyer promised to make me a batch of cinnamon rolls. As we walked up to the Weidermeyers, leaving our bikes up against the garage door, Elder Hampton said that his stomach wasn't feeling well; this would have to be a short visit.

Elder Hampton had some kind of stomach or other condition that made him sit on the toilet for hours. He drank Metamucil several times each day. Metamucil was the third over-the-counter drink or drug that he had tried since being out on the mission. I had never experienced stomach problems or any kind of upset stomach. Therefore, I did not understand and lacked empathy. In fact, I found it quite funny. The thought of being somewhere and being overcome with the need to use the bathroom, and not being able to hold it, had always struck me as funny.

"Hi, Elders. Come on in," a tired Sister Weidermeyer said from behind the screen door. She always looked tired, though, so I didn't think anything of it. She was the sweetest lady. In her early forties with four kids under ten, she was always glad to see us. Her smallest girl, four-year-old Chloe, would hide behind her skirt for the first ten minutes until she remembered us and felt comfortable. Chloe was an angel. I tried to talk to her whenever I saw her at church or her house. After time, she would let me talk with her and sometimes even let me hold her. "Chloe, Elder Dorsey is here," Sister Weidermeyer said as she held the door open for us.

Chloe came in and quickly took refuge behind her mom. "Oh, Chloe, you are so shy around the elders. You are never this quiet," Sister Weidermeyer said as she brushed the strawberry blond hair out of Chloe's eyes. "Why don't you say 'Hi' to the elders?"

"Hi, Chloe. How are you today?" I asked her, getting down on both knees to be at her level. She quickly hid her face in the blue ruffles of her mom's skirt. "I see you, Chloe," I said. I knew she would warm up after about ten minutes.

"Well, Elder Dorsey. I thought about your cinnamon rolls last night and knew you would be by today. I wasn't able to get them done, though. I'm sorry."

“Oh no. Don’t feel bad,” I said. I assured her that anytime would be fine. Even the remnants of another batch would be fine.

“I’ll tell you what. I’m making some for the ward barbeque next week. Why don’t you guys come by and I’ll teach you how to make them? That way you can make them anytime you like.”

“That would be great. I thought this was a secret recipe, though.”

“It is. That’s why you have to promise that you keep it secret too.”

“I will. I promise,” I said, rubbing my hands together. “It will be our secret, then. I’ll be famous throughout the mission for my rolls someday. Don’t worry, though. I’ll always give credit to you.” I sat down at the kitchen table as Sister Weidermeyer went a few feet into the kitchen and pulled some orange juice out of the freezer. I looked over at Elder Hampton and saw he wasn’t sitting. He motioned to me that we had to go. He was casual about it, not insisting.

As we were silently conversing, his facial expression changed and he quickly said, “Sister Weidermeyer, would you mind if I used your bathroom?”

“Of course not. You know where it is.”

I couldn’t keep the smile off my face an hour later when Elder Hampton was still in the bathroom. I knew that without his Metamucil on hand, he could be hours. Hampton and I seemed to have an understanding. He would follow my lead because he didn’t want to lead. He would keep his mouth shut about most things and, when asked about the work, would direct the questions to me. Hampton just didn’t care about outward appearances and would, if I’d let him, go off about other missionaries, investigators, and other families in the ward. As missionaries, we were privy to the meat of the gossip in the wards we served in, and that of the missionaries who served before us, as well as ones being transferred in. I told Hampton he had to keep his negative opinions and thoughts to himself. I also said that if he had anything positive to say, then he was welcome to say it. This arrangement worked, causing many of the members not to know what Hampton was all about. They just thought he was quiet.

When we got back to the apartment, Elder Hampton made a beeline for the bathroom, yelling at me to grab his Metamucil from the kitchen. I did as I was asked, making as many jokes as I could and laughing to myself. Elder Hampton never got mad about the jaunting. This was good. Maybe he realized that it was all I had to laugh at on the mission.

Elder Hampton did hit it off with some of the investigators, though—such as the throngs of young ladies I was constantly pushing him through at church. It wasn't that he was a ladies' man; he just talked about stuff that he shouldn't have and was therefore very interesting to fourteen-year-old girls. I thought this all very innocent, as Hampton wasn't the type to take it too far—at least not out on the mission. Compared with Elder Bell's forays into late-night porn, he was mild.

We canceled splits that night due to Elder Hampton's extreme irregularity, instead opting for a night at the Woodsides. They were always glad to see us. If Hampton was sick, then they could actually go out on a date or something and leave us to baby-sit, which wasn't a problem for us, as it was(1) service and (2) a break from the day-to-day missionary work.

The work was stagnant. We had Andy, of course, who wouldn't commit to baptism. Before Elder Basset left, we had spent some time just hanging out with him. I thought we were making progress. Andy had a '64 GTO and took Elder Basset and me for a couple of rides in it. It was so fast—the fastest car I'd ever been in. When Andy got on the freeway and punched the gas, it was a rush. Not like standard missionary work, which didn't get the adrenalin flowing like a fast car. Since fast women were not going to be a part of my life on the mission or after, all I had was the fast-car adrenalin rush. With the drives and the occasional calls, Andy and I were becoming friends, although I *did* have an ulterior motive in the friendship.

Clarisse, the young woman Elder Basset tracted into, was hard getting a hold of. She didn't want to see us, I was sure, but she didn't realize that she was all we had. It was one thing to have a slacking companion, but if I couldn't back up the lazy days and empty nights with the hopeful thought of future members of the Church, then I would go crazy.

It was a lucky break when the ward mission leader called and said, "Elders, I have a young girl that needs to be baptized. Do you have the time in your schedule?" The young girl was from an inactive family in the ward. Brother Larsen gave me the background information over the phone.

"Brother Benson is the home teacher for the Gables. And when he was over the last week, their fifteen-year-old daughter, Emily, was sitting in on the visit. It came out that she was never baptized."

"How did they miss that fact for the last seven years?" I asked.

"Well, they just started coming back to church in the last year or so, and it just went unnoticed. So we need to start teaching her the Discussions. She's a good kid; there shouldn't be any problems."

"Do her parents want her to have the Discussions?" I asked, still a little surprised at the picture I was seeing.

"Well, yeah. They are the ones that suggested it. This can happen, Elder. If my wife wasn't here I'd probably forget to have *my* kids baptized."

"Hey, I think it's great. I'll give them a call and set something up for next week."

"Great. Now, I was talking with Brother Gable and he said that she is pretty busy with school stuff. I think she might be a J.V. cheerleader or something. So just work around the schedule as best you can." I thought this was funny—Brother Larsen telling me how to work around someone's schedule. I mean, this is what I did as a missionary. I did it every day, and if I couldn't do it now, after over a year of doing it, then there were bigger problems than a schedule. "Also, Elder, involve the members as much as you can in the teaching. This family isn't as active as we would like to see, so the Discussions and the baptism are going to be the springboard to get them back into the fold, you might say."

"Of course, I understand. I'll set up appointments for splits at night. We will need to have splits because of her age; we wouldn't want a time when it was just the two of us and her."

"Well, no. We wouldn't want that," Brother Larsen said carefully. He never had to think of being in a room alone with anyone, and this probably brought back memories that he had suppressed without even knowing it. Although I *did* think it was a good idea to live by, even after a couple got married, how much trouble could you get into in a marriage if you were never alone with the opposite sex? Maybe that's what the Church was doing: training the future leaders of the Church in a way that affairs and divorces would be so random as to never be a problem. "You might want to try to get one of the men from a family in the ward with a daughter her age."

"That's a good idea. I'll see what I can do."

I told Elder Hampton about the new investigator. He showed no sign of excitement. But he did manage a smile and a wisecrack, saying, "Boy, Elder Dorsey, you might get another baptism." Any response from Elder Hampton was better than nothing.

With Emily, we now had three investigators. And one seemed like a sure thing. With Hampton, the weekly numbers were really low. Discussions averaged three to four, and we counted anything—even if we just talked with someone on the street and asked if they would like to learn more. Technically, they were not Discussions, but if we slipped into questions such as "Would you like to learn about the plan of salvation and living with your family after this life?," then we would count it as a First. When we handed out a *Book of Mormon*, we'd circle parts for the potential member to read and count that also. These instances comprised the majority of the Discussions and didn't seem to lead anywhere.

I was dreaming that Elder Hampton was shaking my bed. I thought it odd, as Hampton never awoke before me. But who else would do it? I was getting really mad while I slept. The rage felt in sleep is so much more than when awake. So I wanted to kill him. Maybe.

"Hampton, knock it off!" I said and kicked my feet, trying to hit his face.

"Dorsey!" I heard from the side. Then again, "Dorsey!"

"What are you doing?" I asked, as I looked over at Hampton, sitting up in his bed with a magazine in his hand. "Why are you shaking my bed?" I rubbed my eye with a finger and looked at Elder Hampton. His bed was shaking too.

"Dorsey, it's an earthquake. Not me."

I lay still, thinking that any movement on my part would make the earthquake shake more. I watched as the mattress bounced on the box spring and the box spring bounced on the floor. It was my first earthquake, unlike Hampton, who had experienced several throughout his mission.

Later that day in District Meeting, six of us were listening to District Leader Elder Welch and watched as he bounced on the table he was sitting on at the front of the room. He was giving us a lesson on The Commitment Pattern out of the Missionary Guide. The aftershock felt as big as the earthquake; at least it did to me.

"Everyone under the table!" Elder Welch said, as he felt himself bouncing on the hard cherry table. "Hurry!" We all squeezed in under the table and waited a few minutes until we were sure the tremor had stopped and none followed.

"Well, where were we?" Elder Welch asked, as we got back in our chairs and he took his place at the front of the room again.

"I believe we were identifying each part of The Commitment Pattern, and we left off with Building Relationships of Trust," I said, straight faced with an air of thoughtfulness. Each of the other missionaries looked over at me and started laughing.

"Thank you, Elder Dorsey. Nice to see that you were paying attention and know exactly where we were. Would you care to define the next step of The Commitment Pattern?"

"The second step of eight total in The Commitment Pattern is Building Relationships of Trust with the investigator. This step—"

"Excuse me, Elder," Elder Welch said. "Is it only for investigators?"

"Well, no. I mean it could be used for anything, really. Such as your companion."

"Why don't you give us an example? Maybe something you have experienced, possibly with Elder Hampton?" Elder Welch said, visibly having fun with the serious tone of the conversation.

"OK. Let me think for a minute." I rubbed my chin and looked at Hampton. "How about this? If your comp isn't doing what you want, the best way to see a change is to be his buddy versus his companion. It's a lot harder to disappoint a friend than just another companion."

"Any specifics?" Elder Keene asked. He was trying to get me in trouble, but so far it was all in fun.

"Specifics?" I asked. "OK, here is an example. Let's say Elder Hampton doesn't want to go out on splits and he doesn't want to tell me why. Well, the trust that I've built with Elder Hampton, with the other steps in The Commitment Pattern will eventually enable me to understand exactly why he doesn't want to go on splits."

"And what will that do for you? Remember, it's The Commitment Pattern. Do you have to get a commitment out of him?" asked Elder Welch.

"Well, that's one aspect of The Commitment Pattern. It will be used in different ways. Obviously, for the Missionary Guide, the majority of the examples are geared around baptism and getting an investigator to that commitment. Within a companionship, it simply resolves concerns, thus creating a better atmosphere. For example, with Elder Hampton, the reason he didn't want to go on splits was because his bowels were backed up and he didn't want to get stranded in some stranger's house, sitting on the john for an hour. So upon learning this, I was assured of a valid reason for not going on splits. This enabled Elder Hampton not to feel bad, as we all knew he would, and it would enable me to not feel guilty about not going out on splits, doing the Lord's work, the only true enjoyment out here." The laughs from each of the elders told me that as far fetched an example as it was, it provided one—and laughs along with it.

"Thank you, Elder Dorsey, for that wonderful example. Also, thanks for reminding each one of us where the true joy comes from out here, something that is so easy to lose sight of at times."

"Of course!" I said, and borrowing a line from Elder McDonnell, "I'm only here to help where I can; I think you all know that."

The next few weeks were busy with work for the Lord. We had appointments set with Emily for a Second Discussion. I was already dreading talking with a fifteen-year-old girl about sex. From the first meeting, I supposed that this wouldn't pose a problem, but one can never really tell. I couldn't imagine a girl that age having sex, though. None I ever knew did, so that's all I could base it off of. There was also an appointment set with Andy, and I had decided to get down to the reason why he wouldn't commit to baptism. He had met with missionaries on and off for over a year, and it was time to move on if he wasn't interested. Clarisse was finally reached, and she agreed to have us over during the day for a lunch and formal First Discussion. I had yet to meet her; all conversations were over the phone after she had returned a phone call following several postings of Elder Hampton's missionary business card on her door. It was always the ones you never thought who would whip out a business card with, The Church of Jesus Christ and Latter-day Saints and hand it over so proudly. Elder Hampton had gone with a popular design in the world of missionaries at the time: A small double *W* with an arrow coming off the end, looping up and coming back down, pointing into the open-faced double letter, symbolizing baptism. I had come out with a set of cards that showed the Seattle area temple on the front, with a shiny gloss finish, my name and address as a header, and my favorite scripture on the back. I used the articles of faith. A returned missionary told me how handy they were to have with you. My cards were too personal and flashy to leave on doors, though. They were saved for possible members who wanted to keep in touch and write after the mission. I gave Rachel Barrett one before I left Chatsworth.

Monica had asked about Andy at church the previous Sunday and where we were with him. I told her we couldn't get any kind of commitment out of him even though his enthusiasm over what we talked about in both in the First and Second Discussions alluded to a straight shot to the baptismal font. She listened to what I said, looking into my eyes. Her dark brown eyes were just incredible at that distance. I talked to so many people each day that my eye-contact skills were polished bright. It also helped that missionaries had to study the all-important eye-contact topic in the Missionary Guide each month.

Monica could tell I was struggling with Andy, as if I'd never struggled with an investigator before. She grabbed my arm and said, "Elder Dorsey, there is something you need to know about Andy. He has a crush on me, and I think he is keeping an interest in the Church because he thinks if he is Mormon, then I'll go out with him.

"Have you guys dated in the past or something?" I asked. "No, but one time he told me the reason he is taking the Discussions is to get closer to me. I don't want to prevent anyone from taking the Discussions or anything, but I wanted you to know." She said this with serious concern apparent on her gorgeous face.

"Well, thank you. I'll keep that in mind. Of course, if he wants to get baptized eventually, I wouldn't stop him over something like this," I said, trying to keep eye contact with her, but not for too long, so as not to let on that I was using eye contact to avoid studying her face. From the way she was looking at me, she must have been admiring how well I carried myself for a young man, or maybe she looked up to me because I was a missionary.

"I know, and I wouldn't expect you to. But this may be why he is dragging his feet. He noticed that instead of getting closer to me, he has succeeded in pushing me away little by little, so that now we rarely even talk."

"Do you still want to sit in on the Discussions?"

"I don't think it's a good idea. For me."

"I understand."

"Keep this between us, please. It would hurt Andy if he knew I told you this."

"Of course. Hadn't thought otherwise."

With this new-found knowledge, I thought I had the answer as to why Andy wasn't baptized yet. I planned to ask him probing questions until the truth came out. The desires of one's heart for another person would never surpass the desires for everlasting salvation for one's soul and the desire to sit by God for eternity. It was common sense. Also, I had the spirit on my side. It was a simple matter of bringing the spirit into the room so Andy could get the confirmation needed to make the right decision.

I heard Andy's GTO coming from about two miles away. The headers coming out of those two chrome tail pipes made it sound like a supersonic jet. Hampton was not happy that Andy was coming over on a Sunday afternoon. The start of P-Day had slowly crept into Sunday night, then Sunday afternoon. It was now to the point that we didn't schedule dinners or appointments after church and pretty much started P-Day then. We weren't playing basketball, but the suits came off and Elder Hampton had his Walkman on. I didn't resist this; not with Hampton. It was a catch-22 with Hampton. I'd heard rumblings about Hampton's past. Not that he caused major problems, just his reputation for being lazy. My position was that if he was going to be lazy, then let him be lazy with me. It wouldn't do any good to put him with another missionary and have that companion complain to President Carlson and eventually request a transfer, only to have the president place the lazy missionary with another hard-working missionary, causing *him* to complain to President Carlson. So I kept my mouth shut, worked when I could, and tried to keep Hampton happy and content rather than make an absolute miserable time for both of us.

"It's just Andy. He's *hardly* an investigator. Come on in; it will only take an hour or two, and then we can do our laundry or head over to the Woodsides." I walked over to him; he looked sullen.

Hampton was such a kid, it seemed. "Always good shows on Sunday night at the Woodsides. Come on, if we hurry we can get laundry and head over to the Woodsides, grab some leftovers, and have a great night." This got Hampton rolling his eyes, at least.

"And what are we doing with Andy? We've given him both the First and the Second. He doesn't want to commit to baptism, so what next?" Hampton asked, jumping to the floor from his bed, showing his displeasure by throwing his Walkman on the bed rather than just setting it down.

"I thought we could review the First and Second. Not spending much time on them, as he is already familiar with them. Then we will probe him as to why no commitment." I didn't tell Elder Hampton what Monica told me at church. I didn't see the point. Sometimes I figured that if it weren't a question or statement about the *Greatest Hits* album of Journey, then Hampton would just as soon let me handle everything. So I did.

* * * * *

"Andy, how are you doing today? Come on in," I said, opening the door and waving Andy in. "Missed you at church today."

"I know. Sorry about that. I was up late last night watching *Terminator* and just kinda slept in and then got some things done this morning."

"That's OK. I'm really just giving you a hard time. How was *Terminator*?"

"You haven't seen it? It's out on rental. I should have brought it over."

"Don't see movies, remember."

"No way! I didn't know that. Two years and no movies? Not even rentals?"

"Not even rentals."

"Man, I don't think I could do it, Elder Dorsey. Really, I don't think I could. I can handle all the other stuff, you know. Like going to church and paying tithing." He could see me raise my eyebrows a bit at this statement. "Monica told me about tithing a long time ago. I know you guys haven't taught me anything about it, but I know that she pays money to the Church to be a member."

"Well, it's not *quite* like that, but we will talk about it sometime. So you don't think you could be a missionary, huh?"

"I don't think so. Like today, me coming over is like a big event, isn't it?"

"Well, sure. You are one of our investigators, and that's what we live for. It's fun, though. We enjoy your company as a person as much as we enjoy sharing our message with you."

"I know. I can tell. Both you and Hampton would be pretty normal guys if you weren't on your missions."

"What?" I said with a big grin, "We're not normal?"

"No, no. You *are* normal. But you know, the lifestyle, the day-to-day things you do. They are a little different."

"I know what you mean."

"Where's Elder Hampton?"

"I'm back here! Throwing a tie on for you, Andy."

"Don't worry about me. You guys could wear jeans as far as I'm concerned," Andy said.

The mission rule that stated we had to be in our shirt and ties at all times other than the few hours on P-day was as much for us as it was for the members and investigators. It is known that people act different when they are wearing a white shirt and tie, and they are looked at and treated different. Andy was right when he said that we would be pretty normal guys if it weren't for the mission, and that's what we wanted to portray at that point. We wanted him to see us as different; we wanted everyone to see us as different. One way—an easy way—was to wear white shirts, ties, and name tags, and to keep our hair short.

"So what are we doing today?" Elder Hampton asked as he came into the room with his tie loose around his neck. I thought that wasn't something he should say. He knew we had talked about it, but he probably just wasn't thinking. That was the difference with Hampton—he didn't try to hurt other people (or at least me); he just didn't think. There was a difference when people were smart enough to know better versus when they just didn't know any better and didn't think before they spoke. So it didn't bother me; it was just Hampton. And I still liked him. I'd never keep in touch with him, emulate anything about him or tell anyone in the world about him, but as a companion, he was easy. He was a person who didn't affect me in any way, whether good or bad.

"We are going to review briefly the first two Discussions, like we did last time. We are going to teach the Third and Fourth and see what Andy is willing to commit to." Elder Hampton looked surprised at my candid response and sat down. "Andy, do you remember the First and Second Discussions?"

"Sure. The First talks about being with our families forever and the Second talks about Joseph Smith and his gold plates," Andy said.

"That's pretty good, Andy. I can tell you've had these a few times. Do you know what the Third and Fourth talk about?" I asked. He said he didn't, so I asked the quiet Elder Hampton to explain.

"Well, Andy, the Third talks about the commandments that we need to follow in order to be with Jesus Christ someday," Elder Hampton said.

"Like what?" Asked Andy.

"We will go into detail in a few minutes, Andy. First, just a touch of what they are about," I said.

Elder Hampton continued explaining the Fourth. "The Fourth Discussion explains the law of tithing and the importance of giving what we can."

"The law of tithing? Giving up ten percent of your income? Man, do you guys *have* to do that?"

"The money we get already has had the tithing taken out, so we don't to need while on our mission," Elder Hampton said. I hoped Andy wouldn't inquire further, because technically we should have been paying tithing on what we received each month if we were living to the letter of the law. I made a mental note to ask President Carlson about it during the next interview or in my weekly letter. I wondered whether he would respond in a letter or a phone call. I'm not sure if I'd ever asked him something needing an immediate response.

After reviewing and teaching through the Fourth Discussion and feeling the spirit in the room, I went in for the closure. Andy had agreed with the importance of tithing, the sacredness of abstaining from premarital sex, and the debilitating effects on the body that drugs and alcohol had, to the point where he understood why God had each commandment.

Although we didn't get strong commitments from him concerning the two big ones—sex and drugs—I felt I was prompted by the spirit to progress with the Discussions to find out what was really going on with Andy and where he was with the Church. There was really only one way to do it.

"Andy, you have been taught the first four Discussions and seem to agree with what we are explaining as the word of God. You've read the passage in Third Nephi talking about the visit of Jesus Christ to the people here on the North American Continent. When we asked you to pray about it, you even said you felt the spirit. Would you agree, Andy, that you felt the spirit and feel the teachings we share with you are true?"

"Oh, yeah. I *do* think what you've taught me is true. I believe it."

"Then Andy, at this time, we would like to offer you the chance to follow in the footsteps of Jesus Christ and be baptized as he was."

"I *want* to be baptized Elder Dorsey, I do. There is one thing, though, that I don't think I could give up."

"What is it?" Elder Hampton asked, being more interested in what it was, instead of what this poor man was struggling with.

"I don't know if you guys can relate at all. I'm sure you can't, but what I can't give up is my morning high."

"What do you mean, *your morning high*? I asked. I'd never heard of a morning high.

"I mean my morning toke—my morning marijuana. I like smoking a little marijuana in the morning to get me going. I'm a wake-and-baker."

"Oh," I said, not knowing what to say. "That...ah...would be something that you would have to give up in order to be baptized. You are right about that."

"I know. It came up in the Word of Wisdom. Although you didn't ask about specifics, I knew that marijuana was one that wouldn't be excused. The thing is, I don't have a problem with drinking or any other drugs. And even with marijuana, it's just a little hit in the morning. I mean, it's pretty harmless. I'm not just saying that to rationalize my use of drugs; I really feel like this. And because of this feeling, I don't think I want to give it up."

So many thoughts were going through my head. Not only did I not know what to say, but I didn't know what I thought. Where was the experienced senior companion I needed?

"I know how you feel, Andy," Elder Hampton started saying. "I smoked pot before my mission, and it really is somewhat of a harmless drug. I didn't smoke every day, more like on weekends with friends. It was a lot of fun, though. Made me feel good and made me laugh a lot too. But I can understand it would be tough to give up." This was the *last* thing I wanted Elder Hampton to do, understand Andy's problem. We were not here to tell Andy we understood, even if we did. Andy needed to understand that drugs, illegal ones at that, were an abomination in the eyes of God. They would keep a person out of the presence of God, just like premarital sex or murder. There was no difference. I didn't want Hampton telling Andy—or any investigator—that he had done it before his mission, and here he was—right out in the mission field—teaching the saving principles of redemption that we as missionaries were there to deliver with the spirit of the Holy Ghost.

And then Elder Hampton made light of it, as if it was something we all did and just got over. I didn't know what to say or do. I just let Hampton take over. Among the feelings I had was jealously. Andy was a great guy, and smoking marijuana just didn't seem serious enough to keep him out of heaven. Confused, jealous, and mad at Hampton, I sat back on the couch, taking in the remainder of the Discussion and talk with Andy.

Elder Hampton did a good job making Andy feel OK about being a pot smoker and giving up his chances for eternal life with God. I was glad he did. I'm not sure I would have. I probably would have posed the question "Is pot so important to you, Andy, that you are willing to give up eternal salvation? A seat next to God himself?" This question wouldn't have been fair, but it had been asked of me countless times over the past fifteen years.

With this thought pattern going on in my mind, I realized that these questions weren't fair to me either, at any time in my life, by anyone posing them.

While Andy drove off, the 450 engine purring, I thought about him and his life. And I wondered what I was doing out on a mission.

* * * * *

The Woodsides had gone out of town and asked us to stay at their house for the next week. As missionaries, we weren't allowed to housesit, but as it wasn't in the *Missionary Rule Book*—what we called the "White Bible"—that every missionary carried in his shirt pocket, we didn't ask the President about it; we just did it. Sister Woodside had stocked the pantry and freezer with food for the week. All we had to do was feed the dogs.

We kept it quiet that we were staying there so the members wouldn't know. Once again, the fewer people who knew things, the better. We went to the apartment every day to check our messages and make any phone calls, another attempt to hide what we were doing. I thought about what we were hiding and, really, all we were hiding was watching television. When we got home at night, or if we stayed in late in the morning, instead of being out on our bikes riding around looking for people to baptize, we might watch a little television. I imagined these two twenty-year-old boys, and the worst thing they were doing in their lives was watching an hour or two of television. Oh, if parents had only that problem with their boys growing into manhood, instead of worrying about the girls they were dating, the group of people they were hanging around with, or if they were getting to all their classes in college. All that parents had to worry about was whether their boys were obeying the rules in the mission field. I think the parents' only fear was that their boys might be sent home—not the fear of their boys losing eternal salvation, but rather the fear of their own embarrassment.

Staying at the Woodsides was a break from not only the monotony of the work, but also from Elder Keene and Elder Lampson. The to elders were easy to live with, but even so, a break was a relief.

Living at the Woodsides brought on its own set of discomforts, though. On a night that both Elder Hampton and I decided to stay in, I found out what he was doing alone in the Woodsides bedroom when I wasn't listening or around.

Most of the nights we just watched television or read, in the same room; on the occasional night when we both had our own agendas on television or just couldn't stand being around each other, he would watch television in the Woodsides' master bedroom, the room he had taken to sleep in, and I would be in the front room on the couch. While getting up to grab more free frozen food, I heard unfamiliar noises coming from the master suite. The noises were only unfamiliar because they were so out of place on the mission. The sounds were of people having sex. It wasn't Hampton, which I was comforted knowing, but rather channel 56, the Playboy channel. At first, the thoughts of Elder Bell came back haunting. Was Elder Hampton calling up and getting pay-per-view? Would I have to explain this to the Woodsides? Was he in there on the bed masturbating? Was President Carlson going to find out? Was I going to get sent home? All these questions hit me at once. I was mad and confused, not knowing what to do; mad that I had to even deal with this. I was already dealing with my day-to-day growing laziness towards missionary work and now had to try to consider a companion whacking off to Playboy on a member's bed.

I was very quiet in socked feet on the tiled floor; I was able to get close to the open bedroom door without Elder Hampton knowing I was there. I listened to the noise coming from the television. I think it was two women making out. As mad and confused as I was, it was nice to hear. It had been a long time since I'd actually heard anything like that. I didn't hear things like it before my mission very often, but just by being in the world, a person was exposed to it. So I listened for a few minutes and went back to the kitchen and yelled, "Elder Hampton, what you watching?"

"Oh nothing. Just flipping channels," he said. I heard the noises change as he started flipping channels. I gave him a minute and then went into the bedroom. He wasn't naked and didn't have a big blanket over him. I trusted that he was probably flipping around, came across it, and watched it for a few minutes.

I then remembered that the Woodsides had the Playboy channel. One afternoon, Brother Woodside thought he was being funny. I'd just come in from playing basketball in his back yard, and he said, "Elder Dorsey, come in here a minute." He was in his bedroom and I went in.

"How do you like that?" he asked, pointing to the television as I came in. He was just busting up inside, waiting to laugh. I turned around and looked up at the television, and there were naked girls on it. He started laughing, and I quickly turned around—facing him, television behind me—and played it off like he was just the funniest guy.

"Well I don't see that every day," I said. And that was about it. He was being funny, and I didn't think much of it. I did imagine him and Sister Woodside watching it, though. I had a small crush on Sister Woodside. The image of her and her husband watching Playboy didn't help with my crush, nor being alone with my thoughts.

I let the Playboy channel and Elder Hampton incident pass without any comment to Elder Hampton or anyone else. No zone leader or district leader would need to be informed, and I would never say a word about it; it would have been extremely embarrassing to Elder Hampton.

The habit of taking little action was becoming common with my companions, I realized. I wondered how things would be different if I told the president or a zone leader every time one of my comps broke the rules, or if I told them every time *I* did. As happy as I was with the way I handled things, I did think that if I didn't feel the spirit, it was because of my disregard for the rules. I played basketball on days other than P-Day, wrote letters during the week, and wrote Rachel Barrett back when she'd write me a letter (although the responding letter read like a letter to the president, describing the work going on in the area rather than an expression of romantic feelings when writing a beautiful woman). How could I ever confront another elder with rule breaking when I broke several rules a day? Even sleeping too late in the mornings or not putting in the full thirty minutes of reading the *Book of Mormon* were things I struggled with. With these thoughts came other thoughts—from teaching Andy and how he would not sit by God for eternity because of his pot smoking to how

I wasn't going to sit by God either, because of the countless rules I broke, while fully aware of the consequences. Was I not even more at risk in keeping my place at the side of the Lord? All of these thoughts I tried to keep out of my head, trying not to feel like a hypocrite each night when praying to God. When I did feel this way, I didn't pray.

CHAPTER 13

Once I got the call that I was being transferred, I gave up on Saugus. I was drained. I'd been in the same ward for seven months. I knew all the names of the kids in each of the families. I felt comfortable enough when at a member's home to walk to the refrigerator and open it up to see what was inside. I had the approximate mileage to and from every location in the area—members' homes, church, stake center, or local watch repair store—I knew them all. I had since stopped learning and possibly even stopped caring. It was time for me to move on, and obviously the Lord saw it too.

There was a note on the back door of the small garage apartment:

Elder Dorsey,

We are at Smiths around the corner. Take a left on Soledad Canyon Road and we are at Soledad Canyon Road. Corolla parked in driveway.

Elder Nelson

I hadn't seen Elder Nelson since we served together in the MTC. We weren't companions but did serve in the same district, sharing a room and spending each day together for two months.

Elder Nelson was the oldest missionary in the mission. He was twenty-nine. He had been a member his whole life but wasn't ready to go on a mission when he was nineteen, so he waited. At least that's how he explained it when asked.

Brother Woodside drove me around the corner, and we quickly found the Smiths' house. I knocked on the door and I guessed it was my future companion who answered the door.

"Elder Burton!" I said as he opened the door, "I'm Elder Dorsey." I threw my hand out, and Elder Burton put out his soft, pasty hand.

In a southern drawl, he said, "Elder Dorsey, nice to meet you.

Elder Nelson is upstairs. Should I get him for you?"

"I need to put my stuff in the trunk of your car first. You want to give me a hand?"

"Sure." Elder Burton moved his three-hundred-pound body out the front door and followed me to the Corolla, where Brother Woodside waited patiently by the opened door of his diesel Ford F350 truck.

Brother Woodside rolled his eyes when we made eye contact. "Elder Burton, this is Brother Woodside." I said.

"Hi," Elder Burton said, putting out his hand.

"Hey," Brother Woodside muttered, and shook hands.

I had a car—a red Corolla. We loaded my hard suitcases into the trunk on top of hundreds of pamphlets handed out with Discussions. Light blue, red, yellow, and brown littered the bottom of the trunk like confetti. I was going to suggest to Elder Burton that a box might be a better place for the pamphlets, but I didn't.

Brother Woodside hugged me. I knew I would miss him. We had spent hours talking about his life, and I had spent hours looking at his wife. He wanted me to come and work for him after my mission. I thought about it when he had mentioned it the first time but later thought it would be a pretty miserable life. I was tired of getting dirty from Sheetrock. Working construction before the mission pretty much made the decision for me, although I found it extremely easy work and could imagine falling back on it if desperate.

Elder Nelson grinned seeing me. "Elder Dorsey, how are you?" I'd forgotten how eloquent his speech was.

"Elder Nelson, good to see you," I said, matching his excitement at seeing me. He was striking, with jet-black hair perfectly straightened on his head and high Indian cheekbones.

"So you're the new zone leader? Wow, Elder; good job," Elder Nelson said, looking at me just a moment before being distracted by the mechanical clunk of the printer.

"Yeah," I said, dismissing the "zone leader" comment. He should have been a zone leader and assistant by now; everyone in the mission could learn from him. He had wanted it since leaving the MTC, I'd noticed. "So where are you going? Bakersfield?"

"Bakersfield. I've heard both good and bad: terrible location, but great members. You see my theory: God puts the best members in the hottest weather because that's the only taste of hell they will ever get."

"I'd never thought of it like that. I like that theory."

"It's true, man," he said while getting his printout; that was probably some doctrinal theory on the perception of heaven versus perception of a good life on earth or something understandable by only a few.

"So you're looking forward to it then?" I asked.

"Sure. It's all part of the experience," he said. He could have said "experiment" and it would have been more believable.

"Nice," I said, slowly smiling wide. "Good way to look at it. Going to miss San Luis?" I asked.

He stopped shuffling with his paper and looked at me. "This is a great area. You are going to love it."

The apartment was located above the garage of two Cal Poly Tech professors. It had a sweeping view of the college, Santa Lucia Mountains, tennis courts, and the track. It was unbelievable; I knew it would be a great place to live. It was sad, though. Such a great place wasted on two guys serving a mission. It would have been a great college pad to have girls over. But no, it was lived in by foreigners who wore short-sleeve shirts and ties.

The view also had other added benefits: the women—hundreds of them. There were the tennis players with the short skirts. The California sun had bleached their hair out from their natural colors; their tanned skin shimmered against their faded cotton clothes.

These women were living a dream, it seemed. They were playing tennis at one of the most beautiful college campuses in the world, under a loving sun.

The men with long hair looked silly when they hit at balls—hair going crazy, they looked out of control. And some had shaved their heads. I thought about what kind of hair I would have if I were playing tennis; thought it would be short, like it was. My curls were threatened by those with long, straight hair. And long, straight hair was a foe not to threaten.

The men all had their shirts off, thrown to the back of the court, lying among water bottles, Walkmans, and duffle bags. Their styles of each of plays were as different as their haircuts. One was a double-hander, like Monica Seles, and was the first guy I'd seen play like that. It was a powerful play. Each of his hits sounded as if it were shot from a cannon. Surprisingly, though, the shots were a little softer coming to the other side. It seemed so, at least from my spot on the grass.

I had on a baseball hat, sunglasses, shorts, and a T-shirt. I was incognito—something I'd never done before my mission. It didn't concern me in the least, and I enjoyed it. No one other than the members would recognize me. I never worried. Elder Burton was up in the apartment. He didn't want to watch tennis practice, and I didn't want to sit in the apartment—well, at least not *this* afternoon.

Technically, we were in each other's view because he had binoculars. I told him to look at me occasionally, so I would feel good about what we were doing. It was only for a few hours. Although Elder Burton and I got along just wonderfully, time spent by oneself in solitude is healthy and necessary for thoughts to flourish. So I was flourishing while watching tennis practice.

In high school, I had a friend named Jared, who was known for his ability to watch a sport and then go out and play the sport better than anyone else on the team. Jared was the star on both the football and baseball teams. He had a natural bodybuilder physique and was the strongest one in the weight room. He was in my circle of friends, and all were close in our circle. He was the star of the teams. I was so impressed that he had this ability that I thought I should have it too. I started watching sports differently. I watched and learned what the athletes did. I would slow down in my mind what I saw and practice it later.

With the tennis players in front of me, I had tried each one of their styles in the early-morning hours, when no one else was awake. Elder Burton would stand at the net, acting as a virtual ball machine for my endless bucket of balls. Elder Burton was becoming an extremely good ball machine. He used my oversized racquet, putting it right in front of his wide body on the other side of the net. At five-five and twice as wide as me, he made a fun and forgiving target. As bad as I hit a ball, he was able to reach, scoot, and surprisingly hop to it, getting it back to me on the side I was hitting from. I was impressed with him and knew that his football stories were real. Not that I ever really doubted him, but just from physical appearance, it was hard to believe. I saw his athleticism come out and he saw it too. He never once grumbled about rolling out of bed, throwing on a hat, and walking down to the tennis court. Possibly the ideal situation would have been to have a couple of hot coffees before playing, but we had our hats and the cool morning air.

After hitting four buckets of balls to Elder Burton, I would hit two buckets of serves while Elder Burton enjoyably walked the court, picking up the rolling balls with the bottom of the bucket. He never asked the time, or when we would be done. Not one word ever on what we were doing or not doing. He liked the change from being a companion of Elder Nelson. He tried to tell me these things, but I didn't want to hear about Elder Nelson and him. I really liked Elder Nelson, but I knew him and didn't need any reinforcement from Elder Burton. So I was a poor conversationalist on the topic, but that didn't matter with all the other things we talked about. I insisted on Elder Burton telling me about his football practices after school and the games in front of the lights and the kids on the bleachers. Throughout the day, the conversation was never lacking. He told me about his swimming pool that his mom bought when their dad died. How he and his sister had pool parties. This was a little hard to imagine, as I'd seen the picture of his sister.

After the balls were picked up and with my racquets in their bags, we opened the metal door of the court and walked out. We both felt a little anxious when using that door. It felt so athletic. My game had improved since Chatsworth, and that was reassuring. I thought the biggest hindrance was my inability to watch any tennis. I watched what I could, but without any instructional videos, I was at a disadvantage. So I took lessons, private lessons from a local pro—my first time playing with a local pro. I didn't really know what constituted being a local pro, but he had a flier taped to the court. I tore off one of the perforated number tags from the bottom and called him. He asked me what type of player I was, and I said I didn't know. He asked me how often I broke my strings, and I said every three times playing. "You hit hard?" he asked.

"Sometimes. I mean, I try to hit everything hard, but then they go out or in the net," I said.

"There's a park downtown. It's across from the mission—Edgewater. What time would work to meet?" he asked. I knew what park he was talking about and instantly pictured myself playing there.

It wasn't the most private of places, but who would expect a missionary playing tennis on a day other than P-day?

"I know where that is. Any time, really. My schedule is pretty open during the day. Nights are a little harder," I said.

"How's Tuesday around eleven? That work for you?"

"That will work.

"OK, see you then."

"Oh, wait!" I hoped I'd caught him before he hung up. "What do I bring?"

"Just your racquets, that's it!"

"Great, thanks. See you Tuesday," I said.

My efforts increased for the next two days so I'd be ready for the local pro. Elder Burton was as excited as I was thinking about the lesson with the local pro. He wasn't planning on taking a lesson himself, but he would be right there with me, listening to every word and drilling me on them later. I think Elder Burton resented the local pro in the end for taking over as the current authority on tennis, a position Elder Burton thought he held securely.

The local pro turned out to be everything he claimed. "Why don't we hit a few balls so I can see how you play," he said and started walking towards his side of the court.

I was nervous. I hadn't been critiqued in tennis since a sophomore video for the tennis team. Our coach was a woman, and the guys joked that she got off on the videos after hours. I didn't know if this was true but found the video helpful. We all sat in a room and watched each other return balls. They laughed at my swing. They said I looked like a cartoon. I didn't prepare at all before the swing and waited till the last second. I didn't think I was so bad to warrant such ridicule from an ill-perfected swing. My strength could have at least been acknowledged—the force with which I was able to hit with despite a poor swing. But none of these comments came out; only laughter. So I quit the tennis team. But the jitters quickly passed when I hit a perfect forehand to the local pro. Three more successful forehands and I was feeling good. I was a decent tennis player. I could hit with a local pro.

"Try some with your backhand," he said from the other side of the net as he hit the next shot to the far side, making it impossible for me to run around the ball and hit a forehand.

"Sure," I said and whacked what felt like a softball into the net. He hit another ball to my backhand. Set up so perfectly, I didn't even have to move my feet. The bounce of the ball hit perfect with my swing, and again I hit a two-handed, awkward swing into the net. It worked for Courier and should have worked for me. Jim Courier was my favorite player on tour. He epitomized what I envisioned myself to be as a tennis player. He was number one in the world, on the cover of *Sports Illustrated*, and drove a black Porsche. He played with a strong English forehand and hit with the widest stance in the game, a technique that made him the hardest-hitting player in the game. I had adopted the forehand technique and, although not mastered, it was an incredible weapon of the serve and open court. Courier's serve was a short toss with a powering topspin, causing the ball to kick out of the court on impact with the ground. It was a beautiful serve, and again I brought it into my game. His quick-footed, short, two-handed backhand was a thing of wonder to his peers. Next to Agassi, Courier had the best return of serve in the game. Although the two-handed backhand was a bit constraining, one would think, in reaching for serves, Courier worked it. So in his game I found mine.

"How long you been hitting with the two-handed backhand?"

"A few years. I started with a one handed, but thought I would like the power of the two handed."

"Well you have plenty of power, however you hit. So let's not worry about that. Would you like to get a backhand today?" He asked.

"Yeah. Would love to," I said. Then wrinkling my brow towards the sun, I added, "In one day? Really?"

"Sure. Let's see what we can do." He showed me how he could hit a ball off the bounce anywhere he wanted to with his one-handed backhand. He then powered a couple of rockets to the back of the court. "Plenty of power too. Watch my arm, see the pendulum look of the racquet. I'm just letting my arm swing like a pendulum and it's hitting the ball. You try, without hitting, just letting your arm swing like this." He let his right arm swing naturally like a pendulum. His long arm with golden hair bleached by the sun just kept swinging back and forth, back and forth. Occasionally, he would drop a ball out of his pocket and show me how, without even changing his swing, he could still hit it and position the ball. He started dropping balls for me, his hand just inches away from the end of my racquet. "You are a quick learner, Elder Dorsey." I had hit every ball he dropped perfectly to the other side. "OK, try a little power now. Don't change the pendulum; just use a little more legs." I did and hit with a power I'd never felt on that side of the ball.

He dropped about a bucket of balls with me, encouraging me with each hit. "Good." Bounce. "Good." Bounce. "Good." Bounce.

"OK, I'll hit to you from the other side. Remember, you want to go towards the ball, get it on the bounce; don't wait for it to start falling. You will feel it."

The experience sharpened more when I had balls being hit at me. I'd never felt the power of hitting on the up-bounce of the ball.

That tidbit, along with the new backhand swing, seemed to give me a complete game—or at least the hope to someday have a decent game. My backhand ended up being more highly reliable than my forehand, and I started depending on it for my games—games between the wall and me, mostly. The local pro charged forty-five dollars an hour, and we had spent two hours together. I asked him if he thought I needed more private lessons. He said that I should practice what I learned and try to get some more playing time. I was a little surprised, because I figured this was the way he made his living.

I took his advice and practiced every day. Elder Burton continually told me how much I was improving. We were becoming close in our secrets. He allowed me to have a piece of a life that was off limits to missionaries.

"What are you reading? I said, quickly putting the words together.

"Comics," Elder Burton said, lying on his side on his queen-size bed. The sun had just fallen, and he was going to need a light soon. I got up and turned on the overhead studio light.

"What one?" I asked.

"*The Punisher*."

"Is it good?" I asked.

"Yeah. You've never read *The Punisher*?" He asked, putting it down and looking at me with his big smile. He pushed himself up and sat on the bed.

"I've never read comics. I wish I had, though. I feel I've missed out on something."

"You have missed out. Here, take *The Punisher*." He picked up the comic beside him and showed me the cover. "This guy is really cool." There was a big bodybuilder in a dark blue and black suit.

"I want to read it," I said, reaching for it. I thumbed through it quickly and Elder Burton looked for the signs on my face of enjoyment.

"You'll like it."

"Oh. Aren't you reading it, though?"

"No. You read it. I have plenty."

"How did you get them?" I asked.

"I brought them from home. I packed them in my suitcase."

"You know they are unauthorized," I said, trying to hold my smile in, but at the last word it won and showed through.

"Yeah, that will stop you. Along with everything else we do," he said, to my slight discomfort. I instantly thought how bad we were. Playing tennis in the morning and running at night.

"Where do you get them?" I asked.

"Comic book store. There is one here." "Have you been?"

"Not yet."

I read *The Punisher* that Elder Burton handed me. It was number 112. After 112, I read 110 and 111. Then I read 113. The next morning I suggested we go into town to the comic book store. Elder Burton was thrilled to be my guide. He talked that morning about his love of comics and his first encounter with them. He told me how much he hated the thought of going on his mission, leaving behind his comic books. He didn't mind rereading them. In fact, he enjoyed it. The comic book store was an oasis from the mission. I didn't feel out of place in my shirt and tie—not because I fit in; rather that I was lost in thoughts and sights from all the comic books, posters, glass cases, and the man behind the counter. We were two of a few people in the store. Elder Burton was able to talk freely and point out the different comics. He showed me *The Punisher* section, and I was thrilled to see so many back copies: plenty of reading. Seeing the number, I didn't think I would ever run out of reading material. I bought three back issues, starting at number 97. I was sure that the three would get me off to a good start. Elder Burton had read every issue and had most of them at home. He offered to send for them, but I assured him that it would not be necessary.

I held up my bag of new comic books, "I think I'm covered for a while with reading comics. I need to pace myself."

* * * * *

It wasn't P-Day, but we were downtown with a city to see. We made our way to the mission, the founding building in the small town. San Luis Obispo was named after Saint Louis, a 13th century bishop of Toulouse, France. The whole emphasis on sainthood in the Catholic Church was not shared by the other religions of the world. The Mormons neither celebrated nor, in my recollection, even acknowledged their existence. It was in our name, though: The Church of Jesus Christ and Latter-day Saints. But the saints, in that sense, referred to a congregation or believer, not equivalent to a life-long devotee of the higher law in the Catholic Church.

Growing up, conversations with my non-Mormon friends consisted of frustration on my side and confusion on theirs. The friend would inevitably raise his eyebrows or quickly change the subject when I explained the reason for not being at baseball practice was because I had to go to Priest Quorum. "You are a priest?" Confusion would be the first look, instantly taken over by the bewilderment that I was a priest. I don't think I really did believe it; rather, I just went to Priest Quorum on Wednesday nights, as it was the thing to do.

"Elder Burton, you have some time this afternoon? I thought we could take the tour of the mission. This will help us when building relationships of trust with the future Mormons of the community. With us showing an interest in their town, they may show an interest in us."

Elder Burton laughed. He thought I was funny and told me often. I noticed that he seemed to enjoy the pace of our days. Of course, with comic books in hand, how could he not want to give a little? "I think I can find the time, Elder. Let's go." And he headed towards the small wooden sign that looked antique, as if St. Louis himself had hung it there and carved *Free Tours*. Elder Burton had a bit of a hop in his step. I think he was glad to be on his mission. Or was it that he was glad to be with me, I wondered for the first time. I'd learned that I could live with a person and not get to know them very well. But the companions I had, the ones I shared rooms with and spent twenty-four hours a day with, I could get to know them. It was a good theory, really. The feet of God seemed to be grounded in the theory that if a person is truly known, then all could see his true intentions and would see that they were good. All his intentions somewhere were rooted in goodness towards others. I didn't believe this, but I did notice that I enjoyed my companions more than I did the other missionaries in my zone, district. I didn't have to live with anyone but Elder Burton here. I think what really made the difference was the pillow talk—not cuddled next to each other after passionate sex, no. It was the times after ten o'clock when two young men should have been sleeping with thoughts of future prayers in their heads, but instead stayed up and talked about anything but the Mormon Church and anything but mission life. Like starving in the desert with speech representing food, I enjoyed talking about life outside. Because of this, my companions seemed to open up. I wanted details of what they did and when and who they did it with. And they shared. I noticed I didn't have nearly the fun adventures they'd had, but if they described well enough, then I would be there with them.

It was one thing when stares would follow us down a residential street or on a busy downtown center, but when walking into a Catholic mission—name tags blazing in the sun—we were, it seemed, instantly attacked. Two Catholic priests came towards us as soon as we set foot on the dirt of the mission. We were treated like an unknown power—or a known but unwelcome power—that invaded the mission. We meant no harm to anyone there or to his way of believing in God. We had no intentions to proselytize within the mission. We couldn't anyway, as we were the only visitors. It appeared that weekdays in the mission were reserved as quiet days for the priests.

We introduced ourselves as Elder Dorsey and Elder Burton, with the Church of Jesus Christ of Latter-day Saints. The priest closest to us along with the younger of the two welcomed us and said his name was Father Patrick. He said if we had any questions to let him know and that there was an information desk, which he pointed to, that would be of help also. I explained that we were new in the area and we liked to see the city where we were serving. I didn't explain that we would use this information to help build relationships of trust with the people we met in San Luis Obispo in hopes that they would get baptized and become Mormon. He didn't seem to mind that we were there; after all, we were kids, really. Kids with the power of God, yes, but this didn't seem to worry him. He left us to wander the grounds of the old mission. "It was nice meeting both of you. And again, any questions, feel free to ask."

The mission was composed of several buildings made of wood and stone. The wood was not painted and had taken on the look of an old, unpainted farmhouse. The paths around the mission were dirt. There were some brick buildings, the biggest one being the chapel. I noticed that the chapel wasn't unlike a Mormon chapel. Of course, the mission had been around since before Joseph Smith had even received the vision from God that he was going to be bringing his Church back to the earth. In that respect, the age gave it a sense of sacredness, something that Mormon buildings didn't have. I think the oldest building I'd seen had been in California on the mission, right down in the Valley, the old Van Nuys building, with the raised baptismal font in the back of the chapel. These thoughts quickly led me to thoughts of the Morels, thoughts I went through quickly. How was their addition coming? How was the Jeep, covered in blackberry brambles? How were the kids, and did they ever think of me as I often thought of them? These thoughts abated quickly and I was back in the chapel, following Elder Burton.

"First tour of a Catholic mission, Elder Burton?" I asked.

"Yep. Yours?" he replied, not looking at me but finding the next doorway out of the chapel.

"First one. I'm surprised really that I haven't taken in more of the local history in my areas. Although it's not exactly what we are here for, there seems no better time to get to know a little about a state that is new to me."

It was Elder Burton's first area, so I wasn't surprised when he said he hadn't seen any of the attractions either.

What I noticed was my total disregard for the mission. It meant nothing to me. The history that I was imagining and slowly putting together with the facts in white pamphlets seemed so unnecessary. Did the Dark Ages mean nothing to these people? Would God's Church be so lost and still be on the earth? Why could it be so clear to me? Because God's Church was here, on the earth now, and when the mission was built, it wasn't here. Therefore the whole thing, the whole damn mission, was for naught. The work that went into it, the sweat by so many men and women and their children, was for nothing. Why couldn't the people see it now, at least? Give the Mormon Church a chance; pray to know the truth and it would be revealed. But no, these Catholics believed in their past, their missions, and their traditions—traditions that would eventually take them to hell—that is, those Catholics whom I couldn't save during my short tenure.

On our way out of the mission, Father Patrick wished us well in our journey and hoped we had enjoyed the tour of the mission. I spoke for both of us when I said we had. I wish I could have shared my feelings of the uselessness of the mission today—and even when it was originally built—with Father Patrick. Looking back now, I'm sure his perspective on it would have eased my temperament at the time and opened up my mind to a new way of thinking for the remainder of my days in San Luis Obispo and beyond. But that didn't happen. I stayed ignorant of possible other meanings behind the mission, as I'd been taught to do. I started noticing that we, as missionaries, were not there in California to learn anything, but rather to teach—teach every person we came in contact with yet learn nothing from them, although learning was unavoidable if a certain mindset was reached. It was that mindset that I longed for—constant learning from the people, the places, and the sociology.

From the mission, we walked through Town Square. It was literally a square: four sides guarded by stores, the mission, a waterway, and the street going out of town. There was a fountain in the middle, the water trickling down after rising up from an underground spring. We read the history on the fountain: it had been part of the building enthusiasm of the mission. It was well kept, and the underground spring fascinated me, as I'd never seen one. From the fountain we could see a group of people lined up on the far side of the mission. There was a covered porch with access into the mission's large kitchen.

"Why are all those people lined up there, Elder Burton?" I asked, knowing that he didn't have the answer but still trying to make conversation.

"I don't know. They look like bums, though." And they did. I hadn't noticed. The clothes were mismatched and threadbare, having long ago ceased to function as any kind of weather deterrent and acting strictly as a cover for their dirty, naked bodies.

"They do; you are right," I said. "Let's get a little closer." We walked to a nearby bench for a closer view and sat to rest our feet.

"It's part of the mission. They are probably feeding them. Like a soup line."

"Why don't we do soup lines? The Church, why doesn't the Church do soup lines?"

"I don't know. Maybe we're not that kind of church," Elder Burton said. I was amused at the simplicity and the depth of his response.

"What about back in Kentucky? Did you have soup lines there? I mean, the Church—did it have soup lines? I don't think Seattle did. I don't remember any. Nor was I ever asked to help."

"I don't think we had them in Kentucky. I think I would have known. My mom would have been in on that."

"Who would know? Who could we ask in the ward about this?" I asked Elder Burton. He was still the authority on the people in the ward.

"Sister Day, the Relief Society President, would know about it. I'll call her when we get home."

"Great. I'd like to do this. If nothing else, I'd like to stand in line with the Catholics," I said, thinking about Burton's readiness to help, call, and do anything for me. Although I was the zone leader and could request that he do really anything I didn't want to do, I never had to ask. He volunteered to take whatever he could off my plate. And my plate was never full. He made the calls for appointments, dinners, and splits. He made the arrangements for all of our affairs. I asked him about it once, and he said that Elder Nelson didn't let him do anything. Elder Burton felt like Elder Nelson thought he couldn't handle it. I wasn't sure what this meant, as calling to confirm a dinner appointment or splits for an evening was something that was impossible to do wrong. The only possible wrong would be not doing it at all.

"Elder Burton!" we heard the sound of a woman say. I turned to Elder Burton, who was already walking toward a girl he apparently knew.

"Cami, how are you?" He said, putting out his soft white hand to a beautiful dark-haired girl. She was stunning. And as stunning girls caused me to do, I couldn't speak. I just stared, hiding as best I could, behind my sunglasses, only glancing in her direction so as not to let her know that she had just become the object of my desire. The thoughts of the town, mission, and feeding of bums had all dissipated within seconds. All my thoughts, desires, and feelings were at once melded together in noticing her. I so wished that when I started on the mission, the elders or someone—anyone—would lay their hands on my head and take away all thoughts of beautiful women, enabling me to see the souls of people and not just the outward beauty that would overshadow any tender souls I might meet.

As I still couldn't talk, I was grateful for the small talk that Elder Burton was able to continue for a few minutes, allowing me to hide in darkness behind my tinted shades. The Frog Eye sunglasses purchased from Elder Proude were giving me much-needed cover.

"Have you talked with Jason? Or I should ask, have you finished the Discussions with him?" she asked. I figured Jason was the new member Elder Burton had told me about. As he was the only person in our teaching pool, it wasn't hard to keep them straight.

"We have an appointment to teach him this week. We are on the Fifth with him. You should come."

"What night are you doing it?" she asked.

"Thursday at seven," Elder Burton said, not needing to look at his planner but having it available in his mind.

"That might work. I'll let you know. I haven't seen Jason in awhile. How is he doing?"

"Great. He is moving along in the Discussions and planning on his mission," Elder Burton said.

Jason was a full-time student at Cal Poly. He had met Cami on campus, and they dated for a while. He was introduced to Bishop Baldwin, who was an ROTC recruiter on campus, along with being a history professor. Jason and Bishop Baldwin had apparently hit it off. Elder Burton told me that they had become good friends. Jason moved rapidly through the Discussions, accepting the commitments throughout with alcohol, sex, and baptism. I would learn on my first meeting with him that he never drank nor had sex. He was a virgin when he started the Discussions, rare when sex and drinking seemed the ways of the world to non-Mormons. It was rare to meet a gentile who hadn't partaken of the forbidden fruit without the knowledge of why one shouldn't. And sometimes I didn't know if abstaining was true to bring one closer to God or just simply what I had been taught to believe. So Jason was almost finished with the New Member Discussions and then he would put school off for two years and come back when things were different. Or not different, but he would come back and be accepted into the fold more so than he would have been had he *not* gone on the mission. He would have moved up the ranks, surely, but not as far as he would hope to with a full-time mission behind him. I'd thought a lot about Jason while I was here. I thought about him going on a mission and wasn't sure he was doing the right thing, which raised some questions concerning myself.

The guys who didn't go on missions just had it rough. If they were successful in business, it wasn't because they were smart: it's because they had two extra years to make it when the other men were on the mission. If they were losers, or had no money and lots of kids, then it would forever be attributed to the unserved mission. Anytime the conversation came up about missions, there was a story to follow about Brother so-and-so and why he hadn't gone on a mission.

I was hoping that I was going to be introduced soon to Cami. I couldn't muster an introduction myself, but I could surely reply. My thoughts were losing me in the conversation and I was going to come across like an idiot if I did not engage soon.

"Cami, have you met my new companion, Elder Dorsey?" Cami looked over at me behind my sunglasses.

"Hi, Elder. Nice to meet you," she replied, not using my last name ,and she put out her hand.

"Hi, Cami. It's nice meeting you too."

Cami looked down at her watch. "Guys, I gotta go. I'll see you next week. Bye." And she walked away, her long, dark hair falling down her back and her white knitted bag hanging at her side.

"How did you like Cami?"

"Nice girl. She's in the ward, huh?

"Yeah. She's cool. I told you she dated Jason, right?"

"Yeah, you told me. What happened again?"

"I don't know. I think she might be a little too wild for Jason, but who knows. I tried to find out, but nothing." Elder Burton proved his worth as a gossiping elder. Was there anything worse than a missionary who liked hearing gossip? It was so far from what a missionary should be concerned with, yet I enjoyed hearing it and he knew I didn't mind.

Cami, being "too wild" for Jason, intrigued me, though. If she were wild, what would she be up for?

With no real prospects for investigators or new members to teach Discussions to, or building an addition onto a home, or babysitting a house,

Elder Burton and I tracted. And we did it a lot. When I'd first come into the area, we had a few names on an old whiteboard. We called them and the numbers were disconnected, so we erased the names. We both stared at the clean whiteboard. Then we proceeded to design the best whiteboard in the mission. What made it the best was subjective. Respect was held for straight lines, personal artwork, and daily quote sections. We bought a ribbon to put on it the next day to make it legitimate. What was also intriguing about the whiteboard was its emptiness.

"Elder Burton, we don't have a lot going today, have you noticed?" I asked one morning after tennis practice, personal study, and more time for sleeping, breakfast, and showers. By noon, we had done everything we had wanted to do and had a whole afternoon open.

"We seem to stay busy, though. I mean, we *have* been," he said, not putting down the comic book.

"I think we should tract. I know it sucks, but it makes ya feel good."

"You don't feel good?" he said, putting down his comic book, bringing his eyes around in my direction.

"Well, tracting can be fun." The minute I said it, I regretted it.

Burton's big grin almost wouldn't let the words out. "Tracting can be *fun*, Elder?"

Smiling with him, "Well, it's nice being out there, outside. And not much else we can do."

"OK, I'll tract. I haven't tracted much on my mission, so this will be fun to write home about," he said looking up, imagining himself writing home about the wonderful times we had tracting. It really was the stuff missions were made of.

In my vast experience of going to the best areas for tracting, I put the question to Elder Burton to decide. "Elder Burton, then *you* pick the highest peak with the best view, and we will go at once" I said in the best *Book of Mormon* warrior accent I could muster. I imagined myself one of the Two Thousand Stripling Warriors, who took up arms in the stead of their fathers because the fathers had made an oath to God not to take up arms. So the kids took up the arms that their fathers couldn't—these kids being twelve and fourteen—and they won the battle against the evil Lamanites.

So all Mormon boys grew up wanting to be like the stripling warriors. I don't know what the girls growing up wanted to be like.

"So where we headed?" I asked once we were in the car.

"Well, the hills won't have a lot of houses. There may be some long walks in between the homes."

"Elder, what if the Apostle Paul had never struck out cross-country, later finding the Galatians and converting them?" I asked smiling.

"OK, then. I'm up for it. Let's go," he said, settling into his seat, ready for an adventure.

"Do we have a map?" I asked after a pause.

"What kind of map?"

"One of where we are going," I said.

"Can't you drive on faith?" Elder Burton said, grinning, thinking there were plenty of witnesses to go around.

"Faith without works is dead. The map is the work here. So am I to assume with your lack of usefulness in regards to a map that you don't have one?" I said.

"I don't have one, no. We should get one. I know a map store downtown."

"Good. Let's go." And I put the car in reverse and steered out.

The map store had exactly what we needed for the area map. The state of California, with superimposed San Luis Obispo's streets coming up out of the map in 3D. It was for people who might buy a map as art instead of using it to navigate in their car. I could understand why someone would use a map as art; it would look great on a wall.

"Elder Dorsey, I don't think we need that map. They probably have fold-up ones too. I'll check." And he left me looking at all the maps on the walls. I could have a whole *room* full of maps. I worried, though, that if you had maps, you were expected to have traveled to all the places, like the expectation for a person to read all the books in one's personal library. But then a map of the world had to be open for anyone.

I imagined my room above the garage, overlooking the college track and campus. I could picture the map I was staring at hanging on the wall in my room. The map was a topographic *Landforms and Drainage Systems of the United States*. It was three-by-five feet, black backdrop, with a silver metal continent. It was gorgeous, so I bought it-for seventy dollars.

We left the store with my *Landforms and Drainage Systems of the United States* rolled up in plastic under my arm. Elder Burton had a fold-up travel map of San Luis Obispo neatly tucked under his arm, possibly mimicking me.

With Burton as navigator, we made our way up into the foothills of the Santa Lucia Mountains behind the campus and overlooking the city. We parked the car on a dead-end road and set the emergency brake, slowly turning the engine off. I was expecting a reverent silence, and it was there. It was quiet, except for the wind that was just a different *kind* of quiet. I sat on the hood with Elder Burton standing beside me, looking out over the trees and track, past the greenbelt separating the campus from downtown, beyond where the stalls for the sheep and cattle for the school were kept. I thought what a beautiful place for farmers to go to school. I thought I would someday go to school there and that I would be lucky to be there. I would walk by the apartment I shared with Elder Burton a few years before, thankful that I wasn't there serving on a mission anymore.

"Where should we start?" I asked, noticing there wasn't a house in site.

"Are you ready to walk?" Elder Burton asked.

"You bet. I'm ready. This will be a nice warm-up for the run later. Just think how much walking you are going to be getting in. You might like it."

"I might. Probably will," he said grudgingly, but in good humor.

With four copies of the *Book of Mormon* between us and a stack of First Discussion pamphlets with our names and phone number on the back, we walked to the houses.

Along with being far apart, the houses had really long driveways. Most of the driveways had gates at the end of them, making it hard for our youthful attractiveness to win any unsuspecting gentiles into the waters of baptism. With the first gate, we simply agreed to use our standard greeting, "Hi we are missionaries for the Church of Jesus Christ and Latter-day Saints and would like to share a message with you." This was too long, we learned, after she hung up the intercom and didn't open the gate. It might also have been that she heard Jesus Christ, which would keep *my* gates closed. So we decided to shorten it to "Hi, we are Mormon missionaries" and leave it at that. We tried it at the next gate.

The guy on the other end repeated, "You are Mormon missionaries *and*...." He waited for us to finish the sentence, probably thinking how stupid we were.

Recovering, Elder Burton interjected, "...and we would like to share a message with you." At this. the guy said "No thanks" and hung up. Elder Burton and I just looked at each other for a minute. I knew we were thinking the same thing. Was the view worth it? It was, so we didn't let the gates stop us, although we never did get into a gated driveway. God knew they were going to heaven anyway. Maybe because they lived the closest to him.

Elder Burton was terrible at tracting. He was too polite. With the median income for the city sitting around fifty thousand a year, the majority of the people were out working when we knocked on doors. But the ones we did find home were housewives, predominately—ten to one. So Elder Burton put on this so-called Southern charm that sounded more like he was my boyfriend, and it was Halloween. With his big cheeks, the sun causing him to squint, he put on a big, close-mouthed grin. Once a woman answered the door, looked at us, and said, "Can I help you?" with already a hint of bother in her voice once she realized who we were.

"Hello, Ma'am. How are you today?" Elder Burton said to the thin woman behind the screen door.

"I, uh, I...am...fine. Can I help you with something?" she said in a clear, stern voice. I don't think she liked repeating herself. I wondered if anyone did?

"I'm Elder Burton," he said, leaning forward a little to see through the screen. "We are missionaries for the—" The door was shut in our face. With the number of doors we were knocking on, I knew it had to happen. I don't think Elder Burton had ever had the door slammed in his face. I knew he and Elder Nelson didn't tract. He took it in stride, though, and laughed about it.

"She must not have liked the Southern charm," I said, looking ahead, and patted Elder Burton on the back, "How 'bout I get the next one?"

"All yours, Elder. All yours."

I didn't say anything else again about Southern charm or Elder Burton's tracting abilities, as many people may not have liked his true charm and friendliness, although just as many did like it. I knew, more than anything, though, it was his weight. People looked at him because of it. People, both members and nonmembers looked at him. Then they looked at me because they didn't take him seriously. He was too big to be taken seriously. I hoped I took him seriously, though.

But I didn't say anything. It was unfortunate that Elder Burton couldn't have taken more training from Elder Nelson. Elders Nelson's true elegance was rare, and if in the formidable spot of being trained by him, one would hope to pick up a piece of it. A missionary could do far worse in any conversation, even if he was just mimicking Elder Nelson's voice inflections and manners while speaking. While I received the tutelage of both Elder Nelson while in the MTC and Elder Fischer as a greenie trainee, I felt fortunate to have had Elder Fischer as my trainer. He was one of the most eloquent speakers I'd ever met. I hoped that because of his training, I was smoother than I might have been. Elder Nelson had never allowed Elder Burton to speak, and it was evident at times.

I increasingly liked the stark dryness and heat of the Southern California sun. I enjoyed the sun on my back and face. I enjoyed the sandy earth that dusted my black shoes. The rain in Seattle seemed refreshing at times when living there, but the sun of California was energizing and uplifting. I wondered whether it was the sun that kept me going or God and the Holy Ghost, as I'd been taught. Maybe it was all, but the sun was tangible. And at age twenty, I needed *tangible* in my life. It seemed I'd lived up till then off intangibles, and the sun's warmth, its effects on the dirt and plants were easy to see, appreciate, touch, and feel. Elder Burton and I had walked off the road and again enjoyed the view of the sloping hills towards the city—city that appeared small from where we stood but large when compared with what it had taken away from the foliage that was there first. I knelt down; my knees cracked. They always cracked when I kneeled—too many years behind home plate, catching balls thrown past batters. I settled on my haunches and looked at a small plant, asking Elder Burton what it was.

"What is this, Elder Burton?"

"A plant," he said.

"I *know* it's a plant, but what kind? And how old is it?" I asked the questions, knowing he didn't know, but I wanted to share my thoughts.

"I don't know what kind. We can find out, though. I'll ask Brother Benson tonight at dinner." And that brought me back to my life of tracting and mission life. We had a dinner appointment that night with a family I didn't know and wondered if I even wanted to know. At twenty years old, I was having dinner with people on a regular basis, people I didn't even care about, knowing they didn't care about me either. We were invited simply because the Bensons thought it would help them get to heaven. Before standing up, I pulled the roots of the plant out of the ground. Although its vines and leaves reached out over five feet, the roots came up easily. I laid them down where I pulled it up. Elder Burton didn't see this, and I was glad.

I thought about my all-wise trainer, Elder Fischer, and his comments on tracting. I remembered him talking about how tracting in itself might not be the most efficient way of bringing people into God's church, but God saw the hard work and rewarded us for it. It seemed that way. After just a week of tracting, we had better numbers to send in to President Carlson, along with a few names on our whiteboard.

The door opened to a short, overweight, and apparently overworked woman, with a wisp of hair stuck to her wet forehead. She was probably in her late forties, judging from the lines around her eyes. She was dark skinned; I wondered if she was hired help or if she lived there.

"Hello, my name is Elder Dorsey and this is Elder Burton. We would like to give you a free copy of the *Book of Mormon*."

"No thanks," she said. Her voice was soft and not bothered.

"Have you heard of the Mormon Church?" I asked, continuing to hold the *Book of Mormon* in my outstretched hand.

"I have. I'm sorry, though. I'm not interested." Her genuine concern for saying sorry was evident when she looked directly into my eyes. Her brown eyes sparkled with the sun coming through the big-leafed tree overhead.

"Can we leave you with a flier, then?" I handed the *Book of Mormon* to Elder Burton and pulled out a First Discussion pamphlet from my pocket. It was still early in tracting, and the pamphlets had remained straight and dry, having been in my pocket not more than an hour.

"Sure. That would be fine." She put her hand out for the pamphlet.

"This goes over the plan of salvation that we believe God has given us in these latter days to return to him," I said, opening up the pamphlet and showing her a picture of Jesus Christ. "It also goes over our belief in God the Father, his son Jesus Christ, and the Holy Ghost, which we believe are three separate beings, all working together to ensure our salvation." I hated using the word salvation on a doorstep with the sun on my back in the middle of the week; it seemed a word to be uttered on Sundays in high-ceilinged churches.

"Well, thank you. I'll take a look at it," she said, putting her hand out.

"It also touches on the Prophet Joseph Smith as a modern witness of Jesus Christ and the *Book of Mormon* as another testament of Jesus Christ—and that you can know the truth through the Holy Ghost." I spoke fast but clearly, trying to get the eye contact back that I knew was lost. I handed her the light blue pamphlet. "Our names and number are on the back. If you have any questions about what you read or if you want to talk further, please call."

"Thank you again. Try not to get too hot out there in the heat."

"Well, thank you. Have a good day," I said as she shut the door. We turned and headed down her shaded walkway.

"Elder Burton, did you see what just happened there?" I asked, not looking over at him and lost in my thoughts a bit.

"She was nice. I noticed that. And you were able to get some information to her about who we are."

"Just information?" I asked. I pulled my First Discussion booklet out of my *Book of Mormon* leather case. "Look at this, the doctrinal overview of the First Discussion. What does it say?" And I handed it to him.

"Well, it goes over what the First Discussion talks about—God, Jesus Christ, Holy Ghost, and Joseph Smith. And it mentions the *Book of Mormon*."

"That's right," I said. I couldn't contain the smile on my face. "Elder, did we just give her a First Discussion?"

"A short one. But yes, we did mention what would be talked about in the First. You think it was a valid First?"

"I do. Who are *we* to say what a valid First Discussion is?

Think about it, these Discussions. These six short Discussions are what forty thousand missionaries teach every day. These are what we young men and women, searching for lost souls, are given by God, really. To capture these souls, to somehow intrigue them enough so they'll listen to more, to get them to baptism and beyond. How important are they?

Really, how important? They could hold the key to teaching, well they have to."

"I guess so. So we taught her a First?"

"We did. And if we hadn't, we would have left her with nothing. She said she didn't want the *Book of Mormon*, and in the past, that would have been the end. Think of it like this, the *Book of Mormon* is promised to ring true when read; the Holy Ghost will confirm the truth. That's great and all, but how many copies of the *Book of Mormon* do we hand out?"

"Not many. A couple a week through tracting, and sometimes to the members that need them for friends or something."

"And that's about it though, right? It's been that way since I've been on my mission. Missionaries feel like they got nothing accomplished other than showing God that they are working hard, but nothing accomplished with the people we are here to meet and teach. So what if we use the First Discussion pamphlet as the second tool? Reverse what we've been taught and work towards sharing as much as possible at the door, in hopes that something triggers an emotion or interest. We've been so concerned with putting the *Book of Mormon* in everyone's hands, that we have lost sight of why we're doing it. It is to spark interest, getting them to open it and read and pray. Tough to do on a doorstep."

"Very tough," Elder Burton said.

"I mean, here we tract all day and most times leave nothing for the people to look at later."

"You think they will look at a pamphlet before the *Book of Mormon*?"

Elder Burton asked, holding up the pamphlet in front of us.

"Well, it's not like we don't try to give them the *Book of Mormon* first, but if nothing else, they can take the pamphlet and toss it, or I can see them going back inside, putting it on the counter, and going back to whatever they were doing before we knocked on their door. Now they will think back to when they answered the door and, most likely, remember nothing else. But then later, they walk by this pamphlet, or a kid comes home or the husband, and a four-page pamphlet is something that they can pick up and read quickly to find out what the Mormon Church is about, more so than they could if they were to pick up the *Book of Mormon* and thumb through it, as I do with books all the time and get nothing out of them."

"I can see that. A book is a little imposing. I haven't even read the *Book of Mormon* myself; I can hardly expect someone to read it based on a quick suggestion at their front door."

"Exactly," I said, turning to Elder Burton. I think it is too imposing. Too much to ask in just the few short seconds we have at the door." We stopped talking for a minute and started up another driveway towards the front door. "Let me get this door. I want to try this theory more. How many pamphlets do you have with you?"

"I don't have any. You carry them, remember."

"Well, we will both be carrying them going forward. We will never be without them. There is something in these Discussion pamphlets that people need to hear. Well, they need to hear it all. They are so short and precise and, let us not forget, inspired," I said, pulling another pamphlet out of my case.

Our weekly stats went from zero First Discussions to twenty in the first week of our changed method of tracting. We found the pamphlets were just as easy to hand out when meeting people on the street and engaging them in conversation. College students, especially, were much more eager to accept them, as eager as anyone could be accepting *anything* about religion preached on the street. I toned down the stats, though, keeping them around twenty, even when eventually they were getting closer to forty or fifty.

We went to the Bensons for dinner and asked Brother Benson about the plant we were looking at earlier. Brother Benson was a botanist and taught botany at the college. With a poor description from both Elder Burton and me, he was unable to help. He did say that tumbleweeds were dead plants, though. Although I'd never thought about tumbleweeds as dead plants, I knew if I had, I would have come to the same conclusion. Of all the sights I saw, there was nothing as surreal as seeing a tumbleweed blowing across the road. Brother Benson was helpful in that he loaned me a textbook on indigenous plants of the area. He said to keep it as long as I liked but that he would like it back before I was transferred. I agreed, of course, never thinking he was giving it to me. It was unapproved reading, but I rationalized my reading through my ability to use it in conversation with future investigators. What better way to build relationships of trust than to build on common ground by engaging a local in conversation about the native vegetation? After dinner, we retired to the living room, further discussing botany with Brother Benson.

The daughter, Missy Benson, was pretty. She was a senior in high school and had just accepted a music scholarship at BYU. When she shook my hand, she looked directly into my eyes. I was taken aback by this but then realized she looked into Elder Burton's eyes too. She could have been an angel. She asked questions during dinner, asked why I wanted a plant book, and talked with Elder Burton about Kentucky. She was smart, which I knew before learning that she was getting a full scholarship for not only her music, but her grades too. I'd seen her at church. She played the piano during Sacrament Meeting, and it always sounded perfect. I had a good comparison of piano music played during Sacrament Meeting since my mom would occasionally be asked to play when the regular pianist couldn't be there. My mom was always out of practice, but the congregation was understanding and followed my mom's irregular tempos, slow or fast. But Missy *never* made a mistake. I remember the first Sunday I saw her; I thought she looked like a nice girl. She didn't knock me off my feet, but something was special about her. And then she sang.

After hearing her sing in church, I knew how the hosts of heaven would sound when they finally welcomed me home. Her voice was surprisingly deep. I'd always thought of a woman's voice being a little higher, especially for a girl so delicate. But her voice was unique in sound. And the range she had was something I hadn't heard first hand, even on my mission, where we heard all types of gospel singing. Brother Benson, relaxing on the love seat next to Missy, had his arm around her. Sister Benson was in the kitchen, still cleaning up after dinner. "Missy, why don't you play us a song?" She said.

"OK. What would you like to hear? Elders, any requests?" She asked, looking at me. I'd secretly been listening to *Phantom of the Opera* at night. I had gotten into the habit when I served with Elder Hampton. I'd just about worn out my double cassette of *Phantom*, listening to it every night before going to bed. I hadn't seen the opera when it was touring in Seattle and didn't feel the need to. After listening to the music for so long, I knew every scene and every word to every song.

"How about *Phantom of the Opera*?" I asked. "Can you do Christine?"

"Sure. How about 'Think of Me,'" she said smiling, glad she knew what I wanted.

"That would be great. We don't get the chance to hear music like that; I don't think I've ever heard it live."

"Well I'm no Sarah Brightman, but I'll do my best to make it a memorable experience." She said this while smiling, my heart jumping with the anticipation of the song and from her lovely smile and words directed towards me.

"Can I sing with you?" I asked, surprised that I actually had the guts to say it.

"Of course!"

"Well, I'm no Michael Crawford but…" I said, smiling, wondering if we were flirting.

"This will be fun. You ready?" she asked, standing up and moving over to the piano.

"Sure." I said, standing up and clearing my throat. I'd never sung in front of people, but a few members had said I had a lovely singing voice. I didn't even know if I *knew* how to sing; I just copied the singers.

As she shuffled through a stack of piano music on top of the piano, I slowly made my way to the side of the piano.

"Mom, where is the sheet music for *Phantom*?" She asked, shuffling through a five-inch stack of sheet music.

"I think it's in the bench," Sister Benson said from the kitchen. It was a split-level home, small enough for everyone to hear both the conversation and the singing. Missy got up from the bench and leaned over to open it. I looked at her body, not the way a missionary should. I was very sly about it, though, and no one noticed. She had a mature body for being so young. Her hips could be seen through her thin dress. I thought that she was going to be an incredible wife for someone, but I knew it wasn't going to be me. A girl like her wouldn't *go* for a guy like me. I thought this often and wasn't sure why. I didn't know what women wanted in a man, but I didn't think it was necessarily me. A mission seemed to brew confidence in the young men who served, but I had no confidence that I would be able to interest a girl like Missy, even after the mission. Thoughts raced through my mind of seeing Missy at BYU, asking her out, and then making out with her.

"Here it is!" Missy didn't look at me, and I was glad. She put the music on the stand. I was hidden behind the piano on her side, able to contain myself as the adult I was.

"Great," I said nervously. It seemed that I had just put on a missionary-that-sang hat and just acted. I would never have suggested we sing together had I not been in a suit and tie with a name tag showing that I was a missionary. But something about the moment—there, in that split-level house, grabbed me and I was able to do something that I'd never practiced or even been taught or trained to do.

"OK, Elder Dorsey. You ready?" Missy had her hands on the keys and swung her head around to me; a few hairs hung down on her cheek. She was smiling. She was concerned I might not be ready. She was worrying about me, which felt wonderful.

"Ready," I said. My stomach felt empty, yet it was full.

Missy played the opening to the song that I had heard hundreds of times. Although I had never actually seen Sarah Brightman singing, I saw her singing as clearly as if she were in the room. I imagined what it looked like, there in the theatre, the audience knowing what was lurking below.

It was a love song.

"Think of me, think of me fondly when we say goodbye,

Remember me, once in while, please promise me you'll try..."

"Can it be, can it be Christine? What a change!

You're really not a bit the gawkish girl that once you were..."

The two parts went perfectly. The transition into the duet was magical for the moment.

"You may not remember me, but I remember...I remember her..."

We finished on the highest note I could ever reach or attempt to reach. Missy was an absolute prodigy to my ears. I'd never heard a voice so strong. I wanted to hear her sing some Janis Joplin or Ella Fitzgerald. Brother Benson was the first to clap. "Very good. Very good," Sister Benson said, coming come from the kitchen and standing in the doorway, "Very good. Wow, that sounded just *per*fect!"

Elder Burton got up from the couch and handed me my coat, "Elder Dorsey, I didn't even know you could sing. Is there anything you don't do?" He patted my back and had a big smile on his face. I thought he looked proud to have me as a companion. And that was a great feeling.

I looked over at Missy and told her she was an incredible singer. She said she enjoyed singing with me, looking in my eyes the whole time. And that gave me a very peculiar feeling, as I didn't want her the way I wanted her before we started singing. I wanted her as a friend for life. If I didn't marry her, it was OK, because she would be happy and I would still be in her life. But I also felt that I could marry her now—that she would want to marry me. I knew these were just thoughts of a man who had only thoughts about women and marriage and feelings and friends.

Elder Burton reminded me on the way home that Jason and Cami were coming over for Jason's New Member Discussions.

"Oh, is that tonight? I guess it is. We even talked about it this morning, didn't we?"

"We did, I know. Though I'm not really in the *mood* for it." Elder Burton said.

"No, no, that's not why I sounded like that. I wanted to go and get some music downtown. Well, we can go tomorrow," I said, refocusing on the

Discussion for the night.

"What kind of music? Approved, right?" Elder Burton asked.

"You know me: only approved."

"I know, I know," he said, kidding.

"I wanted to get some classical music. It's all we can really listen to. After singing with Missy, I feel so inept in regards to music, any type of music."

"Do you like classical music?"

"Well, I don't *not* like it. I haven't really listened to it in its entirety. I think if I listened to a whole album—and felt what the artist felt when making it—I think it would mean something rather than thoughts of elevators. I'm like a redneck music guy. Hard rock, man."

"What about country?"

"Well, when I'm in Texas, sure, but when I'm in Washington, I can't listen to country. Country is still kinda new to me. I mean, I grew up on Johnny Cash and Patsy Cline, but this new country is a little foreign to me."

"All I listen to is country."

"Who's your favorite singer?"

"George Strait."

"I like him. My Dad got me into him. He's like the biggest name in country music, isn't he?"

"I think so. Clint Black is pretty popular, but George Strait will go to the Hall of Fame, he's sold so many records."

I looked over at Elder Burton, sitting there in the front seat of the car. "Elder Burton, did you bring any George Strait on your mission?" I asked, sternly with a smile.

"I won't ever tell."

"You did! Elder, as your zone leader and friend, a friend that wants to hang in heaven with ya, I'm going to have to ask that you give me the tapes."

"Yeah, right. I don't even listen to them. Elder Nelson gave me so much crap about it; I put them away for good."

"Elder Nelson didn't like them, huh?"

"No, he didn't. He made fun of the fact that I even listened to country music. I think it was the fact that it was country rather than unapproved music that bothered him."

"Ya know though, that's just kinda Elder Nelson. He doesn't mean to make fun; it just comes out like that from his mouth."

"Well, it didn't seem like that. But it's OK. I don't feel like listening to them now anyway."

"Gotta keep that spirit in ya: no unapproved music."

"What about you and *Phantom of the Opera*?"

"That's approved, I asked President Carlson. *Phantom* is very popular right now.

We were home only a few minutes when Jason knocked on the door, opened it, and yelled up the stairs to us. "Elders? You up there?"

He knew we were; we lived on top of a hill on top of a house. "Jason, come on up." Elder Burton said. He got off the end of his bed and walked to the top of the stairs. Jason's head appeared over the banister, and I got up to welcome him.

"Hey, Elders," Jason said. If Jason had had a white shirt, tie, and black name tag, he could have passed for a Mormon missionary. His hair was short and moussed back. He was in shape and looked like he could have taken my position by putting on my coat. "Elder Dorsey, nice to meet you. Elder Burton told me he was getting a new companion. Did you know Elder Nelson?"

"I did. We were in the MTC together."

"That's so cool. So you came out with him? I've heard that you get to know the guys you come out with pretty good."

"You do. But you get to know your companions also. It's a little different, I guess, but not as much with Elder Nelson."

"So Elder Burton told you I was planning on going soon?"

"He did. You haven't got a call yet, though; right?"

"No, I have to be a member for a year, and I still have a few months. But it works out well because I'll be able to finish this year at school, so it works."

"That's good. I was able to get a semester in before I left, but it would have been nice to get a whole year in."

"Where'd you go?"

"BYU."

"Ohhhh, the old 'BYU before the mission'. One of *those* missionaries," Jason said, a smile confirming his joking.

"Yep, one of those." I said, smiling and raising my eyebrows.

I figured there were some stereotypes surrounding young men who went to BYU; although I didn't know exactly what they were to converts my age. I could only guess.

"So Jason, what are we on here? The Fifth Discussion?" I asked, trying to get to a different topic as I'd tired of school talk and small talk. I was also bothered that this perfectly fine young man would go on a mission when he had exactly what I wanted as a life—mainly not being on a mission.

"I think so. There are six of them, right? So we're going to do them all tonight?"

"We can try. As long as we don't get hung up on any of the commitments," I said, smiling again, Jason and I instantly able to joke with each other.

The commitments for the Fifth Member Discussion were to select and carry out a family reunion or family activity, begin a journal, and complete a family group record.

What I didn't know about Jason was that he had already memorized both the missionary Discussions and the New Member Discussions. Getting through the Discussions was simple in that the questions weren't there.

"Jason, I want you to know that I know that starting a journal is very important, and I know this is what God has commanded us to do. Will you commit to the activity of starting a journal?

"I will, Elder Burton. Thanks for asking," Jason said. I smiled and shook my head.

"Well, Jason, that finishes up the Fifth. We will move to the Sixth if you don't have any questions.

"No questions. You both did a wonderful job on presenting the Discussion. One thing, though: Elder Burton, you didn't bear testimony to the truthfulness of what you shared with me."

Elder Burton smiled and asked, "What do you mean? You don't think it's true?"

"No, no. But if you will look on the left-hand page of your Discussion, it clearly states under Teaching Helps, to 'Express your feeling about' and then proceeds to list the points of interest that require expression of feelings or, in other words, your testimony," Jason stated matter-of-factly. Elder Burton looked over at me as if I would have an answer to this. As much as Jason was kidding, he had a point, a point that was in line with what Elder Burton and I had been working on while tracting: sharing the Discussions exactly as God had inspired them to be written.

"It does say that, Elder," I said.

"OK, OK. Jason, I want you to know that my feelings about starting a journal go very deep and are important to me." Elder Burton was struggling. It was tough to be told not only when to share feelings, but also what to share. I don't think Elder Burton really gave a crap about keeping a journal, but it was going to be fun to hear him try.

"Elder Burton, I appreciate you sharing your feelings with me," Jason said when Elder Burton had clearly finished or just run out of feelings to share. Elder Burton just shook his head. He had direct eye contact with me the whole time while I taught, to the point that it would have been uncomfortable had I not known he was mocking me. He knew the Discussion guided when to look into the person's eyes. And Jason was right there, just smiling away. Although it was all meant in fun, it showed how silly the Discussion's layout was in that not only did it tell us exactly what to say, but also that Jason, who saw the importance of the message, saw humor in the teaching and was able to differentiate between a little fun and the seriousness of the Gospel.

He'd met all sorts of people in the Church, as he'd been going to the singles' ward since converting. Yet Jason was still able to look beyond the bad members, the ones who truly misrepresented the Church, and see the members who truly believed. He admired the true believers.

Cami came over after we had finished the Fifth Discussion. Her dark hair was pulled back smartly in a ponytail. She was going running on the track across the street after the Discussion. She had shorts on—tight, black workout shorts that fit to her skin. Her long, faded college sweatshirt (hiding the chest that I had noticed the other day in town) hung down well past her small waist, letting only her legs show with a thin black strip on top of them, the shorts just peaking out. Her legs were proportionate to her beauty, and I wasn't surprised. She and Jason hugged when they saw each other. She shook Elder Burton's and my hands. I remembered her long, slender fingers, both admired and coveted.

"So how far are you running tonight?" I asked.

"Just a couple miles."

"How long will that take you?" I asked.

"Probably about half hour. I'm not a fast runner."

"Hey, it's faster than I could do. I don't even know what I could run a mile in. I know from watching *Chariots of Fire* that four minutes is something to shoot for."

"I don't think I could ever run a four-minute mile," Cami said, looking to the other side of the room at Elder Burton and Jason.

"Oh, I don't think I could either. I just thought that you might have a goal that you run for?"

"No goal. Just run when I feel fat, which is most of the time," she said, not having to think about it at all. She'd made it clear that she wasn't that interested in running other than just occasionally. I thought I sounded dumb by asking the questions. I thought it would be an easy way to start a conversation, but it quickly turned.

"We should go sometime. I've been meaning to start running down there, and it would be nice to have someone to run with," I said. In my mind I was asking her out.

"Sure. Not tonight, though. I'll probably leave before you are done here."

"Oh, no. I didn't mean tonight. Give me a call next time you go."

"Sure." She almost dismissed it, and I wondered if she was just being polite. Maybe I wasn't her type. I was just asking her to run with me. What was the harm in that? There was harm, though, and I knew it. I had no intentions of running alone with her; Elder Burton would be there walking. But the thought of being alone with her, after the light of the day had cast shadows on the corners of the track, I thought of being alone with her and what could happen, and what I would allow to happen. I knew later, while lying in bed, I would be beating myself up—praying to God, begging for forgiveness, almost being brought to tears, all because I thought it would be fun to make out with a girl on a track. I wasn't thinking about fucking her.

Cami stayed only about twenty minutes before leaving to run. As she walked out the door, I yelled after her like a loser, "Give me a call about going running," and the door might have shut before I finished.

We finished the last Discussion with Jason, struggling through seriously enough so we could all feel good about having completed them. It was the first time that I taught someone who might have known more about the Gospel than I did. Not only did Jason come with his own scriptures, but he also navigated through them as well as anyone I'd seen. Not just the Bible, but the other complete works—the *Book of Mormon*, *The Pearl of Great Price* and *The Doctrine and Covenants*. All of them he used as gracefully as a lifer of the Mormon Church could have. He was as familiar with the scriptures as we—full-time missionaries—were. I sat there looking at him and wondered if he really was a convert, meaning he believed. Could he actually believe it? Did he have a sign, even confirmation that what he read in the *Book of Mormon* was true? Did he get these things? When I didn't get them, it didn't surprise me, but Jason lived like a Mormon by choice, without regret. I thought there was a secret lie in that, although I wasn't sure where it stemmed from. I could only hope to live without regret—to reach an age when living was simply watching movies and television; retired and almost dead. Then I could possibly imagine not regretting having the fun I did and the fun I *didn't* have. It was true that the Mormon religion stunted my fun, but wasn't living with regret still better than not living at all? And if that wasn't the case, then honesty with oneself is put before honesty with God. How does that work? How does it feel?

That night, Elder Burton and I went down to the track. I ran around it three times before I slowed to a walk next to a heavy-breathing Elder Burton, lost in music on his Walkman. I walked beside him for a lap, until he broke away to the high-jump pads. Bending over with my hands on my knees to catch my breath, I watched Elder Burton with his back turned to me, hands in the air, as he fell into the huge pads. He stayed there until I ran three more laps and then announced to him that I was ready to leave. This would turn into a routine we'd practice every night for the remainder of my time in San Luis Obispo. I would run while Elder Burton walked, until he was so out of breath he'd fall into the pads, resting until I was done with my workout. I think it did Elder Burton a lot of good going to the track with me, not just for the exercise but also for the short-lived break from mission life.

The following Sunday I saw Jason and Cami at church. I hadn't been introduced to many of the members in the young-adults ward, so Jason made it a point for me to meet as many members in view. The ones not in our view were quickly corralled into an introduction. As it was with meeting new people, you don't really know which ones will remain with you when you're alone with your thoughts, recalling introductions. The majority of the guys I met were returned missionaries. There was one young man I met who was just getting ready to go on a mission, currently putting a year of college behind him. He was in the awkward stage young men go through right before their mission. The girls are scared to date them, for fear they'd give in to their sexual urges, have sex with the young man, and ruin his life.

The bishopric didn't give them any real jobs in the ward, as they would be leaving soon and needed to concentrate on pre-mission stuff, whatever they thought that was. So you have these young men, living all across the country, not really dating or busying themselves with a job inside or outside the ward. Their fellow members looked at them differently too. They'd tell them stories of their mission and how it was the best time in their life, implying to these young men that if they had doubts about going, they shouldn't. At the same time, they'd explain that doubts were natural, so as not to allow them to question their doubts. It was like an underground mind wash, yet it was out everywhere. Anyone who wasn't Mormon in their lives had been brushed aside for the time, preventing a different perspective from being shared with these young men. These guys were roaming the streets of their neighborhoods with thoughts of short-sleeved white shirts and plastic ties, which they'd have to wear daily for the next two years. Having an impact somewhere—these nowhere boys.

I met the Elders Quorum President Steve Stilson. He greeted me with a big smile and a sharp handshake.

"Nice to meet you, Elder Dorsey," he said while shaking his entire body as vigorously as he shook my hand. He was in good shape—right around six-feet. Lean and athletic, he shook like he looked.

"Steve, nice to meet you. Look forward to working with you."

"Oh sure. It will be fun!" Then his voice lowered a touch to add emphasis. Leaning closer to me, he said, "Ya know, though. We don't have a whole lot that happens in this ward in regards to missionary work."

"Well, maybe we can change that," I said.

"Anything you need, just let me know. Love to work more with you guys than we have in the past," Steve said, and I thought he was kissing my butt for some reason.

I'd never experienced it, really, being only twenty-one, but it felt like he was kissing butt. Steve was a nice guy and, as Elders Quorum President, he must have been a pretty good Mormon. At the very least, he'd have to be following the Word of Wisdom and paying tithing. Giving up ten percent of income was hard for some, especially those in their early twenties, as I myself had noticed. But Steve was a bit of a smart ass, an attribute that I found unequaled in the dumb faults of people. I knew he would be on my mind throughout my time, in a pestering, annoying way. After Steve had proceeded down the hall to his Gospel Doctrine class, which he would probably teach, even if he weren't at the front of the room, I noticed a tall, dark-haired man leaning against the wall in the foyer. I walked over to him and introduced myself.

"Hi, I'm Elder Dorsey. New missionary in the ward."

"Hello, Elder Dorsey. You enjoying the area?" he said in a quiet, mysterious voice.

"I am. It's gorgeous here."

"And you probably haven't even been out to the beach yet, Morro Bay?"

"Not yet. Going out there this week to see the rest of the zone."

"Oh, you are the zone leader?"

"Yep. Made me a zone leader when I transferred in."

"How do you like that? More paperwork?" he asked, but somehow I knew he didn't really mean paperwork; he meant the other annoying responsibilities that went along with the title.

"It's OK. Not a lot of paperwork. Just weekly stats from the companionships. You seem to know a little about missions. Did you go on one?"

"I did. I've been back about a year now. Went to Japan."

"Wow, Japan. I think that would be a fun place to go."

"Fun? I'm not sure about *fun*."

"Well…I mean somewhat all inclusive of the experience. You know, you get the language, the different culture, the different people, and the opportunity to see a totally different part of the world. I think the experience of it would be fun."

"It was OK. Ate a lot of rice; now I can't eat much else." David's breath smelled of parsley. His hair was wet. His complexion was perfect, and the darkness of his skin shone against its smooth surface. His jaw was cut out of a box; his sunken cheeks out of clay. He belonged in an ad for jeans, not in the foyer of a Mormon church.

"So what are you doing now?" I asked.

"Planning on going to school."

"Here at Cal Poly?"

"That's the plan. I just came here to hang with some friends I had before the mission. I went here then."

"How do you enjoy being back?"

"It's OK. It's different."

"In what way?"

He looked at me and smiled a little. "Just different."

"Hey, you want to go on splits sometime?"

"Not really. I'll give you a call if I do."

"OK. Hey, I'm going to get going. It was nice to meet you."

"You too, Elder Dorsey," he said and shook my hand. His long, slender fingers tightly gripped my hand; his stark blue eyes tried to hide behind his squinted eyelids.

Young-adults wards were odd. They had all the same callings, such as bishop, elders, quorum president, and relief society president and her counselors. Of course, there was no need for a primary or Sunday school, but other than that, it ran like a real ward—an adult ward. I thought it so strange that these young men, barely older than me, could handle such responsibility. Of course, the freedom of choice was removed with the fear of *Do what you are called to do or go to hell.* With that consequence in mind, maybe they didn't choose; they just "did." And they "did" to the best of their ability. Wasn't how a person utilized the best of his or her abilities subject to question by all, as well as by the person him- or herself? But with the lay ministry of the Church, young-adult members had no other options. Where else would they train the future leaders of the Church, after all? Unless, of course, it was in the mission field. Maybe it was all part of the Church's plan, run truly like a large corporation. Files were kept on people, and references were always made when people moved in and out of the ward. The first thing the bishopric would do is sic the missionaries on the unfamiliar person. Generally, that was enough to get information on where they came from and, put in polite terms, answer "What brought you here?" As soon as the bishop had information on the person, he would proceed to call their previous ward and start the search for information on the unknown Mormon. They didn't just float around.

I figured I would be in a young-adults ward when I got home. I thought it would be cool to be dating the relief society president. And maybe I could be the elders' quorum president. We could be the *perfect* before being-married-Mormon dating couple.

Bishop Giles snuck up behind me while I was lost in thought, an enjoyable thought. "Elder Dorsey!"

I turned and looked at him, putting out my hand. "Bishop Giles, Hi."

"Hi. Hey, I saw you talking with David."

"Yeah. We talked for a few minutes. Nice guy."

"He is a nice guy, but we don't know much about him."

"What do you mean?"

"Well, I think he's homeless and lives in the woods."

"Oh. Is that a problem?" I honestly didn't know. I didn't know if Mormons couldn't live in the woods or be homeless, or was it just that the

Bishop just wanted to know.

"Well, we'd like to take care of him if he needs help. We could always make arrangements so he wouldn't have to sleep outside."

"I see. Well, he said he had friends here and that's why he came back. Other than that, we talked a little about his mission."

"I've asked a few of the people he has gotten to know, and they don't know any of his friends. He doesn't share much information about himself. But I thought he might have told you where he lived. Then at least we'd know he wasn't living outside."

"I can ask to come visit him. I'll do that and get back to you."

"Thanks, Elder. I've asked him casually, yet he kind of dodges the question."

"I understand. I'll see what I can do." It felt good to say "I'll see what I can do" with the zone-leader's status. I felt powerful for a minute.

David had left after Sacrament Meeting, so I didn't get a chance to talk with him again. I said goodbye to Jason and Cami, while Elder Burton tracked down the dinner calendar. The dinner calendar was a bit of a joke in the ward. Any of the dinner appointments we got at the young-adults ward pretty much consisted of college kids with limited funds. If there *were* any appointments, they were lunches at In-and-Out Burger, which was fine by both Elder Burton and me. We enjoyed the break from the monotony of dinner with members. Not all dinner appointments were like the Bensons, and not all families had daughters like Missy.

The fruits of our labors in tracting had produced a twenty-year-old student at Cal Poly, studying agricultural business. He was planning on taking over the family farm after graduation. Rob was hesitant to talk to us when we approached him on the street. We were walking back from tracting, cutting through the campus. We never tracted to people on the campus, but once off campus and close to our house, we met Rob walking past us. We gave him the First Discussion using the convenient First Discussion pamphlet, along with two passages marked in the *Book of Mormon,* which he took home to read. We called him a couple of days later and invited him to a Family Home Evening Night at the ward building on Monday. Much to our surprise, he accepted the invitation and said he would meet us there. We were anxious.

The ward building wasn't really a ward building. It was the campus institute. All college campuses across the world had Mormon institutes off campus. It's where the young-adults wards met if it was a college town. If not, then the family wards were shared. The institutes had a chapel, sometimes added on after the Church had more money.

But the majority of the institutes were a building of classrooms and a gym. The classrooms were for daily religion classes that students were encouraged to take. Unlike BYU, they weren't required classes for a major, but still the encouragement could be equal.

Our last P-Day had been about as perfect as they come. It started with our usual ritual of me pounding balls to Elder Burton on the other side of the net. He continued to improve each day. If he were a hundred and fifty pounds lighter, we would make great doubles partners, with his play at the net being unequaled to anything I'd seen. Well, at least it was impressive. But it might have been impressive just due to his weight. We hit balls, then sat on the court while the mist lifted off the grass onto the hills behind us. We talked lightly on tennis, comics, and the day. All we had planned was the Family Home Evening Night at church, and we were going to that only because Rob was meeting us there. I couldn't imagine Rob really meeting us there, as I'd had hundreds of planned meetings ending quite one-sided. I never blamed them, either, understanding they'd agree to anything just to get rid of "those damn missionaries." But we still planned on the meeting, penned it in our planners and talked about it in both our Daily Planning Meetings and our Ward Mission Meetings. How funny it was that he probably never gave *us* a second thought, yet he consumed time from countless individuals, from the ward mission leader to our own president going over the stats, reading about our so-called investigators in weekly letters. The president knew, though, that one week a companionship might have a baptism planned and the next week there was no mention of it. This happened often, and sometimes no questions were asked. I had mentioned that we met a person through our tracting efforts in my brief weekly letter that got sent with Elder Burton's letter (including the stats) to the president. These were all folded, enveloped, and mailed. Little did

Rob know that he would be part of history: he was talked about in a letter that was mailed.

I saw Rob walk in while the Bishop was corralling everyone into seats to start the evening's festivities. I saved a seat for him beside me. He had on a coat, heavy for the mild spring weather. Perhaps he was using the coat as protection from things other than weather, though. The rough outer shell of the coat made raking sounds while he walked, announcing his arrival a few feet ahead. He didn't need the coat to bring attention to himself. It was enough just being an investigator. I introduced Rob to a few of the young adults sitting near us. I could hardly remember their names, so it was a bit awkward. I consoled myself with the thought that Rob probably didn't want to meet them anyway.

Seeing Bishop Giles reminded me of our conversation earlier, causing me to look around quickly for David. I saw him leaning against a wall, talking with Steve Stilson. I settled back into my seat, focusing my attention on the bishop in the front of the room.

"What I thought would be fun tonight," he said, rubbing his hands together in front of him, "is to open up a discussion on any gospel topic you would like."

My heart leaped a bit in anticipation of some deep, doctrinal secrets that would come out of the evening. I thought quickly of what I could ask to sound really smart. And then I just thought of something I could ask that I didn't understand. The whole idea of the Atonement of Jesus Christ bothered me. It made no sense. I thought of asking about that but knew I had to hone in on a direct question, rather than the broad topic I saw in my mind. I put my question to rest and listened.

"I have a question!" Steve Stilson said from a couple rows behind me.

"OK. Great, Steve. What is the question?" Bishop Giles asked.

"Why do men have nipples?" Pretty much everyone laughed.

Even the Bishop smiled and laughed slightly.

"I don't think we can answer that tonight," Bishop Giles said, sincerely wishing he had an answer. And I thought it an excellent question for my mom's list of unanswerable questions she was putting together for her first meeting with Jesus Christ. I looked over at Rob, glad to see him smiling.

Hopefully, it was a sign that he was enjoying himself, even if the subject matter was on the level of grade school.

After the laughter died down, I asked the bishop to explain the difference of having the Restored Gospel on the earth versus the other churches having the Gospel passed down from Christ to his apostles. He explained that the teaching and beliefs of the majority of the Christian sects today are similar in that they were handed down from Christ himself, but what was lost in the apostasy in those dark ages was the influence of the Holy Ghost, both as an interpreter of scripture and as a constant guide through this life—a guide in which God himself had intended that each person have to show them the way to salvation. I thought the bishop did a wonderful job in addressing a broad topic with a broad answer.

After the meeting, I introduced Rob to the bishop. I always liked introducing the investigators to the bishop or his counselors. They made a good impression for the Mormon Church, being generally well kept and, most importantly, well spoken. The random member's mouth was no friend to missionaries' fragile investigators. The Bishop introduced Rob to Steve Stilson, who I'm sure was now infamous in Rob's eyes from the nipple question. Rob was quiet. After he met Steve, he looked over at me.

"Elder Dorsey, I've got to get going."

"Oh, OK. Well, thanks for coming out tonight," I said.

"Rob, it was nice to meet you," the Bishop said, extending his hand once again to say goodbye.

He said goodbye to Steve with a simple "Maybe see you around campus."

It was an easy exit. He knew where the door was, and I didn't want to offer to walk him to his car. We were both guys and both of the age that escorts weren't needed at any time. He gave me a mini-wave goodbye and walked to the door and left.

I looked around for David, but didn't see him. He was becoming somewhat elusive.

On the way home I talked with Elder Burton about Rob. "So what do you think of Rob?" I asked.

"Seems like a nice guy."

"Well I *know* he seems like a nice guy, but what about him being baptized? That's really what we are wondering always, isn't it?" I asked. I sensed a little bit of irritability in my voice and was surprised.

"I don't look at everyone we meet as to whether they will be baptized. It hardly ever happens. I think I would get depressed having that expectation," Elder Burton said.

I laughed inside my head, thinking, "Elder, you are depressed about everything, from being fat to not having a girl waiting to marry you when you get home and knowing (that because you are fat) you have very limited options in this life. All this and you wouldn't want to get depressed when thinking of too few baptisms?"

"That's true. I don't think that everyone we meet will get baptized, but if that's our job out here, then it makes a person wonder what we are doing if we don't get baptisms. I've only had, like, two or three. Does that mean I suck as a missionary?" I didn't think that I sucked but was thinking out loud and liked getting Elder Burton's opinion.

"You don't suck at all as a missionary…" Elder Burton started to say.

"Hey! Whoa down there, cowboy! I wasn't looking for stroking on that statement; just putting a question out. What determines a good missionary, given the criteria that they obey the rules and work?"

"Well, there's got to be measures other than baptism. Think of this—I wasn't happy at all on my mission until I started serving with you. I like my mission now. That has to say something for a missionary. Not to say you are the only one either. I'm sure it happens pretty often."

"I can see that. But I think that speaks of the person versus aptitude of the missionary. I mean, if we worked together in a job and you liked working with me each day, I'd still have to do my job in order to keep it. It would make no difference that you liked working with me."

"Yeah. Mission is different, though. It's not all about baptisms and conversions. It's got to have something to do with you and me as people. We both know that if the Church wanted converts, the best way isn't to send out young men. So it's got to be about us," Elder Burton said, looking forward as he mulled over what he had just said. I thought about it too. I'd heard of the Church sending out young men and, of course, the theory behind it. But what struck me was Elder Burton's simplicity in understanding that it had to have something to do with us as people. He had something there. And I wondered where I had lost that—or if I'd ever had it? My irritability soon passed as my thoughts moved to what I was going to read while I lay in my bed.

Other than seeing the zone members at Zone Conference, we had only one other companionship weekly—Elder Brady and Elder Kenny. They served in Atascadero, only thirty miles south of us. We were able to spare the miles to see them for District Meetings.

Unfortunately, with a zone leader in the district, the zone leader had to act dually as the district leader, preventing another missionary's parents from receiving a letter saying what an outstanding leader he was among his peers, causing him to be "called" officially as a district leader.

Elder Brady was a "baller." That term had never been used lightly by me, reserved only for true natural basketball players. I walked into the small classroom on the side of the gym. "OK, guys! Let's get the missionary business taken care of, and then I'll continue the schooling on the court." I was never able to trash-talk without having a big grin on my face, impressing myself with my wittiness. I was never taken seriously enough to be coined a "baller." I did think of myself as a player, though, and would rather have been on the court with the rest of the district than going over weekly stats, baptism hopefuls, and limited monthly miles. It was a great group of elders, we leaders. We each had quiet personalities that were expressed in a joking, sarcastic manner.

"Whatever, Dorsey. I'll school you!" Elder Kenny said. He knew he wasn't a player, but this didn't stop him from talking trash with the best of them. Elder Kenny was a garbage player, picking up points that fell into his hands. When he did try to make moves, he was knocked down—literally, sometimes. Everyone needed something to define him as a player; otherwise, one had no game.

"Let's go, Elder Kenny! I'll see *you* on the floor," I said, putting my books on the table, acting as if walking to the court.

"Anytime, Elder. Anytime." Elder Kenny said, getting the last word.

"OK, guys. So what do the stats look like this week?" I asked, sitting on the edge of the table.

"We have one First Discussion," Elder Kenny said.

"One First, huh? Is that good or bad?" I asked.

"What do you mean?" Elder Brady asked.

"Well, did it result in a baptism, or was it somewhat dismissed by the recipient?" I asked, impressed with my approach.

"We didn't get a baptism, but it was a First. We met the guy in the park, and we taught him right then and there," Elder Kenny said.

"Now that's cool, teaching a guy in the park. That's like the Apostle Paul, man. So how did it go?" I asked.

"His name was Frank," Elder Kenny started saying. I thought Frank was the perfect name for a guy in a park. "His family lives in Utah, of all places."

"Utah? But he's not Mormon, right?" I asked.

"No. He lived there only a few years before coming out to California. He got a divorce, then came south to work. Ended up in Morro Bay."

"Morro Bay is a strange place to end up looking for work. Was he a bum?"

"I don't know," Elder Kenny said.

"What makes him a bum?" Elder Burton asked.

"I don't know. I guess whether or not he has a job," I said.

"What if he doesn't *need* a job?" Elder Burton asked.

"Well, if he didn't have a job and needed a job, then he might be a bum," I said.

"OK, that makes sense," Elder Burton said.

"I don't know if he has a job," Elder Kenny said.

"Are you going to meet with him again?" I asked.

"We set up a time for the Second in the park," Elder Kenny said.

"In the park, huh? During the day? This guy might be a bum. Not that it matters, though. Invite him to church," I said, thinking it would be an experience for all involved, and I would love to hear about it.

"Just invite him to church? Just like that?" Elder Brady asked, finding my proposition humorous, laughing to himself.

"Sure. I don't think we do that enough. Just think of all the lovely members that we know and love. We need to share them," I said. The early trash talk had set the mood for fun, and it hadn't dissipated. "Well, guys. Let me know if there is anything I can do for you. Remember, myself and Elder Burton are just here to help where we can."

"Dork." Elder Brady whispered, respectfully.

"OK, let's discuss any other pertinent information over the hardwood," I said, cradling the ball in my arm.

"It's carpet, Elder Dorsey," Elder Burton said.

"Over the carpet, then." I hated the carpeted courts of Mormon gyms.

We started to shoot around, our ties flipping back and forth from shoulder to shoulder. I took my tie off to get serious. We never played basketball during the week; only games like bump or around the world. We opted for H-O-R-S-E that day. Elder Brady would casually shoot the ball, his wrist flipping perfectly, with the ball going through the net, missing the rim entirely. He made Elder Proude's form and follow-through look childish. Elder Brady stood around six-three (although a *small* six-three, as he seemed to slouch or wear baggy clothing). On the court, though, his height was apparent. Standing under the basket, he could easily flip a ball into the hoop, even while close to the rim. His arms hung to his knees. This not only gave him an advantage in the game, but added to the delicate form and touch he had on the ball. Some people were just made for one thing, their bodies somehow perfected through genes to make them the ultimate baller.

While Elder Kenny chased down errant shots and Elder Burton took on the role of rebounder, I was able to sit out in three-point land with Elder Brady and have a shoot-out. I had the touch, sinking the majority of my shots. My jump shot was awkward at times, rarely fluid, but it happened to be fluid at that moment. Elder Brady matched me for three-pointers and pulled ahead when going on a tear of six threes in a row as fast as Elder Burton could put a ball in his hands.

"Can you dunk?" I asked like a little kid.

"Ahh, sometimes," Elder Brady said shyly.

"Come on, man. Do it!" I had no tact in asking. I wanted to see a real dunk.

"Let me warm up a little," Elder Brady said. He took the ball in one hand and started stretching with the ball palmed in his right hand. He then went under the hoop and jumped for a few minutes, just reaching up to the backboard. I watched in anticipation of a dunk.

"Dorsey, you can't dunk?" Elder Burton asked.

"No. I wish. I can grab the rim and hang, but that's not close to dunking."

"Thought you would be able to. After all, you sing," Elder Burton said. I hoped no one had heard him—or if they had, wouldn't comment. No such luck.

"Elder Dorsey, you sing?" Elder Kenny asked.

"No, I *sang*. I did it once on the spur of the moment, and that was it."

"Where were you? Like in Sacrament Meeting?" Elder Brady asked, stretching.

"I was at a member's home, Burton. I'm going to kill you!" I said, clenching my teeth a little.

"Hold it—you sang in a member's home? You've got to tell us about it," Elder Brady said.

"Will you sing for us, Elder Dorsey?" Elder Kenny asked, amused with himself.

"No, I won't! It was a duet. I happened to know the song she was playing, so I sang it with Missy, the member's daughter."

"Oooh, *Missy*. Was it a love song?" Elder Kenny asked, just loving the topic.

"I don't know if it was a love song. What classifies as a love song?" I asked. They both looked over at Elder Burton.

Smiling, Elder Burton, enjoying center stage, said, "Yeah, it was a love song."

"Burton, you're killing me here. No more. Brady, you dunking?" I asked, hoping to divert their attention.

"OK, I think I'm ready," Elder Brady said. We all stood looking at him, much more interested in his dunking than in my singing.

He took a step and flushed the ball through the hoop. It happened so fast, I had to think about what I had just seen. There was no running start, no superexaggerated body pump. It looked as if he took off from his ankles, simply flexing to gain momentum.

"Whoa! I gotta see that again!" I said, the gym quiet.

He took a few steps, bounced the ball and took off from the baseline, moving his arm to the side to avoid the backboard. He put the ball down over the rim as easily as he had the first time.

"Dang, Brady! You can leap. I've seen Smith and Proude dunk, but it's nothing to this. Do you know them?" I asked. I figured he didn't; this was only his second area in six months.

"No. I've heard they were ballplayers, though." He gave them respect, probably knowing they weren't in his league.

"Take off from the foul line," I said.

"OK." Elder Brady walked to the far end of the court, bouncing the ball between his legs, looking loose. Elder Brady came to a rest at the far corner, bounced the ball, and looked at the ground. He took a couple hops and then started sprinting with the dribble looping beside him. He was a foot behind the foul line when he took off. He was parallel in the air instantly, and at the last second, his head almost ducking under the backboard, he threw the ball through the hoop, the breakaway rim banging back into place. Elder Brady landed on both feet softly, leaving him momentarily remaining on his haunches for balance. I then noticed his well-worn black wingtips, well worn for an Elder out only six months. I was sure it wasn't the first NBA Slam Dunk Contest dunk that he'd mimicked in those shoes. The rest of us in the gym just stood there in shock.

"Elder Brady, that was incredible! How long you been dunking like that?" I asked.

"About twelve."

"Twelve years *old*?" I said, raising my tone.

"I was, like, five-eleven and could jump. So I started practicing my dunks."

"And then you got even taller?" I asked, wishing so badly it had happened to me.

"Yeah. Grew another four inches through high school."

"Man. You can fly. Really, you can fly. Did you get a scholarship for college?" I asked.

"I got a few. Took the year off to take a break, though."

"What are you going to do when you get home? What school?" I asked further, wondering why he would need a break from being a star basketball player at a Pac Ten college.

"I don't know. Go play somewhere," Elder Brady said. He wasn't going to volunteer any information for my pleasure.

"Man, Elder Brady. You can play. I'll watch for you in college. Maybe I can say, 'I knew him when.'"

"I don't know about that. I'm a little small for ball, even at six-three. Lot of guys can do what I do at that level."

"Then what makes these small guys able to get into the NBA?" I asked.

"They are just incredible. Most of those guys are guards too. And I've been bred as a power forward and center. So they have quite a head start on me already," he said.

"But you are still young. You have time," I said.

"I hope so, I do. Just serving the mission now, though," he said.

"Well, I think you got it. I've never seen a better player, even in the little bit I saw here," I said honestly.

"Thanks. Always good to hear," Elder Brady said, flipping a final three-pointer into the still net. "Look at that," he said as it went through. "If only I was as good a missionary as I was a three-point shooter. If it was all just that easy."

We talked about the picnic we had planned at Pismo Beach on P-Day, an afternoon on the beach grilling hot dogs. Grilled hot dogs tasted so much better than microwaved ones. We split up what each companionship was to bring, then made carpooling plans. Elder Burton and I would pick up Elder Brady and Elder Kenny, and Elder Wagoner and Elder Baldwin would get a ride from the sisters. The sisters lived in Pismo, so the Elders would just meet them at their place—only outside, of course. Per mission rules, there couldn't be elders and sisters in the same house paired up equally. I could have looked at the car arrangement and noticed that it was against the rules also, but it was a short drive, so I decided against questioning it. The mission area bordered the Pacific Ocean. There were few missionaries who served in coastal cities, and even when serving there, the beach and water were off-limits. Against the rules, even. No one could ever explain the damn rule for staying away from the water, though. By following the path in the Bible dictionary and *Book of Mormon*, it led me to a couple of scriptures, one in the *Book of Mormon*, where Nephi uses the analogy of the great Church being the whore of the earth. And this whore of the earth sits on the water, having dominion over it. So this might explain why missionaries were to stay away from the water. I'd asked several members, and the question was usually dismissed. I heard a story that some prophet had said the devil has power over the waters. I couldn't find anything to back this up, though it agreed with what I read in the *Standard Works*. I looked at the sixty-first section of *The Doctrine and Covenants*. Joseph Smith and his elders were canoeing down the Missouri River when, as I imagined it, when Joseph said, "I have a revelation coming" and proceeded to be the mouthpiece of the Lord. He then spoke. "There are many dangers upon the waters, and I, the Lord, have decreed many destructions upon the waters." He goes on to say, "Nevertheless, all flesh is in mine and he that is faithful among you shall not perish by the waters." After reading this, I was even *more* confused than when I started researching it. I put *The Doctrine and Covenants* away for another time, to read and ponder the revelations given through Joseph Smith the Prophet.

My T-shirt flapped hard against my skin as I walked on the beach. I thought how different the California coast was from Washington's. The jutting rocks and smooth holes were intriguing. I walked along the rocks with my rubber-soled tennis shoes providing traction against the dark brown and black rocks. As the water came up to my shoes, I jumped out of the way to keep them dry. With the churning waters fifteen feet below, contrasting colors of white and black from cresting waves crashing against the side of the seawall, I could sense doom—as if the devil *did* own the waters. But it was cold, dark water, so of course it felt like doom. It was a little scary in that I wasn't sure what doom the water would bring upon me. Was I too close to the water? At what point did the Holy Ghost stop on the beach when I got too close to the water? Having been warned and still getting near the water, was I in more danger than others? All these questions I asked myself, as I wished my mind would instead be centered on enjoying the moment. With a full stomach of casing-burnt hot dogs, I let my thoughts and feelings became more lackadaisical, and I started to have fun.

Surprisingly, for as little as we saw each other, we elders and sisters got along quite wonderfully. There were never any problems in the zone. All companionships got along perfectly, at least from what I could see. I think the congeniality of the companionships just carried over to the time spent on the beach. Each of us had a camera and took turns getting shots with one legs buried in the sand, looking like a one-legged pirate, or posing as a surfer while standing out on one of farthest rocks rising up out of the ocean. We got wet and the sisters' hair stuck to their small heads.

I took the opportunity to have an ad-hoc Zone Meeting. I went over the stats of the week for each of the companionships.

"Sister McCoy, would you like to explain how you taught *zero* First Discussions?" I asked, sitting on a picnic bench. "Do we need to go over the First Discussion, as maybe that's the problem: that you don't know what a First Discussion is?" Sister McCoy had been out three months. She was small and all her dresses went down to her ankles. I didn't know if it was because she was short or because she didn't want to show any leg. I thought perhaps the skirts the sisters wore could be no higher than the knee. I did find that the sisters liked baggy-looking dresses that seemed to hide their large curves.

"Well, we did a lot of proselytizing, though. Visited members and tracted," she said seriously.

"Sister McCoy, good to see that Sister Soren has taught you the right answers." I shot a quick look at Sister Soren and saw she enjoyed the jesting. "I'm just giving you a hard time. I don't worry about whether you guys are working. Not my job," I said, smiling at Sister McCoy.

"And what is your job, Elder Dorsey?" Sister Soren asked in defense of Sister McCoy.

"I'm not sure what my job is. Let's open it up to the zone. What's a zone leader's job?" I asked the seven missionaries.

"To take weekly stats," Elder Kenny said, enjoying the simplicity of the summary of a zone leader's job. He then looked up and thought about it a little more. "The fourth man in P-Day basketball.

"Both very good points, Elder Kenny. Any others?" I asked.

"Well, you pass on the stuff you learn in the Zone Leader Meetings," Sister McCoy said.

"All of which you hear in Zone Conference. Pretty much word for word. If anything, they think the zone leaders need to hear it twice. The coolest thing about those Zone Leader Meetings is the spread put out by the office staff and Sister Carlson," I said. "But good point again. Possibly, I relay pertinent information at times." I thought about the spread put out and my mouth watered. With the spread came the relationships of the zone leaders themselves. The first time I went, I enjoyed seeing Elder McDonnell. We hadn't seen each other since the Valley. But even more, I enjoyed seeing some of the seniors and the way they interacted with each other. That was where the joy came on those days. Although I didn't feel like one of the elite, the rest of them there—in their full suits, trimmed hair, all seemingly taller than me—I could see were the future leaders of the Church. There, in that group.

"You pick up foreign copies of the *Book of Mormon* and mail sent to the office," Elder Burton said.

"This I do, all of which you could do. So, seeing what zone leaders do, do we need them?" I asked.

"Well, about seniority within a zone. Like Sister McCoy looking to someone who has been out for a while, it's the experience you bring," Sister Soren said. I hadn't thought of that, and it felt good to hear it, especially from Sister Soren.

"Well, there is Elder Baldwin. He's been out longer than I have. Sister Soren, we were within a month of each other. I don't know if I bring any more experience than the other people in the zone. Although I liked the sound of it."

"Maybe you are more for the president and the mission rather than for the zone? The president can watch the zone more efficiently with zone leaders than just calling each of the missionaries himself." Elder Kenny said.

"Now that makes sense. Does that change your views on zone leaders if you knew they were in place to assist the president, rather than here to assist you?" I asked.

"Well, it's one and the same. The better the president runs his mission, the more available he is for what is really important," Elder Wagner said. I was impressed with his insight; he'd been out only six months, and this was his first area.

"Yeah. He needs the zone leaders and the APs to actually run the mission while he does the work of praying for companionships and getting inspiration on what to speak about. Also, his family is here and that's as important to him as tending to the mission. So he does need the zone leaders as much as we do, really," Sister Soren said.

"All points I'm not sure I'd thought about, guys. I think I even understand my job more. Whoa, that was good." I wrapped up the Zone Meeting with a toss of the Frisbee to Elder Brady, after telling him to go long.

As I got up to walk to the water, I heard Elder Baldwin say my name. "Elder Dorsey, you got a minute?"

"Sure. What's up?" I asked, hardly moved from the picnic table.

"Can you ask the president a question for me next time you see him?"

"Sure. You can always put it in your weekly letter if you don't want to talk with me about it." I offered this as a token of friendship rather than a way out.

"No, this is fine. Maybe you have some insight also. I want to know why I was overlooked as the zone leader here."

"Oh, OK. I hadn't thought of that. You are district leader and could have easily moved into position as zone leader."

"That's what I thought. So will you ask the President?"

"Sure. No problem," I said.

"Thanks," Elder Baldwin said, making his way to the water, where the sisters were writing in the sand with sticks.

Sister Soren started making her way back to the table, which I hadn't left yet. I slowly picked away at a bag of Ruffles. I sat down on the bench and looked out over the beach and saw we were the only ones out today.

Sister Soren and I were sitting on opposite sides of the heavy, shellacked-wood picnic table. The surface of the table provided a topographical history of Morro Bay Beach: *who loves who* and *who sucks what*. Burn marks in the deep-pitched surface bore witness to young boys smoking cigarettes bought from a stranger. Knife cuts showed someone waiting for a lover, only to have them not show up, left only to whittle.

"Elder Dorsey?"

I looked up from behind my Frog Eyes. "Yeah?"

"Today was fun. It could have been the funnest day of my mission."

"Sister Soren, it's only a day at the beach. You're mission hasn't been that fun, then."

"It hasn't. Has yours?"

"Well, none of this is really fun. It's not even meant to be, I think," I said.

"It should be a little, though."

"A little, I guess. This has been fun, though. Possibly one of the funnest days on my mission too."

"See? Maybe it's just a really fun day and doesn't need to be compared to other fun days to be any more fun."

"That's the best thing I have heard, unrelated to the Church, in a long time," I said, thinking about what Sister Soren had just said.

We sat for a moment, looking out at the water and our companions on the beach.

"Elder Dorsey?"

"Yeah, Sister Soren?"

"Let's do this again."

"OK."

"Let's do it again before anything changes."

"OK."

We threw the last Frisbee between the two cars on the way out of the parking lot, the tires crunching on the rocky drive and the downing sun lighting the waves behind us.

* * * * *

Elder Burton bought a weight-loss-powder drink from the Millets. He'd started taking the supplement shortly after arriving in the area. They approached him, which I learned when I asked Elder Burton how he started taking the drink.

"So does it work?" I asked, sitting on my bed, showered and dressed, relaxing before starting the day.

"It sure does. I've lost fifteen pounds since I've been here."

"Hey, that's pretty good," I said dishonestly. "What about the last couple months walking the track? Have you seen a change from that?" I asked, truly wondering.

"Ten pounds in the last couple months. I think it is the supplement finally kicking in along with the walking," Elder Burton said, and I thought it sounded scripted.

"It's probably the combination of the two. You are right; it's hard to tell with losing weight because it's so retroactive. It's hard to think what you were doing, like, three months before, which the results are showing now. It's like hard work: real pain while doing it, and sometimes takes years before paying off," I said.

"I'm looking good, Elder." Elder Burton stood up and sucked in his gut, his XXX T-shirt hanging out over his stomach into the air. "Look at that. I think I can lose it," he said, proud of the lost fifteen pounds and his newfound physique.

"I think you're looking good. How do you keep track of the weight, though?" I asked.

"Whenever I'm at members' homes, I use their scales."

"Really?" I was intrigued. "Are they different?"

"Oh, yeah. They are all different. I like the electronic ones with the digital display."

"Who has that one?" I asked.

"You know the Snows? They have the two teenagers that had to go to soccer practice that night we ate at their house."

"I remember. Man, and they're all in good shape."

"I've noticed that." Elder Burton looked up. "It's not necessarily the ones with weight problems that have the scales right there."

"We always kept ours under the bathroom counter. Same scale since I can remember. My mom still has it. It's looking pretty old."

"I've seen some of those. Most of them are just the dial scales."

"You hope it's not the difference in the scales," I said in fun.

"Well, sometimes it's more than it should be."

"Maybe they do that on purpose to freak them out or something."

"I don't know."

"I'm going to start using the scales too."

"OK. Then we can compare the weights. Does yours fluctuate much?"

"Some. I haven't weighed myself regularly, though, since I was home. Then I weighed myself every day."

"I don't weigh myself every day. I don't want to."

"It might be fun now, though, while you are losing weight.

Maybe it would even help," I said, concerned.

"Maybe, but they're, like, thirty bucks."

"Oh, That much? That kinda sucks," I said, thinking I shouldn't say "sucks" while on a mission. But then I thought about the words that some of the missionaries used. I noticed them first at BYU, when guys would get mad on the basketball court and yell a word foreign to me: *frick, flip, flipping-yang, fudge,* and, little better, *freak*. Eventually, I heard them all and was used to them, although I never picked up any of the BYU slang. It was all the same, though. When I heard those words, I instantly thought *fuck, fuck an egg, fuck it*, and *motherfucker*. These words I'd hardly heard in my life, but when thinking of what the slang words were replacing, I ended up with quite a vocabulary in my mind, but not in speech.

"Go take a shower and we will go to the Millets to get the magic powder," I said, trying to get Elder Burton going a little faster.

He was surprisingly buttery when getting ready, taking far too much time.

I've always thought it a good indication of the importance of what a person is doing when they don't care how long it takes them to get to where they are going. The Millets lived about twenty miles from the apartment, up in the hills behind the campus. We had tracted there and knocked on their door, but no one was home. I had insisted that Elder Burton at least call them and make sure they were home. They weren't, but we drove up there anyway. Oh, the life of a full-time missionary, wasting perfectly good time. Supposedly the most important work in the world, and yet we acted in such a manner as if the *Pits of Hell* weren't such a bad afterlife. If a mission sucked and a marriage sucked and pretty much life sucked, then *Pits of Hell* sounded more like a backyard barbecue.

The sun was almost at its highest for the day before succumbing to the darker side. We had dawdled all morning and looked forward to an afternoon of mundane tracting and talking. It didn't really matter, though, whether the focus was morning tracting or afternoon tracting, it was all part of the workday: a missionary's work stops only in sleep.

Sister Millet was pulling a garbage can in from the front of the driveway, towards the garage. The house sat on a small hill. The college and town were spread out below, looking small from up here. The mountain the house was backed up against was brown in reality, but it looked red to me. The trees gave way to boulders and steep dirt cliffs. I wondered if the Millets ever climbed up the mountain? Sister Millet was attractive for a fifty-something-year-old. Her pulled-up hair made her look younger than she did when she wore it down, which she did at church on Sundays. Sister Millet was so busy she was always doing stuff when being talked to. Or at least she was always doing something when we missionaries spoke to her.

"Hi, Sister Millet," Elder Burton said as we walked through the opened iron gates to the drive.

"Oh, Elders. Hi," she said, dragging the plastic-bottom garbage can up the aggregate driveway. "What are you guys doing way up here?" *Scratch, scratch.* I wanted pick up the damn garbage can and carry it for her.

"I came by to get some more Metrolax-A. I ran out a few days ago," Elder Burton said. I wondered why people shared information that wasn't needed. Sister didn't care when he ran out. It made Elder Burton look a little pathetic, and that was not what he was.

"Oh, I wish you had called," she said in a beautifully concerned voice. "We stopped ordering that a few weeks ago. I'm sorry I didn't call you. I'd forgotten that you were getting it."

"Well, can you order me some more, then? I'll get extra since you have to order it," Elder Burton said expectantly.

"The problem with that is that we always ordered in bulk. That was the only way we could get the rate we did. So if you were to order in the small quantities that you do, it would almost triple the price."

"Well could I just call the company and order direct from them?" Elder Burton asked quickly. He was holding his own against Sister Millet.

"Let me get back to you on that. You may need a business license to order from them, and I'd hate to get in any trouble. Can I call you later about it?" She said, knowing Elder Burton had no choice but to say "Of course."

"Sure, that would be great." Elder Burton was thinking she was doing him a favor.

"OK. I have your number in the directory. Has it changed?" She asked, still dragging the garbage can. We'd moved to the back of the house, where they had a concrete pad and a top over the garbage cans.

"Hasn't changed. Should be around tonight. Thanks again," Elder Burton said, then turned and looked at me.

"Good to see you, Sister Millet. Talk to you soon," I said, peaking out over Elder Burton.

"Have you over for dinner soon, Elders." And she locked the side gate behind us.

It was going to be Elder Burton's birthday in two days, so I bought him a scale as a present. I thought he wanted one and couldn't buy one. It was a dial scale—white with a black background with white lettering. It looked like the dashboard of a fancy sports car. Elder Burton seemed to like it. He didn't want to get on it, but I did.

CHAPTER 14

Zone Conference snuck up on Elder Burton and me. We were having so much fun with our lives in San Luis Obispo, the thought of a pep talk from the center of the mission wasn't even on our minds. Yet, I still looked forward to Zone Conferences as a chance to see some of the elders I hadn't seen in a month. With transfers each month, we didn't really keep in touch by phone or through letters. It was simply seeing each other at the Zone Conferences that kept us in touch.

It was a sea of dark suits, with both tall and short suits standing next to each other. The colors that jumped out were those of the dresses worn by the sisters: yellows, pinks, and purples. Most of the men's ties were red or blue. Everyone looked nice in their "missionary best." The sisters and elders were all talking in the chapel, between the pews and in the aisles, groups of two, and three, and four, all laughing. I looked for an elder I knew so I could walk up to someone, say "Hi," and join in on the laughter. I saw Elder Anderson from Saugus. He was hard to miss, with his striking blond hair and six-five frame. He still wanted me to go down and live with him at BYU. Maybe that's what missions were for, to find your future college roommate, as I'd had offers from just about everyone. Elder McDonnell was going to go to Utah State. He tried convincing me to go there and be roommates together, with promises of riding motorcycles. It sounded intriguing; I told him I'd think about it.

"Elder Anderson. How are ya?" I asked, throwing out my strong zone leader hand.

"Elder Dorsey. Man, good to see you. I'm so glad to be out of Valencia," he said with a relieved look and grin. Elder Anderson served in Valencia while I was in Saugus. His companion and the companionship they lived with were notorious for bad behavior.

"Oh, I hear you on that. That place was bad!" I said, not wanting to share too much, as I wasn't sure where exactly Elder Anderson was coming from.

"Question for you, Elder Anderson—now that it's behind us, is it hard to love your companion when he's Elder Lampkin?" I asked sincerely.

"Oh, Elder Dorsey! You know I can't answer that," he said with a loving grin. Elder Anderson's smile lessened the impact of his intimidating frame.

"Thought I'd try. I think we can love everyone, of course, especially once we get to know them. But you still come across people that may weaken the theory."

"Ah, Lampkin wasn't *that* bad," he said. "So how have you been? You like being a zone leader?" He asked.

"It's OK. You know, not much to it," I said. "I bet you're good at it."

Elder Anderson made me feel great every time I talked with him. "Well again, not much to it, so isn't hard to be good at if that's the case." We could hear Elder Pratt at the microphone telling us all to sit down as politely as he possibly could. I thought that his ultrapolite tone might have been because he was the junior AP. He had been speaking in front of the mission for only a month, and he was probably still getting used to it. I knew I wouldn't want to do it.

"I'll talk to you later. After..." Elder Anderson said as he went to sit down next to his already seated companion. Then I remembered the bandana that I had in my pocket. I was sitting down with Elder Burton when I pulled it out and looked around at Elder Anderson; he saw it and smiled in anticipation of getting his favorite headgear back. I knotted the bandana and threw it through two rows of surprised missionaries into Elder Anderson's mitt of a hand. It was my favorite bandana, although it was never mine.

Elder Pratt went over the Zone Conference Program, after tapping on the microphone. With the amount of time it took us to sit down, he wasn't sure if the mic was working. After a couple thumps from the speaker above, though, he couldn't doubt the integrity of the speakers. "Hello elders and sisters." He had a contagious smile, backed by a striking, athletic face and slicked-backed hair. "Thanks for finding your seats so fast. We are going to start off with an opening song. I understand Sister Soren—" He found her next to Elder Burton and me on the pew. "There you are! Understand you play the piano. Would you be willing to play for us?" he asked, knowing she would have to oblige.

"Oh sure," she said as she got up and walked to the end of the pew.

"Let's start off with *Called To Serve*. I'm sure you all have the page number memorized, but for those who don't, it's page forty-three," Elder Pratt said, then moved four feet to the right and held up his hand, ready to lead the music. He stood there with feet together, his long legs shorter than his even longer torso, his arm poised to lead us. Sister Soren played an extended introduction to warm herself up. By the time she was finished, I was in the mood to sing. I had wanted to be able to bust out in song ever since the time I sang with Missy. My tenor range was limited, I felt. I couldn't go high and couldn't go low without coughing and needing water. I thought to myself how nice it would be to find something you were a natural at and could do better than 95 percent of the people in the world. With Elder Burton on one side of me and an empty seat between myself and Sister McCoy, I could risk my voice cracking, as it would get hidden or lost in the group.

After the song and the prayer, given by one of the other zone leaders in the audience, we heard from Brother Emery, the Fleet Coordinator for the mission cars. He had ceased counting the days of no accidents, as we'd had a string of accidents in the past few months. It was no fun keeping track of a record that sucked. We then split up into two groups led by Elders Westra and Pratt, while President Carlson conducted one-on-one interviews.

I shook Elder Westra's hand when I walked in to my group. We exchanged bonding pleasantries as I proceeded to find a seat somewhere in the middle of the room. Seats quickly filled up in the Relief Society room we were using. I spotted Elder Burton saving a chair…for possibly his favorite companion? I took the seat beside him. Elder Westra then spoke to the group in a quiet voice. Whether in conversation or in front of a room, he demanded attention, perhaps since it was the only way his soft voice could be heard. His small, round glasses looked out of place, as if he was fitted with the wrong pair. I thought he'd look better with square ones, to accent his sharp jawbone. He had a strong face, but with his small frame and round glasses, he looked a lot smaller than he really was.

"Elders and sisters—thanks for being here today," he said, "I'm going to start off by asking a question. And before you answer, I want you to really think back through your past as an adult—or young adulthood, I guess—and as a child. OK, the question is: What is your favorite story in the *Book of Mormon*?" The room was silent as we thought of an answer to his request. Finally, he broke the silence, "OK. Now that you've thought of it, I'm going to go around the room and ask each of you what story it is." He started with the elders in the front row. "Elder, go ahead."

The elder shut the *Book of Mormon* on his lap and said, "The story of the wars between the Lamanites and the Nephites."

"OK. Anyone in particular?" Elder Westra asked.

"No. All of them."

"OK. I like them too," he said, and then looked at the next person in the row. "What about you, Elder?"

"I like the one where the brothers go back to get the plates of brass from Laban, and Nephi has to kill him."

"Well, let's hope it's not the killing that you like about it," Elder Westra said, getting a few laughs from the group, including one from me. "Thanks, Elder. Great story! Ever thought of why you like it?"

"No, not really. It shows how the Lord can work, though—in commanding Nephi to kill another man."

"That's true. As we see throughout the *Book of Mormon* and the Bible," Elder Westra said, summing up perfectly and restating what the elder had said, just saying it better. Elder Westra went around the room as each one of the elders and sisters shared their favorite story, gave it some thought, and listened to the rest. By the end, I had a burning feeling to read the stories that I'd heard from the others. I was familiar with them and knew where to find them. After the last missionary shared, Elder Westra explained the reason behind the exercise.

"Can you feel the spirit in the room right now? It's here! It's here because we have been talking about the *Book of Mormon*, and it's here because we have been talking about it with the enthusiasm and excitement that is perfect for the spirit to feel welcomed." He shared a couple of scriptures from the *Book of Mormon* on feeling the spirit and inviting it in. I shared his thoughts as well. I thought how he had brought the feeling of the spirit just by having each person share. I envisioned the possibilities: sharing with members while at dinner, sharing stories with investigators before a Discussion, even sharing stories with my family someday, to have the spirit in the room like it was there tonight.

Elder Pratt gave a smiling talk from the Missionary Guide. I recognized it instantly as the writings on Charity from the Christ-Like Attributes section. As much as I liked Elder Pratt, I had a hard time believing that a guy my age, with what I assumed was a similar background (public schools and little college) could possibly add knowledge to anything that wasn't already in the book.

Therefore, I sat back and enjoyed what I heard and didn't worry about taking notes. What I wasn't prepared for was how much I enjoyed having Elder Pratt teach. It was like getting a professional teacher for the morning study. He was good. He didn't go off on tangents; he shared a few personal stories from his experience in the field and stuck right to the Missionary Guide. My heart was light in feeling, but my mind was heavy in thought. I noticed that I was able to think clearly on what I heard.

President Carlson had finished his interviews and was sitting on the stand by himself. We were the northernmost zone in the mission. I thought that might be why Sister Carlson wasn't with him. It was one thing to drive an hour and speak at a Zone Conference, but a three-hour drive there and back.... Some people couldn't lose full days. President Carlson was in a hurry, shaking hands on the run, but he always looked into the eyes of us missionaries. His talk was poignantly directed, it seemed, at me. My stomach dropped from this awareness.

"I want to talk today about actively searching out people to teach, which comes down to actively working each day," he said, listing off scriptures from the Old Testament, the New Testament, *Book of Mormon*, and *The*

Pearl of Great Price, finishing with three different quotes from the First Presidency. He then told stories of how he had languished from hard work on his farm one summer but how he felt so proud and worthwhile of his work in the end. It was a beautifully given talk, with sternness in the words showing the truthfulness of what he was relaying to us all. There is a story in Mormon history that was written shortly after the Prophet Joseph Smith was killed. In the story, President Young, still somewhat unknown in the Mormon community, was speaking before a congregation, when his face suddenly took on the appearance of the Prophet Joseph Smith. That's what I felt President Carlson's face doing, although it wasn't the Prophet of God I saw, but God himself. I felt as if he were speaking directly to me, telling me to get busy. All the trips to the beach that Elder Burton and I took casually throughout the weeks came to mind. The lack of speediness throughout the days, the afternoon naps, and comic books in the sun—they all showed me how I had misprioritized my time. The missionary work came second, only after I had exhausted all rationalized distractions. As I listened, he carefully pulled out a letter from his coat pocket.

"I would like to share a letter with you today from one of the parents of a missionary in our zone. If there is ever a question as to what kind of letters we want from your parents, well, this should be a good example of one."

Dear President Carlson,

I am writing to you to thank you for putting a wonderful missionary with my son. I'd been worried about him for some time. With his letters home and the few times we talked, I could tell he wasn't happy and thought he would come home. Since you have put him with Elder Dorsey,…"

I was hoping I hadn't heard that right. *Oh no!* I thought, this is not what you want your peers to hear in a Zone Conference. Why couldn't he have just shared it with me in an *interview* or something? Not that sounding like the best companion in the mission was bad, but I'd rather have the missionaries hear it straight from Elder Burton instead of from his mom. I could have gone with never even *having* it said—acknowledged coolness dies. President Carlson read the rest of the letter. It was short and thankful. She said I had saved her son's mission. I made a mental note to start screening Elder Burton's letters home.

"Elder Dorsey," Elder Pratt had caught me while walking down the steps of the church building. "Hey! Elder Westra and me are coming over tonight for splits. Did he talk to you yet?" he asked, while putting his hand on my shoulder.

"No, but that's OK. When are you guys coming? We'll make sure to be there," I said, as I noticed my heart beating furiously.

"We're going to pack up here, then get going." It was the closest that Elder Pratt I had come to talking at length. "Can we get some directions? I know it's up the 101, but what exit?" he asked, pulling out a small notepad from his white shirt pocket.

"Yeah, it's exit 177. There is only one San Luis Obispo exit; just don't miss it," I said, with my voice relaxed and my words trailing at the end.

"Great! We will see you in a little bit," Elder Pratt said.

Then, looking at Elder Burton beside me. "Elder Burton, look forward to getting to know you a little better," he said, putting his notepad back in his pocket, while sticking out his other hand to shake Elder Burton's.

"I look forward to it too," Elder Burton said, his words bouncing with Elder Pratt's hearty handshake.

"You didn't know they were coming?" Elder Kenny asked from the back seat, as I thought about what it was like riding with four elders in a Toyota Corolla.

"No. I think it will be kind of cool, though. Just dropping in on missionaries like that," I said.

"You do? I think it's kind of rude," Elder Kenny said. "It's not like the army or something."

"Well, it kind of is. Hadn't really thought of it like that. It wouldn't be fun to drop in on cool elders, but bad ones—it would be kind of cool," I said, hoping to dig myself out a little.

"Maybe. So is your place ready to have them over?" Elder Brady asked.

"Yeah, I think so." I looked over at Elder Burton. "What do *you* think, Elder Burton?"

"Yeah, it's pretty clean. I think I have my comic books on the bed, but we have some time to straighten up."

"You think they would mind seeing your comic books?" I asked, knowing I wouldn't want them lying on my bed.

Elder Kenny started laughing and threw his hands on Elder Burton's big shoulders, shaking him. "You wouldn't want them to see those after that *nice* letter from your mom, Elder."

Elder Burton turned a quick shade of red, high up on his fatty cheeks.

"Yeah, yeah, yeah. I didn't know about it, guys. I really didn't," he said in his defense. I was looking at him, smiling slightly, watching him struggle with the embarrassment that he brought on himself

"Elder Dorsey, you came across like the perfect companion from that," Elder Kenny said, always ready with the obvious.

"Yeah, that couldn't hurt. I'm *the man*, guys," I said, reveling.

"Elder Burton, is he really that good of a companion?" Elder Kenny asked.

"He's a pretty good companion, he is. Easy to get along with," Elder Burton said.

"OK guys, OK. I think that's enough. It's going to start sounding weird here soon." I said, hoping to muzzle Elder Burton's words about me as a companion.

"Did you know he was going to read it, Elder Dorsey?" Elder Kenny asked.

"Elder Kenny, you have a lot of questions. I didn't know. I wouldn't have let him read it. It was very nice," I said, looking at Elder Burton, careful not to hurt him, "but I wouldn't want it read. It's kind of personal, more than anything," I said, happy with my final statement, hoping to diminish the talk that would ensue and the nonstop jesting from other elders throughout the rest of my mission.

Elders Westra and Pratt were only twenty minutes behind us. It was still early afternoon, and the plan was to tract for three hours, then double up on the dinner appointment and splits. The AP's caught us on a busy night. I was able to confirm splits once we got home, relieved to find they were both still on. We even had two appointments scheduled with the splits. It was the only night in two months that we had two teaching appointments on the same night, with splits scheduled. Just looking at Elder Burton, I could see on his face that he wasn't happy about his little world in San Luis being interrupted. This was hardly a life to be interrupted, I thought. Of all the lives I could possibly live, I think I'd want the monotony of mission life with a companion to be broken by strangers or acquaintances.

We split up—Elder Westra and me in our car, and Elder Burton and Elder Pratt in their AP wagon. I had taken Elder Westra's place in Chatsworth. He was a very popular missionary there. The fact that I was both popular *and* from the same city was not only unique, but also bonding for the both of us. We had plenty to talk about with respect to home, past areas, missionaries, and families.

"So, you still keep in touch with Rachel Barrett?" He asked, after we had knocked on a few doors.

"Oh, not really. She wrote me a couple letters while I was in Saugus, but that's about it. I broke the rules and wrote her back. Nothing big, though."

"She's a cool girl. She likes me, you know," he said, concerned with my thoughts.

"I know," I said, confirming his statement "All she does it talk about you," I lied. "You were very popular there in Chatsworth. You couldn't have laid low until I got there, so the transition for the ward wasn't so painful. I felt they'd replaced Michael Jordan with World B. Free. Just wasn't right."

"Hey, I couldn't control that. Wasn't Elder Fisher fun to serve with? I loved him," Elder Westra said.

"Oh yeah, he was probably my favorite comp so far. I've had some good ones, but more so, just easy to get along with. Elder Fischer was like serving with a prophet or apostle. He kind of had it all."

"He was good. Just super nice and considerate to everyone he ever met," Elder Westra said.

"He gave me this advice one day, and I've constantly gone back to it on the old mission so far. He said, 'You might as well work hard for the next two years. You are out here already; might as well work hard and see what becomes of it.' It made a lot of sense, especially when you consider how hard he worked. Did you guys work hard while you were together?" I asked, already guessing the answer.

"We did. We were only together a month, but we worked hard. Didn't you see all the work that was there when you came in?" he said, throwing his arm over my shoulder, shaking me slightly.

While he was taller than me, his real presence was that of an AP "So, you think you are going to take Rachel out after the mission?"

"Oh I don't know," I said.

"Elder Dorsey, this isn't an interview."

"Well, we have really kept the whole thing a total friendship, not even touching any other subjects. You know how it is on the mission; it feels weird to even *think* a girl is pretty. It's hard enough trying to keep in touch with one. And she's pretty."

"Yeah, she's pretty. Well, just to let you know, I don't plan on taking her out. I think she wishes I was planning on it. We got pretty close there in Chatsworth."

"Not too close, though, right?" I asked.

"Oh no. Not like that. We just had a lot of fun talking in the end. You know how it is, if women can talk to you, then they are willing to spend the rest of their *lives* with you," he said, surprising me with his expert perception after two years on a mission.

"Rachel and I hardly talked: a few times while I served there and then a couple letters. So we would have to talk a lot more before I decided to take her out or anything," I said, leaving out the late-night phone calls I received from her about once a week, and the talk of past relationships, and the fact she was a virgin but almost wasn't. Rachel and I had gotten close, but no one knew. Well Elder *Burton* knew, but he wouldn't say anything. He liked having that secret.

We walked and talked. Elder Westra was going home the next month. He said he was going to BYU after stopping off in Bellevue. He said he didn't want to spend too much time at home, that *things* happen after the mission at home. He said this jokingly, with the obvious hint of truth. It instantly brought forward my thoughts about life after the mission. For some reason, I assumed I would go home and then go off to BYU. But as much as I thought this, and said it, and planned for it, I knew it wasn't going to be what happened. I truly didn't know what would happen.

"Dorsey, if you head down to BYU, call me. I'd be happy to be roommates with you. I think we would have fun," Elder Westra said.

"I'll let you know. That would be fun," I said, secretly thinking how boring it would be.

"Funny talking about it when it's so close. It seems for so long they've been more of dreams than plans."

"I can see that. It would be a little weird thinking about it. A good weird, though."

"Yeah, a good weird," Elder Westra said, lost in his thoughts. He then advised me he would give me the next door.

"Thanks, Elder. Very thoughtful of you." No one liked tracting.

"No problem," he got out of his mouth, right before the door opened. A young girl opened it slightly, her small body filling the space.

"Hi, is your mommy home?" I asked. I hated being a stranger talking to kids. She left the door open, turned, and ran into the dark space behind the door.

"Baby, who's at the door?" I heard a woman's voice, her heels banging on the tiled floor. I heard the hint of frustration in the question to her daughter. She came from behind the door and opened it further so she could see us. "Hi, can I help you?" she asked. She had straight, short brown hair that hung partially over her eyes. "Oh, you're the missionaries. Well I'd invite you in, but I'm right in the middle of something. Can you come back later? My parents will be home then," she said cutely.

"Uh…Uh…Uh…." Of all times for the hot-chick stutter to come out! "Sure. I don't know who you are, though." I spoke so honestly, I loved it. A bold statement that in the past would have been a time of harrow.

"Oh, I'm Melissa Black."

"OK, I know the Blacks. Well, it's nice to meet you, Melissa. I'm Elder Dorsey, and this is Elder Westra. We were just out tracting, and here we are."

"Nice to meet you guys," she said smiling, her classic features accentuated. "I'll tell my parents you stopped by."

"Thanks. Well, I guess we will see you around." I said, not knowing if she was going to church or not. I knew I hadn't seen her there before, though. She was unforgettable.

"Bye," she said, the small girl at her side, peeking through the open door while we walked down the drive.

"Pretty woman," Elder Westra said. It surprised me a little.

"She was."

One First Discussion came from the afternoon tracting, but it was a short First out of the pamphlet that I had taken over from Elder Westra, when he was about to relinquish the open door to the rejection of a free *Book of Mormon*. He was somewhat stunned at first, at what I appeared to be able to do—teach a complete First on a doorstep.

"That explains the high number of First Discussions you guys are reporting each week," he said.

"Yep. Burton and I have been working on it and told the rest of the zone about it too. It's actually kind of fun. Makes tracting more fun at least," I said.

"I think it's great. Why not? I wish I had thought of it."

"You can claim it if you want." I said this, not meaning it. I knew it had potential. I wasn't sure to what extent, but it had potential in something, somewhere, with someone.

I'd called the dinner appointment, advising them that there would be four hungry, twenty-something men at their table that night, not two. I didn't give them a choice in the matter. It was a luxury I had as a full-time missionary in the Church that they had chosen as their path to righteousness. They had lots of bread and butter out on the table. When the meal was over, there wasn't any food left.

The splits were scheduled to pick us up at our place, and they were waiting there when we returned. Elder Westra and Elder Pratt were going to head back to Ventura and skip the splits. I was relieved again. I couldn't have planned it better, though, to have the splits sitting there waiting. While I thought that, I wondered why I even cared. I wanted to talk with Elder Burton about his day with Elder Pratt, but it would have to wait until after splits, making for a long night of splits.

"Elder Burton!" I said, running up the steps, grabbing my books for the night, "Who do you want to split with tonight?" I asked. Brother Morrison was waiting in his car, a Ford Escort. He was a big man, appearing even bigger in a compact car. It looked a little cramped for both Elder Burton and Brother Morrison, and I was sure that Elder Burton would have rather gone with Dale anyway. Dale was twenty-three, going to school, and laid back about missionary work. He was a little goofy, so he and Burton got along great.

"I'll go with Dale," he said, already up in the room, getting his things together.

"OK. You know where you are going and everything?" I asked. We had just gone over the directions in the car, so I knew I shouldn't have asked.

"Just went over it. I have it."

"OK. Let's meet back here at eight thirty. Short visits, quick Discussions, in and out," I said, knowing it would cheer him up.

"Sounds good."

When both our teaching appointments weren't home (or didn't answer the door), I suggested we go downtown and talk to people on the street. At the last minute I added, "Or we could go back to our place and wait for Elder Burton to get back. It won't be a long wait."

"I think that would be better," and that's all he said as we started the car and drove back to our place slowly, in no hurry to get there, seemingly enjoying the drive, the conversation, or both.

With my thoughts racing at times about what I would be doing after the mission, I thought it a good opportunity to ask some advice from an adult.

"So, Brother Morrison. Are you where you thought you would be when you got home from your mission?" Brother Morrison had served a mission in Canada; I couldn't remember what part, though.

"Where I thought I'd be now?" He asked, either not understanding the question or needing more time to formulate the answer.

"Had you planned on being where you are today? Family, San Luis Obispo, on a split with a missionary?" I said.

"Pretty much. I went to school after my mission and knew that I'd take my small family wherever I got a job teaching."

"That was pretty serious, wasn't it? Not knowing where you were going to live and what you would be doing?" I asked.

"Not really. After going to school, a person has a lot of options. I could have taken a job anywhere, but my wife and I were able to not only get the job I wanted, but also a beautiful place to live and raise a family."

"Lots of stress going through it? School and family and working?" I asked.

"Again, not really. I had school loans, and Tami took care of the kids. It was tight but stable. It was a fun time, not a bad time at all."

"So you are where you want to be and have what you imagined?"

"I am. For the most part, I am. I haven't done all the things I wanted to do or seen all the things I've wanted to see, but there is still a lot of time, and the things that you wanted to do change."

"Yeah, I guess they would. I hadn't thought of that."

"So, how was the split with Elder Pratt?" I asked Elder Burton after Brother Morrison had left.

"It was alright. He asked a lot of questions."

"He did? About what?"

"What we did."

"What did you tell him?"

"That we tracted a lot."

"Well, we *do* do that." I said. "Anything else?"

"He wanted to know whether we worked hard. And I told him we did."

"Do you think we work hard?" I asked in fun.

"I think we do. What do you think?" Elder Burton asked, getting surprisingly serious.

"I don't know, Elder. I don't know. Sometimes I'm just trying to get through the days."

* * * * *

We had planned a hike with the zone. I gave Elder Burton the chore of finding a trail guide from the ward. We found out about an old mine in one of the higher hills behind the campus. It wasn't far from our apartment, so we met there and convoyed up the roads to the trailhead. The sisters were wearing shorts; it was warm. There was a sign at the beginning of the trailhead.

"This it, Elder Burton?" I asked, wanting to treat him like the tour guide for the day, the master of the trail.

"This is it," he said.

"OK. You're sure, though? I wasn't sure if the Hikers' Trail sign was what we were looking for."

"Elder Dorsey, is it going to be one of those days?" he asked.

I really didn't know whether he was joking or not.

Always ready with a comment, Elder Kenny said, "Hey, you guys sound married!" That could be the absolute last thing a missionary wanted to hear about his relationship with his companion.

"Burton, I was just having fun." I said, making sure he understood, while thinking Elder Kenny was a pain—a funny pain, but a pain nonetheless.

"I know. It's fine," Elder Burton said, shaking his head a little in wonderment of my constant taunting.

The trail went down to a stream spanning seven feet. Although it was several yards from the street and the cars, we had hoped for a longer hike. There was a faint trail on the other side of the stream that we agreed to follow. Crossing became a comic scene when Sister Soren slipped into the stream. She was able to catch herself with her long legs before falling into it entirely. She was wet up to her waist, but trooper that she was, she wanted to continue the hike. The rest of us were dry, finding the rocks sufficient as stepping-stones. The trail went sharply up, with exposed roots acting as handholds up the steep embankment. The trail had been traveled on recently, as the fresh dirt was exposed before we even reached it. The trees and undergrowth were dense, but the small, worn trail offered enough room to progress. When the trail split in two, we took the worn trail to the right and came upon a camp. We were high on the hill, hidden behind trees and dense bushes. The only sounds were those of a running waterfall down to the stream we had crossed and heavy breathing from the elders behind me. It was Elder Brady who came upon the top of the hill first and stopped, standing in the middle of the small camp. It was a clean camp: no garbage or bags or dishes. There was a small wood table next to the aluminum cot, with a toothbrush on it. I knew it was David's camp and thought about telling the bishop.

"You think someone lives up here?" Elder Brady asked, with an inquisitive smirk.

"I don't know. Don't think I could do it," I said. Elder Burton was the last one to get to the small camp. He was slow and out of breath.

Breathing heavily and leaning on a walking stick he'd acquired on the trail, he inquired, "What's this?"

"Looks like someone lives here," Elder Kenny said.

There was an out-of-place reverent feeling throughout the group in the trees.

Elder Burton moved his body over to the cot and sat down. "Elder Burton, you can't sit on someone's bed!" Elder Brady said.

"He lives in the woods. I don't think he will mind," Elder Burton said.

"So what if he lives in the woods? It's still his place, here, this place!" Elder Kenny said.

"We should go, guys," I said. It was eerie there in the woods, in David's camp, the sun hidden behind layers of leaves.

"I agree. Let's go, this is a little creepy," said a dripping Sister Soren, her quiet companion near.

"Hey, Sister Soren. Would you date a guy that lived in the woods?" I asked.

"I don't think so. Not really into that."

"What? Why? You would discount a guy for living in the woods? What about Moroni?" I asked, trying desperately to flirt, but struggling.

"Well, I'd date Moroni, but I doubt this guy is Moroni," she said. I thought how striking David really was—"out of her league" striking. She would be shocked if she knew.

"Maybe it's one of the Three Nephites' camps," Elder Kenny said smartly.

"Don't you think they travel together?" I asked.

"I doubt it. Don't you think you would get a little tired of traveling with the same two guys for thousands of years?" Elder Kenny asked.

"Yeah, I guess. It's hard to imagine them getting tired of each other, but I guess they are people," I said, feeling grossly inadequate in my knowledge of the Three Nephites.

The trail followed the small, cascading stream up the steep hill, as we continued to climb. There were parts of the stream where the water was high enough for the sisters to somehow end up in the middle of the stream, with water coming down onto their heads. The elders stood on the side, still dry, just watching the sisters getting wet, their hair making them look sad as it lay flat against their small heads. By the time we got back to the car, several hours had passed and we were all tired. The hike made us hungry, so we went to the local Wendy's and grabbed burgers and milkshakes, all the while talking about the harrowing experiences on the hike and the small camp we had found. The sisters had brought a change of clothes, and we all felt better having them dry, without their clothes sticking to them. Before we split up at Wendy's, Elder Baldwin talked with me in private about why he was overlooked as a zone leader.

"I talked to President Carlson about it, Elder Baldwin. He said it's because you hadn't passed the scripture memorization requirements in the mission," I said, feeling a little sheepish, as I had spent only a couple hours on the whole thing and hardly thought about them, but they did seem to be more available in my head since learning them.

"I passed those with Elder Nelson when I first transferred in. He never reported it."

"Oh, that would suck. Well, I'll go ahead and sign off for you then. Did you pass off the Discussions only? Or did you get the overachiever award for Discussions and Missionary Guide Scriptures?" I asked.

"Just the Discussion ones. But if you think it will make a difference, I'll get the Missionary Guide ones signed off too."

"I don't know if it will make a difference in anything. Do you mean whether you are called as a zone leader or not?" I asked.

"I don't know. I would at least like to be considered and not have the lack of memorizing scriptures be holding me back."

"OK. No problem. I'll sign off on the Discussions, and next week sign you off on the Missionary Guide Scriptures. You will be one of the Master Scriptoriums in the mission. Very few of us," I said in a serious tone, denoting playfulness.

"Just what I want. Did you pass them all off?" he asked.

"Yeah, but remember I told you I learned them and passed them within a day, so it was pretty easy being so fresh in my mind."

"Well, I shouldn't have a problem," Elder Baldwin said. I felt stupid for telling this guy how to study; he was probably an even better student than I was. I considered myself a lazy student. I did the minimum amount of work, unless I had a real interest in the subject or project.

"Cool. Sorry about that, Elder Baldwin. That wasn't cool of Elder Nelson. I'm sure he didn't do it on purpose, but still he should have caught that."

"That's OK. No hard feelings. I liked Nelson and he was just a busy guy. Always had something going, different than the rest of us." Elder Baldwin said.

"He does, doesn't he?" I responded.

"Elder Burton, do you think that was David's camp there in the woods?" I asked him as I made noodles on the plugged-in single burner above the minibar fridge.

"Nooo…, I don't think so. Does he not have a house?" Elder Burton asked, surprised at my small theory.

"If he does, no one knows where it is. The bishop even talked to me about it; asked me to find out where he lived."

"It was a nice camp. I could live there even. So is it bad if he does live outside? I don't think he does, though."

"It's not bad, but I'm sure the bishop would rather have him living somewhere else. That's kind of a bishop's core responsibility: keeping everyone in the fold sheltered. If nothing else, you will always have a roof over your head if you are Mormon, and you can bet it's a pretty nice roof if you are a returned missionary."

"Yeah, it probably is like that a little. But David is a smart guy. He's going to school and goes to church, nice-looking guy."

"And…"

"If he's living in the woods, he probably wants to and doesn't really want to be bothered with the bishop finding him a place."

"That's kind of what I figured, too. For now, Elder, let's just keep this between us. OK?" I asked, thinking I was doing the right thing, living the higher law rather than running to the bishop, telling him what I found. That really wasn't my job, asked or not.

* * * * *

Our stats were the highest in the zone. There were no problems between any of the companionships that I knew about. Other than the call to action by President Carlson in Zone Conference, my guilty feelings had subsided a bit, making this one of the best times and places I'd been in my life. I couldn't have asked for more, other than the obvious. And then it all came crashing down one moment, when I woke up from a relaxed sleep to answer the phone.

"Elder Dorsey, I didn't wake you, did I?" It was Elder Westra, and I remembered it was Friday night: transfer calls. Not expecting any transfers in the zone, Elder Burton and I had gone to bed early.

"No, no. I was reading and thinking about it with my eyes closed only," I said, getting my voice back with the few extra words.

"Good, good. Well, I have some news for you Elder Dorsey. You are moving to Ventura," he said. I was confused.

"What do you mean? I'm being transferred?" I asked, annoyance building in my head at the thought of such a quick transfer. My annoyance showed in my response.

"Elder Dorsey, Ventura. You know what's in Ventura?" Elder Westra asked, laughing.

"I guess I'm not following you. I wasn't expecting to be transferred; I just got here."

"Elder, your new companion is Elder Pratt."

"Elder Pratt?" I asked, and then it clicked in my head. "You are the new assistant to the president, Elder Dorsey. Congratulations!" Elder Westra said, excitedly.

"Whoa, are you sure?" I asked. "Are you serious?"

"Yeah, you are it. I know you like it there in San Luis, but the mission needs you in Ventura."

"Wow, I've got to let this sink in," I said.

"Elder Dorsey, you had no idea?" Elder Westra asked, surprised.

"No. I didn't even know your time was up there."

"Oh, and what's cool, I'll be serving in the Ventura second ward, so we will be in the same stake. But even better, we can play ball on P-days."

"Oh, that will be cool. We haven't played much on our mission," I said with thoughts of playing ball, being AP in beautiful Ventura. "You know I'll school ya," I said, always there with the trash.

"Yeah right, Dorsey. I'll just shoot over you. You can't block the Three," he said. "Hey, I got to get a few more calls out. You'll know soon enough about these late nights. Elder Pratt will call you with details for next week."

"OK. Well, thanks for the call," I said, thoughts swimming.

"No problem. Congrats, Elder Dorsey. You are one of the best missionaries in the mission. You should be here. Have a good night."

"Will do. Thanks. Talk to you later," I said and put the receiver back into the cradle on the side of the built-in message machine. I looked over at Elder Burton, who had turned on the small reading light clipped to his headboard. "That was weird. I'm being transferred," I said looking at him, with both joy and sadness in my eyes.

"I knew it. The whole APs visiting: they were scoping us out; scoping *you* out for the job. I think it sucks. I'm probably going to get some lame companion."

"Come on, Elder Burton. You probably won't get a lame companion. I've had tons of companions and I haven't had many lame ones. Only a couple, really. And they weren't that bad."

"But it's so easy with you. Everything is easier," he said, putting his hands behind his head, cradling it, thinking. The phone rang. It was late, so I was surprised.

"Who the heck would be calling this late? Maybe it's the APs again," I said, turning to the phone away from Elder Burton.

"Hello?"

"Elder Dorsey, how you taking the news?"

"Who is this?"

"Elder, come on. I'm only here to help where I can; think you know that."

"McDonnell!" I said enthusiastically. I hadn't heard from Elder McDonnell since Zone Leaders Meeting, but he had never called me. It was against the rules for elders to call elders.

"Hey, Elder. Just wanted to call and say congratulations on the new position. Pretty cool," he said. It must have been hard for him to say.

"Oh hey, thanks. Not a big deal, though. I was surprised," I said.

"I wasn't. Elder, you're just one of those kinds of guys that, well, everyone likes. This doesn't surprise me at all."

"Well, thanks. Don't go and get gay on me there, Elder," I said, trying to be funny, smart, and witty in order to equal the man on the other end of the phone.

"Hey, Elder. That's not nice to say. But hey, I gotta go. Can't talk on the phone, you know. Just wanted to say 'Hi' and congrats. I'll see you at ZLM."

"OK. Hey, thanks for calling, Elder McDonnell. This is cool." My mind and heart had settled down since talking with McDonnell; he had a calming effect.

"Talk to you later," Elder McDonnell said and hung up the phone. The minute I put it down, it rang again. This time it was Elder Jameson. He had heard the news and wanted to call and say "Hi" and congrats. After his call, it was Elder Barney, my greenie. He thought it was cool that he was trained by an AP. And after that, Rachel Barrett called. She had heard too. And she seemed to come on stronger over the phone.

It was a blur, looking back, with still glimpses into self-analysis, self-indulgence, self-realization, self-improvement, and a self-portrait. A time and place where I would look back to and long to be again. A time I felt great.

I'd lost myself in thoughts of San Luis Obispo while I lay there on the grass hill above the tennis courts. Since I'd arrived and found a place to myself, away from others, it had now filled up, and I noticed I was surrounded by unknown onlookers at the afternoon's match. In my sunglasses, hat, and shorts, I blended well but was still starting to get anxious. I looked at my watch; it was four-thirty. The Morels were scheduled to pick me up at four forty-five. I got up, stretched, brushed off the short pieces of cut grass that clung to my legs, and looked out at the courts. As I started to turn to walk back to the apartment, I heard my name.

"Elder Dorsey, is that you?" It was Missy and her mom. "Oh, hey, hi. Yeah, it's me," I said. It wasn't P-Day; it was transfers. I was by myself, I had shorts on showing too much leg, and it was sunny. And I was done trying to impress others with a good, Mormon missionary attitude.

"What are you doing here?" Missy asked. I hated that question in any context.

"Watching tennis," I said, shrugging my shoulders. With palms forward, arms at my side, I said, "You caught me." And I walked off towards the 1964 Lincoln with suicide doors pulling into the drive at the house.

CHAPTER 15

I met the bureaucrats of the mission on my first day in Ventura. Elder Pratt introduced me to each of the office staff: Brother and Sister Morgan from Arizona, the bookkeepers; and Sister Jefferies from Michigan, the clerk—all ninety pounds of her. Brother and Sister Freeman were split up in their duties, Sister Freeman acting as President Carlson's personal secretary and Brother Freeman acting as the zone leader.

Elder Pratt and I were part of the small zone. President Carlson, when in the office, sat in on meetings. We had lessons out of the Missionary Guide and role-played more than I'd done since my time at the MTC.

The much-anticipated basketball match between Elder Westra and me came shortly after arriving in Ventura. The man I had followed upon entering my mission I was now following out of the mission. Always the underdog against the strong Elder Westra, I could only hope to show off my skills on the court. His reputation preceded him, as I'd heard of the three-point tears he could go on.

Although he didn't have hopes to dunk, he had a smooth touch inside, which made him a deadly force, it was said. He played with glasses and sweats, disregarding even with his attire, it seemed. A lazy approach to gearing down before the match, he was a trash-talking fool at his best. I was in my shorts, flipping the ball close to the rim.

"Oooh, the much awaited match," Elder Westra said, coming into the key, close to me.

"The match. You know, Elder Westra, I never claimed to be a baller," I said, the downplay deep.

"Whatever! You've been talking trash since you've been on the mission.

I hear it."

"Hardly. I've been nothing short of dreading this confrontation. *You* are the better player; I know that. We really don't even need to play today," I said.

"Oh, let's go ahead and play anyway," Elder Westra said, not letting me take my banter further.

There were six of us—Elder Westra, Elder Pratt, and myself; Elder Hardy, Elder Foster, and Elder Jenkins, our companions.

Although Elder Pratt and I were companions, we did proselytize with companions on a trial basis. Elder Pratt was a southpaw and had a beautiful Chris Mullin–like shot. Everything looked better left-handed; everything sounded better in another language; everything looked better off the mission. Elder Pratt had an inch and ten pounds on me, and Elder Westra would bounce off me in the paint. I reveled in my paint play. If the three-ball wasn't falling, then I could resort to the paint and pick up points all afternoon from put-backs and clever passes overhead. The extra few inches I had in my arms gave me enough confidence to play like a big man. Not that I was good; rather, the other players didn't play against post-and-pivot players often and didn't know how to guard them. Going over my repertoire on the hardwood, I felt I could compete against this group. The first game had me going against both Elder Pratt and Elder Westra, two players who had played together for the past few months. Elder Hardy and Elder Foster were with me, and they were less than mediocre players, who hurt more than helped. It quickly turned into a shooting match from the outside between the players on my team. Trying to put points on the board, I quickly shot every time I got the ball, whether driving it in or pulling up for a three. As this was keeping my team in the game, it wasn't fun for the other two players, who unfortunately cared more about shooting the ball than winning, something I'd noticed in nonathletes. My team members, thinking that my shooting was an open invitation for them to launch their uncontrolled shots—some hitting the top of the backboard even—shot away whenever they got ball. All hopes of winning lost, I became a Gary Payton assist-king and started passing to each of the team members and letting them miss their shots. We got killed 12–6 and split up the teams. Elder Westra and I were matched with each other. We both hit each other for easy lay-ups and tossed for assists to each other behind the arc. We were on fire, quickly running the score up 10–2. Elder Pratt's three-ball put a few points on the board, but he was more concerned with letting the other players on his team get some kind of satisfaction out of shooting, rather than entertaining thoughts of winning. We played about three more games, then called it a day. Each of us wanted to get back to our apartments and do laundry, relax, and nap before appointments that night. I'd come away with a new respect for Elder Pratt as an athlete. Basketball wasn't his first sport; baseball was. But he was a true athlete and carried himself in basketball better than most who played.

Elder Pratt had a full-ride scholarship to BYU for baseball. He played there before his mission and was planning on going back. He was a real baseball player. He wasn't good because of his speed, his arm, or his defense—he could simply hit a ball. No truer athlete was there than the man who was born to hit a baseball.

"So what's the plan tonight?" Elder Hardy asked when we were back at the apartment. The four of us lived together. We were the only whites in a five-hundred-unit apartment complex. It was noisy, with a rooster living nearby that woke me up every day.

"What do you mean?" I asked, hoping for the best.

"I'm not going with Foster," Elder Hardy said.

"Elder Hardy, I told you that Elder Pratt and I are working at the office tonight. It will only be a few hours. Maybe it will be a good dinner," I said.

"I'm not going. You guys just have to take us with you to the office and cancel the dinner. I refuse to go with him."

"Why can't you just be cool about this and go to dinner?" I asked, both frustrated and bothered. It surprised me how quickly my feelings came out in the tone of my voice.

"Be cool? Whatever. You have been doing this since you got here. And before that, Elder Westra did it. Not as much as you, though."

"So what do you want to do? Not go to dinner? You want me to go the office another night and go to dinner with you? What do you want, Hardy?" He hardly deserved to be called "Elder." It was an adjustment to serve with two companions. Elder Pratt and I wanted to serve full-time together, and we made that pretty clear. Elder Hardy and Elder Foster, our proselytizing companions, wanted to serve with us because they couldn't stand each other. This was understandable, as they were both real pains in the ass. Neither of them wanted to be Elder Pratt's and my companions, but that was better than the two of them spending time together. It was a boring, disheartening, emotional drag and a time-consuming mess.

"I don't care what happens or what we do. I'm just not going with Foster," Hardy said, echoing the words of Elder Foster in the next bedroom over. I could hear Elder Pratt trying to be diplomatic about it.

"Fine. I'll go to dinner with you, and then we will go to the office late. Of course, you don't mind hanging out at the office?" I asked, knowing he didn't. It was their favorite place. Elder Hardy would sleep in big chairs, and Elder Foster would go around and go through people's drawers while Elder Pratt and I worked on the computer or mapped out some joint teaching on a wallboard. It would always surprise me what some people could bring out in others. I always thought it was easier to just get these people out of your life—solves the problem, no one loses—but I couldn't get rid of Hardy.

My parents got a letter from President Carlson explaining that due to my hard work and outstanding service in the California Ventura Mission, I had been called as an assistant to the president. I thought it was interesting that the president signed it, yet referred to himself in the third person. My parents weren't allowed to phone me, but I got a letter from my mom telling me how proud she was and that she wasn't surprised at all by my success. She took all the credit for any leadership calling I would have in my life, as she was the one who earned the Eagle Scout. My Dad said how proud he was of me and that he was least surprised that, out of all of his kids, I was being called as assistant. He reminded me that he had been an assistant on his mission and that I should prepare for lots of work ahead. As I'd done in the past, I kept my companion problems to myself, not sharing with the family. My letters home could have been carbon copied, as they were all expressing the love I had for everything and that the work was great.

Dinner with Hardy was uneventful. I watched him stuff his face for thirty minutes while not speaking a word. He was very quiet, except when it came to voicing his opinion on whom he would and wouldn't spend time with. When we arrived at the office, Elder Pratt and Foster were already there, Elder Pratt working and Elder Foster in front of the computer, making a greeting card for his Mom's birthday.

"Nice card, Foster," I said, noticing my increasing slack towards using the title Elder. Or maybe it was due to the lack of respect I had for Elder Foster.

"Thanks. You guys need to go work. Hurry," he said, swooshing me away with his big hand.

"OK," I said, not sure what had tipped him off already.

"You guys have a good dinner?" he asked as I walked away.

"Roast beef." It was always roast beef that members served, I thought. Overcooked, dry roast beef.

"Where is Hardy?" he asked. Hardy had stopped in the commissary to avoid even seeing Elder Foster.

"Commissary."

"Oh. How long we going to be here?" he asked, acting as if he had some place to go.

"I don't know. Not long, though. Maybe an hour," I said, trying to be as sincere as possible.

"I don't know what you guys have to do all the time."

"AP stuff, man," I said, hoping to put a stop to the talk by providing him with what he wanted to hear.

"Well, go do your AP stuff. I think *AP* stands for *Arrogant Prick*," he said, continuing to stare into the computer.

"Thanks, Foster," I responded rudely, and walked into the office to a smiling Elder Pratt. Smiling, even though he had just heard what had been said.

"Isn't that fun?" he said, quietly sarcastic.

"Let's do some splits soon," I said.

"Good call. We could arrange something for tomorrow night. It's going to be tight to get splits in before Zone Leader Meeting and Zone Conferences," he said, looking at the calendar on the wall. He called one of the zone leaders and set up a split for the next night. It was in the Valley, close enough to go one night and come back. It would be a needed break from Elder Foster and Elder Hardy, for both of us. It also showed them, I hoped, that if they bitched all the time, we would just leave for splits and stay busy. It was stupidity on their part for not seeing how it worked and made it easy to manipulate the system. The four of us had tried to adapt to the arrangement of split companions. When we were in town, not working on mission stuff, we would proselytize in the ward we covered. We were always in town on Sunday, available for the mandatory Ward Mission Meeting. It confused the hell out of the four of us as to where our allegiances fell. But it came down to the fact that Hardy and Foster were miserable missionaries and Elder Pratt and I weren't. We wanted to serve together full-time. After all the bitching and complaining we had endured, we reached a point where we didn't care *what* Elders Foster and Hardy wanted. And as long as we had that attitude with those two people, then there were going to be problems.

I'd been on a couple splits since I'd been there. I'd gone with the Junior Companion both times. It was always awkward, and not really fun. They were just like splits when I was zone leader, doubling up on dinners and teaching appointments. The time that was fun was time spent with Elder Pratt. We had fun—possibly the most fun I had with any companion. Elder Pratt made everyone feel smart and funny. He laughed at my jokes; really laughed. He seemed to understand the words I said when describing feelings or people.

Preparing for Zone Leader Meetings was simply putting together forty-five minutes worth of material for the group. Elder Pratt and I each took the time to share something relevant to the missionary work. I'd ask him what I should talk about, and he said that he and Carlson always split up a Missionary Guide Lesson and a "Christ-like Attributes" lesson. I quickly opted for the Missionary Guide Lesson, which went well with Elder Pratt's plan, as he had already started on a talk about forgiveness, a topic I wouldn't have broached. The longer I was out, the more I struggled with the core beliefs—repentance, forgiveness, plan of salvation, and especially atonement, which I thought there was no explanation for. I would agree with anyone that the beliefs I struggled with were ones everyone truly struggled with, but that wasn't enough for me. I needed to gain from them more than what I had simply read and been told. Missionary Guide topics were safe, though, rarely ever having to bring God or the spirit into the room. I chose to share my insight into *The Commitment Pattern The Commitment Pattern*, a pattern of commitments common to not only the Church, but also to the business world. A common set of questions and common-sense steps walked a missionary through what could be called manipulation, but in the Church was called *The Commitment Pattern*. This tool was force-fed to us since the first day on the mission field. I was going to stand in front of a group of five-hundred missionaries and explain to them what it was, as if they didn't have the same Missionary Guide at home by their bed that I did. But then I thought of Jesus and his teaching in parables, thinking I could teach like that. I could illustrate the concept with a story, something the missionaries had never heard before, as it was an original thought of mine. I quickly thought back to the different talks I had heard over my mission. The one that came to mind was the one that Brother Simpson had used back in the Valley, speaking on the Gospel and relating it to hearing out of only one headphone, when the music should be in stereo. The not-true gospels of the world were those listened to on a mono headphone, while The Restored Gospel of Jesus Christ, the Mormon Church, came in from both sides in stereo-surround sound.

I didn't want to do that at all. I was alone with my *Book of Mormon* and the cross-references on the bottom of the page, and I wanted to come up with something original. I decided to go with the sons of Lehi going back for the plates of Laban, the story still fresh in my mind from Zone Conference. I would compare Nephi convincing his sniveling older brothers not to go home without the plates, the sole reason they had come back from the desert. He convinced them, and if I did a little ad-libbing from the Missionary Guide, I could show that Nephi used every step of *The Commitment Pattern*. Within an hour, I had a rough draft penned out on the back of a Ventura First Ward sacrament program that had been left in the breast pocket of my suit coat. Since becoming an AP, I wore my suit

90 percent of the time, as opposed to maybe 20 percent when I had been a zone leader.

Elder Foster came to the doorway of the small office. "I'm ready to go, Elder Pratt."

"Oh, well OK. Uh, Foster, I'm not quite done here. Can you wait about another thirty minutes?" Elder Pratt asked.

"I really don't want to wait."

"Why don't you ask Elder Hardy if he will go home with you?

You think you guys can be in the same car for a minute?" I asked.

"I'll ask. I doubt he will, though."

"Thanks, Elder Foster. You are *so* helpful," I said facetiously. He hardly looked at me. I think it was one of the things he did to show me he didn't approve of my being called as an AP We heard the door open, shut, and the car start, telling us they had miraculously agreed to leave together. Elder Pratt and I worked in silence as he finished his presentation. I moved over to the computer, working on a cleaner outline. I sat there, typing out a presentation on *The Commitment Pattern*, even as my thoughts were on my companion. I saw that he was fine as long as he was by my side. The more time we spent together, the more we enjoyed the time. Maybe not *enjoyed*, but rather didn't notice any conflict. I wondered if I should cater to his needs or continue on with my own agenda? I was tired of the day-to-day missionary work of door-to-door, whether they be members, gentiles, or other missionaries. But these thoughts would do nothing for Elder Hardy. I needed to decide if I cared, because decisions would be made according to my decision over the next several months. What we did have was a family—a golden family—an entire family just ready to hear the Gospel and convert. Elder Westra had told me about them, saying how lucky I was. That was really what the whole mission was quite possibly about—what I would witness with this family.

Elder Hardy and I hadn't spent much time together since Elder Pratt and I had gone on our split. We stretched our split into the following day, as long as we could, going to the office when we were back in town, only to get caught there by Elders Foster and Hardy. It was awkward being there and having them show up. We did need to take care of a few items before going back home, as we wouldn't be back for a couple of days.

"So, were you guys going to tell us you were back?" Elder Hardy asked. Elder Hardy didn't raise his voice and didn't look at me when he talked. He was a football player and had locker room conversations. He counted on his teammates to play hard, and when they didn't, the coach would handle it. He wasn't a diplomat within a companionship.

"We just stopped for a few minutes before heading back to the apartment. It looks worse than it is, man," I said, hoping to avoid any type of argument or future inconvenience in my life.

"'Kay."

"You have a good time while I was gone?" I asked.

"No, not really. Would *you* if you got stuck with Foster?" He asked.

"No, not really. You are right. Well, at least you get *me* half the time."

"Yeah, sure Dorsey." I sat there on the couch with my planner opened in front of me in attempt to go over our schedule, yet I saw nothing on the pages in front of me. I was too struck by the thought that Elder Hardy saw right through me. He saw me not as an AP or zone leader or senior companion: he saw me simply as a guy who made his life harder through the decisions that were mine to make for the companionship.

"We have a Third tomorrow night with the Harrisons. You ready for it?" I asked.

"Sure."

"Do you think they will get baptized?" I asked. Elder Westra had told me he thought they would.

"I think so. But it doesn't matter; they are a cool family," Elder Hardy said, correcting my judgment. I knew my judgment wasn't off from the standpoint of a good Mormon missionary It *wasn't* OK if they weren't baptized; it was their only hope for salvation—the only way they would be together forever in eternity—and even if they were a cool family, they had to be baptized someday. Cool family or not, without being baptized into the Mormon Church, they would go to hell.

The pinnacle of baptisms was to get a whole family. It rarely happened. The Harrisons were tracted into by Elder Westra and Elder Hardy. I'd heard the story from Bob, from his recount the first night I met his family.

"I was home for the day, a random day I took off to get some paperwork done at home. Well, I finished everything I wanted to finish early in the afternoon and was just thinking about what I could do the rest of the day, or a least the next few hours before the kids got home from school. And then Elder Westra and Elder Hardy knocked on the door. They explained who they were, and I invited them in. They didn't know that my wife was a lifelong member of the Mormon Church. We talked and I really enjoyed the conversation. They taught me the First Discussion then and were finishing up by the time Jake got home from school. They were walking down the driveway when he was walking up." Brother Harrison thought for a minute and said, "I talked to Nancy that night and asked her everything she had remembered about the Church. We talked for hours, coming to a decision that we should all take the Discussions, if for no other reason than to learn about a religion and to learn about Nancy's family's beliefs and upbringing. And here we are," Brother Harrison finished, putting his hands out slightly in front of him and opened them. "Here we are." They had the First and Second as a family. I was impressed with Elder Westra for going ahead with the baptism commitment on the Second as the Discussion states. They all had accepted the Discussion eagerly, wanting to talk as a family before agreeing to get baptized, making us aware of their interest by stating they looked forward to getting the remaining Discussions.

Brother Yule from the ward sat in on the Discussions; it was picture perfect, the way the family, ward, kids and missionaries interacted. Brother Yule was a convert and therefore had never experienced a mission and would always wish he had gotten that chance. He had a family and looked forward to the day when his son would go on a mission. Brother Yule was about five-foot-seven and bald. When he got out of his car in front of the Harrisons' house, the light reflected off his bald head. It was the three of us: Elder Hardy, Brother Yule, and me. There was no way Elder Hardy or I were going to miss even one of the Discussions with the Harrisons; at least Elder Hardy understood how rare a thing it was to get a family baptized.

We were teaching the Third Discussion, which was going to bring up tithing—next to sex, the hardest concept to teach. It felt a little like we were asking them to pay for their salvation. I was at ease with Brother Yule there. I had asked him previously if he would like to present the tithing concept and get the tithing commitment from the Harrisons. I thought it was more appropriate if it came from someone who actually worked full-time and paid tithing

Nancy was baptized at age eight. She was raised in the Church and stopped going when she was in college at Utah State. "Sunday was the only day I had to ski," Nancy would say when recounting why she stopped going. She and Bob had met while skiing, fell in love, and got married. They had talked about coming back to the Church but had never made a move. Nancy said, "We were happy. We *are* happy, and when you're happy, you're really not looking for anything." She spoke softly and her kids' eyes lit up when she looked at them. She had a natural beauty that was brilliant when she spoke, and I got the feeling Bob knew how lucky he was. It was for *her* that he was listening to us. He wanted her to have everything. He worked hard and was a gentle man. Their kids were polite, always shook our hands, and looked us in the eye. They were strong in their views and ideas, speaking the only truth they knew. We were introducing them to God. We were teaching them the boundaries of God, this God they would grow to love and fear. We taught them about the fear of God, masking it by putting their parents, their Mom, there at the side of God.

Jacob was going to be trying out for the school basketball team. We agreed to come back Monday and play with him. It wasn't something I needed to check with Elder Hardy about; he loved the family. He smiled when we were around them. Brother Yule had taught the principle of tithing with the respect that only age could bring. The Harrisons were well versed already from their readings on tithing. Nancy had grown up tithing on her few pennies from a young age.

They had discussed tithing prior to our arriving, making the agreement to give the Church 10 percent of their income. I wondered if it would have been easier for them to give if they had a testimony of tithing and how it worked? Although it was impossible to prove, as was any of the Gospel, testimonies on tithing were somewhat unique. In one of many ill-ventured testimony meetings that we had taken an investigator to, one woman stood up and said how she had the choice to pay tithing or feed her three children. She said she paid her tithing, and that night baskets of food showed up on the door of her home from the local ward members. The last thing missionaries wanted investigators to hear was a testimony of tithing that got investigators to believe that they could never fail to pay it, or question paying it. The Harrisons didn't have the experience to lend to testimony, so they were going off blind faith in the matter. But then it was all blind faith. They had committed to the principle, putting us well on our way towards baptizing the most coveted new members of all: white, middle class, English speaking, and handsome.

We hadn't spent that many P-Days with Elder Pratt and Foster. They washed their clothes at a member's house, and we washed ours at a laundromat. Even if I had members offer their washer and dryer, I would not have accepted. The three dollars a week it cost to shop, read, and write, sitting on top of the washers while watching the other people watch us, was worth every penny. We wore our shirts and ties, per request from President Carlson. He felt the mission was starting to slack in the dress code, and in reigning this in, he suggested that APs wear their shirts and ties even on P-Days, which was going back to the standards that I'd grown accustomed to while serving with Elder Fisher. Elders Hardy and Foster simply did what they wanted on P-Day, dressed in P-Day clothes, leaving us to our morals. I knew if they had to sit in front of President Carlson as often as I did and look into his eyes, with his looking into mine, they would do as I did. A guy simply couldn't live with himself if he didn't. It was on one of the afternoons that we had been left to sit on top of our washers to enjoy time to ourselves when the thoughts of Zone Conference came to me. I was as nervous as I could be about the talk (or call-to-arms). I was always thinking that I had to practice what I preached. I got off my washer and walked to a woman on the far side of the laundromat folding kids' clothes, which belonged to the four children running around her legs.

"Wow, these all yours?" I asked. She was polite enough and gave me a surprisingly cute smile from a needy face.

"Yeeeeah, they are," she said, showing her yellow-stained teeth with another smile—a cute smile that brought on another smile from me. And I think she thought I was flirting.

"And it looks like you have another one on the way," I said, pointing to the perfect basketball-round belly protruding out over her sweats, revealing a large flash of skin.

"No, no. That's just my fat," she said. An embarrassed feeling went to the bottom of my gut, I didn't even know how to get out of it. I had no idea what to say. There was silence for several seconds before I put my hand out and introduced myself.

"I'm Elder Dorsey. Would you like to learn about the Mormon Church some evening?" I asked, getting on to words and conversation I knew.

"Sure. I don't know much about the Mormons. You want to come by my place?" she asked. I was surprised by her willingness, but grateful for it after my gross blunder.

"Great. What's better for you? Tomorrow night or the next?" I asked, knowing I was on a roll with The Commitment Pattern.

"Oh, tomorrow night will be fine," she said, keeping stride with me.

"Wonderful. Just wonderful. I'm going to give you this to look at before we get there tomorrow. It goes over the plan that our Heavenly Father has for us here on Earth…." I finished the entire First Discussion in ten minutes. I had her read from the Bible with a commitment to read the passage in Third Nephi in the *Book of Mormo*n at the end of the Second. Coming off the high of teaching and committing the Harrisons, I could feel the power of conviction in me. The power to convince—to have people yearning for what you are teaching—was overwhelming. There is glory in people looking at you like you know more than they do; more than they ever hope to know. I went back to the washer and switched the clothes to the dryer, hanging my shirts. "We have an appointment to teach her the Second tomorrow night. She will have read Third Nephi already. We will get a commitment for baptism from her tomorrow night. She smokes and will struggle with the Word of Wisdom, but she'll still commit."

"All right, Dorsey," he said without looking up from his *Sports Illustrated.*

* * * * *

The following night we went to the address that was written in the margin of my blue planner.

"This must be it, Brother Lot," I said, the cars lights shining back from a decrepit house, "Lights are on; someone's there."

"Hi Bernice. It's me, Elder Dorsey, from yesterday in the laundromat," I explained after reading the expression on her face.

"Oh yeah, forgot about that. So you *did* come by."

"I did. I've brought Elder Hardy and Brother Lott from our ward."

"Oh. Well, come on in. Have a seat." She motioned for us to sit on the orange and brown rendition of a lakefront couch. It was worn out. I sunk down to the springs. I'd left my suit coat on, and it was now bunched up behind me, digging into my back. Brother Lott had a hardback chair that Bernice had gotten from the kitchen. She sat down by me. There was hardly any room in between Elder Hardy and me, with an empty chair a step away. "So, what do you guys want to talk about?" The ashtray on the dark coffee table looked like a porcupine, so full of cigarette butts. I thought how funny it would be if a porcupine, instead of shooting quills, shot cigarettes from its ass. There was a small trail of smoke rising from the stack. The room smelled of cigarettes and perfume. Bernice's smile wasn't so cute when wrapped around a cigarette.

"Well, we talked about God and his plan of salvation and how he restored the gospel here on earth today through prophets, just like he did when he was on the earth. We would like to talk with you about the prophet that he restored the priesthood through. Have you heard of Joseph Smith?" I asked.

"No, I don't think so." She picked up a book from the coffee table. It was a pictorial of Neil Diamond's motorcycle trip across the country, with lyrics and notes in it that he had actually written while on the road. I looked at Elder Hardy; he was smiling and not making an attempt to move the focus of the conversation. "I want to show you this when we are done talking. It's a great book," she said, her yellow teeth showing between her lips.

"Sure. I like Neil Diamond, I'd love to look at it," I said, meaning it. It sounded like more fun than going through the stories in the *Book of Mormon*.

We went through the Second Discussion. Afterwards, I threw out the baptism commitment. I threw it out, knowing there was no spirit present; knowing that she was hardly listening; knowing the only reason she had us there was in hopes of getting lucky with me.

She returned with a weak commitment to pray about it and a promise by us to come back and teach her a Third. She asked me if she could call me.

"Sure. If you have questions on what we've taught you, give me a call."

"Can I call you late?" she asked.

"Well, we turn in pretty early. And well, we…" I stammered over my words, trying to tell her that missionaries couldn't get calls from girls after hours.

She then turned to Brother Lott, "Can I call you, Brother Lott?" She flashed a smile in his direction.

"Sure." He said it calmly and then said we should go.

In the car, Brother Lott suggested that we not go back to her house; that she might have other ideas than learning the gospel. I agreed and knew I wouldn't miss her. She never called, and I never tried to contact her. Brother Lott later said she never called him either.

"You knew she was drunk that night, didn't you?" He asked.

"I smelled alcohol, but I didn't know she was drunk."

"She was gone. Her eyes were glossy, and that wet smile she kept flashing at us, the slurring of the speech: she was hammered. I'm glad you guys didn't go back."

"Me too," I said.

The missionaries enjoyed the talk on The Commitment Pattern. I was surprised when they came up and shook my hand afterwards, almost all of them. I was standing by the door, thinking I had never experienced such an outpouring of gratitude before. I think the missionaries who knew me before I was AP liked being loosely associated with me. Elder Burton announced that he was getting married. Only a month after I had left, and he was engaged! I wondered where the hell his head was.

Changes were starting to show in my attitudes towards other missionaries. I saw the time and energy that the president spent in dealing with their problems, their parents, and their unlikely salvation. It was more difficult trying to get the troops together and organized. I found I was able to be mean and judgmental in ways I had never thought possible. Whether they were elders, brothers, or sisters, I had no patience or leniency: it was impossible, it seemed, in the role of an AP. The very skills of compassion that got me to this position became jaded when the skills of leadership took over. This dichotomy didn't seem right, and I knew it would have to end badly.

Elder Pratt and I had been on a run of arranging "shotgun transfers"—midmonth transfers resulting from something bad, usually when a big rule had been broken. We simply picked them up and dropped them off at the Mission Home. We had absolutely no details as to why they were being transferred. The missionaries in the field were always better informed than the APs; they talked. I really didn't want to come back to silent treatment from Elder Hardy. My only comfort at times was thinking that maybe God had big plans for me; maybe that's why he gave me a companion like Hardy. It had to be the case; I needed to learn something from this misery.

I'd just gotten a call from President Carlson asking if Elder Pratt and I could go pick up Sister Crayton in Bakersfield, a two-hour drive east into the desert. I, of course said yes and told him we would get started within the hour. We had a fourth appointment set up with the Harrisons, and Elder Hardy wouldn't go with Elder Foster. I explained to him I didn't want to miss it, but I had to go pick up a sister. He didn't care that I was missing out on something I wanted to do; he simply didn't want it to ruin his time. It didn't make sense to me how he could think like this with such limited options available. I told him to go with Elder Foster or go with a split from the ward, but he had to figure it out for himself.

"You're a little shit, Dorsey!" Elder Hardy said as he lay on the bed, finally having had enough of whatever I was giving him. He leaped off his bed and came at me. I was ready for him but not for the weight of his 230-pound body. I'd planned to quickly push him right back onto his bed, but succeeded only in pushing him down to the floor.

"Fuck you, Hardy! I'm so sick of your shit."

"Ooohhh.... Elder Dorsey swore. You going to tell the president?"

"God made swear words to use with people like you," I said. Elder Hardy was up after regaining his footing. I had moved out to the living room, knowing if we were going to fight, we would need some room. "I'll take you on, Hardy. I know you can beat me, but I'll fight till I can't move anymore. I'm not going to take your shit anymore. That's it!" I was pissed. Elder Hardy came into the room, laughing at me.

"I'd kick your ass, Dorsey!"

"It's not really about that, though, is it? It's about you getting tired of doing it. Getting so tired of kicking my ass that you finally give in to everything I do. Which would be nothing you're not doing now, but you would have no more fight in you and would become a vegetable for the rest of your mission."

"God, you're a dork," he said as I grabbed both his upper arms and tried to throw him against the wall. He was surprised by my strength and hopped on one foot to get his balance back. I pushed him as he was getting his footing, but he was ready for it and quickly shifted his weight, pulling me through the push into his waiting fist. The uppercut took the breath out of me. I doubled over instantly and sank to the floor, gasping for breath. "Don't fuck with me, Dorsey! I know your kind; I don't mind kicking your ass every day. Don't forget that. I could kick your ass every day!"

"Fu…ck you." I said, gasping with pain, as I'd never felt.

When I had recovered, after lying on the floor for forty minutes, I called Elder Pratt at the office. He came home and we left to get Sister Crayton. I didn't say a word to Elder Hardy after the "Fuck You" I left as my dying words. I had gotten my ass kicked, but I walked out on him that night and didn't give a shit what he thought of it. I didn't tell Elder Pratt about it. I wasn't in a contemplative mood, other than trying to figure out the feeling in my gut and the thoughts in my head.

I knew Sister Crayton from Chatsworth; she was in the zone.

We had talked several times while at Zone Conferences, and I always felt that we had a bit of chemistry and could possibly date. She wasn't my type, but becoming fast friends blurred the lines. The question never came up, though, and we simply enjoyed our few talks and smiles. There was only one reason why a sister like Sister Crayton would get transferred: she had met a guy. It was an assumption based on rumors and stories of past shotgun transfers. Surprisingly, I learned more about the transfers from Elder Hardy than anything Elder Pratt told me. I was informed somewhat while out in the field (with Elder Burton as a companion it was easy, as he let me know what was behind the scenes). With what I learned from Elder Hardy and what I'd heard, I was able to imagine what happened. I had called Sister Crayton before we left, so she knew we were coming to get her. She probably didn't want that, as I wouldn't want it either. I was sadly comforted in knowing it was her being transferred, not me. We had a minute in the car alone while Elder Pratt went to get the luggage from her room. The windshield wipers struggling to keep the rain off and the silence thick, she said, "Elder Dorsey, it's not what you think."

"I don't know," I said, turning around from the front seat and shrugging my shoulders. "I really don't know. I can only assume."

"I asked to be transferred," she said softly.

"Sister Crayton, you don't have to tell me anything. We are just taking you to the Mission Home. President and Sister Carlson will be there."

"Come on, Dorsey, don't be like this. Just believe me! I asked to be transferred. I didn't have to be transferred."

"OK, whatever that means to you, OK. You requested a transfer," I said, finishing quickly.

Elder Pratt slid the door shut on the mission minivan. He then hopped into the front seat and gave Sister Crayton a big "Hello," wiping the rain off his suit coat. We listened to mission-allowable gospel music on the way back. I thought of the country music song by Merle Haggard and how nice it would be to have a girl with faraway eyes right there, with the lights from Bakersfield fading in the back. That was what I wanted. I didn't have anything close to what I wanted. I was so far from what I truly wanted. I saw myself on a never-ending sailing trip with only the sun, the blue sky, and black water, all coming together at night in a sparkling blanket to roll into and sleep, but then I'd get tired of sleeping with the stars and sailing with God's toys and would want my own. I'd end up cold at night, looking ahead to even colder days

It was late when we got back from Bakersfield; we didn't have much to say, and went right to sleep.

The Harrisons were scheduled for the Fifth Discussion the following week, when we'd go over the baptism with them. We would ask them whom they wanted to baptize them, and we would print up baptismal programs with our names on it. I felt I was in good running with Elder Hardy, and possibly Brother Yule. The P-day basketball had helped me connect with Jacob. He had a decent shot but was soft inside. After I showed him that I could shoot from the outside, he respected my game. I went inside and tried to get him to use his body when guarding me. I didn't think it was too much for a kid to know about using the body, but I thought back to learning ball from older, bigger, and better players, remembering that everyone has his own game. If a guy can shoot the ball, he has game, and all the rest is just a part of his game. So I stopped trying to coach him and just shot with him. He had game and would figure it out someday.

I knew Elder Hardy was going to get transferred at the end of the month. Elder Pratt and I had presented enough evidence showing our need to work together without other companions. We assured the president that the amount of time we were gone wouldn't impact the work in the wards we served in. He agreed. I wanted the Harrisons to be baptized before Elder Hardy got transferred but was trying to hide my wishes. We were only on the Fifth Discussion, so I suggested we combine the final two. They agreed. We taught them and were a bit exhausted by the end. It was nice to finally sit back on the couch with a Mormon-appropriate drink in my hand, instead of the *Book of Mormon*.

"Hey, guys. Do you want to see my room?" Benjamin asked.

"Sure," Elder Hardy said, starting to stand from the couch.

"No thanks. You go ahead, Elder," I said and looked back to Nancy and Bob.

"You don't want to see his room, Elder Dorsey?" Nancy asked.

"I'm not sure if we should. I don't think we are supposed to be alone with kids like that."

"Oh, Elder Dorsey. It's *nothing* to look into a child's room. It's their way of expressing themselves; it's just their little homes."

"Oh, I know. It's not that. I'm just not sure on the rules." I had dug myself in pretty deep and was hoping for a way out. Nancy rolled her eyes a little and I could hear Elder Hardy's deep voice below those of the kids. It didn't seem like the right time to talk about the baptism, so I sat there and let Brother Yule talk. Sometimes I was just worn out talking about church—so worn I didn't have anything else in me. The family had committed to baptism, and I was ready to go to bed and be alone with my thoughts.

"Well, it would mean a lot to the kids." She picked up her tea and took a sip; the break in the conversation was needed for person to gather one's thoughts.

"Did you have fun the other day with Benjamin? Shooting the ball?" Bob asked.

"Yeah, he's a good little player. I was impressed."

"Yeah, he does pretty good out there."

"He's got a really smooth shot. Where did he learn that?" I asked.

"Well, I'd *like* to think he got it from me," Bob said, flashing a quick smile.

I thought back to the Discussion we had, relieved no questions had come up about work for the dead. From past experience, investigators didn't understand exactly why we baptized dead people, and I didn't want to try to explain it again. Try was all I could do, as I didn't know why we baptized dead people either.

Elder Pratt and I talked about Zone Leader Meeting when we got back from the Harrisons. We agreed that I would present Finding People to Teach and he would teach Trustworthiness, which I quickly learned was an amalgam of honesty, integrity, and reliability. At least this was the approach he took. It was a pretty heavy topic. What person wouldn't want to possess those attributes? We set up a time to go to the office and work on the upcoming talks, discussing our splits for the week. We liked to go on splits at least once a week. President Carlson left it up to us, how often we would go, and whom we would see. We simply looked at the map and went the obvious route, starting at one end and going to the other. The missionaries on splits treated us differently; even the missionaries I had *lived* with and *knew* treated me differently. They surely didn't share anything other than missionary work, not because they were scared of what I'd report to the president; rather, they didn't think I wanted to hear anything but missionary work. I thought that this wasn't so bad. It was, after all, the air I was putting on, and it seemed to be working. I wasn't lost in the work—I was hiding in it. Missionary work, broken down to its truest form, is simply a multilevel hierarchal business. I was just one of the bureaucrats brought in to help motivate the workers because their free coffee had gotten taken away.

I walked into the room, and Elder Hardy was on his bed listening to music on his headphones. I motioned for him to take them off, and he did. "What?" He asked.

"I'm going to the office tomorrow night to work and then leaving Friday for splits. Be back late Saturday."

"That's bullshit! You don't have to do as much work and as many splits as you say you do."

"Probably not, but you see I can, and you are an asshole. What did you think would happen? You want to hit me again, Hardy? Will that make you feel better?" I was surprised at myself for taunting him. I could count on one hand the number of times I'd digressed to the point of humiliating and taunting someone. "You know what gets me in this, Hardy? Because of your ignorance, you are ending up having to spend more time with a guy you don't like, and less time with the guy you do. You don't *get* that I liked you. But now that you have been such an ass, I don't. And I don't care how much time you have to spend with the guy. I was looking out for you before," I let it sink in and let the silence seal it. "How's that make you feel? You not only make another guy's life miserable, but then you hang with someone you hate." I figured I was done.

"You're the asshole, Dorsey!" he said, putting his headphones back over his head. He didn't look at me or talk to me for the rest of the night. I felt both good and bad.

The problems I was having with Elder Hardy were at the forefront of all other activities. I was able to spend very little time thinking about what I was doing; I never worried about a Zone Conference presentation; I didn't worry about talking in Sacrament Meeting; I didn't worry about how successful we were in our efforts to bring people into the Restored Gospel: I simply brooded over my relationship with Elder Hardy, how miserable he was, and how miserable he made my life. And I wanted him out of my life. I had no compassion for him and no hope of getting any. The ward wasn't big enough for both of us; it was up to me to take control. So he was going to be transferred the next month, along with Elder Foster. Elder Pratt and I would move into another apartment with proselytizing missionaries. I was excited that a change was going to happen. Any change while under such confines was welcomed.

Jacob Harrison looked into my eyes when he told me he wanted me to baptize him. I wondered if I should? My heart wasn't in it. I had to, though, to make him believe he was making the best decision possible. I thought he was too young and his sister was too young. Bob was old enough to make his own decisions, though, and although I didn't agree with what he had decided, I supported him. I thought it odd that I questioned the very principles I had just introduced to them. I had told them their eternal salvation was dependent on baptism, that I had first-hand knowledge of its truthfulness as I had prayed about it, and had gotten the warm feeling equated to the Holy Ghost manifestation.

The sun was bright on the day of the baptism. The women's flower-print dresses looked shiny, blowing in the wind along with their hair. Everyone was happy and smiling, saying, "Wait! Let me get a picture," or "I want to get a copy of that picture."

After Mary's baptism in the Valley, I knew all baptisms in comparison would go perfectly. I could have dropped Jacob into the drain and it *still* would have been better than what had happened with Mary. But the baptism *did* go perfectly. I didn't like bestowing the Gift of the Holy Ghost, though. I laid my hands on Jacob's wet hair and felt nothing. I pulled phrases from all the blessings I remembered to make his baptism sound as if the Holy Ghost was present in me. There weren't many blessings to recall, as I was never a kid who yearned for a blessing to make me better (whether I was sick, saddened, etc.), and that feeling, in and of itself, was enough to discredit God and blow the blessing. Yet as a good Mormon,

I gave blessings when asked. I couldn't imagine myself giving a blessing after the mission. The only reason I did it *on* the mission was because it was my job. Not only would I have looked really silly refusing, I probably would have been sent home for not complying with given orders.

Elder Hardy baptized both Bob and Jennifer. They had requested him. I didn't feel badly about them not choosing me. Yet, I couldn't imagine why, if they had a choice between Elder Hardy and me, they would choose him? Who would want to remember him and his face the rest of their life? Expecting to look back on it with fond memories? Elder Pratt and Foster were there; Brother Thule and his family, Brother Lot and his family, and some other members of the Ward who didn't know the Harrisons but read the program the previous Sunday (and had nothing to do on a Saturday afternoon or felt it was their obligation) also attended. Elder Hardy and I did beautifully together, as we generally did in public. He did a wonderful job with both the baptisms and bestowing the Gift of the Holy Ghost. He didn't stumble over words and even used some phrases I hadn't heard in some time. The bishop shared his thoughts and admonished the new members to live the Gospel and help other people. They'd been through months of Discussions and had made big decisions. And, in the end, the leader of their ward said simply "Be good and nice." If we shortened the Discussions to just that, we would not only reach more people, but the message would hit home fast.

I had a dinner appointment with the Olsons the following evening. They had a daughter, Teresa, who was going to BYU and asked that I give her some pointers as a former first-year student. I said I would, although I had nothing in mind to say. I figured I could make something up. I could tell her that the first girl I went out with said she wouldn't have sex before marriage but would be willing to give me a blow job. The girl was gorgeous and I thought how *perfect* it would be if she just gave me blow jobs every day until we were married. I wasn't sure how the logistics of me going on a mission factored in, so I passed on the nightly blow jobs, for fear of tainting me prior to entering the mission field. When we got to discussing school, I talked about the buildings and the prophets they were named after, describing each of the five different floors in the library.

I advised her where the good places to study were, how the dorm food sits in one's stomach a full hour after eating it, along with all the stuff that no one told me and that I had to figure out on my own. I wanted to tell her that figuring this stuff out on my own made me cool and that she, herself, had to figure it out to be cool. But she wasn't cool; she was coming on *way* too strong. I didn't know if it was my AP status or my good looks, but this girl was sitting close to me with her leg showing. It wasn't that great of a leg either. It was good, considering I hadn't seen one in some time, but in a magazine of legs, it was average.

"Elder Dorsey, are you going back to BYU after the mission?" Sister Olson asked.

"Probably. Haven't given it too much thought lately."

"You are going home soon, right? What, in six months?"

"Five. Five months. Oh, I agree. I should have some things figured out at this point, but I don't. Most likely, I will go back to BYU," I said quickly.

"You should look Teresa up. That would be fun," Sister Olson said. I felt a little on the spot.

"Sure. I'll make sure and get your address before I leave so I can write you. I'll probably be there within a few months after the mission."

"Is it weird thinking that the mission is going to be over?" Teresa asked, and I was impressed with her honest question.

"Not that it's over, but that I'll be doing something different. That's a little hard to imagine."

"Doing the same job full-time for two years, and so different from a regular job: no outlets. People that work forty-hour or sixty-hour weeks have outlets after work and on weekends. Missionaries don't. It's really great training to receive early in life to prepare for a life of working," Brother Olson added to the roundtable.

"I hadn't thought of it like that, Brother Olson. Interesting," I said, understanding further that age had nothing to do with smarts.

"Elder Hardy, did you go to school before your mission?" Brother Olson asked.

"Yeah. West Valley Community College. A little community college close to my home town."

"Did you play football there?" Brother Olson asked.

"Yeah. Fullback."

"Tough position."

"Loved it, though."

"You look like you can handle it."

"What about you, Elder Dorsey? Any sports in college?" Sister Olson asked. I was starting to feel a bit on trial, but I had a fairly stacked résumé at such a young age for a Mormon kid. I knew I was up for the questioning. I was no scholar, but that fact wouldn't come out in my answers.

"No. I skied. Kinda played while I was there, heck,..." I stopped short for a second, time feeling frozen, and I replayed that I'd just said "heck." I knew then and there the impact the mission might have on me. And I had lived too long with Elders from Utah. It felt good to be honest with myself.

"What did you play in high school?" Teresa asked. Again, I was impressed by her questioning. I'd always thought that a few pertinent details about one's life in high school told a lot about a young person.

"Tennis, baseball, and golf."

"You didn't want to take any further than high school? Brother Olson asked.

"I probably wasn't good enough at any of them to take any further," I said.

"Well, you *look* like an athlete," Brother Olson said.

I didn't know what to say; it was a strange sort of compliment. One I didn't feel comfortable receiving from another man. "Uh, thanks."

"You Elders want some pie and ice cream?" Sister Olson asked, getting up and walking into the well-lit kitchen.

"Sure," Elder Hardy said.

"Just pie for me, thanks."

I watched Elder Hardy finish eating his last supper and felt a little like Judas Iscariot.

CHAPTER 16

We both just played dumb when the calls for transfers were made. We called Elders Foster and Hardy, who were probably sitting at home, rubbing each other's feet and enjoying the fresh breeze coming off the Pacific, the seagulls sounding perfect.

"Elder Foster, Elder Dorsey here. How ya do'n?"

"Fine. What's up?"

"Transfer calls. Both you and Hardy. I'll bring the addresses home. You are going to Bakersfield with Hardy. Different zones, though; don't worry."

"I wouldn't care," he said smartly.

"Your comp is Elder Gast and Hardy's is Elder Isaacs. Here are their phone numbers if you want to call them. You don't have to; it's pretty late."

"It *is* late. Why did you call us so late? You waited till last?"

"No, just worked out that way. Talk to you later, Foster" I hung up before he could say anything. He was one of the few people I really didn't like in the world.

"So how was that?" Elder Pratt asked.

"Wow. Did *that* feel good. It shouldn't feel this good."

"Ahhh, don't worry about it. Not everyone gets along."

"You have any problems with companions?" I asked, surprised that this question never came up in the past.

"No, not really. Foster has been one of the hardest. I struggled with a few guys that didn't want to work, but it wasn't too bad."

"Why is it that some missionaries have problems with all their comps and some never have any problems?"

"It's gotta just be perception. We can trust that everyone acts about the same to each other, so it's gotta be what's perceived as pissing them off."

"That's it! Well, in that case, these guys will probably struggle their whole lives with relationships."

"Living with a guy for two years has got to be one of the hardest. So I wouldn't base his whole life and all his relationships on it; surely some, though. But it does make a person wonder why some people struggle with the mission rules more than others. I used to think it was rules, but then I look at how Elder Foster and I obeyed the rules, yet he was always pissed off. So that doesn't hold true anymore."

"I think that too. If no rules are being broken, then there shouldn't be any problems, right? But these companionships illustrate that's not the case."

"I don't know what it is, but I'm sure glad it's over."

"Me, too. I think I will sleep better tonight," I said.

Elder Hardy didn't say anything to me the following two days. He simply lived out of his bags, having packed them the night he heard of the transfer. I didn't say anything either. And when he left, he walked out of the apartment and didn't look back. He didn't say ""Bye," or "See ya," or anything; he just left me sitting there. I thought I had really messed up our companionship and hoped I hadn't messed up his whole mission. I wondered if where he was going, would he be considered different since his last comp was the AP?

We moved into another apartment, further from the tracks, the freeway, and the Hispanics, and closer to the centralized front where the whites protected themselves by keeping the enemy in the fields. The new apartment had a greenie and a training companion. Elder Mortensen was from Portland, Oregon. It felt good knowing that he was even closer to home than I was. Being only two days away by car from family, friends, and the easy life made me think of running home sometimes. I knew I wouldn't, though; I couldn't. That seemed so outrageous, to pack up and drive home. Elder Mortensen drew pictures in his spare time. He had a drawing pad and special pencils, items I hadn't seen since my Fischer days. He was a hard worker and did everything Elder Kramer asked him to. Elder Kramer was the best damn trainer I had ever seen. He was a stickler for the rules, constantly quoting from the white missionary rule bible he kept in his front shirt pocket. "Elder, what does it mean when we are asked something from our senior companion?" He looked at Elder Mortensen sitting on the couch after he had just asked him to clean the dishes for dinner.

"*Do* what he says. I'm going, I'm going." Elder Mortensen was a good sport about it, and we all ended up starting an ongoing mission joke of quoting the White Bible in all Discussions.

With his constant rule quoting, I wondered why it was so easy to break or follow the rules at any given time. I'd done both on the mission, and both had turned out fine. Both were fun, other than feeling like *shit* about the breaking of rules. I'm glad I did it, though. I thought if I could break the rules and get away with it, I would—only because the rules took the innocent fun out of life.

There was a grass courtyard that was as big as a football field, where we'd throw the football. We got to know each other pretty quickly out on the grass field. Elder Kramer had a girl back home in Pittsburgh. He didn't talk about her too much but had a picture of her that he kept packed. He showed it to us one evening while we were talking and thinking of home.

"Do you think you will marry her?" I asked.

"I think so. We've known each other since we were kids. We've dated and always thought we would get married. I don't see why we wouldn't."

"Don't you think you should date a few women? Go away to school and date and see what else is out there? There could be someone else out there and you wouldn't know," I said.

"Maybe…but she might be it. I mean, maybe that's why God made it so easy—because it was going to happen anyway. She is perfect for me and she loves me. God let us grow up together so there would never be a question as to whether we knew each other well enough. We *know* we do."

"I don't think there is anything wrong with knowing you have found the One, even if she is from your home town. It happens all the time. It probably works out well. The people know each other, their lifestyles, have something in common. That's a lot to go into a marriage with today."

"Well, I don't think that commonalities surrounding locale and lifestyles and knowing each other are necessarily good criteria to rate a marriage on. As good as it might be for a couple to really know each other, the flip side is that they might hold each other back in life. And neither would *ever* know it."

"I don't know. I think any relationship is better the more you know the other person. I think Elder Kramer would be further ahead starting out than many of us would be years after being married."

"I like to think of it more like Elder Mortenson—a little more positive than Elder Dorsey's idea. I'm really not sure, though. I have another year out here and imagine my feelings towards women, marriage, and life might change."

"Probably will. I know mine have since I've been out," I said, looking up at Elder Pratt as he walked into the room. "Elder Pratt, you are going home soon, in a few weeks. What has changed in your thinking in regards to women, marriage, and life?"

"What has changed, huh? I don't think much. I still feel about the same. I haven't thought much about any of those questions."

"What about women? Do you think you will date different type of women after your mission than you did before?" Elder Kramer asked.

"Sure. I want someone that is pretty serious about the Church, at least as serious as I am. So that's changed. But that would come naturally, like with school. Generally people marry someone that has similar school goals. I don't know."

"Elder Kramer, undoubtedly you will come home from your mission and know more than your girlfriend. Will that make a difference?" I asked.

"I would think that it might. But since sitting here, I realize she would have grown also, in ways that I hadn't, and she won't hold that against me. So I shouldn't hold it against her."

"It's not a matter of *should* or *shouldn't*, but *will* or *won't*. I don't know if it's something a person can control, the feeling of not being accepted on a matter," I said.

"Sure, you can. Forgiveness. That's it," Elder Pratt said. "From God, sure.

But from people? They…*we* aren't that good. We all hold grudges. Sure, God doesn't, but we still are stuck living down here on this earth, and pissing people off, and holding grudges, and not measuring up, and basically feeling bad our whole lives because we let people down—like Kramer is already thinking of doing to his girlfriend back home," I said.

"I'm not letting her down. I might change."

"And she could probably take that change in you and love you even more. So you would have gotten so much smarter that you couldn't live with another daughter of God unless she was as smart as you. And where is the line? What if she memorized all the mission scriptures and knew them as well as you? Then, would she be smart enough?" I was keeping my tone soft and we were having a little fun with the conversation. If things didn't get heated in simple discussions, then concepts could be grasped and things really thought about. Elder Kramer wasn't taking it personally that I was asking about his girlfriend and his intentions with her. He was being a sport, like Elder Mortenson was a sport, and Elder Pratt was a sport (and hopefully *I* as well).

Elder Pratt's mom was picking him up to drive him back to the East Coast. She was renting a convertible. I asked him about it on our way to visit the Goldmans. Barry Goldman was raised in the Church, and his family was from the Valley. His wife, Stacy, never joined the Church. They had been married four years and had a baby girl.

Barry was impressive, at six-four and broad shouldered. He had hair that hung several inches past his chin, which helped him retain his surfer look from earlier days, and he got away with it. His wife was as tall as me and had long, blond hair. She had a full figure with a skinny waist and looked about perfect. Each time I met them, not only was I impressed with their level of conversation, but also with the beauty the two brought into the room. They were a stunning couple; Hollywood couldn't have put together a better couple.

"What do you want to go over tonight with Barry and Stacy?" I asked.

"I talked to him earlier. He said he had this cool video on the Last Days. He suggested we watch it and I said sure."

"Sounds good," I said, looking forward to seeing Barry and his wife.

Their view-condo was hidden in trees, located in the hills above Ventura.

"You can see the islands on a clear day," Barry said, one of the few things I'd heard him brag about. Their baby girl was already put to bed. I felt that both he and Stacy were excited to see us and watch the video with us. It was a video that, had I been home, I wouldn't have seen nor cared to. We had briefly touched on why Barry didn't come to church. He explained that he had some hang-ups with how the Quorum of the Twelve ran things. He didn't want to give too many examples, but the one he gave stayed in my thoughts. He said that the twelve apostles had to have their talks approved before they gave them during general conference. "These guys are the closest thing to God on earth, and they are saying to the members that they can't receive inspiration on the spot like Joseph Smith and Jesus Christ. Hell, the bible and *The Doctrine and Covenants* were written by immediate revelation. And what of today? Is it obsolete?" He wasn't asking us to explain it or even try to understand it. He clearly understood the concepts of the Church more than any missionary I had met. His single example pushed me even further into confusion in regards to the Church, though. And that confusion was getting harder to hide.

The video was of a famous actor explaining how some of the major events in the Bible could have happened, scientifically speaking. It was good, and I asked Barry for a copy of it. I thought I'd like to take it home and show the family. He said sure, and I thought we had bonded a little. After the video, we talked about coming to church the following Sunday. He was hesitant but honest and said he would be there. Stacy didn't say anything, but she would have supported him in any decision. I would have supported him in any decision. He was that kind of man who could make a decision, and people automatically thought it was the right decision—a better decision than they could have made themselves. These types of people are described as leaders, but in reality they are just really cool people others want to be like. He talked about his own mission briefly, and I marveled at his speech and experiences he described.

"We actually healed a blind woman," Barry said. When he told me this, I wondered how he could fall away from the Church after seeing a miracle like that.

"Do you still keep in touch with her?" I asked.

"No. She didn't even get baptized. She had committed to, but didn't."

"Why not?" I asked.

"She didn't believe it was the Church that made her see. She agreed that God was working through us but that God wasn't only in the Mormon Church."

"Well, she had a good foundation for an argument there. After being healed and not being Mormon, it would be hard to argue with her," I said.

"I don't think I would have argued with her. I'm not sure her getting her sight back had anything to do with the Church. I think it had to do with two young men and a woman and God. So I couldn't fault her for thinking the way she did."

"That whole thing probably happens to very few missionaries," I said.

"What whole thing? A blind person seeing? We met her and planned on going back and healing her. The two weeks prior to the healing, my companion and I prepared ourselves. We fasted for two full days, doubled up on prayers, and studied the Gospel more than we normally would have. So, we weren't surprised when it happened."

"Yeah. I've only read about that in the Bible, and here you are telling me about an actual occurrence. It's really a testimony booster. Not of the Church, but of the love that God has for us," I said.

"There was an article or story that came out when I was on my mission. It was published in the *Ensign*. It was about people coming to church on Sunday and the different comments that the people in the congregation might make about them. I think the article was called Jesus Wept. Have you guys heard of it?" Barry asked.

I looked at Elder Pratt, and he looked at me with the same confused look. "No, haven't heard of it," Elder Pratt said. "Pretty good though, huh?"

"It is. It would be impossible to find a copy of it now, but if you guys ever run across it, will you get me a copy?" Barry asked sincerely. I thought instantly that I would call my Mom and she would locate a copy, and I would be the hero of the day—Barry would like me and remember me forever. I also wanted to see what a man like Barry thought was a great essay.

It was raining and the simple logic behind windshield wipers was helping me sort the thoughts from the evening with Barry. I was staring out at the blurry streetlights when Elder Pratt, noticing my thinking, asked, "You OK, Dorsey?"

"I'm fine."

"Barry says some things that make sense."

"He does. Does it get to you?"

"Sometimes, but I've been coming here for months now, and I kinda got over it."

"How does a person get over thoughts and feelings they're confronted with almost every day?"

"I know, it's easier said than done. Barry did affect me at first, which Elder Westra noticed it. He told me something, though, that made a lot of sense. He said, 'What makes the difference between Barry and me is that I have a testimony. I know that God lives and that Joseph Smith was his prophet.'"

"Whoa. That's pretty perceptive of Elder Westra."

"Kinda what it all comes down to."

"Yeah, it really does. It's the testimony. We will meet other Barrys in our life, won't we?"

"Yep."

There wasn't a better companionship in the mission. I hadn't seen nor heard of one. Elder Pratt and I were magnificent in our efforts to show the mission how a companionship should work. We didn't have to try; it came as a result of what I figured to be two decent guys serving together. Elder Pratt was loved by all missionaries. He shared thoughts and feelings when speaking that were noticeably void in my talks. I was able to present with such enthusiasm. I thought this enthusiasm masked the lack of testimony or feeling towards what I was presenting.

We talked well into the night, most nights, about people we knew and what our plans were after the mission. Elder Pratt was looking forward to seeing his family. I felt I knew them from the way he talked about them, but also because I saw a video of a family dinner and he pointed out all the faces that went with the names. On the same tape of the family dinner was a tape of him playing baseball in high school. He didn't know it was on there, and when it came on the screen, he quickly shut it off.

"You guys don't want to watch that," he said. Elder Mortenson said he wanted to, Elder Kramer wanted to, and of course, I was up for what the majority was doing. It was P-Day, we had time, and it seemed like a fun thing to do. I also wanted to see if Pratt could hit a ball like he said he could.

"Put it in, Pratt," I said. "Come on, you know you want to. I bet you like seeing yourself play ball."

"I don't guys! I'll put it in only because it might be fun to watch. I haven't seen it."

"Yeah, Yeah, Yeah. Just put it in," Elder Kramer said.

"OK, OK."

The video was a championship game from his senior year in high school.

"This guy throws about ninety-five miles an hour," Elder Pratt said, providing stats for the various players. The stands were full, and the overhead lights shone off the men's uniforms. Elder Pratt was batting; he swung and missed.

"What's this, Pratt? You going to strike out on us? Your debut on the mission?"

"I don't remember. I don't think I struck out this game, though."

The next pitch was a ball, followed by another. He got the count to full, swinging at and missing another fastball. On the next pitch we were all anxious to see what happened. He hit a high fastball—out of the park! He had a swing to match his stroke on the basketball court. He was a good-looking man. He was the perfect height, with straight hair and a smile that everyone smiled back at. He was able to hug each one of the office staff and brighten their day, simply by looking into their eyes.

He was one of the most perfect men I had ever met. I waved goodbye to him pulling out of the apartment complex in the sporty little convertible that he and his mom would become reacquainted in. I saw in her eyes how much she liked her son. The way she looked at him when he talked, her eyes marveled.

CHAPTER 17

Before Elder Pratt left, he and I attempted to talk to one thousand people each week. I got the idea from a statistic I found in an old copy of the *Ensign*. It simply said, "Speaking of missionaries, if you ask a thousand people to be baptized, one will say yes." I thought how easy that would be: no thinking, no planning, just ask a thousand people to be baptized. So we tried it. The first day we asked fifty people between us; the next day, a hundred. We kept track of the number on the small notepads we kept in the shirt pocket of our short-sleeved shirts. People backed away when they saw us coming.

They changed sides of the street to avoid us, and I hated it. I hated seeing the look in people's eyes, like I was crazy. I was starting to think I *was* crazy; crazy for being out on a Mormon mission, asking people if they would like a life like mine. A life I had grown to despise. I couldn't imagine anyone wanting my life if they knew the drudgery they would go through over the next few years. There would be the ward calling as soon as I got back. They assigned the calling fast, so as not to lose the missionary.

Then there would be the speaking engagements, every Sunday driving to a different ward, sharing the mission experiences and what it meant to be an AP on the mission. This would further indoctrinate the young fence-sitters, questioning their own loyalty to the Church and to their families, and push them finally to the side of the Lord and preparation for a mission. Young Mormon women would then walk up to me at the speaking engagements, trying to get to know me, as I was a young, returned missionary with an obvious testimony that would certainly pull them into heaven if they were to go awry. That was the drudgery that no one would have signed up for, had they known. But I went on asking a thousand people a week if they too would like to have my life.

My new companion, Elder Lee, was supportive of my new approach to finding people. At first I just started talking to people and offering them a *Book of Mormon.* And if they didn't want it, then I offered them a pamphlet outlining the First Discussion. It was easy enough to teach a First in five minutes on the street, causing the numbers for First Discussions to quadruple in the mission, while I pushed my new baby. The Firsts were taking too long, though.

Although plenty of praise from the president came from the increase in First Discussions, I still wasn't able to obtain my thousand contacts a week. I had to modify what I was sharing with the people I met. I simplified it down to two things: What did *I* want, and what was the counsel of the Twelve? What I wanted was to baptize people, and what the Twelve said in the *Ensign* was that a person needed to ask a thousand people to be baptized.

"Elder Lee, you go to that side of the street and I'll stay here," I said, looking over the small, two-lane road.

"Don't you think we should stay together?" Elder Lee asked. "It's just across the street; we are less than forty feet apart. I think it will be OK. Plus, I'm saying it's OK."

"Well, I think I'll just stand by you if you don't mind. You talk to people first and then I will."

"It's a waste of time."

"We have time, Elder," he said.

"Fine," I said, bothered but not willing to fight Elder Lee on the rules. He knew them better than I did. I didn't really care about the rules. I was forced into living them, so they were meaningless to me.

A woman with a bag with small handles befitting her small red hands approached. "Would you like to be baptized into the Mormon Church?" I asked, stepping in front of her on the small sidewalk. Her head moved back slightly to the side, and then her body followed her head. She stepped around me, looking at me only briefly as she was passing, so as not to touch me.

It was easier asking women because they weren't as scary. I didn't think I would get my ass kicked by a woman. So naturally, I tended to ask more women. I tried to avoid long periods of eye contact; I thought people might see the doubt in my eyes from what I was sharing with them. Briefly, on initial contact, to avoid running into each other, our eyes met. I quickly asked my two-second question, and they responded with a one-second answer, then stepped around me.

"Hello, Sir. Would like to become a Mormon?" I asked a man about my age.

"No thanks," he said and was just about by me when he turned and said, "You know, there might be a better way." He didn't smile but said it with kindness in his eyes. I didn't know if the man meant there was a better way of proselytizing or a better way of life. So I wrapped myself up in it and thought.

"Hello, Ma'am. Would you like to become a member of the Church of Jesus Christ and Latter-day Saints?" I asked an older woman. She was pretty, very tan; probably in her fifties.

"No thanks," she said, flashing me a small smile, hoping that I wouldn't persist in my questioning. Of course, I wouldn't. I learned the key was to make oneself enough of a presence so as to not scare, like a Walmart greeter. What I didn't want to look like was a man leaning against a street sign and nonchalantly asking, "Hey, man. You got any change? How 'bout a cigarette?" or a shoe-level pinching for money. If it weren't for writing down the numbers at twenty-people intervals, I would have lost track of time. Losing track of time was a nice reward for working hard. Elder Lee was keeping pace with me. I couldn't tell if he enjoyed it, or was putting up with it because he thought I was inspired, or thought I was smarter. He went to Yale before the mission. He had two years behind him and was planning on law school. He was fluent in five languages: Spanish, Chinese, Korean, French, and English (his first). He was brilliant with his note taking and assiduous in his studies. He was different from me and didn't want to be like me. He knew himself and didn't expect others to know that. He shared few thoughts and asked many questions. He tried to be liked but couldn't because he was smarter than the rest. And he was foreign.

I showed him how to pick up the missionaries from the airport and drop them off at the Mission Home, how to drive around in a circle at the airport while I ran in and grabbed the missionaries.

President Carlson had always insisted on meeting missionaries off the plane, but in the past two months he let the APs handle the logistics. He just said to bring them to the Mission Home when you can. There we would talk in the front room and in the kitchen to President Carlson's daughters and wife, along with the senior missionaries and the greenies. We ate cheesy potatoes and casseroles as the women tried to make the new elders feel comfortable. I explained to Elder Lee that we would go get ice cream from the local dairy for dessert.

"Elder Lee, it's sooo good. You have no idea," I said. "Do you like ice cream?"

"Elder Dorsey, I like ice cream," he said. I was enjoying Elder Lee's company. It was one of the few times, though. He was a stickler for rules, and I was quickly dealt a blow when he insisted on perfection from me. We timed our study times on his wrist; we role-played out of the Missionary Guide each morning. We took one-hour lunches and mapped out a schedule accordingly, faithfully sticking by the schedule. We tracted every day for three hours: half spent in English-speaking Ventura and the other half in Spanish-speaking Ventura.

My Spanish was as good as any missionary's. Elder Lee insisted that we take the extra hour that all foreign missionaries got to further my Spanish-speaking capabilities. He had his books from the MTC, so I did lessons each day. He was a great teacher, and the time we spent together learning was the most enjoyable time two such men could have. With the words changing, my mind awakened again. I took in the Spanish words and irregular verbs and tracted in Spanish, loving what I was doing. I worked harder than ever before. It was like working with Elder Fischer, but at a faster speed. I hated the guy and I loved the guy. He kept me quick and called me on the shit I said. We were downtown, talking with the homeless, and I said if they would get baptized, then we would get them food. I figured we could if they were members, and I wanted the baptisms. They were as good candidates as any, so I thought it might work. But Elder Lee made sure to tell me that we couldn't do that. When I asked him why, he looked at me with wisdom in his eyes and said, "We just can't do that." I relented and wasn't all that mad, as somehow he told me without making me feel like an ass. I understood how a person could love and hate something at the same time.

Elder Lee was waiting in the car for me as I finished reading a letter from Rachel Barrett. She had continued her monthly correspondence after adopting a system of sending the letters to the mission office and just having them forwarded. I didn't like that she did it; it didn't look good to have a letter coming through the mail from an area that an Elder had served in the past. I hoped nothing was noticed, though, and didn't say anything to Rachel. I wrote her back sparingly, a 1-to-4 ratio at best. I wouldn't have written back at all, but I was so close to going home and I wanted to make sure and hook up with her after my mission. I knew I didn't want to marry her, though. I just wanted to make out with her and have that fantasy behind me, the *make-out-with-girl-from-mission* fantasy. She would be perfect for the undoing. She was very pretty, but I couldn't imagine marrying her, as her ankles were too big. We were going to the bishop's house for dinner and I wanted to be in a good mood when I went, so I read the letter. It was P-Day, too, and I wanted to read it on P-Day.

The Channel Islands were big and the skies clear. "This is a nice view, Bishop."

"Thank you, Elder Dorsey. Do you spend much time on the Hill?"

"Well, not visiting members. I think you know you are the only member on the Hill," I said, hoping to flick away his pretentious manner.

"There is a park or lookout spot up farther, isn't there?" I asked, remembering back to my Pratt days and spending time together on P-Day. It was a fun day of goofy pictures with the ocean in the background.

"There is. You have been up there, then?"

"Sure," I said, hoping he would grow bored with me. Elder Lee was walking around the room, looking at different pieces of furniture.

"You have a lot of nice knick-knacks," he said to the bishop, standing in the doorway as his wife prepared dinner behind him.

"I don't think we have any knick-knacks," he said. I was enjoying the mood change in the room.

"The things you have around. Like this," Elder Lee said, holding up a small, round rain hat. It was a cone and looked like it was made out of grass, yellow grass.

"That is a traditional hat from Hue, Vietnam, the capital city."

"The capital city before the Americans blew it up in the war.

I believe it's just a tourist attraction now," Elder Lee said. I had no idea he had that kind of knowledge available for retrieval from his mind.

"Well, the locals still consider it the capital city. The neat thing about these hats in particular is that they have pagodas woven into the brims," the bishop said, trying to show Elder Lee that he knew more than him. Elder Lee handed him the hat. The bishop held it in front of the window, showing us the temples woven in that could be seen only by holding it up to the light of a window.

"I see them. So did you guys go there?" I asked, knowing that's what he wanted me to ask.

"We did, last year. Incredible trip. Have you traveled abroad, Elder?"

"I went to Hawaii. That's a pretty long plane ride," I said tired, knowing he really wanted to ask Elder Lee anyway.

"Elder Lee, have you traveled?"

"I haven't," he said with a sincere smile. I'm not sure I could have taken the abuse from the bishop like he did and still been sincere with a smile. But he was; I saw it in his eyes.

"That is a very nice hat," Elder Lee said, sounding a little sarcastic, but it was from his tone and dialect versus any notion to insult.

"Thank you," the bishop said. I wished it were after dinner and not before.

"Elders, why don't we sit down to dinner? I think it's just about ready," the bishop said, showing us to a small table for five, motioning us towards our seats. The table was set in front of a picture window. We all had a view from where we were sitting. Elder Lee had mentioned that he went to Yale before his mission; the Bishop didn't say anything in reply. With a lack of question from the Bishop regarding this, I wondered if he had graduated? He probably hadn't graduated from an Ivy League school, but maybe Pac-ten or private school.

"What about you, Bishop? Where did you go to school?" I asked, surprisingly enjoying the questioning, wondering why I had not asked other members more about themselves.

"I actually didn't finish. I went for a couple of years and dropped out."

"Oh. What do you do know?" I asked.

"I manage my father's construction company."

"Oh. How do you like that?" I asked, keeping a brisk pace on the questions.

"I like it. Something I knew I could always do and be successful at."

"It looks like it worked out well for you."

"It has," he said, his glasses not making him look as smart as they did before.

"Elder Dorsey, you go to college before your mission?" The Bishop's wife asked.

"I did. BYU. Probably head back after the mission," I said, trying to get all the answers in, in one outburst. We talked about college and the importance of it. Surprisingly, the Bishop relaxed and had very good insights into the types and levels of education, and the importance of each. It was nice having a conversation about something other than missionary work.

* * * * *

Elder Kramer and I were getting along nicely, one benefit of living with other Elders and not solely with Elder Lee. I worked splits a majority of time when in town; the other times I was usually splitting with other zone leaders. Elder Lee was usually with the Junior Companion. When not on splits with zone leaders, I was traveling in separate cars, making deliveries of vehicles across the mission. I successfully studied with Elder Lee, eating dinners with him and praying with him; that was it and it worked perfectly.

Elder Kramer wanted to be an AP on his mission. His theory was that if a guy was a hard worker and that's what he wanted, there was no reason why he couldn't get it.

"What's wrong with wanting to be the best missionary you can be?" he asked, thinking for a minute and then continuing. "Isn't that really what an AP is—one of the best missionaries in the field?"

"Well, *I* don't feel like the best missionary in the field, I know that. I think there are a lot of factors that go into who gets called as an AP And I think it's different for each President. I think what President Carlson might want in an AP is different than the next President, the one you would serve as AP under," I said, pausing for a minute to think about what I said. "Is it weird thinking you will have a different president before you go home?"

"A little. It would have been cool to serve my whole mission under President Carlson, but that's OK."

"It's probably not that big of deal. I personally would have liked the experience of having two different presidents to serve under."

Later that afternoon, the weather turned cool, with leaves blowing off the trees, onto the grass. Elder Kramer had suggested we go tracting. I enjoyed tracting more and more, the further I got in my mission. It became a time more for personal pondering than an attempt to find people to sit next to with Christ in eternity. Elder Kramer was a good companion for tracting; he was quiet and seldom asked questions.

"So, Elder Dorsey. What are you going to do after your mission?" Elder Kramer asked for the first time in the months of living with him.

"I don't know. I really don't know."

"You have no plans?"

"I have a decision that other decisions depend on, so no. Right now I have no plans."

"So, what's the decision?" Elder Kramer asked, surprised that I didn't provide the information. But I had purposely left that information out. I didn't want to share it, not because I was lacking complete thoughts. If I shared the decision, it might make it awkward at home, and I didn't want that. I already had to tell Elder Lee to loosen up on some of the missionary rules: that I would not shower with the bathroom door open, and that the prophet-authors of the White Bible did not intend that to be an issue when they wrote *Don't ever be out of sight with your companion*. So with that out there, I couldn't take a chance on further opening myself up. I swayed the conversation just a bit. I had gone many months without having any ire in the apartment. No dreaded silence with squeaks from unapproved music being pumped into a deceptive missionary's ears. Although our discussion, I'm sure, wouldn't have resulted in that type of behavior, what I *didn't* want to risk was the silence after a heavy discussion—the bad silence.

"Hey, let's cruise down and visit Larry."

"You guys still teaching him?"

"He's my favorite investigator. Why would I want to stop teaching him?"

"I don't think it works like that, does it? You're just trying to pad your Discussions."

"Elder Kramer," I said, with subtle surprise in my voice, "I would never think to pad." Then, in a soft, serious tone I added, "And why would I need to? I'm already the AP"

"Dude, I want that. I want that title."

"I'll let you wear it today," I said, slipping my black name tag off my shirt pocket, handing it over to him.

"Oh gee, Elder Dorsey! Really? Can I? Can I wear your name tag?"

"Of course, my son," I said, keeping my smile at bay.

"You dork, Dorsey! Let's go see Larry."

"Up for a little ocean-front property?"

"If you want to call it that. You don't find it strange that we sit in the bushes on logs and it's someone's home? And then a train comes within feet of where a person sleeps? It's very strange there."

"It's a trip, I agree."

Larry was one of four vagrants who lived in the blackberry bushes next to the railroad tracks. We met him while asking people to be baptized downtown; he was number forty-seven. He had grown up in Ventura, his family being one of the founding families. His family also included prominent Mormons. He was said to be crazy. He had schizophrenia, and the

Church did everything they could for him. The first time I met Larry, he stopped me after I asked him if he would like to be baptized Mormon and said, "They won't let me. I believe it, but they won't let me." He floored me with his response, and we went from the street corner to the park and sat on a picnic bench. He taught me what I believed. It was like encountering the writings of C. S. Lewis and having so many questions answered all at once that you couldn't even keep track, but it gave you hope to get up the next day and keep living. It was this type of engagement at first. Over the months that I visited him, I saw that he drank heavily and smoked butts of cigarettes. He had mentioned prior that he wasn't opposed to any type of drug. He also had a vicious side that lashed out at God and cursed the earth.

For a homeless man, he was surprisingly clean. He lacked a mate to cleverly tell him he smelled bad, so I let him shower in our bathroom. Elder Lee hated it, so I stopped allowing it when he threatened to tell President Carlson. People were very scared of Larry. He was a handsome man, not forbidding in the slightest, but the good looks and charm were so smooth and genuine that his very situation insisted there were serious problems in his life. People regarded homelessness as a state of mind versus a state of being, putting heavy hopes on the man-made structures of the world. Larry didn't work because he didn't want to—at least that's what he told us.

"Why work? I guess if I really needed anything I would work, but I don't need anything right now, so why go do something all day I don't want to do?" He asserted, with the butt of a cigarette hanging from his mouth.

"What about family, though? You can't have a family like this."

"That's a good point, and it's mine exactly. Until you want something, there is no point in working for it. If I wanted a family, I would work to be prepared for one. I don't want one, so how could I motivate myself to get up and work for it?"

"But there's got to be something you want more than *this*," I said, sweeping my arms in the air to include the tent behind us.

"At one point I did, but now I don't. I'm sure someday I will want something again, and at that time I will go get it."

"Larry, come on. A person can't live like that."

"Oh, yes they can. And many do every day. That's why you have the hard workers and the middle-of-the-road workers. Some are motivated; some are not. It's all about finding your motivation in life. The sooner you can find it, the better off you will be. And soon all your decisions will be grounded in that motivation. In the end, you will have what you wanted and what you have dreamed of your whole life."

"If it were only that easy. I think work is just part of life.

Whatever the work might be, it's part of life. It's like dying—no reason to fight it."

"I agree, those are the people who are working for something that doesn't motivate them. You can't work just to work. You have to find something that pays *and* that you enjoy doing," Larry said, becoming more pleased with himself as the conversation continued. I thought he rationalized his position poetically. It amazed me how well a person could make a stand to justify one's station in life. As low as they might be, they might think it the top of the world. I thought the beer in his hands was helping him pontificate on the intricacies of the workingman. My age was that of indelible ideas and theories that guided me though life, as the God of my fathers slipped slowly away from me. I didn't think that Larry had all the answers, though. I wanted to be smart like him, but I didn't know what I would be willing to trade. I'd rather take the chance that someday I could be smart like him and still have a house without railroad tracks running through my front yard.

"Larry, you want a Discussion tonight? You know that's we came over for."

"How about a video, Elders?" He asked laughing, spilling his beer in his lap. I knew the beer would dry and stain, turning hard before it ever made it to the laundry.

"Larry, you want to go to the laundromat with us on Monday?" I asked

"Sure. I don't have any money to wash my clothes, though."

"I'll give you the money, man."

"Thanks, Dorsey," he said. Then, holding his beer above his face, "Here's to you!"

"We will meet you there. The one off Ventura Boulevard."

"OK. What time?"

"Nine thirty, morning."

"Wow, that's early. Well, I usually wake up with the eight thirty train ,so I might as well just get out of bed too. I don't plan on making a habit of it," he said, grabbing his lower back as he stood up. He was in very good shape for a middle-age man. He had six-pack abs showing from his opened, flower-print shirt. I couldn't tell if he had gym muscles or lack-of-food muscles. But he was in better shape than I, and I lived in a house, ate three meals a day, got eight hours of sleep, and had medical coverage.

I'd called Barry and set up a time to visit after the article from my mom arrived. She said she couldn't locate a copy, but then she called Salt Lake and they found one for her. She made it sound like that had a red button on her phone that she pushed, with the prophet instantly on the other end. The article was from 1971. I would have liked the whole magazine, but she sent me only a photocopy of the article. I made another photocopy and gave one to Barry. He was surprised—the kind of surprise like when I've met a girl and she buys something for me and gives it to me. It might be the smallest thing I've mentioned—"I like them too" in reference to a music group—and voilà!—she buys me the album. I say "Thank you" and it's awkward—the surprise that someone cares so much about your happiness. It was a little freaky to me and to Barry as well.

After Barry read the essay out loud, I sat back in the couch and relaxed a little. I was so tired of never being relaxed, always with someone—members, nonmembers, companions, other elders, other elders' companions. I looked at Stacy. She was talking with Elder Lee about school and didn't notice me looking at her. I was able to appreciate how stunning she was. Her long, blond hair fell just below her shoulders, with strands catching on her ears, giving her hair and her manners a wistful feeling. Her strong, yet delicate, facial features were accentuated by the leanness of her muscles on her well-proportioned body. She was the kind of woman I imagined myself with if I looked like Barry. They got married when they were older, midthirties. Barry worked his way through college by writing for the school paper. He had hope when he talked about his earlier days, before and shortly after his mission. Lisa's family was Mormon, but inactive when she was born, so she never went to church and was never baptized. She knew as much as any convert, and it was clear from her questions that she and Barry didn't discuss the Church Doctrine before sleeping each night. I wouldn't have either, though, with a wife like Lisa. She was five-nine and smiled when I asked her how tall she was because she knew she was a pretty woman.

Elder Lee was studious and knew his scriptures. He knew the Missionary Guide better than any elder in the mission. Even with everything he *knew*, he could hardly talk without putting an entire room to sleep. He did have an accent, but it wasn't a Chinese accent. It was an accent that came by knowing five languages from a very young age. I imagine some of the younger Elders might have even said he talked funny. Even if this were not the case, he had no sense of eloquence in front of people. He was studying to be an electrical engineer and probably didn't intend to be a professor or a spokesperson for an engineering company. I believed if he had thought it important to be a good public speaker, then he would have worked to become a good speaker. But without needing speaking skills, as far as he saw, he didn't spend any time on it. Also, he was a convert and didn't have to speak in primary classrooms, Sunday school, at Sacrament Meetings, to Boy Scouts, or at young-adults wards. Each of those organizations had its hierarchy of leaders, with each of those leaders having people under them. Pretty soon, everyone in the Mormon Church would be trained to be a leader, to take over the world with Mormonism as the only religion, and then on to his own world someday, where they to would be gods themselves, populating their universe with their many wives.

During Zone Conference, I shared with the missionaries the results of asking a thousand people a week to be baptized. I wished I could have shared with them that I had baptized someone as a result of my asking, but that wasn't the case. I hadn't even started teaching anyone from it. It was something I did and had rallied behind, now trying to get the whole mission around it. I pulled out a clicker counter from my pocket during my talk and explained how I was keeping track of the number of people I was talking with daily. I also explained that I didn't expect a companionship to ask a thousand people per week and start cranking out baptisms, but rather that they simply start keeping track of the number of people they talked with and work to improve on it daily, as that was the reason we were out—to talk with people and ask them to be baptized. The talk was funny, at times. Just slightly bordering on serious. I bore my testimony on the importance of what I was doing and what I'd hoped the missionaries would do also. It was an energizing talk, leaving the sisters and elders with laughs in their bellies and smiles on their faces. All except for one I didn't know, Elder Shamley. He was from Mexico City and spoke English as his second language.

"Elder Shamley, how are you today?" I asked as he walked up to me after the presentation.

"Elder Dorsey, you disgust me."

Shocked and not believing what I had just heard, I said, "Excuse me, Elder?"

"The way you push numbers and not people. This mission is not about how many people we can talk with, it's about helping others feel the spirit, with the hope that feeling will bring them into the waters of baptism."

"I agree. I'm simply taking a different approach; that's all."

"Your approach is disgusting. I can't believe I have to serve *under* you," Elder Shamley said, refusing to shake my hand as he walked off. I stood there in shock, glad he was one of the last ones in the room so I didn't have to put up an AP front any longer. I could stop and consider what just happened. I thought he was joking. I wasn't sure what to do or make of his comments, so I asked President Carlson what he thought.

"Elder Dorsey, don't worry too much about Elder Shamley. He is just like that," President Carlson told me when I had a chance to pull him aside, outside of the church, with missionaries dispersing around us.

"Do you think I push numbers and that's all? Should I change the way I teach and what I present to the rest of the mission?"

"No, No. I don't want you to change at all. I want you to continue to do *exactly* what you are doing in Zone Conferences. Elder Dorsey, you are one of the most gifted teachers I have ever seen. When we get back to the Mission Home, I'd like to sit down with you and talk a little about what your plans are after the mission. I think you would make a great institute teacher at BYU."

"Well, thank you, President. That is quite a compliment coming from you. I look forward to sitting down with you."

"Good, and don't worry about what Elder Shamley said. He says things like that."

"OK. I wanted to check with you, though. If there was ever anything I was presenting to the mission that you didn't think appropriate, I would hope you would talk with me."

"Of course, I would. I've never had a problem with anything you have presented. Your new plan to talk with everyone you meet about the Church is a wonderful idea. It's what should be happening every day among missionaries. Elder Dorsey, keep up the good work!" he said, putting his hand on the back of my shoulder and squeezing it. This fatherly show of praise something my own father had never done, felt wonderful.

"Thanks, President."

"Don't worry about it; just keep doing what you are doing."

"Oh, I can do that," I said, smiling and looking directly into his eyes. He got into the mission van and rolled down his window. "See you elders in the Valley! And good job today."

I was anxious, going back to the Valley for Zone Conference. The letters from Rachel Barrett kept coming in the mail each week, leaving little doubt about what her intentions were when I was done with my mission. She was going to BYU the next semester and wanted to see me there. Although I wasn't able to write her back, per mission rules, I did talk with her a couple of times when she called after hours. It was hypocritical of me to talk with her and then tell the rest of the mission to support President Carlson in his attention to the rules, but she was gorgeous and I was desperate. In the Valley, being so close to Rachel and to freedom made me want to go home and get back to Utah, and BYU, and a date with Rachel. I wanted it all that day and didn't want to wait any longer. I wondered if I could get out of the mission Could I leave? Could I tell the President that I wasn't sure what I was doing anymore—that I wasn't sure what I even believed anymore?

With my last Zone Conference and last Zone Leaders Meeting behind me, I relaxed and settled down, something I hadn't been able to since San Luis Obispo. I didn't take on the lackadaisical life that I had with Elder Burton, but I didn't think about the missionary work either. All I thought about was going home. I went on splits as often as I could with Elder Smith, avoiding talk about missionary work or the Church. He noticed it but didn't say anything. He was a good friend, one of the best I had.

I played tennis hard, enjoying the members who shared my interest in the sport. I met Norman. He was a member of the Ventura ward who wasn't so popular. He was forty years old, married to an eighteen-year-old girl who had grown up in the ward. They lived together before they were married in his modest wood house near the water. He had a small gray truck with a foot-high rhinoceros horn on the hood and a leather tail out the back. There were tennis courts close to his house, a park with lots of green grass, and a fountain where children played. He was in excellent shape, showing a six-pack of abs when he took his shirt off to warm up. He had a scream'n serve, and I was lucky enough to return it consistently enough to enjoy a match. His eyes were soft and warm, with a gentleness that made it obvious how a woman would, at any age, fall in love with him. Norman and I got to know each other slowly, finally playing tennis after I'd been in the area for over four months. We bonded one afternoon after I moved up to the net to put away some softer ground strokes. His ground strokes quickly turned hard. He was passing me at the net, taking the lead in the match.

We didn't talk while we played, a sign of true athletes, I thought. But on one particular passing shot, or what was hoped to be passing shot, I was able to stop the ball. It plopped down onto my side of the court, inches from the net. I followed it instantly with my whole body plopping onto the court, my racquet hand going limp, first from the ground stroke then directly into my balls. It was slow motion, really. The small, fuzzy yellow ball went over the net and into my groin. Upon impact, I just stood there as first my legs turned in; my wrist went limp, dropping my racquet to the court; and a wave of heat flashed from my groin up through my torso. Then my head got dizzy as I melted onto the green court, lying there while Elder Smith and Norman burst out laughing. When I had regained enough composure to talk, they were still laughing.

"I don't think I can play anymore." This phrase got even more laughs from them. We all bonded, though. And if a man has to go through a little pain to bond with another man, it's worth it.

I respected Norman for what he did; falling in love when it was a taboo and going after what he wanted in life, possibly understanding the consequences and not caring, or caring more for the life he saw was possible with his eighteen-year-old bride. She was one of the most stunning women I had ever seen: tall, thin, and fuckable—extremely fuckable.

Norman was a bit of an anomaly. He had long hair and didn't shave every day. He drove a little beater truck and kept a new red Corvette in his dilapidated garage. He went to church each Sunday and said "Hi" to everyone, with the members saying "Hi" back to him, even though I knew the people in the ward didn't want to. I asked him why he lived in the same ward with his wife's parents. "Isn't it a little awkward at times?"

"Maybe. I don't notice and don't really care. I've grown up in Ventura and love it. I surf, and work here, and see no reason to change any of that to make someone else's life easier. We are happy here. Why change that? We rarely see other people, so it's not worth basing decisions on them."

I spent as much time as I could with Norman. He took some of my pain away. He didn't answer any of my questions concerning the Church, people, life, or anything else, but he did tell me why he opted for a red Corvette versus a black one: "If you are going to do something as impractical as buy a Corvette, you might as well get a color as impractical as red."

I said my goodbyes to the members after giving a talk to the ward on my last Sunday. I tried to hide the lack of bearing my testimony by delving into Isaiah, hoping to lose people to sleep, tending to their kids, and program doodling. I tried the "not-bearing-a testimony" approach in my final missionary testimony meeting. Rachel was there, looking edible in a short-short skirt. The Morels were there, as was Norman. The Austins showed up, which surprised me, as did Barry and Lisa. Even Larry showed up in his beer-stained pants along with a few others who had heard my mission was coming to an end. I had to remember their names and act thrilled to see them, as if their being there was the most important thing in my life. I shared a funny story about tracting: how a dog jumped through a screen door and onto me after I had taunted the dog. Everyone laughed. We talked about the future together, which was sad.

CHAPTER 18

As I walked down the aisle scanning for my seat, I saw a beautiful young woman.

Once my bag was in the overhead compartment and I was seated, I looked over at the woman and said, "Hi. How are you?"

Looking over quickly, she returned my "Hi" and smiled.

As we taxied, the pilot welcomed us, advised us we would have a quick stop in Portland before heading on to Seattle. Then the steward showed us how to buckle our belts.

"What's scarier, taking off or landing?" the woman next to me asked.

"Landing," I said. "I hate it."

"Me too." She gave a small, scared smile-frown.

We were pushed back in our seats, both gripping the armrest, waiting to level off.

"Not that takeoffs are all that great though," she said, keeping us engaged.

When the pilot announced the fasten-seatbelt sign was turned off and advised we could move about the cabin, the woman next to me turned her head and smiled.

"I'm Janet," she said, sticking out her hand. "What is your name?"

"Ray. Nice to meet you, Janet."

"Nice to meet you, Ray. Coming or going?"

"I guess coming home. Although it doesn't seem like it."

"Why?"

"I've been serving a Mormon mission for two years. So I don't know what I'm going home to or frankly why I'm going back to where I left from."

"Are you into it?"

"No. That's the problem. I took two years and learned I want no part of this life."

"Then why are you going back to it, literally the first chance you get? Right now is the first chance and you are going right back to it?"

Coming down into Portland, I could see the city and mountains as clear as anything I'd ever seen. The seatbelt sign came on and the captain advised the crew to prepare for landing. I wasn't worried about the landing at all.

Janet looked back from several people ahead, "Ray, you coming?"

"Yeah."

She was smiling as she saw me throwing my bag over my shoulder. I tossed the worn-out Bible and Book of Mormon on the seat behind me and walked up the aisle.

"Sir, are these your books?"

I turned around, quickly surveyed the books, and looked over at the stewardess.

"No," I said, knowing the gold embossed name had worn off a long time ago. "Those aren't mine."